Steve

Wilson

Tempest
of
Fire

Published by White Feather Press. (www.whitefeatherpress.com)

ISBN 978-1-61808-071-4

Printed in the United States of America

Cover design created by Steve Wilson and Adam Wilson Design

This is a work of fiction. The characters and incidents are not to be construed as real. Any resemblance to actual events or persons, living or dead, is entirely coincidental. While some technology is grounded in reality, certain liberties have been taken in the interests of creating a compelling story.

White Feather Press

Reaffirming Faith in God, Family, and Country!

For Bill and Charlene Collier

Tempest
of
Fire

Prologue ✳ Commendation

Headquarters Marine Corps,
Virginia

I T WASN'T THE WORDING OF THE COMMENDA-
tion that was unusual. Marine Corps Lieutenant Colonel
Nicholas Terryton had crafted the citation himself, and as
the CO of the International Office of Investigations, it was only
fitting that the job had fallen to him. What struck him as odd
was the collaborative nature of the document.

Ordinarily the citation would have been written by a junior
officer, the Sergeant Major, or some other trusted senior NCO.
This case was different. Dozens of pages of paperwork crossed
the Colonel's desk daily, but he was especially proud of the job
he'd done on this one. In deliberating over it, he had relied on
examples kept in a filing cabinet behind his desk. He used those
as templates. The source material had been provided by another
officer—from Ukraine, no less—so the narrative only needed
to be re-told in a format that followed the prose of the United
States Naval Services.

The Navy and Marine Corps Commendation award was
sheathed in a soft vinyl case. With the official party assembled,
Terryton adjusted his uniform slightly and then stood more
erect as he began reading aloud the words from the parchment.
Standing at attention before him was Lieutenant Michael Neill,

and at his side was none other than the Commandant, General Bradley Cole. The General's office was just down the hall, and he enjoyed attending ceremonies for his top-tier staff. Only one enlisted member was present, Marine Sergeant Christina Arrens. Her role was largely administrative, and she was there to ensure the ceremony went smoothly.

"For meritorious service while serving as a liaison in the former Soviet Union—" Terryton intoned, enunciating the dates—*"Lieutenant Michael Neill was instrumental in establishing the verification of disarmament procedures in the nation of Ukraine."*

There was more, but that information was compartmentalized, and on a need to know basis. The Colonel had exercised great creativity in listing Neill's accomplishments, omitting some details. Only a few individuals beyond the walls of Terryton's office were privy to those.

Neill stood patiently as the citation was read. Sergeant Arrens, directly across from him, was immobile as well, but turned her head slightly and caught his eye. She allowed herself to smile at the Lieutenant; it was a demure expression, but conveyed her approval. Neill caught her look and smiled back.

Terryton continued at length, and then proceeded to the conclusion. *". . . His professionalism, devotion to duty, and personal initiative reflect credit upon himself, and are in keeping with the highest traditions of the Naval Service."*

Arrens stepped forward and presented the hexagonal bronze medal, which Terryton took and pinned to Neill's breast pocket. The Colonel smiled and extended his hand.

"Congratulations, Lieutenant."

* * * *

It was nearly noon. Sergeant Arrens and Lieutenant Neill had exited the Colonel's office and were headed down the hall to their work space. The IOI had recently moved from its former location at the Marine Barracks at Eighth and Eye to the more robust Headquarters Marine Corps complex in Arlington, Virginia. The change in facilities afforded the IOI staff an environment that was closer to the heart of its world-wide operations.

"Very nice, Marine," Arrens teased, now wearing a wide grin. She was in a playful mood. "Pretty soon you'll have as many medals as I do."

Neill eyed the awards the young woman wore on her uniform. Displayed on her blouse were the Marine Corps Good Conduct and the Navy and Marine Corps Achievement ribbons, among others. The most recent one was in recognition of her service in Afghanistan. He couldn't let her comment go without some ribbing of his own.

"Well, I doubt that," Neill quipped. "You admin types have the inside track on hogging the glory." His look suggested admiration that went beyond her decorations.

Christina saw the smile on his face, but returned it with a stern expression. She balled up her fist and softly tagged his arm. Each enjoyed the slight physical contact more than they let on.

"I hear he's wearing a star now," she remarked.

"That's right—*General* Andrei Alexandreyevich Ulyanov," Neill confirmed. A lot had happened in the months since Michael had returned from Ukraine. "He's also been re-instated as the commander of the airbase in Nikolayev."

The Ukrainian President had given Ulyanov a few additional duties prior to Neill's tasking there. With Neill's help, Ulyanov had successfully fulfilled the assignment, and as a result, Pavlovsk had rewarded the Colonel with a promotion.

The International Office of Investigations had been the starting point for that mission. Arrens and Neill had individual cubicles in the IOI shop that occupied the second floor, but shared responsibilities for the Eastern European/Russian desk. Arrens secretly wished they shared more, but fraternization between the ranks was discouraged, so she kept her thoughts to herself—aside from the occasional comment that hinted at her true feelings. As for Neill—she just couldn't get a read on him. He was friendly enough, and polite. And always a gentleman. But sometimes she wished—

"What about you?" she asked. Her dark eyes turned to meet his. "Has Terryton approved your request?"

There was very little daylight between the Sergeant and a direct question. Neill took a deep breath. "He has."

She held his gaze for a moment longer and then turned as they entered their own office. "I see." Her disappointment was unmistakable. As naïve as he was when it came to women, even Neill recognized the tone of her words.

"Christina, consider things from my point of view."

Using her first name got Arren's attention. She folded her arms and faced Neill, noting that the Lieutenant's eyes were focused on hers. She put aside bruised feelings and decided to hear him out.

"I've been in the Corps for over three years now," he continued. "Most of that time has been in this office. Or acting as a liaison in some old Soviet republic. Those roles have very little to do with being a Marine."

"You want more time in the field?"

"I need to shoulder my share of the load. And I can't do that here. The closest I've been to a real war zone was the three months I spent in Manas—watching everyone else flying into Afghanistan."

Arrens couldn't argue with that. She'd been deployed twice herself. Her own reasons for joining the Corps had a lot to do with a desire for adventure, a need to be a part of something bigger, and for assignments that would take her far beyond the routine of an eight-to-five job in corporate America. While her administrative duties kept her tethered to a desk most of the time, at least that desk could sometimes be found in the far-flung corners of the world.

Christina had seen the paper trail for Neill's visit to Ukraine—it was one of the perks of having a top secret clearance. And he was right. His language skills and background had been a factor in his last two deployments.

"Any idea where you'll be assigned?" she said at last.

"The Thirty-Second MEU is headed out in a few months. They'll be fielding some new battlefield technology. The Commandant wants an honest assessment of its effectiveness."

Neill continued looking at her. There weren't any words that would make her feel better about this. A silent moment passed, and her eyes held his for just a few seconds more.

"Keep me in the loop," Christina told him. She was all business now. "I'll make sure your orders get put into the system."

"Roger that." Neill watched her face, but her expression remained the same. Even with the imposed barrier between them, there was no denying the fact that she was a beautiful woman. While he was thankful for her friendship, and that they worked together, he sometimes wondered how things might be if the circumstances were different.

There was no point in pondering over hypotheticals. Their paths paralleled each other, but they were distinctly separate. Both were committed to a career in the military. She had chosen the enlisted route, while Neill's commission pointed in another direction. Michael knew that as long as they maintained their focus, there would be very little change in their respective journeys.

* * * *

"I MIGHT BE A LITTLE LATE GETTING BACK."

Christina was headed out for lunch. The smile she wore made her even more appealing, and her mood seemed improved since their earlier conversation.

Neill was going to reply, but she was already moving down the hall. He considered the workload on his desk, but then turned his head and watched her go with an appreciative glance. He was a disciplined man, but a man nonetheless.

Alone in the office, Neill stared at the paperwork scattered in layers before him. He smiled to himself. A field assignment was becoming more attractive by the minute. Six months earlier he'd been in Ukraine and helped avert a disaster. But back in the States, he analyzed political and military trends in Eastern Europe—much of the time behind a desk. He had been born in that former Soviet republic, and when he flew back to D.C., he regretted leaving.

Michael shook his head and began sorting through documents. The morning had started well, but he had a feeling it would be a very long day, and his focus lasted all of five minutes before his stomach reminded him of how hungry he was.

Chapter One ✶ Demon in the Depths

Late September, the South China Sea

THE SUN HAD NEARLY SET, AND THE SEA AND sky blazed with a fiery glow as the submarine surged through the waters. The bulk of the vessel was hidden beneath the waves, and had been submerged for most of the voyage. Now the sub was cruising on the surface, its big, rounded bow displacing tons of seawater as she sailed south.

Today the sea had a light chop. Occasionally, a breaker would wash across the black hull, rolling aft until it was cut in half by the long, rounded hump of the ship's conning tower. The sub had an almost natural look to it—sleek and organic, mimicking the shape of a whale or some other streamlined sea creature. The tower itself was bristling with periscopes and electronic gear. At the top, dwarfed by the masts that loomed above, stood a lone figure.

He wore the uniform of a Chinese naval officer, and the rank on his collar identified him as a Senior Captain. Over his clothing was the standard issue heavy jacket common to all of China's submariners.

Captain Wu Chang scanned the horizon as a chill south wind blew into his face. The summer had barely passed and winter was already signaling its approach. To the west, just over the horizon and out of sight, lay the Huo Shan island chain, a tiny cluster of volcanic rock that jutted up out of the sea. Like every other sailor who plied these waters, Chang knew them to be a no-man's land of thick, impenetrable jungle—and the home of a dark legend.

The Captain was well aware of the mysticism that surrounded the sea, but would never admit that to his officers or crew, and as such, would also never acknowledge anything other than a tacit respect for the stories everyone had heard about those islands.

Chang pulled his jacket around him a little more tightly and turned to survey the sea beyond the stern. Twilight had almost overtaken the day, and as he peered into the distance, the Captain could still make out the southern shores of Taiwan. The twinkling of city lights along the coast reminded him that he was once again leaving the comforts of civilization far behind, trading them for the mysteries of the deep.

But Chang was far from somber about that. The deck plates beneath his feet reassured him, and the prospect of heading out to sea thrilled his soul. Chang and his crew—only twenty-six officers and enlisted men for this shakedown cruise—were embarking on China's most technologically advanced warship, the prototype of all attack subs to follow.

At forty-three hundred tons and three hundred feet long, the *Gansu Province* was hardly the world's largest submarine. Western military experts might have sniffed disdainfully at some of her design characteristics, but Chang's new command was a cut above China's older boats. The bulbous hull was encased entirely within a blanket of specially designed skin. This rubber coating was intended to defeat the sonar equipment of vessels that might try to track the sub. It also acted as a muffler to hide the sounds of the ship's machinery.

There were other innovations; safety was the main concern. In years past, being assigned for duty aboard a submarine of the People's Liberation Army-Navy was nearly a death sentence. Losing a boat to the crushing depths, or to fire, or some other accident—usually involving nuclear reactors—

was commonplace. With over a billion citizens, Beijing appeared to care little for the small percentage of sailors serving below the waves. Chang sought to change that. Using every bit of political capital he had, the Captain had pushed hard for features that would safeguard the lives of his comrades.

Chang's demands also included a focus on competing with western navies. Remaining hidden from the more advanced subs of the U.S. became an obsession for him. His efforts paid off. Not only did she have the advantage of stealth, the *Gansu Province* was fast—she'd already surprised the engineers who designed her. In addition to her speed, the ship's strong titanium hull enabled her to dive to incredible depths. But these improvements came at a high price.

The Captain had seen a report on her building expenditures and smiled to himself as he recalled the figures. The cost of materials alone for the ship represented a sizable chunk of the Navy's budget, and many had opposed its construction for that very reason. Chang's superior officer, Admiral Xian Lee, had fought the hardest to deny funding for the new boat, arguing that better submarines could be bought—more cheaply—from Russian shipyards.

The Admiral had nearly convinced everyone, but not the Premier. Tao Chengdu, the leader of China, rejected Admiral Lee's advice and pushed ahead with his plan to revitalize the nation's military. *"Chinese weapons for Chinese troops"* became his rallying cry, and few dared challenge him when it came to national policy. Lee grudgingly relented, and with some stern prodding from Chengdu, he joined the bandwagon of support for the sleek new weapon.

STANDING HIGH ABOVE THE CHILLING SPRAY that lashed at his ship, Chang couldn't have been happier with the results. He had every confidence in his new vessel, and secretly hoped that the ship's maiden voyage would silence once and for all the Admiral's muted opposition. Chang also had the pleasure of commanding a top-notch crew as well, and he knew that when the *Gansu Province* returned to port, a new chapter would be written in Chinese naval history.

He mused on that for some time, but then was interrupted by the buzzing of the ship's telephone. Chang reached below to retrieve a handset from a small watertight locker secured to the bulkhead.

"This is the Captain," he answered.

"Song here, sir." It was the voice of the ship's XO, or Executive Officer. Lieutenant Whe Song was new to submarines, but a highly competent sailor. Chang intended to mold him in his own image, forging the young man into a skilled undersea warrior. "We have arrived at the test area."

"So soon?" Chang replied. He turned to look at the horizon behind him, but Taiwan had now completely faded from view. "What is the depth below the keel?" The receiver pressing against his ear felt like ice.

"Nine hundred meters, Captain."

Chang pursed his lips. "Very well," he said at last. "Make the ship ready for diving. I'm on my way."

He sealed the phone back in its case and took one final look at the darkening sky. A canopy of stars danced brilliantly overhead. The glittering display reminded Chang that mariners of old used those lights to steer by, and he smiled once more. Hidden in the depths, the *Gansu Province* used other means of navigation.

The Captain drew in the crisp sea air, and then descended the narrow ladder to the control room below, dogging the hatch behind him. He reached the command center seconds later. All around him, his officers and men busied themselves with their duties, and Chang could see the quiet pride in his crew as they prepared to submerge. A bank of lights on one of the ship's monitors flashed green, and First Officer Song turned to his Captain and nodded.

"Take her down," Chang ordered. He removed his jacket and

stowed it in a locker. "Twenty degree angle on the dive planes. Descend to four hundred meters and set course due west."

Song repeated the order and the crew moved to obey. Within moments, the deck below their feet took on a more inclined angle, and on the surface, twin jets of spray shot into the sky as the ballast tanks were emptied of air. Like a whale making for the bottom, the *Gansu Province* plunged downward, leaving only a phosphorescent wake to betray her presence.

THE FRIGID SEAWATER HAD NOW FULLY EM-braced the ship, and the bulkheads creaked as the pressure built up around the hull. In the control room, Chang and his First Officer moved to the navigation console and studied a map of their present position.

"Today's test will end here." Chang marked the navigational chart with a grease pencil. "In two hours we will be well past Huo Shan. At that point we will alter our course to the south."

The Captain was plotting their path carefully while Song looked on. "There is a deep water basin here—" he made another mark with the pencil "—and after our third test dive we will set sail for Hong Kong at flank speed."

Chang waited for a reaction from Song, and after a long pause he got it.

"Perhaps we should bypass the Huo Shan islands complete-ly," Song offered thoughtfully. "We could reach the basin half a day earlier if we maintain a south-westerly plot."

The Captain laid the pencil on the chart and straightened up. There was more to Song's suggestion than just expediency. "Lieutenant, you surprise me," he smiled. Looking the junior officer square in the eye he said, "Surely you don't believe in ghost stories."

Song was startled by such a direct statement. He tried to appear indifferent, but he knew exactly what Chang was getting at. While the Captain deferred to his crews' views regarding Huo

Shan, and would never openly mock them for it, he couldn't resist this gentle prod of his XO.

"I am not a superstitious man, Captain," Song said evenly, his voice much lower now. "But some of the men may not be so enlightened. If word gets out that we are to approach Huo Shan—"

"Have no fear, Whe," Chang laughed softly. He had a mischievous look on his face, and couldn't help the amusement he felt at Song's reaction.

The two officers worked well together, blending Chang's knowledge and experience of the sea with Song's youthful exuberance. Chang normally presented a no-nonsense, professional demeanor, but from time to time he would surprise his First Officer with something unexpected. The Captain's levity was rare, to say the least, and Song was caught off guard by his disarming humor.

Unfortunately, the light-hearted moment was not to last.

Song opened his mouth and was about to respond when the world aboard the *Gansu Province* was turned on its ear.

* * * *

AFT OF THE CONTROL CENTER, THE SHIP'S CHIEF engineer was a busy man. He checked and double-checked a dozen gauges, dials, and digital displays, then walked the decks of the reactor room, peering into the nooks and crannies between complex machinery. Satisfied that everything was in order, he started forward. The old officer arrived in the ship's control center just before the chaos began.

* * * *

THE LEAD SONAR MAN, ONE OF THREE ON DUTY, heard it again; first a creaking sound, followed by a groan. Then a distinct grinding that sounded like metal on metal.

"Captain," he kept his voice steady but had already risen halfway from his seat at the sonar console, one hand pressed against the listening phones wrapped around his ears. "Transitory contact, port side."

Chang turned immediately. "Bearing?"

"Course is two-eighteen," the young officer replied. His scope now showed a more persistent return; clearly the contact was now no longer transitory. "Moving west at eight knots. Distance is two kilometers."

The crew instinctively adopted a hushed tone. Captain Chang was now at the sonar man's shoulder, peering at the contact's image on the scope.

"Make your speed twelve knots, and give me negative twenty degrees on the dive planes," Chang ordered his First Officer. He intended to go deeper. Song repeated the order as his eyes fell on the helmsman and Diving Officer. He waited to see that his commands were obeyed, and then turned his attention back to the sonar suite.

Chang was about to issue another order when the sonar man bolted up from his chair and pulled the earphones from around his head. Even from where he stood, Song could understand why; the sound that erupted from the young officer's listening device was loud and unearthly. The sonar officer nearly fell backwards, but the Captain's hand steadied him. Again, Chang started to speak, but the officer cut him off.

"Sonar contact bearing two-twenty one; moving to intercept us, Captain." In spite of the assault on his eardrums, the sonar man quickly regained his wits and focused on the task he was trained for. His eyes were now glued to the console. "Distance is six thousand meters . . . directly behind us. Speed is—no, that *can't*—"

Chang's eyes were also attuned to the display. They were under attack, but what the instruments told him clearly wasn't possible. At the moment he didn't have time to reason it out and instead acted on instinct.

"Best possible speed," he ordered. "Maintain course and bearing; stand by to angle diving planes—we may have to take her deep." Chang felt that by turning, the sub would present a

larger target for the mysterious sonar contact to home in on, so his intentions were to move in a direct path away from their attacker. He turned to a wall-mounted intercom and grabbed the microphone. "This is the Captain speaking; aft torpedo room, load two weapons and standby for firing protocols."

Song gave Chang an alarmed look. "Captain—we have no war shot ordnance aboard; just practice torpedoes."

Chang nodded. "I know, Whe." Dummy warheads. Chang pushed the mike back into its cradle. The Captain was also aware that each torpedo weighed several thousand pounds, and while inert, an impact with whatever had targeted them still might save their lives. Chang looked directly at the Fire Control Officer. "Activate the targeting computer and prepare to launch."

The officer didn't have to be told twice; he was already moving to the weapons control station when the Captain issued the order. With the touch of a few buttons on the key pad, the computer automatically tied itself to the information being gathered by the sonar systems. Within seconds the launch protocols were ready.

"FOUR THOUSAND METERS AND CLOSING, Captain," the sonar man called out. "Impact in . . ." Again, what he saw on the instruments just couldn't be. "Sir, it's moving at nearly *three hundred kilometers an hour*." He winced as he held his earphones as close as he could. "And it screams like a demon from hell!"

Chang looked to the Fire Control Officer, saw him nod, and picked up the intercom mike again. *"Torpedo room*—the target's plot has been computed. *Launch the weapons."*

All eyes turned to the weapons display as first one, and then another light went from red to green.

"Weapons away!" Fire Control called out.

"Captain?" The voice was quietly subdued. Chang looked to his First Officer. "Nothing can move that fast underwater. What is it?"

"I wish I knew, Whe."

There was nothing to do now but wait, and at the speed this demon was approaching, that wouldn't take long. Chang turned again to the sonar display and watched as the electronic signature grew closer to the ship. Sonar called out a warning.

"Brace for impact!"

* * * *

SOUND AND VIBRATION ABOARD ANY SUBMA-rine was an unwelcome phenomenon. Taken together, and in great magnitude, the two could only be regarded as an indication of disaster.

The Captain and his First Officer heard—and felt—the low, rumbling *whump* at the same time every other member of the crew did. Without warning, the *Gansu Province* lurched forward, shaken violently by what felt like a collision from astern. Chang reached out instinctively to steady himself, but as the ship rolled to starboard everyone standing in the control room found themselves thrown to the deck. Just before his head struck a bulkhead, Chang felt something pop in his ears as the pressure in the hull was radically altered.

First Officer Song felt a sense of dread. He remembered reading about submarine calamities during his early training. The United States had lost two nuclear subs during the 1960s, and each boat had gone down with all hands. The safety record of Soviet boats had been even worse. The sea was an unforgiving mistress that tolerated no mistakes when it came to submarines. As he wondered about what had happened, the groaning hull stopped its pitching roll and slowly righted itself.

His forehead bleeding, Captain Chang jumped to his feet as the ship's emergency claxon sounded. With the alarm ringing in their ears, the crew picked themselves up and scrambled to their posts. Song reached the damage control console ahead of his Captain, and the glowing monitor before him told a horrific story.

"*Explosion in the engineering spaces, Captain!*" Song was wide-eyed. One—or both—of the torpedoes must have hit their target, resulting in an explosion of some kind. But it had been too close. The blast must have caused a breach in the hull. "We are taking on water in the reactor room. Temperatures in the compartments aft of the main generator have reached three hundred degrees and are climbing."

Chang wiped the blood from his face. "We are on fire," he replied calmly.

A hull breach was bad enough. Fire aboard an oxygen-rich environment like the *Gansu Province* was equally deadly, and Chang and his crew would have to deal with both.

"Seal all watertight doors aft of the reactor. Get on the phone to Engineering and find out if anyone is still alive in there."

As Song moved to obey, Chang addressed the helmsmen. "Do we still have power?"

One of the two men charged with guiding the sub turned to Chang. The Captain saw the perspiration and fear on his face.

"Negative, sir. Helm is unresponsive. We are losing forward momentum."

"What is our current depth?" Chang barked.

"Two hundred meters, sir," came the reply.

Chang frowned at the news. Without forward motion, and with the ship taking on water, the sub would fall to the bottom. Their only hope now lay in somehow reaching the surface.

"Song, who's left in Engineering?"

The Exec jammed the phone back in its cradle. "No response, Captain."

Chang quickly scanned the damage control monitor. The temperature in the spaces behind the reactor room had now reached five hundred degrees. The Captain turned to the Diving Officer and ordered him to blow the ballast tanks fore and aft.

* * * *

AS THE VALVES WERE OPENED, THE CREW HEARD the reassuring sound of compressed air being forced into the bow compartments. The nose of the ship lifted slightly, but the airlines leading to the stern had been severed. Water continued to pour into the sealed spaces aft, and the *Gansu Province* began to sink.

There was only one option now. Chang lifted a microphone from the bulkhead. "This is the Captain," he announced firmly. In the face of disaster his first concern was to calm his crew's fear. If he could do that, Chang knew, they still had a chance. "All hands muster amidships—near the main hatch—and prepare to abandon ship."

Song knew what the Captain had in mind. Built into the sub's conning tower was a pressurized compartment, with enough room for the entire crew. The capsule was designed to detach from the hull and carry the men to safety. The *Gansu Province* was the first Chinese submarine equipped with such a device.

Things were happening much more quickly now. As the crew scrambled into the escape capsule, the blaze aft raced forward. Temperatures in the stern compartments were pushing one thousand degrees. The ship's electrical system began to overload, and small explosions and fires erupted in the command center.

As the lights began to flicker, the last crewman squeezed into the conning tower. Chang pulled himself up the ladder behind him and sealed the hatch. He was amazed that most of them were still alive. In the cramped enclosure, the men could hear the hull groaning beneath them as the pressure of the depths increased.

Chang took hold of the lever that would release the clamps and free the chamber. He pulled with all his might, but the mechanism held fast. Undaunted, he tried again, this time aided by several of the crew; but the handle refused to budge.

Chang had taught his crew that there were always options. Even now, he knew there was still one more alternative, but it would require sacrifice. Without hesitation, he opened the hatch that led below and swung his frame down the ladder. Song watched incredulously, but before he could protest the Captain's actions, Chang had dogged the hatch and was gone.

* * * *

EVERY SYSTEM ABOARD THE SHIP—EVEN THE capsule's release mechanism—had a back-up. Chang groped his way through the darkness, occasionally guided by the light of sparking equipment or a burning panel. He found a flashlight and dropped to his knees as smoke began to fill the command center. Astern, the flooded compartments could hold no more, and the weighted vessel began to descend at a steeper angle.

Chang found the back-up release and threw the lever. This time it worked. The ship lurched slightly as its mass shifted, and Chang heard a terrific *ka-klunk* as the conning tower broke free. But with the escape capsule headed toward the surface, the *Gansu Province* lost the buoyancy that kept it fighting for life. The ship slipped deeper into the sea.

* * * *

SUDDENLY, THE SUB'S INTERIOR WAS A MUCH emptier place than Chang had grown accustomed to. He was truly alone now, trapped in a sinking steel coffin, surrounded by darkness and smoke. He could hear his ship crying out, as if in pain, as tons of water pressed against the hull.

A less resourceful man would have given up, but the Captain pressed on.

* * * *

ONLY THE COMMAND CENTER AND THE SUB'S forward compartments remained intact, but the crushing depths would soon change that. Chang headed toward the bow through the central passageway that ran the length of the ship. Along the way, he resorted to a practice not condoned by the Chinese military.

He prayed.

Everything seemed to move in slow motion. Chang tried to remain as calm as he could while maintaining a sense of urgency. There wasn't much time left, but if he hurried, there was still a chance he might survive.

* * * *

IN THE SHIP'S FORWARD TORPEDO ROOM WAS an escape trunk. The tiny compartment was designed like the conning tower chamber, but on a much smaller scale. Chang hoped to reach the trunk, seal himself inside and break free from the doomed sub. But he was racing against the clock.

Several thoughts flashed through his mind in those last moments. *What disaster had befallen his ship? What type of weapon had attacked them?* Clearly there had been a detonation of some kind, but with no explosives in the torpedoes, the blast must have originated with their attacker. He shook his head. Everything had happened so quickly. *And what about his crew?* Would the untested escape capsule carry his men safely to the surface?

Chang forced those questions from his mind and squeezed through the torpedo room hatch. He pointed the beam of the flashlight ahead, past the undersea missiles lashed to their racks. Above him, and at the end of the passageway, Chang could see the escape trunk.

* * * *

THE HULL GROANED MORE VIOLENTLY, AND AS the Captain reached his only means of escape and climbed inside, the final blow came. The ship's titanium skin was designed to withstand tremendous pressure, but the *Gansu Province* was mortally wounded. With the hull vented to the sea, the unrelenting grip of the depths closed in.

Starting at the stern, the bulkheads that divided the ship's compartments began to fail. Seawater forced its way into every seam of the dying ship, and the raging fire that had consumed much of the sub was snuffed out in an instant. The pressurized spaces forward lasted only milli-seconds longer.

In the wink of an eye, the hull collapsed in a series of muffled implosions; a cloud of bubbles formed around the hull as the wreckage descended, and by the time she reached the bottom, the *Gansu Province* was nothing more than a crumpled mass of twisted metal.

Chapter Two ✴ Questions and Answers

Six months later
Heathrow Airport
London, England

THE POLICE ESCORT WAS THE FIRST TO arrive. Two British officers on motorcycles rolled onto the flight line through an entry control point—or ECP, using one of the acronyms commonly employed these days at military and commercial airports. A pair of diplomatic limousines followed close behind. The lead car was a Mercedes; the second, a Lexus. Painted black and heavily armored, both were sleek and outwardly featureless with darkly-tinted windows.

The vehicles moved away from the main terminal complex and edged along the pavement at an unhurried pace. Finally the escort slowed to a halt at the runway boundary. The limos did the same.

There was activity in the air as well; quite a bit on this unseasonably warm day, but only one aircraft captured the attention of the occupants in the waiting cars. At the other end of the tarmac a Gulfstream VC-20 swooped down from the sky and lowered its landing gear. The pavement rushed up to greet the descending executive jet, and in a moment its wheels brushed lightly against the runway, a testament to the piloting skills of the Air Force Captain at the controls. As the pilot reduced power and began taxiing, the American DV—or Distinguished Visitor (another military acronym)—sighed his relief.

"I hate transatlantic flights," he grumbled to no one in particular, but loud enough to be heard by his aide and the two Secret Service agents who accompanied him.

Across the aisle, his comment elicited a grin from Richard Aultman. The Special Assistant to the National Security Advisor looked away from his window and smiled at his boss.

Willis Avery, the President's right hand man, grunted and shifted his bulky frame in the seat he was strapped to. "Blasted chairs," he muttered. "Never could get comfortable in these."

Aultman raised an eyebrow. "Maybe next time we'll come over in Air Force One. I'll make a note to ask about that when we get back."

Avery gave him a stern look. "I'll bet it's that dry wit of yours that makes you such a hit at parties. Tell me again why I keep you around."

"Who else would buy your souvenirs?" Aultman asked.

Avery looked pensive. "That reminds me—my daughter will be expecting something when I get back." He stared downward as he often did when he was deep in thought. "Something very—*British.*"

Aultman's eyes lit up. "How about a snow globe? With the Tower of London in it."

"Too macabre," Avery said. "Maybe Big Ben."

"Yeah. Very classy."

* * * *

THE WHINE OF THE TURBOFAN ENGINES RECEDed. In just a few moments the little jet was parked on the ramp, parallel with the waiting limousines.

The cars emptied first, a diplomatically appropriate gesture for the host nation's representatives. Four security agents emerged from the Lexus and fanned out around the aircraft. A British diplomat stepped casually from the Mercedes, donning a pair of sunglasses to shield his eyes from the noonday sun. An aide followed. After a brief pause, the door of the jet swung open and its passengers disembarked.

The two Secret Service agents exited first, followed by Aultman. The National Security Advisor squeezed through last, bending slightly at the waist to avoid bumping his head. The diplomat stepped forward and extended his hand.

"Mr. Avery," he said with a broad grin and a distinctively English accent. "So good of you to come. I trust you had a pleasant flight?"

Avery gripped his hand and smiled back. "Pleasant enough," he lied. "Brian Weston, correct?"

"Quite right," Weston answered, visibly surprised. "We met at the Embassy in Washington last year. You remembered."

Avery chuckled. "First rule of diplomacy—*never forget a face.*"

Aultman noted the differences between Weston and Avery as they exchanged greetings. It was quite a study in contrasts. The young Weston was impeccably dressed, wearing a smart ensemble undoubtedly purchased at some Piccadilly clothier's shop; Avery wore a rumpled suit, and his unruly head of hair seemed forever out of place. Next to their host, the National Security Advisor was a big man, with broad shoulders and an imposing presence.

Avery turned. "Brian, this is my assistant, Richard Aultman." The two shook hands. "Richard, meet Major Weston."

"Major?" Aultman said.

Weston looked almost embarrassed. "RAF, Mr. Aultman. Intelligence branch." He fingered the lapel of his jacket. "These days I don't wear the uniform much, I'm afraid." His toothy grin told Aultman that he wasn't quite as disappointed as he let on.

WITHIN MINUTES THE TWO CARS HAD EXITED the ECP and were rolling through the streets of London. Avery and Aultman sat in the back of the Mercedes for the trip in. Weston was across from them, facing toward the rear of the car. As the landscape raced by, the Major got down to the business at hand.

"We'll arrive at your hotel shortly," Weston said. He paused and pulled a thin folder from a leather satchel at his side. "In the meantime, I thought you might like to see this; you certainly wasted no time in getting over here."

The long flight had worn Avery down, but the sight of the dossier in the Major's hands seemed to perk him up. Reaching across, Avery took the file and scanned a newspaper article that was attached to the front.

"*American envoy to meet with Prime Minister.*" The headline was in bold type. A subhead ran below it. "*Officials to discuss Middle Eastern security concerns.*"

Avery smiled. "News travels fast, doesn't it, Major?"

Weston frowned. "I'm afraid Lord Mallory doesn't share your glee, Mr. Avery," he said, referring to the British Prime Minister. "He prefers to keep matters of State private. He's very serious about protecting the realm."

Avery made note of the Major's remark; as an American, he would have said *homeland security* or something similar—but in a monarchy, the choice of phrase was different. The subtleties in terminology always made international discussions just a little more interesting.

"Leaking this visit to the press wasn't entirely my idea," Avery replied. "But it's a tactic that I'm hoping will work to our advantage. Something's not right in the Far East, Major—it seems that elements of the Chinese military are up to no good. We suspect Admiral Xian Lee is at the heart of it." He tapped the newspaper clipping with his index finger. "This story will divert attention from the real purpose of our visit."

"Admiral Lee?" Weston asked. The Major knew that the man was head of Chinese Naval Forces in the Pacific. "It would appear your intelligence services are a step ahead of ours, then."

Avery nodded. "Lee is ranting about Taiwan again," he

sighed heavily. "Problem is, more of his countrymen are starting to listen." While Taiwan had asserted its independence for years—with the lukewarm approval of Western nations—China still regarded the island nation as a rebellious child that they desperately wanted under their sovereign control.

Weston looked thoughtful. "I see your point. That would certainly explain quite a bit."

Aultman sat up a little and began to take an active interest in the conversation. The car sped along Bayswater Road, passing Hyde Park as it went. But by now Aultman wasn't paying attention to the scenery.

Avery had opened the folder and pulled out a photograph. "We knew we had something when MI:6 contacted our intelligence services." He was referring to Her Majesty's Secret Service, the branch focused on foreign threats. "Especially when we discovered the location of what you'd found." He studied the photo in his hand. "Is this your asset in the Pacific?"

Aultman craned his neck and got a glimpse of the black and white glossy.

Weston nodded. "She's the HMS *Bradford*, an *Astute* class attack boat. Presently on station off the coast of southern China." Another grin. "*Well* off the coast, in international waters," he was quick to add.

"Nice place to be this time of year," Avery noted.

"Yes, quite," the Major replied. "She's been nosing about there for the past three weeks."

"And we appreciate it," Avery said. What the Major didn't know was that the *Bradford* had sailed to the Pacific at the request of the U.S. Navy—America had intentionally kept her vessels out of the area, hoping the absence of U.S. ships might cause the Chinese military to act a little more freely—and possibly reveal their hand. "Turn up anything interesting?"

Weston leaned forward slightly. "Six days ago the *Bradford's* sonar acquired an unusual submerged contact."

"Submarine?"

The Major nodded. "A very evasive one, too, it would

seem. Our boat tracked her for some time. They lost contact with it only yesterday."

Avery pursed his lips, deep in thought. The Mercedes turned right onto Regent Street, and Piccadilly Circus lay just ahead. "Any idea whose sub it was?" he finally asked.

"Her Majesty's ships are all accounted for," the Major answered, and then a sly grin spread across his face. "And we're reasonably sure where you chaps have *yours*. That narrows it down a bit."

"Leaving who?"

"The *Bradford's* skipper believes she's an old Soviet Oscar class boat," Weston continued. "But we don't think she's flying the Russian flag."

"Then whose sub is it?" Avery asked. Aultman had an odd feeling his boss already knew the answer to that question.

"At first we weren't sure," Weston replied. "Years ago, the Russians sold a number of Oscars. Some of their clients were less than reputable—Iran, Iraq. And *China*." Weston enunciated the last nation slowly and deliberately. "And now you mention that you have your own suspicions regarding the People's Republic."

"Yes." Avery said simply. "We keep coming back to our friends in the East, don't we?"

The operation tasked with keeping up with the submarines of hostile nations was code-named SHELL GAME. Since the end of the Cold War, it had given a great deal of job security to the American intelligence community.

The Major moved on. "In any case, British security services got involved, and this morning—" he reached into the leather satchel, producing two more photos, "—they gave us this to chew on."

Avery looked them over and grunted in satisfaction. "Satellite imagery," he muttered aloud. Squinting at the pictures, he studied every detail. The high resolution photos pinpointed an area that looked familiar, but Avery couldn't quite place it. "Where is this?"

Weston leaned in again, tracing a finger down the middle of one of the shots. "This is the Chinese coastline. *These*—" he pointed to three specks of land, about one hundred kilometers due south, "—are the islands of Huo Shan."

"What's so special about them?" Aultman asked.

"Next photo," Weston answered. "A much closer shot."

Avery shifted his focus to the second image. "Appears to be some construction on the southern tip of the largest island," he said. "Right on the water; probably a small naval facility. A helipad, fuel depot here on the left, and this—"

"A pier, nestled in that small inlet," Weston finished for him. "Enclosed, at that."

Smiling now, Avery looked up. "That's a submarine pen."

The Major nodded. "Our assessment as well," he said.

Aultman was catching on. "You think the mystery sub is based there? Does it belong to the Chinese Navy?"

Weston frowned. "That's a bit tricky. Huo Shan is supposed to be uninhabited. China has laid claim to the islands, but for some reason they've been ignored by Beijing. And if the Chinese are operating an Oscar in these waters, why base the submarine there, when they have numerous ports along their coastline?" He shook his head. "And if that wasn't enough, there's another mystery; her acoustic signature reads like a diesel boat."

"I thought Oscars were nuclear powered."

"Quite right. We don't know if the sub belongs to China or not, but given our current intelligence, that is the most likely conclusion. The *Bradford* tracked the boat for days, and she never strayed far from this island chain." He leaned back in his seat. "When they lost contact, that's where the sub was headed."

"What about the possibility it's an Iranian boat?" Avery asked. "Or maybe someone else's?"

"Iran has two Oscars at present." The Major replied. "Both are in the Persian Gulf. Syria has one, somewhere in the Indian Ocean. And we know where all of Russia's submarines are."

Avery sighed at the mention of those three countries. Each had been a thorn in his side over the past few years, with Iran and Russia drawing most of his ire. He was about to editorialize when Aultman chimed in.

"What if it's something else?" Richard asked slowly. "Suppose this boat doesn't belong to the Chinese Navy at all, but a faction of their military that's under the radar. Maybe some ultra-nationalist group." He reached across and took one of the photos. "This naval base suddenly appears on an uninhabited island; the very nature of it seems secretive. It's possible the Chinese high command doesn't even know it's there."

Weston was thoughtful. "Those islands are well outside of their normal patrol routes; if someone wanted to hide their activities, Huo Shan would be the perfect place." Another thought came to mind, but he kept it to himself. "Rather puts us back at square one, doesn't it?"

The three men were quiet for a moment as the cars passed Trafalgar Square, then crossed the river Thames. Finally Weston broke the silence.

"What piqued your interest in Chinese naval activity? You mentioned earlier that something was afoot there; could you elaborate?"

Avery looked up and nodded. "You've been more than forthcoming, Major. I guess it's time we returned the favor." He looked out on the city. The Tower of London appeared in the distance as the traffic began to slow their pace.

"Six months ago, our underwater listening nets in the Philippines picked up something we've never seen—or heard—before." There was still quite a bit he hadn't told Weston. "As a result, we've stepped up the alert status of our fleet around the world. Our consulates and embassies are keeping their eyes open, too. Additionally, we've deployed the *Victory* to Pearl Harbor, along with her control ship."

Weston's eyes widened. The *Victory* was America's newest class of warship, an unmanned, frigate-sized vessel armed to the teeth with cruise missiles and controlled remotely by another ship from miles away. She was designated as an arsenal ship; an upgrade to the battle wagons the U.S. Navy currently had sailing the world's oceans. Sending the *Victory* to the Pacific—and possibly farther—meant two things to Weston. The first was that the United States intended to send Beijing a message. The second—combat action against the Chinese was unthinkable. Clearly tensions in the region must have escalated for the Americans to consider such a move.

"Do you think she might actually be needed there?" the Major asked.

Avery reached into his briefcase and produced several photos of his own, then handed them over to the British officer. The Major studied them before offering a comment.

"Debris field? Where were these taken?"

"South China Sea, in about eight hundred feet of water." Avery answered. "We believe that's what's left of China's most advanced submarine."

Weston's frown returned. "Accident?"

"Not according to the experts."

"Then what?"

Avery sat back in his seat, and for the first time in the conversation, he had no answer. The silence that followed left Weston chilled.

Chapter Three ✷ Assignment at Sea

Three days later
Aboard the amphibious assault ship,
USS Lexington,
Off the coast of Northeast Africa

"I'M TOO OLD FOR THIS."

The Second Lieutenant was huffing and puffing as he ran. "Let me get this straight," he managed between breaths. "You do this seven days a week, right?"

As he plodded along he was flanked by three other Marines. Each was deeply tanned, the result of physical training on the flight deck and daily sessions spent on the fantail practicing rifle marksmanship. One was First Lieutenant Michael Neill. The other was a Second Lieutenant, fresh-faced and straight out of Officer Candidate School. The third was a Sergeant, about the same age as his comrades.

It was Neill who answered. "Well, not quite," he replied. "I take Sunday off. That's the Lord's day."

Second Lieutenant Nathan Crockett nearly lost his stride. Neill's faith was no secret, but Crockett was unprepared by his reference to God.

"Sit-ups?" Crockett asked, pressing on.

"One hundred, every morning."

"Pull-ups?" Sergeant Douglas Butler spoke up. It was getting harder to run and talk at the same time.

"Twenty or so," Neill said.

"So in other words, you run the PFT six days a week," Crockett responded.

Michael shrugged and wiped the sweat off his brow. "Look at it this way; every Marine has to pass the PFT twice a year." He drew in a deep breath as Crockett grunted. "Then there's the combat fitness test. You've got to be in shape for that too. If you do it every day, the PFT is a piece of cake."

Winded as they were, the men could see the wisdom in Neill's words. The PFT, or Physical Fitness Test, was a twice yearly examination required for every Marine, General to Private. Failure to pass was not an option—for anyone.

Lieutenant Crockett struggled with the physical demands of the PFT just a little more than those he was running with today. He was older than he looked. After high school he'd started down a path of scholastic achievement. His university studies bored him. He stuck it out long enough to earn a bachelor's degree, but the prospect of a career in the family business didn't inspire, so he surprised everyone by enlisting in the Marines. In a twist no one saw coming, Crockett excelled on the rifle range and was fast-tracked from the School of Infantry to one of the Corps' elite scout/sniper platoons. At the end of his formal training he received the coveted title of HOG, or Hunter of Gunmen.

His thirst for challenge didn't end there. Conquering everything the Corps threw at him, he used his college education to further his military career—deciding there was no point in throwing away a perfectly good degree. Crockett selected an officer candidate program that fit his level of progression, and after the Basic School he found himself aboard the *Lexington* as a newly-minted Second Lieutenant.

The Leathernecks continued to run around the outer perimeter of the *Lexington*'s flight deck. The forty thousand ton ship was anchored in calm seas, the overhead sun beating down on the non-skid coating underfoot. They rounded the ship's stern and moved forward, along the starboard side of the vessel. Up ahead lay the enormous bridge structure, housing the *Lexington*'s command center and other vital equipment used to navigate and protect the ship.

As they headed toward the bow, a big troop-carrying helicopter blocked their path. The runners angled around it, and the other officer, on Crockett's right, spoke for the first time.

"What about the Commandant's new policy?" he asked. Second Lieutenant Ben Shipley held his side as they edged past the chopper. He'd experienced cramps during PT before, but this— "Are the rumors true?"

"Afraid so," Neill chuckled. "General Cole intends to push for a quarterly PFT," he caught his breath— "starting next year."

Neill heard a collective groan. The Corps was known for its emphasis on physical fitness, but the Commandant seemed obsessive about it. As a member of General Cole's staff, Neill had witnessed that compulsion first-hand.

The four men had nearly reached the bow of the ship, and Lieutenant Neill picked up the pace. Crockett struggled to keep up.

"I guess the PFT is the least of our worries," he remarked, looking out over the horizon. "Especially if this Somalian thing gets any hotter."

Crockett had a point. The Marine Expeditionary Unit—or MEU—had spent five uneventful months at sea, but now things were heating up. The brewing African crisis might have been out of sight, but it was never far from anyone's mind.

"Guess you're right," Neill replied, again wiping the sweat from his brow. "Hey, Ben, you okay?"

Out of the corner of his eye Neill had seen Shipley stop abruptly. Mike did the same and turned to face the younger officer. Ben was now clutching his right side with both hands, a look of indescribable pain etched on his face. He let out a stifled yelp then collapsed to the deck.

Neill and Crockett reacted instantly, kneeling beside the groaning Second Lieutenant. Shipley continued to grip his side.

"Ben," Mike's voice was urgent. "What's wrong?"

A frown darkened Crockett's face. "Heat exhaustion?"

Neill tried to get some reaction from his friend. "Don't know," he answered. Ben was now breathing in short, labored gasps. "Let's get him to medical. He needs to see the doc."

Crockett nodded and they draped Shipley's arms over their shoulders. The Lieutenant moaned in pain as they carried him into the bridge superstructure and then below decks into the heart of the massive ship.

* * * *

AFTER TAKING BEN TO MEDICAL, MICHAEL stayed close, hanging around until he could speak to one of the medics working on his friend. The passageway was narrow, and Neill felt awkward as he waited. Finally the ship's physician appeared with lab work in hand. Catching his eye, Michael asked, "How's he doing, Doc?"

"Looks like you got him and his appendix down here just in time. He'll be just fine—but no more PT for a while."

"Can I see him?"

The doc shrugged. "He's sedated, Lieutenant. Won't even know you're there. But be my guest."

"No worries," Neill said. "Only be a minute."

He entered the pre-op area and found Ben sleeping peacefully. With a light touch on his friend's shoulder, Michael bowed his head in prayer.

NEILL COULD SMELL DINNER EVEN BEFORE HE reached the chow hall. Two hours had passed since Shipley collapsed. Before heading to the mess deck, he showered and put on a fresh set of camouflaged utilities. By then it was time to eat, and he was pleased to find chopped steak with mashed potatoes and gravy on the menu. Steamed vegetables and corn on the cob rounded out the meal. The Navy never failed to impress when it came to serving chow.

The big room was full of hungry sailors and Marines. At one end of the compartment Neill spotted Crockett and Butler wolfing down their food. There was no one sitting across from them, so he headed in that direction.

"Got room for me?"

Crockett looked up. "Have a seat." He popped a buttered roll into his mouth, his round face stretching to accommodate it. After chewing for a moment he managed a question. "How's our boy?"

"I just left him. The doc says he's got an inflamed appendix." Neill took a long draw on his milk. It was cold going down, and helped him forget about the humidity in this part of the world.

"Ouch," Butler winced. He scooped up some mashed potatoes. "The doc gonna operate?"

"Looks that way. He'll be out of circulation for a week or so."

"Then he'll miss all the action."

Neill looked up. "*The action?*"

Crockett grinned as he chewed his food. "Colonel McLane and the Skipper were seen headed for the briefing theater. Scuttlebutt is that something's up—big time."

"That *is* news," Neill said thoughtfully. He picked up his knife and fork, attacking the steak on his tray.

Crockett had finished his meal. "Word spreads fast around here. I just keep my eyes open." He wiped his mouth with a napkin. "You really oughta stay in the loop, Mike."

Neill smiled. "That's what I keep you around for, Crockett."

In a few more minutes Neill was finished too. He was thinking about going back for a slice of apple pie and coffee when a Marine entered the mess deck and made his way to the table where he was sitting.

"Colonel McLane wants to see you, Lieutenant," the Lance Corporal said. "He's down in the wardroom."

Neill nodded in acknowledgement and picked up his tray. Dessert would have to wait.

* * * *

THE WARDROOM ON THE SECOND DECK WASN'T far. On his way there Neill passed the Skipper in the passageway and came to attention. The ship's Captain threw him a casual salute and headed forward.

Inside the wardroom a podium had been set up with an overhead projector near the front. Rows of chairs were neatly arranged for the numerous briefings held throughout the course of the ship's deployment. In one corner was a desk with a laptop computer, and bending over it, peering intently at the screen, was a familiar figure. He turned when he heard Neill enter the room.

"Come on in, Lieutenant," the tall officer intoned. He strode across the deck with a purposeful swagger. Colonel Dennis McLane was a broad-shouldered man with a hawkish nose and penetrating blue eyes. Silver eagles were pinned to his collar, reflecting the overhead lights as he shook Neill's hand. As commanding officer, McLane was in charge of the fifteen hundred Marines who made up the Thirty-Second Marine Expeditionary Unit. The MEU was a fast-action, rapid response crisis team that waited for trouble to rear its head. When it did, the Marines—with a lot of help from the U.S. Navy—would be prepared to intervene.

"At ease," he barked. "Take a seat."

Neill pulled up a chair and did as he was ordered. "I just came from medical," the Colonel said as he leaned against the desk. "Commander Santorini says Shipley's going to be fine." Santorini was the chief medical officer on board. "Surgery's scheduled for nineteen hundred. He'll be good to go in no time." McLane looked at his watch, then pulled the chair away from the desk and positioned himself across from Neill. "We've got about fifteen minutes, so let's make use of the time and have ourselves a little conversation."

Aside from small talk and the occasional briefing, Michael couldn't recall any significant discussions he'd had with the Colonel. There was a decidedly odd tone in McLane's voice that instantly put him on guard.

"I've been looking over your file, Neill," he went on. "Good stuff. On the Commandant's staff, yet you volunteered for sea duty with the Thirty-Second. A field assignment to assess the combat effectiveness of new technology." From his front pocket McLane fished out a white, translucent object, about the size and shape of an ordinary playing card. "This tevlite is pretty interesting. Might even save some lives where we're going."

Neill nodded. "Body armor has come a long way in the past ten years. The Commandant hopes that wafers like this will be a part of that."

"Agreed. I've been reading up on this." He laid the wafer on the desk. "Of course, it's not true body armor; and it'll have to be proven in combat."

Neill understood the Colonel's skepticism. Tevlite was made of several composite materials layered together. In some circumstances, it could be nearly bulletproof. Several hundred wafers could be sewn into the linings of a Marine's uniform, sandwiched between the layers of fabric. Where the wafers overlapped they created even greater protection.

"They'll have to be proven to the individual Marine, too, sir," Neill added. "A heavier uniform is a hotter uniform; these don't add a lot of weight, but it is a consideration."

"True; but from what I've heard, it's only meant to supplement the battle rattle we normally wear." Both men seemed a bit more relaxed now. "Time will tell, as with any other advancement." McLane turned the laptop so he could better see the screen.

"In any case, I appreciate you being here with us. I could use more officers like you in the Thirty-Second." He tapped a few keys, and the screen displayed a popular internet browser. "And it seems you've made an impression in other places, too."

Neill almost grinned. He had a feeling he knew where this

was going.

"Not too many Marines get hand-picked for assignments by the National Security Advisor," he added casually. "Is it true Willis Avery sent you to Ukraine last year?"

Michael sat back in his chair and tried to convey a relaxed, but respectful, posture. "Not exactly, sir," he answered. "I was sent over to verify nuclear disarmament. Avery asked me to look into something else while I was there." He measured his words carefully; his mission to the former Soviet Union wasn't exactly common knowledge, and there were certain—*aspects*—of that trip that were highly classified.

McLane smiled. He enjoyed an occasional game of cat and mouse. "Pretty dry stuff, nuclear disarmament and all that. What's it like over there?"

"Beautiful countryside," Neill replied. "You might have heard that I grew up there."

McLane's eyes widened. "No, I hadn't," he lied. "You speak Russian?"

Michael nodded again. "Fluently. My Ukrainian's not bad either." A subtle parry.

McLane folded his arms and looked up at the ceiling. His smile suggested that he knew more, but he decided it was time to shift gears.

"Thirty minutes ago I received a message from the Joint Chiefs of Staff. As you might guess, Operation HEAVY ANVIL is a go."

Neill was glad to change the subject. Some secrets were just too hard to keep. He was more than willing to drop the whole thing and focus on the country—and the mission—just over the horizon.

The CIA had frequently described Somalia as a government in anarchy. Years earlier, a civil war had split the country. Competing factions took control of the southern half and set up a military dictatorship, creating two separate nations: Southern and Northern Somalia. The south had experienced one bloodbath after another. Atrocities were widespread. Famine and starvation became the order of the day. The north had fared some-what better; a fledgling democracy was taking root, but it was a shaky prospect at best.

"As you know, relations between the United States and the two Somalias have been strained of late," McLane continued. "This morning, our worst fears came to pass; a militant rebel faction in Southern Somalia attacked our embassy with rock-ets and gunfire. Fortunately, our people were prepared. There were no American casualties. However, that could change very quickly."

The Colonel turned to the computer and accessed the SIPRNet—the Secret Internet Protocol Router Network. McLane glanced at his watch once again. "The rebels show no signs of retreating at this point. It is the combined opinion of the Joint Chiefs that these people mean business. That's where HEAVY ANVIL comes in."

The Marines of the Thirty-Second had all heard the rumors; some of them were true. The U.S. had been expecting a move by Southern Somalia—and now the rebels had acted.

"So far, you've heard of this operation by name only. Now it's time for details.

"Operation HEAVY ANVIL is a two-pronged offensive. Colonel Hooper and his Marines will commence the attack by sweeping in from the east, moving toward a landfall on the beaches of Mendari. The faction we're dealing with is called the Urudisi Party, the most heavily armed group in the nation." At this point McLane pulled out a map from beneath the laptop. He laid his index finger on a position circled in red. "The American embassy is located here, in the city of Pashay. That's ten miles inland."

Neill studied the map. "You said this was a two-pronged of-fensive; where does that come into play?"

McLane nodded. "As I said, Colonel Hooper's group will move toward the beaches near Mendari. His people will com-mence firing on the rebels' shoreline batteries at a point safely out of their range. Since this assault is a ruse, it will only be necessary to get their attention."

"I think I see where you're going."

"I thought you might." McLane was clearly enjoying this. "The Urudisi Party has already divided its forces; a contingent on the shore, where they suspect us to attack, and another surrounding the embassy ten miles away. Our aim is to divide them further."

"What's the plan, sir?"

"Hooper's sea-based assault will draw their forces to the beach in an effort to repel our attack," McLane explained patiently. "With the rebels focused there, it should be easier for the second wave to slip in through the back door."

Looking at the map, Neill was beginning to understand.

"Here's where it gets a bit tricky," the Colonel said. "Three Ospreys will enter Northern Somalia's airspace from the Gulf of Aden." The V-22 Osprey had already distinguished itself in Afghanistan. "They will proceed south, crossing the border into Southern Somalia. One of the Ospreys will break formation and approach from the west, drawing the attention of the troops around the embassy. But that's just the bait—with the bulk of the Urudisi forces on the beach, the other two aircraft will swoop in, land in the embassy courtyard and effect the rescue of our personnel. We'll be in and out before the rebels know what hit them."

The plan sounded simple enough, but a dozen questions flashed through Neill's mind. McLane expected that and waded patiently into the mission's finer points. After clarifying a few details, the Colonel pressed on.

"I tell you all that because I know how much you'd hoped on participating in this mission." Neill wasn't sure he liked the sound of that. "Unfortunately, the Department of Defense has another assignment for you, Lieutenant—and it looks like our fifteen minutes are about up."

Neill was about to respond when the Colonel turned back to the laptop and tapped a few keys. The red splash screen of the SIPRNet disappeared, replaced by another official-looking DoD site. "I've been told to expect a secure transmission from an old friend of yours."

Both men watched as the screen winked in and out, then static, until finally the image resolved to reveal the interior of a plush office that Neill knew was nowhere near Somalia.

"Good to see you again, Lieutenant." Willis Avery's frame now filled the screen. "You still sticking your neck out for little old ladies?"

Neill grinned. "Not lately."

"Navy been treating you right?"

"Chow's great, sir." Neill replied. His response got a laugh from the National Security Advisor.

"You Marines. Always thinking about food," he said. He paused and patted his own stomach. "I guess we're a lot alike in that respect. Colonel McLane, we've got a few things to discuss. I'd like you to stick around for this."

McLane nodded. "Wouldn't miss it."

Avery adjusted his bulk in the chair he sat in. "I've just returned from London; security briefing with the Prime Minister and MI:6. Between our two respective countries, we've uncovered some disturbing activity in the South China Sea." He paused, and then added, "Along with a somewhat unexpected scenario."

The two Marines were now glued to the screen as Avery continued.

"Six months ago, the Chinese Navy lost their most advanced submarine—a boat called the *Gansu Province*." The image on the screen froze, pixelated briefly, then returned to normal. "She was attacked on her maiden voyage and sunk about a hundred kilometers from the Chinese mainland."

"Attacked?" McLane wasn't sure he'd heard right.

Avery looked away long enough to direct someone off-screen. "Richard, punch up those first photos."

Instead of Avery being in the picture, a series of black and white images were now being displayed on the monitor.

"This is the wreckage. One of our deep research submersibles got these. As you can see, there's not much left."

Neill whistled softly. The *Gansu Province* lay in a debris field littered with twisted shards of metal and titanium. He wouldn't even have known he was looking at a submarine if Avery hadn't clued them in. "Who attacked them?"

Avery's face returned, with a frown. "The who, what, and why are somewhat of a mystery to us. But we suspect a rogue element of the Chinese military is behind it. Next photo."

A new image appeared; an Asian man wearing a Chinese Naval officer's uniform.

"This is Admiral Xian Lee," Avery went on. "In charge of China's Pacific fleet. Old school, hardline Communist, and from what our sources tell us, not a very nice guy."

"You suspect Lee is behind the sinking of one of his own submarines?" McLane asked. "What's his motive?"

"Money. Power. Maybe even his own distorted sense of self-importance," Avery replied. "We've been able to connect him with several Russian industrialists and ship-building firms in the old Soviet empire. Even before the loss of the *Gansu Province*, he's steered the Chinese Navy to buy their ships and submarines. Over the past few years, China has built very few of their own—and after this incident, they'll probably be building even less. We suspect that's his plan—undermining confidence in the Chinese ship-building industry."

"Is he taking his orders from the top, or does the Chinese senior leadership even know about it?" Neill asked.

"Lee has managed to keep this very quiet," Avery answered. "With his rank and power, he's in a position to control the flow of certain types of information. And he collects a boatload of money—pardon the pun—every time China purchases a naval vessel from the Russians, thanks to his nefarious associations."

"Why not just tell his bosses in Beijing?" McLane asked.

"I doubt they would believe us," Avery answered. "Hardliners like Lee keep getting between their leadership and our diplomatic efforts."

Neill began thinking out loud. "So Lee is secretly aligned with Russian profiteers—enriching himself at the same time."

"That's right," Avery replied. "It's the old story of having absolute power and being corrupted by it."

McLane shook his head. "And killing the crew of a submarine is the price for getting more."

"Not quite, Colonel," Avery said. "That's the only silver lining to this whole catastrophe; only four members of the crew died. The rest escaped before the boat went to the bottom. The survivors—including the ship's Captain—were picked up by a Chinese destroyer the next day." He affected a humorless smile. "They testified that whatever attacked them ignited a 'scorching wind' on board. I believe their exact words were a '*tempest of fire*.'"

Neill was surprised to hear that. "How is that possible?" His mind went back to undersea disasters suffered by the United States and Russia during the Cold War years. "Usually no one survives the sinking of a sub."

Avery nodded. "Normally you'd be correct. But this ship was built with a specially designed escape pod—which the crew made good use of."

"What do we know about how the ship was sunk?"

"The crew testified that something came out of nowhere and targeted them. They managed to launch two torpedoes in a counter-attack." The screen froze briefly again and then returned. The satellite feed hadn't quite stabilized. "Details are sketchy, but it would appear that at least one torpedo hit its target. The resulting explosion damaged the sub and caused a breach of the hull."

"What did the torpedo hit?" Neill asked.

"The sub's sonar detected an incoming—well . . . something—approaching the boat at a speed well over three hundred miles an hour." Avery stopped and let that sink in before continuing. "Only quick thinking by the ship's Captain saved the lives of the crew."

Neill was a little confused. "You're saying they detected an inbound missile—*before* it entered the water?" Even he knew that sonar only worked below the surface.

Avery shook his head. "No, Lieutenant," he answered firmly. "I'm saying that whatever attacked the *Gansu Province* was underwater the entire time."

Both Marines sat slowly back in their chairs. McLane was the first to respond. "God Almighty. Traveling at a speed of—what the Sam Hill was it?"

The frown returned to Avery's face. "A new weapons system," he said flatly. "And a rather destabilizing one at that. Given the crew's testimony, we've code-named it TEMPEST."

"And you think Admiral Lee is behind all of this, acting on his own?" Neill was trying to clarify his thinking.

"Yes; he stands to profit if China abandons its own shipbuilding programs," Avery said. "His alliance with the Russians has already paid off. And we've learned that he opposed the construction of the *Gansu Province*. We found further evidence of this on a small, three-speck island chain called Huo Shan. We suspect Lee's private navy is based at a secret facility quietly tucked away on the largest of the three."

"What exactly does Lee have at his disposal?"

"Our intel suggests the Admiral has acquired a Russian Oscar. We think he used that in the attack."

"How do you know all this?" Neill asked. The intelligence being laid out was certainly wide-ranging. "A lot of this information is pretty comprehensive—the speed of the weapon; the number of crew lost—"

Avery raised a hand. "Hold on, Lieutenant," he replied. "I'm getting to that."

"FIVE MONTHS AGO, THE CHINESE NAVY CON-vened a board of inquiry into the fate of the sunken boat," Avery continued. "According to their official report, the sub's Captain acted prematurely in launching his weapons. They found fault with his actions and laid the blame squarely on him." He could see the look of disbelief on the two Marine's faces. "We found that to be a bit odd, too, until we discovered who chaired the board."

"Let me guess," Neill offered. "Admiral Lee."

"You don't disappoint, son," Avery smiled. "Even though the Captain survived with the rest of his crew—saving their lives—the loss of his ship cost him his career." The National Security Advisor shook his head. "Admiral Lee stripped him of his rank and drummed him out of the Navy."

"A scapegoat," McLane said. "One that gave Lee an excuse to continue buying subs from the Russians."

"And here's where things took an interesting turn," Avery said in a somewhat dramatic tone. "Right after the board's findings were released, our ambassador in Taiwan received a letter—written in Russian."

"And?" Neill perked up at this news.

"It contained most of the information we have about the sub's sinking," Avery answered. "And it also included the findings of the board of inquiry."

"You think someone in Russia sent that letter?" McLane asked.

"We do," Avery replied. "The letter also detailed Admiral Lee's involvement with the Russians, and his plans to have the Chinese government buy ships from them."

"An informant inside Russia," Neill said. "Someone involved in their shipyards?"

"Possibly," Avery answered. "Maybe somebody handling the financial arrangements. We just don't know—yet."

"AND THAT'S WHERE YOU COME IN, Lieutenant," Avery said, straightening up in his seat. "We need to know more about what Admiral Lee's up to—specifically, we need some good old fashioned human intelligence."

"Boots on the ground," Neill replied.

"Exactly," Avery answered. "And some eyes on the islands of Huo Shan—focused on that naval facility. Get close—land if possible. Take some pictures; monitor radio traffic to and from the big island. I can't stress this enough, Neill—it's imperative that we find out more. Think you can do that for me?"

Neill thought it over. "I'll need a little help," he said finally. "One or two more Marines, if Colonel McLane can spare them." He had Crockett in mind.

The Colonel's eyebrows went up. "With a major operation about to start, that's all I can spare. I've already got one of my platoon leaders in medical." Then he raised his hands in mock surrender. "But I just follow orders; if you say jump, I ask 'how high?' "

Avery nodded as the screen skipped, then pixelated again. His image returned along with his reply. "Appreciate that, Colonel—no worries, a small team is all we need. This is a high-visibility mission, but we want it to remain well below the radar." He looked at Neill. "Get your people assembled, Lieutenant. You could probably use someone who speaks Mandarin. I'll see what I can do. And I'll see to it your travel arrangements are cleared through the DoD." He checked his watch. "You'll fly to Diego Garcia aboard an Osprey; from there, a C-130 will take you east to the Philippines. The Brits have offered their assistance and have a carrier making for Taiwan as we speak—you'll chopper from the Philippines out to her location. Specific instructions will be waiting for you when you arrive. The Royal Navy will take you where you need to go from that point." Avery turned to McLane. "Colonel, HEAVY ANVIL kicks off in a few hours; I'll get out of your hair so you can get your game face on."

"Just one thing, Mr. Avery," McLane asked. "The person who sent the letter to our ambassador—he didn't sign his name, did he?"

Avery looked back at the Marines from thousands of miles away. "Actually, Colonel, he did—" he picked up a pad and peered at some notes he'd taken. "He signed the letter—now let me see if I can say this right— '*Byeh-neh Drakon.*' " He looked up. "How's that sound, Lieutenant?"

Neill smiled. "Byeh-*leh* Drakon," he corrected.

"It means White Dragon."

Chapter Four ☆ Probing

North Island Naval Complex,
Office of Cyber Defenses
San Diego, California

ENSIGN KELSI PRESSMAN STUDIED THE COM-
puter screen in front of her, intent on ensuring the
software was operating properly. With the click of
her mouse, she ran a systems diagnostic check, and satisfied
with the result, she eased up from the seat in her cubicle and
motioned to her supervisor. Nodding, he got up from his desk
and began making his way across the room.

Tall and lanky, Lieutenant Commander Ronald Fitzroy
crossed the space quickly. "Did you confirm it?"

The young sailor pushed herself away from the screen. "Yes,
sir," she said, satisfaction in her voice. "It's not an electronic
anomaly or a system glitch. Not an echo, either. This looks like
the real deal. DEFENDER has detected a breaching operation directed at the naval grid's firewall." She rolled her chair closer
to the computer and pulled up a display. "It's very subtle, but
as you can see, the system is being interrogated by an outside
source."

Fitzroy leaned in. "Sure looks like it," he replied. Still, some
of the data was over his head. "You wrote this program, didn't
you, Pressman?"

"Yes, sir. She's my baby."

The Commander was impressed. The Navy had its own concerns about cyber-attacks, and no small sum of the DoD budget had been spent protecting their systems from espionage. Cyber counter-intelligence measures had been brought online after several nations suffered damage from computer-based attacks. The greatest risk was to the command and control operations of military networks that relied on computers to function effectively. USCYBERCOM was born, and acted as a shield against a mounting wave of attempted incursions.

To blunt the electronic assault required extensive knowledge of the threat, so defenders in the San Diego office learned how to go on the offensive. As a result, the command became very good at not only anticipating aggression, but also in tracing it back to its source. And given the level of sophistication, the list of suspected perpetrators was very short.

Ensign Pressman had played a role in that, acting as a *white hat*, a friendly hacker looking for weak spots in the Navy's electronic defenses. She learned a lot from her experience and spent nearly a year perfecting her own software to guard against malicious activity; her efforts were rewarded when the Navy began utilizing DEFENDER at the North Island facility. The software had paid off in spades; four attempted intrusions like this one had been caught early and the attacks thwarted.

"Any idea what the source is?" Fitzroy asked.

Pressman suppressed a chuckle. "I'll re-direct the system's resources. See if it can pinpoint where it's coming from. As if we couldn't guess." Again, she clicked the mouse and loosed the electronic bloodhounds. "Right now it's very early in the process. They're attempting a port scan to determine our vulnerabilities. Our firewall will prevent that." She looked up from her monitor as the software did its work. "What about that report from Seattle, Garcia?" she asked.

Her colleague in the next cubicle, a Petty Officer Second Class, regarded his own computer. "Cable company in Washington state reported an interruption to all bundled service.

Half a million customers are affected; internet, telephone, cable TV—all on the fritz, and they can't identify the source."

Fitzroy nodded. "Anywhere else?"

"Same thing in Oakland," Pressman answered. "It's a coordinated attack; whoever's doing this is testing the limits of their own software, hitting a variety of targets—including us."

A dialog box appeared on Pressman's screen. The information it relayed didn't surprise anyone.

"DEFENDER can't identify the source; whatever it is, its shielding is far too advanced." Then she smiled. "But that's all we need to know."

Garcia was new to the office of cyber defenses. "I don't get it."

It was Fitzroy's turn now. "It's the *complexity* of the attack that tells us who's behind it. If you've gone to this much trouble to hide who you are, you're definitely not some college kid in a dorm somewhere."

"It's at the nation state level, which probably means China," Pressman explained. "Their military academies have blocks of instruction dedicated to training in cyber warfare."

"That's true—but so do we," Fitzroy added. He felt the need for full disclosure on that point. Officers were like that.

"Only because we have to," Pressman countered. Fitzroy's remark left her a little hot under the collar. She eyed an empty cubicle near his office and then broke into a smile. "Lieutenant Chau would have a field day," she said. "This is right up his alley."

Fitzroy noted the lilt in her voice at the mention of the Lieutenant's name. It wasn't common knowledge—both officers were very discreet—but Fitzroy was well aware of the relationship Pressman and Chau shared. In fact, he silently encouraged it.

"Roger that," Fitzroy replied. "I'm sure if he wasn't playing with remote-controlled boats right now he'd consider this a real challenge."

Naval Forces Garrison Academy,
Beijing, China

AMONG THE GROUP OF TWO DOZEN ANALYSTS
in the science department, Lin Yuan was more than just a
technician. His peers and supervisors had recognized that
early on. They had even given him a nickname—*the Prober*.
With an aptitude for electronics, Yuan believed that the fates
had gifted him with a special competency—reserved for a select few—and had dictated the time of his birth for the computer age.

Lin's young life had been steeped in the internet. As part of
a generation that had grown up in the digital era, he steadily
advanced his knowledge to a point where the Chinese military
took notice. By his twentieth year, the brooding, tight-lipped
son of a shopkeeper received a commission in the PLA-Navy
and made his unpretentious family proud. Four years later, Yuan
asserted his skills to become the pre-eminent operator within
the expanding world of the PRC's cyber community. There was
no denying most of that was due in large part to his abilities.
But behind the scenes, and known only to a few, Lin's rise to
the top could also be traced to a powerful benefactor within the
Admiralty.

Yuan sat quietly and nearly alone in a sea of cubicles dedicated to this new branch of warfare. Only a handful of his col-
leagues manned their stations across the floor. Outside it was
dark, and the soft glow of his monitor was the sole source of
illumination in this part of the room. Lin reveled in the solitude
and enjoyed the level of concentration afforded by the early
hour. It was rare to find him here at this time of day, but he had
been instructed to apply his training toward targets during peak
operation, and that meant altering his schedule.

Yuan started with an analysis of his quarry's vulnerabilities. He needed to determine avenues of attack, and he had
several tools at his disposal. The first was an application that

detected data being passed over a network. With an over-arching view of a server's information environment, a hacker could direct his programs to intercept the passwords and usernames needed to gain complete control. Yuan's job was sometimes made easier by the fact that the wrong data was often protected. That was the case for two of his targets; the companies he'd selected in California were formidable, but not beyond his expertise. The third, on the other hand—

The task had begun well after midnight and Lin was almost finished. With this assignment nearing its end, the young officer thought it might be possible to wrap things up before sunrise. He pushed those thoughts aside for the moment. There were still a few details that required his attention.

Yuan tabbed through the applications running on his machine. This morning's forays into the electronic grids up and down the west coast of the United States yielded the expected results. The software he used allowed him to gain nominal control over the infrastructure of his targets in both Seattle and Oakland. To his disappointment, Lin was unsuccessful—*for the fifth time*, he reflected—in penetrating the firewall at the naval base in San Diego. Functional access to that facility just wasn't going to happen.

He sighed heavily. Lin wasn't used to having his efforts denied. He would have to re-tool the applications and adjust the algorithms *again*. And there was no way to tell if this attempt got any closer than the previous ones. It was like trying to open a combination lock—without the combination. He reminded himself that the American Navy's defenses *were* military grade; getting in to their servers required a whole new way of thinking. But Yuan—*the Prober*—was confident he would figure it out eventually. Destiny decreed it. It was a narcissistic view, but as time went by he would not be persuaded otherwise.

Entry channel to Pearl Harbor, Oahu, Hawaii
Aboard the escort vessel USS Meyer

IT WAS A STRETCH OF THE IMAGINATION TO consider the USS *Victory* as just a remote-controlled boat, but technically speaking it was somewhat accurate. At three hundred and fifty feet long, and with a low profile that whispered 'stealth,' the swift and silent unmanned vessel was the newest addition to the U.S. Navy's inventory. Even though she was technically classified as an arsenal ship, her outer features weren't bristling with weapons or anything else that would hint at her true purposes. The vessel's deadly cargo of cruise missiles and special weapons lay neatly hidden behind rows of hatch covers and below decks protected by heavily armored plating. Her futuristic looks and unorthodox piloting and navigational systems made her the flagship of a new class. She'd been sailing at nearly full speed since departing San Diego, but now, as she entered the channel, the *Victory* had slowed her pace, leaving only small, nearly imperceptible swells behind her stern as she passed Aloha 'Aina Park.

From a mile away, just off Ewa Beach, the USS *Meyer* maintained a watchful eye on the *Victory* as she moved through the channel. In the command center located near the bridge, Lieutenant (Junior Grade) Simon Chau monitored the *Victory's* progress, using a sophisticated GPS system that not only tracked the vessel, but also controlled her every move.

Hovering at Chau's shoulder was Senior Chief Petty Officer Malcolm Richey, arms folded across his barrel-like chest as he slowly weaved from side to side. Square-jawed, with a salt and pepper flat-top, he was powerfully built, and sported a narrow waistline that had grown slightly since he'd reached the age of thirty-five. Navy chow did that to a man.

Chau was muttering to himself, his words practically unintelligible, tapping the electronic display before him with a grease pencil. A candid photo of Ensign Pressman was stuck to one corner of his monitor. Half a dozen other sailors manned their stations in the small compartment. The Lieutenant spoke again, but his voice still lacked clarity.

Richey continued his slow, side to side motion. He knew Chau was given to occasional wanderings within his own mind. "Say again, Lieutenant?"

"Before the Japanese started their aerial attack," Chau's voice grew louder, and he leaned back in his chair. He seemed a little more relaxed now, and no longer oblivious to those around him. "The USS *Ward* was patrolling the mouth of the channel. The crew spotted a Japanese mini-sub and shelled it, sending it to the bottom."

"Is it still there?"

A shrug. "As far as I know," Chau replied. "But the exact location is classified—the State Department has an agreement with Japan to keep it that way."

Chau turned his attention back to the screen monitoring the arsenal ship's progress. The *Victory's* extensive optics array and radar suite told him that the traffic in the harbor was ramping up. Two ships had begun their transit to the mouth of the channel, and were headed for the open sea beyond. The Lieutenant thought it prudent to give these vessels a wide berth.

Using the controls at his fingertips, Chau directed the *Victory* toward Hospital Point, a position closer to shore and clear of the sea lane. He double-checked the depth below the arsenal ship's keel to ensure there was sufficient draft. He didn't want her to run aground. *Somewhat ironic*, he thought to himself. The spot he chose was very familiar to him.

Chau's mind conjured up images from the past. On December 7, 1941, the battleship *Nevada* had raced down the channel in a desperate attempt to escape the Japanese attack. Enemy aircraft swarmed after her. Their plan was to sink the warship, and block all traffic in or out of the harbor. To avoid that, the *Nevada's* Skipper had run his ship aground, near the very spot where the *Victory* now idled.

The historical significance of Chau's action was lost on the Senior Chief. During his eighteen year career with the Navy, Richey had only visited Hawaii one other time, spending most of his sea-going career in the Atlantic and Mediterranean. His intention had always been to return to Oahu and bring his wife, but those plans were dashed now.

Navy spouses were steadfast for the most part, but after ten years, Allison Richey decided she'd had enough of waiting for her man to return home from the sea. Malcolm had always assumed just the opposite, and maybe that was his biggest mistake. The wedding band he'd worn was gone now, just like his marriage. With a few strokes of a pen, the latter had dissolved, and a judge had decreed the legal action complete.

Richey wasn't as big on history as the young, hard-charging officer of Chinese descent. Chau's parents had encouraged an inquisitive nature in their young son. Hu Chau, Simon's father, had been a university professor in Shanghai. A journalist at heart, the elder Chau had dared to expose the abuses of the People's Republic. His first essay focused on the student protests in Tiananmen Square during the late 1980s. More followed, and in the years to come, his writings gained an everwidening audience.

At the dawn of the twenty-first century, the professor was jailed briefly for his published efforts. Censorship was a way of life in China, and after being released, Hu decided it was time for his family to escape the restrictions of the government.

The professor had a brother living in Taiwan, and along with a boatload of other dissidents, the small family left the mainland for more emancipated shores. A storm in the Strait had swamped their tiny vessel; several of the refugees drowned before a U.S. Navy frigate happened upon the survivors, desperately clutching the remnants of their craft and each other. Six year old Simon would remember that day for the rest of his life.

Despite Chau's ancestry, and relatively short time in the States, the young man had embraced all things associated with his new home, and constantly surprised the Chief with his knowledge of U.S. history, naval customs and heritage. Richey found him to be a curious mix of enthusiasm and passion against a more subdued and introspective calm.

"Attention on deck!"

From behind the two men, the Marine security guard manning the hatch appeared in the compartment. As the sailors stood to their feet, Chau saw the ship's commanding officer enter the room out of the corner of his eye.

Captain Robert Beacham strolled purposefully into the small room. For a man with his responsibilities, the ship's senior officer always seemed to possess a relaxed air about him. It was a quality that put his men at ease, and that suited Beacham just fine. On the other hand, the crew also knew that their skipper could adjust his temperament and become laser-focused when necessary.

"As you were," Beacham ordered. "Status report, Mr. Chau. Is the *Victory* on course?"

"Yes, sir," Chau fixed his eyes back on the monitor he'd been studying earlier. "She's at station keeping now while the *Parrish* and *Gibson* exit the harbor. Holding true and steady—" He checked the display. "—point seven five miles astern of the *Missouri*. She'll be ready to dock shortly."

"Mooring party?"

"Spoke to the harbormaster ten minutes ago, Skipper," Richey replied. "The crew on the pier is standing by to tie her up." The Chief's voice sometimes seemed more like a growl than anything else.

"Outstanding," Beacham replied. He liked what he heard, and rubbed a hand across his chin as a smile appeared on his face. The brief delay in the docking operation gave him just the opportunity he'd been waiting for.

"Did you find that Japanese mini-sub, Lieutenant?"

Chau blinked. "No, sir," he admitted. "How did—"

"I figured you'd try your hand." The Skipper said. "Had a lot of junior officers have a go at it. And one of them actually succeeded." He pulled a small notebook from his pocket. "Of course, it's outside the rules, but I have the coordinates right here. Now let's see if you're up to the challenge."

Richey watched as the Captain selected a page from the pad, and then fixed his eye on Chau.

"You ready for some mental gymnastics?"

The young officer was puzzled at first but was gradually becoming more aware. "Ready when you are, sir," he sighed.

Beacham looked pleased. "Very well then," he announced. He picked up a grease pencil from one of the workstations and then turned to a navigational chart on the bulkhead. The Captain surveyed the map and selected a point slightly northwest of their current position.

"Pearl's here—" Using the pencil he circled the naval base. "And these are the coordinates for that position." Beacham extended his hand so Chau could read what was written on the pad. "The air base at Hickam is here." He was referring to the Air Force base next to Pearl Harbor, a few miles distant. Again he identified the location, and the Lieutenant nodded as he read the corresponding numbers for longitude and latitude.

"Now let's plot one more position so you can triangulate."

The Captain leaned in to study the console Chau was manning. One of the displays monitored the position of the arsenal ship in relation to the *Meyer*, constantly updating the information using a network of GPS satellites orbiting overhead. Beacham jotted down their location and then turned back to the chart. Seconds later another mark identified the spot where the *Meyer* was anchored.

"Now as I understand it," Beacham began slowly, "Your brain perceives numbers as shapes and colors. Is that correct?"

Simon looked a little embarrassed. He was quiet by nature and didn't like the spotlight. "That's a little simplistic. But yes, sir. That's correct."

"And you process spatial coordinates in much the same way,

right?"

"Most of the time," Chau answered.

"Okay," Beacham smiled. "Here's one more set of digits for you to chew on." He looked at the notepad once more and recited a new series of numbers. "Given the three coordinates you already have, I want you to pinpoint this last position on the chart."

There was an awkward silence. Richey had heard about Chau's unique abilities, but had never seen those skills put to the test. The Chief suspected that the Lieutenant's sensory gifts were a highly spontaneous process that rarely performed on command.

Chau's eyes were now closed. A few of the other officers in the compartment were now watching the demonstration playing out before them. Richey wasn't sure if the Lieutenant was thinking or merely pained by the sudden scrutiny that came his way. He decided it was probably a combination of both. Captain Beacham patiently folded his arms and leaned against a stanchion.

"No pressure, Mr. Chau. Take your time."

Richey wondered why Chau wasn't studying the navigational chart. Three of the locations were clearly marked. The Chief reasoned that by using those as a guide, it might somehow be easier to determine the fourth position. That seemed like the logical approach, but this whole exercise was unorthodox.

Chau's lips moved slightly and it appeared as if he were talking to himself. In truth, his mind's eye had begun processing the data he'd been given. The Lieutenant gave all the indications of being in a trance-like state. For a full thirty seconds nothing happened, then his eyes opened and his whole body seemed to relax. The look on his face conveyed a sense of defeat.

Richey winced silently. He'd almost expected something, but so far Chau's performance had devolved to the level of a failed parlor trick. Even the Captain seemed slightly embarrassed.

"That's quite all right." Beacham's words were intended as a salve. He'd put the young man on the spot and it just hadn't worked out. "This kind of thing—"

"*There.*" Chau stepped forward. He placed a finger on the chart at a point outside the mouth of the channel leading in to Pearl and turned to the Skipper. "May I?"

Without waiting for a reply, Chau took the grease pencil from Beacham's hand and made a tiny 'x' on the chart. He stepped back, his confident grin still in place.

"I might be off by a few yards, but that should be close."

The Captain's eyes narrowed as he compared the coordinates on the chart with those on the notepad. He checked them twice before shaking his head.

"Bingo," Beacham announced. " 'X' marks the spot. That's absolutely amazing."

"Normally I only use a total of three positions, not four," Chau said sheepishly. "Too many coordinates can be confusing—and it *is* a triangulation."

Richey grinned. The Lieutenant's words suggested an explanation, but to the Chief they carried just a hint of pride.

WITH THE EXHIBITION OVER, EVERYONE IN THE compartment got back to work. Beacham pocketed the notepad and cast a glance at the screen in front of Chau.

"All right," Captain Beacham answered. "Lieutenant Chau, is there an officer on duty who can relieve you?"

Chau stared. The question had caught him off-guard. *Had he done something wrong?*

"Relieve me, sir?"

"That's correct. I know that getting the *Victory* docked is your primary concern right now, but we're on a tight schedule. I just got off the phone with CINCPAC." Beacham referred to the Commander-In-Chief, Pacific. "The Department of Defense needs a qualified Chinese linguist. You're it. The plan is to chopper you over to Hickam and fly you from there out to the Philippines."

"Direct flight, sir?" Chau asked.

Beacham shook his head. "A series of hops." Which meant the young Lieutenant could be in transit for up to three days. "First leg's scheduled to leave tomorrow afternoon—sixteen-thirty—so get a room at Pearl for tonight."

This was certainly sudden. It was one of those rare occasions when Richey had actually seen the young officer speechless. The Captain saw the look of surprise on Chau's face and decided he might have been just a bit abrupt with his announcement. "Relax, son. All the arrangements have been made." He smiled. "Once you're in the Philippines, you'll be flown somewhere else—right now, your final destination is classified."

"The Philippines?" Richey frowned. "What's the mission?"

Beacham shook his head. "They didn't tell me," he turned to Chau. "Some kind of field work. You'll be briefed en route. The helicopter will be ready to pick you up in two hours."

The younger officer seemed to blanche. He was more comfortable in an office environment.

"What's the rush, Skipper?" Richey pressed. "His flight doesn't leave till—"

"I know, I know," the Captain said, raising a hand for patience. "Mr. Chau leaves tomorrow. But we're leaving Pearl—" he checked his watch, "—in about three hours."

Richey could almost imagine hearing a collective groan from the crew in the compartment—but no one made a sound. San Diego was always nice, but everyone on board had hoped for at least a couple of days in Hawaii.

"Sorry for the inconvenience," Beacham said aloud. His comment wasn't directed at anyone in particular. "CINCPAC wants us in the western Pacific in four days. If we push our luck a little, we might just make it in five." Beacham's voice trailed off and he regarded Chau once more. "You better get down to your stateroom and pack your sea bag."

Chau knew that wouldn't be difficult. He'd been aboard barely a week and hadn't had much time to unpack. The Lieutenant stood to his feet and wondered what this classified mission just might be.

"I'll be ready." He recovered from his distracted state and motioned to another officer working nearby. "Lieutenant Sanchez can relieve me." He moved past Beacham and nodded at Richey. "Take care, Senior Chief."

Richey folded his arms again and watched as Chau exited the compartment and practically double-timed down the passageway—only to stop in mid-stride. He turned back and re-entered the control room. With a slightly embarrassed look on his face, the Lieutenant plucked Kelsi Pressman's photo from the monitor and slipped it into his shirt pocket.

* * * *

"You have something on your mind, Senior Chief?" Beacham eyed his enlisted counterpart thoughtfully. "You're not worried about him, are you?"

"And you aren't?" Richey sighed heavily. "He's smart as a whip, no doubt about that. And he knows this new technology better than anybody," he continued. "But you saw him when he came on board," he smiled. "That kid didn't know the bow from the stern."

Beacham laughed softly. "Well, it wasn't that bad, Senior Chief. Granted, he's still getting his sea legs, but he'll adapt."

"He's not a blue water Navy man, Bob," Richey added softly. "They yanked him out of an office in San Diego because of his aptitude with all this," he waved a hand at the electronic gear and GPS systems installed around them. "Not to mention his knack for pinpointing locations on a map." A frown darkened his face. "And what's that called again?"

The Skipper thought carefully before speaking. "*Synesthesia*," he answered slowly. "Kind of a hyper-functional autism." Beacham shook his head. He knew that definition barely scratched the surface and searched for a better one. "He has a savant-like gift for fixing numerical coordinates on a given landscape."

"I'm sure there's more to it than that."

Beacham grinned. "Cut me some slack, Malcolm. There are brain surgeons and rocket scientists who don't understand his—*condition*. And I'm just a lowly ship's Captain." He eyed the Chief seriously. "So what's bothering you?"

Richey set his jaw. "It's one thing to pull him from a cubicle—unannounced—and send him across the Pacific. Now they're giving him a field assignment?" He shook his head. "I know the Navy's spread thin these days, but they could at least let the kid change his socks before they ship him someplace else."

"What do you recommend?"

Richey shifted on his feet. The Captain was good at this. Presented with a problem, he liked to get his people working on solutions instead of taking care of the issue himself. Pushing issues down the chain of command was one way he trained his leadership to take on bigger roles. The Senior Chief had walked right into this one.

"Well, someone should go with him; he needs a wingman. Somebody to watch his back."

Beacham considered the Senior Chief's recent marital problems. Suddenly he had an idea. He nodded slowly and once more drew a hand across his chin. "Seems to me that's what a good NCO does, Senior Chief; looks after his people, trains them up, shows them how it's done in the Navy. You volunteering for the job?"

Richey drew himself up to his full height. "Well, Bob, since you put it that way," he growled, "Maybe I am."

The Skipper shook his head. "Dunno, Malcolm. I should probably send somebody else. At this stage of your career, you should be sitting behind a desk." He glanced at Richey and saw the Senior Chief bristle slightly at that remark. This was something else the Skipper was good at; needling his staff, then gauging their reactions. "You think the *Meyer* can survive a few days without you on board?"

Without coming right out and saying so, Beacham had just

offered the Senior Chief a choice. Richey was already moving toward the hatch.

"Probably not. Which is why I think you should stay here and run things," he smiled broadly as Beacham chuckled. "So if you'll excuse me, sir, I've got a sea bag to pack too."

Chapter Five ✳ Alliances

Luzon, the Philippines

I T WAS A BURN PHONE, CHEAP BUT CAPABLE. IT had arrived that morning, delivered by a commercial courier service, swaddled in bubble wrap in the center of a manila envelope and without any indication of where it had come from. Like half a dozen others that had been sent over the past few months, this one would be used once, maybe twice, and then discarded. Its singular purpose was to communicate with only one person, and about only one subject.

Surrounded by luxury and solitude in a country where both were at a premium, Emory McBride III reclined on a couch and stared at the phone as it lay next to him. He was not a patient man. McBride considered his time as much too important to be wasted by delays, and preferred to maintain control over his own schedule rather than have it dictated by others. Meeting someone else's timetable was a completely foreign concept.

There were two reasons for his presence in the Philippines, and it was difficult to distinguish which was the most crucial. For one, his father and grandfather had sent him to Luzon to oversee the company's Far East operations. McBride Defense Industries operated bureaus all over the world, but the Philippine branch was the fastest growing of them all.

Working closely with the Department of Defense, the company supplied a wide array of software and hardware to the U.S. and her allies. Emory McBride—the *second*—decided his son needed experience in running the business, and the family agreed. Emory McBride III was extremely talented with software and electronics. But he had also run afoul of the law back in the States, and it was decided that to keep him out of trouble, a little responsibility—and some time away from home—just might do the trick.

McBride took his eyes away from the phone to glance at his watch—impatiently noting that the appointed time had come and gone—and when he looked back, the call he had been waiting for finally came through. He flipped open the device, exchanging pre-arranged phrases with someone on the other end. Assured of each other's identity, the two could now speak more freely—although neither would use their names during this conversation. They could never be sure who else might be listening. And there would be no attempt at small talk. It was safer to keep these calls short and to the point.

"I have coordinates for you." The voice was brusque and heavily accented. A filter on the other end altered it, making identification difficult at best.

McBride could feel a level of tension building. The last call hinted at travel—he wasn't comfortable with the idea, but he did as he was instructed.

"I'm ready," he said.

The voice relayed the information, and then added, "My representative will meet you there. You'll find a landing pad for your helicopter. Bring the drive."

"Timetable?"

"Forty-eight hours."

"And why am I making this trip?" In the past, instructions and information had been relayed by messenger. It was a convenient arrangement that benefited both parties.

There was a heavy sigh and a pause before the voice spoke again.

"Because someone familiar with the software needs to install it," came the reply. "It needs to be tested on-site. And I assume you want to be paid. But if that's not the case—"

"I'll be there," McBride assured his contact. He would have preferred it to be sooner. "Make sure you do your part."

"Half the deposit will be made in the morning; the rest when I have the drive."

The click he heard told McBride the call had ended. He tossed the phone on the couch and stared at the jumble of letters and numbers he'd written down. McBride knew they weren't true coordinates. Safeguarded by a complex cipher, the actual location could only be revealed using a key. His contact had provided that as well; along with the burn phone, the courier envelope contained a single sheet of paper with the decryption code typeset in the middle of the page.

McBride retrieved the envelope and spent a few minutes with pen in hand. He was able to translate the coded alphanumeric message into a fixed position that used longitude and latitude. He then walked to the desk where his computer sat. The machine was already powered up, and he accessed an internet mapping site. He typed in the location and waited for the computer to do its work. It didn't take long. The image on the screen changed to display a topographical map of the South China Sea, and a red flag pinpointed the coordinate's position.

McBride smiled. "There you are."

The little red flag on the screen even identified the location for him: *the islands of Huo Shan.*

He did a little math in his head; it would be a little longer flight than he would have liked. The rendezvous point chosen by his contact was remote enough. Flying alone, it would test his endurance. But the money would be worth it.

Little did he know the high price he would pay for his greed.

* * * *

ADMIRAL LEE LAID THE CELL PHONE IN THE TOP drawer of his desk and poured himself some tea. The first stage of his bold enterprise had begun. He disliked placing too much reliance on those outside his own inner circle. In this case it was necessary. McBride would suffice, and once the American had completed his task the critical phase of the operation could start.

Huo Shan had been a good choice, he told himself. Too small and out of the way to draw attention, it was the perfect place for his plans. Even in this day and age, his countrymen still regarded the islands as haunted. Lee snorted indignantly and shook his head. He had no time for such superstitious nonsense—but in this instance, the archaic beliefs had served his purposes.

Lee now picked up a landline phone and punched in the number of his aide, whose office was around the corner and down the hall. There was work to be done, and Lee knew just the man to do it.

* * * *

TASKED WITH COLLECTING SIGINT—SIGNALS IN-telligence—TANGENT/CASCADE-6 sat in a geostationary low-earth orbit directly above the South China Sea and used an umbrella-like dish to listen in on selected conversations. This vehicle eschewed cameras and telescopes and relied on special-ized software that intercepted, processed and passed on elec-tronic communications to a ground station in Australia, which in turn forwarded the information to the National Reconnaissance Office in Chantilly, Virginia.

TANGENT/CASCADE-6 had been put in place to sort through radio and telephone traffic between selected points in China, Taiwan, the Philippines and a host of other Asian nations. The vehicle was primarily focused to look for patterns that devi-

ated from the normal flow of routine communication. Its main
mission wasn't to snoop on U.S. citizens, but if an American's
activities crossed a line, the spacecraft was well-equipped with
a weather ear. While one or two exchanges between disparate
parties weren't enough to raise suspicion, anything beyond that
did. And the call between Admiral Lee and Emory McBride was
one of several that had been intercepted.

The satellite wranglers at the NRO took their orders from
various agencies in the American intelligence community. Their
most persistent customer lately had been the CIA, which had
taken a very keen interest in anything related to Emory McBride
III. Over the past year the analysts in Langley had grown concerned. Covert software—designed to *protect* the U.S. military
infrastructure—began to show up in use against American interests.

All of the incidents were attempts at probing the lines of
naval defense systems. The interrogation code that was used
had a very unique signature, one that pointed back to McBride
Defense Industries, and specifically to their Far Eastern branch.
Once they had identified the source, the CIA decided to dig
deeper, and started their scrutiny at the top of the company's
hierarchy. It was a good call. Almost immediately, they were
able to pinpoint Emory McBride as a high-probability suspect.
From that point on, the intelligence agency began quietly collecting evidence and tracking the frequent flow of low-level,
classified information to McBride's unknown source on the
Chinese mainland.

Like all the other calls the satellite intercepted, this one between McBride and Admiral Lee would be passed along to a
signals officer at the NRO for analysis. The officer would assign
a priority code to the intercept based on his interpretation of the
content. At a higher level, a supervisor would flag the call for
appropriate action. At least that was how it normally worked,
but on this occasion there were variables in play that would delay that process.

For two days, the National Reconnaissance Office had been

warned by the U.S. Geological Survey about an impending coronal mass ejection from the sun. These types of solar events created electromagnetic radiation and projected it away from the sun's surface, generally playing havoc with orbiting satellites. TANGENT/CASCADE-6 had built-in shielding to protect itself, but the most prudent course of action was to simply shut down the spacecraft's delicate instrumentation and wait for the geomagnetic storm to pass.

All of the normal precautions had been taken. The wave of ejected protons and electrons was carefully monitored and at the appropriate time the satellite went dark. The technicians at the NRO intended on re-activating it within four hours, giving the vehicle a wide margin of safety. Unfortunately the USGS had vastly underestimated the strength of the incoming plasma.

Even in hibernation the spacecraft was still vulnerable. Not everything on board was completely protected against the massive, terawatt discharge, and a relay shorted out. The most affected systems were the receptors that processed commands from the controllers on the ground. An algorithm designed to further shield the central processor sent the satellite's electronic brain into an even deeper sleep, but also encoded a command to re-initialize all onboard systems at a point still far in the future. While the data stream was interrupted, everything that had been collected so far was safely stored in an information buffer.

TANGENT/CASCADE-6 would re-awaken from its self-induced coma in forty-eight hours. The satellite would eventually transmit the call between McBride and Admiral Lee to the technicians and analysts of the NRO and the CIA, but by the time they received the intel, it would be too late.

Chapter Six ✵ Boots on the Ground

S TAFF SERGEANT DOUGLAS BUTLER AND HIS platoon watched as the last Osprey climbed into the sky. In the courtyard below, the dust storm kicked up by its ascent caused the Marines to shield their eyes. In less than a minute, the aircraft's massive tilt-wing engines rotated to a vertical position, and the plane sped off to the east and out to sea for a rendezvous with the USS *Lexington*.

On board the Osprey were the last embassy personnel extracted from Southern Somalia. All had left in good spirits; uninjured, grateful—and extremely happy to be leaving the inhospitable and violent patch of desert behind. Another V-22 was thirty minutes out, and would retrieve Butler and his men when it arrived. While they waited, Butler went man to man, making sure everyone stayed sharp, providing perimeter security for the compound and waiting for Corporal Perez' squad to return from the area beyond the high walls.

The first phase of the operation went smoothly enough. Major Hooper's forces engaged the rebels at Mendari, while the second part of the ruse was unfolding near the embassy. Just as Colonel McLane had planned, one of the Ospreys flew in from the west, getting the attention of the Urudisi militia that had surrounded the compound. These troops moved to counter what they thought was an attack on their flank. It took them almost an hour to realize they'd been duped.

In the meantime, Butler's Marines swooped in and began the rescue. The rebels returned and started a disorganized attack on the walls of the embassy, but they were easily repelled. All in all, it was a textbook assault—and with no friendly casualties.

There was only one slight deviation to the plan. During the firefight, one of the combatants shouldered a rocket launcher and pointed the business end toward the embassy. It was the last mistake the Somalian ever made. Butler's men brought their weapons to bear on the rebel before he had a chance to fire. He slumped to the ground dead, but his comrades managed to grab the launcher as they retreated to their fallback position. Corporal Perez and his squad slipped through the gate in pursuit—Butler didn't like it, but sometimes there was just no stopping the hard-charging young NCO.

* * * *

AS THINGS SETTLED DOWN, PEREZ AND SOME of his Marines returned. The junior enlisted ranks filed in first, weapons drawn, more relaxed now but still focused after their initial contact with the enemy. Butler did a quick head count, but by his reckoning the squad was one fire team short. This alarmed him. The Staff Sergeant moved to the gate and then surveyed the ramshackle urban environment outside with his night vision goggles. At least a dozen bodies littered the streets.

Perez was the last man through the gate. Once inside, he released the chin strap on his Kevlar and pushed the helmet back on his head, grinning broadly and wiping away sweat. Grabbing the drinking tube from the hydration system he wore on his back, he drained the last of the water inside, checked his weapon and then made his way to the Staff Sergeant.

Butler gave the younger Marine a stern look. "You forget the rules of engagement, Perez? Our orders were to defend the embassy and get the personnel out—not chase the cockroaches back into the woodwork."

Perez nodded. "I got that, Staff Sergeant." He knew it was best not to argue with this particular senior NCO. "But one of those cockroaches had an RPG."

"Orders are orders, Perez." Butler held firm. "One day you'll be in my shoes. How would you deal with a non-commissioned officer who went off the reservation? And would you be prepared to write a letter home to his parents if he took a bullet?" Perez lowered his eyes and seemed to get the message.

There was a pause, but Butler wasn't waiting for Perez to answer. At that point the Staff Sergeant seemed to moderate his tone. "Still, I admire your initiative, so keep talking," Butler relaxed his stance, signaling his willingness to hear the Corporal out.

Perez almost smiled. "Our air assets were ready to leave, Staff Sergeant—it just wouldn't do to have them shot down."

Butler grunted. It sounded like agreement, so Perez continued.

"So I'm like, *you take a shot at my ride, we're gonna talk.* You follow me, Staff Sergeant?"

"I'm trackin'." Butler could no longer conceal a smile. "You catch up with him?"

"Oh, yeah—*big* time." Perez was breathing easier now that he knew he wasn't in trouble. "And we found something you might want to see, Staff Sergeant. You up for a tour?"

"Lead on."

Motioning to a few of his men, Perez turned on his heel and led Butler out of the compound, using hand signals to communicate. *This way.*

PEREZ LED BUTLER AND HIS MARINES BLOCK BY block. He seemed to be driving toward one building in particular. It was a two-story structure with a direct line of sight to the embassy compound. Butler recognized the last fire team taking up defensive positions near the entrance. Perez stopped and looked through glass-less windows, making sure the room on the other side of the open door was empty. Even with his men on station, he wasn't taking anything for granted.

Satisfied for the moment that it was safe, he pushed through the entrance and swept the interior with his weapon. The Marines followed him in, with Butler bringing up the rear. A Lance Corporal moved to the rear of the room and looked low—if this place was booby-trapped, he didn't want to find out about it the hard way.

There were no IEDs. The room was mostly empty, but the tell-tale remnants of a pitched firefight were everywhere. Empty shell casings, broken glass, and shattered plaster littered the floor; it was impossible to step anywhere and not find something underfoot. Bullet holes in tight groupings decorated the walls, beginning about waist level and becoming more concentrated higher up.

"Looks like you fought your own private war here, Perez," Butler noted. "You take fire from this building?"

"They were real intent on making a stand. So we lit 'em up."

Butler noticed a couple of open crates in one corner. Perez approached one of them and pulled a flashlight from his gear. He clicked it on and pointed the beam down inside.

"See what I mean, Staff Sergeant?" Perez asked as Butler joined him.

Butler reached inside and pulled out a rifle, one of several at the bottom of the crate. There were other weapons as well, and ammo boxes stacked six high.

"Chinese SKS." The Marine turned the automatic weapon over in his hands, admiring the rifle's assembly. "Bunch of 'em, too—with several thousand rounds. And I do mean several thousand."

Perez nodded. He was sweating. Even at midnight, the temperature here was well over one hundred degrees. "More in the other box; mortars, grenades, small arms. Assault rifles out the ying-yang."

"Chinese, like the ones here?"

Again, a nod. "That's right, Staff Sergeant."

All the Marines in the MEU had fired Chinese infantry weapons for familiarization. Like Russian arms, these were sturdy, dependable—and lethally efficient. It was commonly believed that these heavy weapons weren't as accurate as the rifles used by Western nations, but Staff Sergeant Butler—and most of his men—could easily fire a lethal grouping at more than two hundred yards.

Butler was sweating now too. This was a different heat than what he'd felt jogging on the flight deck of the *Lexington* with Neill and the other officers. "What about the bodies in the streets? Were they armed with stuff like this?"

"Roger that, Staff Sergeant. We already policed up their weapons."

Butler did a quick inventory of the crates' contents. "We can't leave all this here." He knew the Somalians would be back after his men left. Butler considered using C4 to destroy the cache of arms, then decided against it.

"Corporal Perez, you and your Marines will transport these weapons to the LZ—I'll bring two fire teams back and we'll provide cover for you. Till then just hang tight."

Perez nodded. He knew the Staff Sergeant would have his back; Butler was good people.

There are an awful lot of weapons here, Butler thought. *And God knows how many more in buildings just like this one.* Colonel McLane would be very interested in what Perez and his men found.

"I'll radio the *Lexington* to send another Osprey. We're gonna need it."

Chapter Seven ✳ The Industrious

THE LUMBERING C-130 HERCULES WAS A notoriously loud beast, and with good reason. Hanging from the wings on each side of the big cargo plane were four six-bladed turboprops capable of enormous horsepower. Their durability was reassuring to the flight crew and kept the bird in the air, but while aloft, the droning of the powerful engines was constant, making casual conversation a practical impossibility.

Since its original design, the inelegant aircraft—while extremely reliable—was not known for its creature comforts. Brutally hot while on the ground, the Hercules required altitude before it could offer its occupants a respite from the heat. The majority of the onboard space was taken up by the cargo compartment. Side facing, canvas seating lined the interior. In certain configurations the plane could hold more than a hundred combat-ready troops, although it made for a tight fit. And in spite of the noise—or maybe because of it—most passengers spent their time aloft trying to sleep.

Senior Chief Richey had always found it easy to doze while flying. Now that they were ascending, the air was a chilly sixty-five degrees. For this trip Malcolm was wedged in a corner of the airframe, against a bulkhead just behind the flight deck. Arms folded across his chest, he stretched out and rested his boots on an empty berth in the center aisle. Seated several feet away was Lieutenant Chau. Unlike Richey, the young officer was wide awake, wearing ear buds and staring intently at his laptop. Music filled his ears and helped him ignore the din reverberating around them. Fortunately for both men, the two sailors were the only passengers manifested for this flight, giving each man ample room to stretch out.

Simon started to watch a movie, but grew bored with his selection after about half an hour. Digital photos came next. Chau was an amateur camera bug, and had uploaded some shots he'd taken during a recent trip to the beach. Kelsi Pressman had tagged along, and her smiling face was featured in most of those images.

As the plane ambled westward, Simon became aware of movement in the seats to his right. Malcolm Richey stirred from his nap and stretched, then leaned over and cast a glance at Chau's laptop, his eyes widening slightly.

"Very pretty," he said approvingly, lifting his voice to be heard. The woman in the photo was quite a looker. "That your girlfriend?"

Simon nodded proudly. He tabbed to a few more images and shifted the screen to give Richey a better view. "We've been seeing each other for about six months."

The Senior Chief grinned. " '*Seeing* each other,' " he repeated. "Not just dating. Sounds serious."

"Maybe." Chau was smiling now too. "What about you, Chief? You married?"

Richey's expression soured. He settled back in his seat and seemed much less buoyant. "Not anymore," he answered.

Malcolm replayed the sordid story again in his mind. Fourteen months earlier, the Senior Chief had redeployed from a cruise in the Adriatic only to be served with divorce papers. The legal proceedings were amicable enough—Richey truly loved his wife and refused to give in to anger or retaliation. Stung with pain, he fought to keep her, but it was too little, too late. He blamed himself mostly, but in the months that followed he rarely gave in to self-pity, focusing instead on advancing his own career.

An awkward silence followed; Malcolm eased the sullen moment by stretching out again and resuming his nap. After noting the look of pain on Richey's face, the Lieutenant went back to his laptop.

Chau tried the movie again, but his thoughts were elsewhere. Richey had always given the Lieutenant a fair shake, and behind the Senior Chief's gruff exterior, Simon had sensed a compassionate heart.

For some, that was a vulnerability; but for Malcolm Richey, it was far from being a weakness.

* * * *

TRUE TO HIS WORD, WILLIS AVERY MADE ALL the arrangements. The trip still took days. After hop-scotching from Diego Garcia to the Philippines, Lieutenants Neill and Crockett found themselves aboard a CH-53 Sea Stallion helicopter as it approached the HMS *Industrious*, Britain's newest aircraft carrier.

While Crockett slept, Neill was invited up to the cramped flight deck for a look ahead. There was little to see until the big chopper broke through the cloud cover and began a slow descent. The aircraft banked to the northwest and the pilot leaned forward, pointing out their destination. Far below, Neill could see the box-like, rectangular shape of Her Majesty's ship as she sailed choppy waters, a wide wake trailing astern.

Neill returned to his seat and roused Crockett. The inclement weather created some turbulence, and the Sea Stallion hit a few bumps on the way down. The two Marines cinched their seatbelts a little more tightly, and after a few minutes they felt the deck below their feet angle back as the pilot flared the aircraft for a textbook carrier landing.

The roar of the engines diminished a bit as the chopper reduced power. The Marines looked aft; with the helicopter resting on the deck of the *Industrious*, the air crew lowered the ramp. Neill and Crockett got to their feet, checked their gear and then trudged to the back and disembarked.

THEY WERE GREETED BY TWO MEMBERS OF THE ship's crew, a female officer and a lanky seaman with a clipboard. Both stood near the ship's superstructure, their feet planted firmly against the wash of the Sea Stallion's massive rotors.

"Watch your step, gentlemen!" The young woman spoke first and seemed in high spirits as Neill and Crockett came off the chopper. "Leftenant Amanda Templeton, air operations officer."

Each carried a rucksack, with Crockett brandishing a shooter's bag containing his weapon. Neill was armed with a pistol, and a rifle slung over his shoulder for good measure. A light rain swept across the deck as the ship rolled slightly under cloudy skies. Even in this new age of blended responsibility between genders, neither man expected to be welcomed aboard by a female officer. Neill threw Templeton a salute.

"Permission to come aboard."

Templeton wore rain gear—a windproof smock, not unlike the Gore-Tex worn by the Marines. "Permission granted, Leftenant," she cheerfully replied, then added, "We're having a bit of weather today."

Weather, indeed—Neill scanned the horizon as Templeton escorted the group across the flight deck. Clouds obscured the farthest reaches of his vision, and there was no land in sight. Near the 'island', as the control superstructure was known, a flight crew secured a Seahawk helicopter—*was that what they called it in the British Navy*? He wasn't sure, and as tired as he was from the trip, he was beyond caring at that point.

Fatigue hadn't prevented either man from noting Templeton's fresh-faced beauty. As they got their sea legs, Crockett edged up beside Neill and gave his friend a nod.

Neill couldn't help but smile. *She is definitely easy on the eyes*, he thought to himself.

* * * *

LIEUTENANT TEMPLETON LED THE MARINES through a hatch and into a super-cooled, brightly lit corridor running parallel to the flight deck. The Americans began unzipping their rain gear as they moved into the ship's interior. Templeton pulled back the hood of her own jacket, revealing a bun of auburn hair. As she peeled off the smock Neill saw that she also wore the new PCS—the Personal Clothing System uniform—recently adopted by the Royal Navy and officially called the number four dress. The dark blue outfit sported zippered boots and Velcro fasteners, and conformed to the Lieutenant's frame as if it had been tailor-made. Soon they arrived at one of the *Industrious'* ready rooms, and Templeton ushered them inside.

"Let's get you squared away first—just drop your weapons case and kit right there," the Lieutenant instructed. Then, almost as an afterthought, "And I'd like your IDs as well; we need to document your arrival for the ship's log."

Neill and Crockett produced their CACs—Common Access Cards—and handed them over to the seaman with the clipboard. He dutifully recorded their names and returned them. Templeton read what he had written, and then dismissed him with a nod. Her attention turned back to the two Americans. "Good flight?"

Neill couldn't help but grin. British pleasantries seemed both out of place yet oddly appropriate coming from Lieutenant Templeton. *Next thing we know she'll be offering us tea*, Michael thought.

It was Crockett who answered. "Long flight is more like it—nothing good about it." The reply sounded a bit brusque. Crockett was never one to hold back an opinion. "Where's the head?"

"Back of the room," Templeton said, not the least put off by

Crockett's tone. "Are you hungry? Some tea, perhaps?"

Neill laughed. "Sounds great, Lieutenant. But I'm forgetting my manners. Michael Neill, USMC." He extended his hand. "And this is Second Lieutenant Nathan Crockett. And yes, some chow would be fantastic."

Lieutenant Templeton nodded as Nate moved toward the head. "Very well, Leftenant—I've been told to extend to you every courtesy of the Royal Navy."

"I appreciate that. We left the *Lexington* in a bit of a hurry." He reached into his ruck and pulled out his cover. Over the past three days he'd hardly worn it; doing so on a flight line or aboard an aircraft didn't sit well with air crews—there was always the danger of having it blown off and getting sucked into an air intake. "There are a few items we might have need of."

"Let's get you gentlemen fed first, and afterwards—" Neill hadn't noticed, but Templeton had been carrying a satellite phone—"I expect you'll want to ring up your people in Washington."

Hungry as he was, Neill decided that dinner could wait just a little longer.

✳ ✳ ✳ ✳

THE OFFICER'S WARDROOM WAS EMPTY. NEILL took advantage of the solitude it offered to make a few calls. The first went to the office of the National Security Advisor.

Willis Avery didn't have much to add to the briefing he'd given days earlier. He did tell Neill that two Navy personnel were being added to the team, one of those being the linguist they might need. Michael informed him that he and Crockett had arrived on board Her Majesty's Ship and were awaiting transportation, but beyond that he had nothing else to report. With that out of the way, his second call went to Colonel McLane aboard the *Lexington*.

The senior officer was still pumped about the MEU's success in Somalia. Neill was relieved to hear how well the operation had gone. McLane was concluding his summary of the mission when Michael saw Lieutenant Templeton poke her head through the hatch. The young woman smiled as Neill gestured for her to enter the compartment.

"I can come back later if you'd like more privacy." Her voice was very pleasant, and barely rose above the level of a whisper. It wasn't intentional, but her stance accentuated just how lovely she truly was.

The Marine ended the call and laid the phone on the table dominating the center of the room. "Not at all. I just finished—I've had a little catching up to do." He stifled a yawn but it was clear that fatigue was overtaking him. "And I appreciate the use of the phone, Lieutenant."

"Please," she began. Templeton pulled out a chair across from him and slowly lowered herself into the seat. There was a slight hesitation, and then her smile widened. "My name is Amanda."

Neill nodded with a grin of his own. "And mine's Michael," he reminded her.

She laughed softly and then reached across the table and the two shook hands for the second time since they'd met. *A bit awkward*, Neill thought; still, after nearly three days of travel, the sensation of a woman's touch was a welcome one. Amanda seemed to be blushing slightly.

"I'd suggest you get a little food and some rest, Michael." She seemed to fine tune her professional bearing just a bit. Her soft tone and British accent were having a very tranquilizing effect on Neill's exhausted nerves. "Tomorrow morning we can go over what you might need for your excursion."

"Roger that," Neill answered. "A decent chart of the target area would be greatly appreciated." He couldn't come up with anything else at the moment; hunger and drowsiness were beginning to cloud his thoughts.

She would have liked to spend more time with this American, but his drooping eyelids told her that he could use some quality time with a bunk.

"You need a meal and some sleep," she told him. "You'll find the mess on deck three." She was referring to the dining facility. "Just follow your nose—the food on board is really quite good." Neill wasn't sure but she seemed to have a sparkle in her eye. "I believe your comrade has gone ahead without you."

* * * *

"OPERATION HEAVY ANVIL WAS A COMPLETE SUC-cess," Neill announced, finding a seat across from Crockett in the *Industrious'* mess. "No American casualties, and the embassy personnel are safe aboard the *Lexington*. Shipley's surgery came off without a hitch." He checked out the food on Crockett's tray. "What is that?"

"Bangers and mash; real British food," Crockett said, motioning toward a group of Royal Navy sailors in the hot chow line. "You should try it. A lot better than two days' worth of box nasties."

"I thought it was three." Neill leaned forward slightly. "Is it any good?" he asked. He eyed the Brits almost as suspiciously as they regarded the two Marines.

"Heck, yeah—go on, grab a tray," Crockett said. "You've been making phone calls this whole time?"

Neill nodded. "Lieutenant Templeton loaned me her sat phone."

"Uh-huh." Crockett wore a sly grin. "I see how it is. You couldn't join me for dinner, but you found time to charm the local ladies."

Neill ignored the comment and pressed on. "You remember Corporal Perez?"

Nate nodded. "Assault man from Staff Sergeant Butler's platoon."

"That's right." The food was starting to smell really good. "His fire team found a cache of Chinese weapons near the embassy—assault rifles, mortars, grenades."

"Chinese?" Crockett asked. "Not Russian?"

Neill shook his head. "McLane says it's not the first time. Arms from China have been surfacing in third world countries for almost a year. Oh, and I talked to Washington—" he added. "We can expect our team to grow by two," Neill said. He watched to see what kind of reaction Nate would have. "Navy personnel from the USS *Meyer*—a Chinese linguist and some Senior Chief."

"Anchor clankers?" Crockett groaned. That was one of many nicknames given by Marines to sailors; sometimes as a term of endearment, but usually just an expression of rivalry between the two branches of the military. In turn, the Navy had equally colorful labels for Marines. "You have been busy. Is our mission still the same?"

"Yep. Survey the island's facilities and monitor any communications we can," Neill replied. But that was just the big picture; Neill hadn't clued Crockett in on the fate of the *Gansu Province* and the weapon that sent her to the bottom. He decided the time for full disclosure could wait a little longer.

"How are we coordinating with the Brits?"

"Templeton filled me in," Neill said. "The *Industrious* is steaming into the South China Sea now; we'll be in range to launch a small reconnaissance boat in twenty-four hours. We'll go in, do the mission, and then return to the ship. If there aren't any complications, it should be pretty straightforward. The Lieutenant's offered us support with gear and intel." He eyed the food line hungrily. "I think I'll get some chow."

Neill pushed himself up from the table and got a tray of food. Within twenty minutes he and Crockett had finished their meals and headed below deck to a stateroom that Templeton had made available. The two decided to get some sleep.

Crockett was a bit more experienced with field work, but neither Marine was naïve. They both knew Neill's summary of the mission was optimistic. In most military operations—even the small ones—nothing ever seemed to go exactly as planned.

Chapter Eight ✴ Introductions

THE MARINES HAD SLEPT FOR TEN HOURS and felt completely re-charged. After getting cleaned up they were looking forward to breakfast before moving on to the next stage of their mission.

Crockett double-checked his ruck and pulled out a fresh set of cammies. Next he made sure his weapons case was stowed in the corner next to his bunk. Marines could be very obsessive about their rifles. "What's the plan after chow?"

"We'll check with Templeton about transportation to the island," Neill replied, lacing up his boots. He bloused his trousers and then tightened his belt. "But before we do that, there are a few other details about this assignment that I should share with you."

It didn't take long for Neill to recite what he knew about the loss of the *Gansu Province*. Crockett stopped adjusting his own uniform long enough to take in the full story and then let out a low whistle when Neill had finished.

"You sure about all that?" the Second Lieutenant asked. "I mean, just how good is our intel?"

"Pretty solid," Neill replied. "Got it straight from the National Security Advisor himself. Now let's go find our *Leftenant* and see where the rest of our team is."

* * * *

AMANDA TEMPLETON JOINED THE TWO Marines near their stateroom, and then the three of them descended to the hangar deck and began to make their way toward the stern. Crews were busy at work on a variety of planes and helicopters; maintenance went on long before—and after—air operations were concluded. Transiting the open spaces where the aircraft were kept, the small group continued aft, squeezing through knee knockers—passageways in a bulkhead—appropriately named for the effect they had on the shins of the uninitiated. Within a few minutes they reached the fantail; a wide, open space that extended nearly three decks high and offered a spectacular view of the sea from astern.

Completely rested now, Neill decided to engage their hostess in some conversation. "What made you join the Navy, Lieutenant?"

Templeton gave him a puzzled look, but smiled nonetheless. "A sense of duty, mostly." She looked out to sea as the wind picked up. "And tradition—my family has a long history with the Royal Navy. My father served during the Falkland Islands campaign."

Neill decided to go out on a limb. "Then I take it you're a fan of Margaret Thatcher."

Amanda turned to him as the wind caught her hair, her eyes bright. "We were both born in Grantham in Lincolnshire. She's one of my biggest inspirations for joining the service."

"I have an uncle who shares your admiration," Neill said with a smile. "You two would get along just fine."

Amanda turned again to face him, and seemed to move slightly closer. An obvious question remained unspoken on her lips. She was looking at him the way she had in the officer's wardroom the day before. The blush in her cheeks suggested something more than just mild interest.

The moment didn't last. She adjusted the bun of hair on her head as the sea breeze threatened to dislodge it. "Let's go topside. The rest of your team should be arriving shortly."

＊ ＊ ＊ ＊

ONCE THEY EMERGED FROM THE SUPERSTRUC-
ture and onto the flight deck, Templeton pointed a finger skyward and directly aft of the big ship. Just over the horizon,
following the *Industrious'* wake, was the distinctive shape of
a Marine V-22 Osprey.

"Right on time," she announced.

Neill, Crockett and Templeton watched as the tilt-rotor
aircraft closed the distance with the carrier. The weather was
much better today; the sun shone brightly and there was no
rain in sight. Within minutes the pilot had brought the Osprey
over the stern and then set it down gently amidships.

＊ ＊ ＊ ＊

SIMON CHAU WAS THE FIRST TO STEP OFF THE
Osprey's ramp and onto the *Industrious*, followed closely
behind by Senior Chief Richey. They'd only found out they
were headed for a British vessel a few hours earlier. The seaman with the clipboard appeared again and escorted the two
men carefully around the rear of the aircraft as Lieutenant
Templeton and the Marines made their way toward them. The
Navy men each carried their sea bags and M-4 rifles, drawn
from the *Meyer's* armory before they left. Chau also held his
laptop, protected in a waterproof case.

Templeton greeted the American Navy men as cheerfully
as she'd done with Neill and Crockett the day before. With the
roar of the Osprey's rotors drowning out anything but a shout,
she guided her guests back to the ship's superstructure and
through the main hatch. Once inside, Neill introduced himself, Templeton and Crockett to the newcomers.

"Pleased to meet you, El-Tee," Malcolm growled softly.
He removed a pair of sound reducing plugs from his ears.

"Senior Chief Malcolm Richey; this is Lieutenant—*Junior Grade*—Simon Chau."

Neill reached out and shook Chau's hand. "You must be our linguist."

"And historian," Richey grinned.

"Outstanding," Neill replied. "Where are you from, Lieutenant? Originally, I mean."

"The Chinese mainland," Chau answered. "I still have family in Taiwan." It occurred to him that Neill might be able to answer a question. "Where exactly are we headed?"

"We'll get to that. We've got about ten more hours before we shove off. I'll fill you in after you're settled."

"Fair enough," the Senior Chief drawled. He looked over at Nate. "How about you, Marine? What's your special skill?"

"Scout sniper platoon leader, Senior Chief." On the other side of the bulkhead they could faintly hear the Osprey as it lifted off and headed back out to sea. "Besides doing paperwork, I shoot people."

Richey seemed surprised, and then grinned again. "Okay. I guess that could be useful." He liked the young Lieutenant's candor. "What is it you guys say? *You can run, but you'll only die tired?*"

"Roger that, Chief. How about you?" Crockett asked.

Richey looked around, regarding the rank on everyone's collars. "They said you had too many officers for this party—so here I am."

Richey's response got a chuckle from all of them, which also helped to break the ice.

* * * *

IT WAS A SMALL TEAM, BUT THEY ALL SEEMED TO click immediately. With the introductions out of the way, the Senior Chief felt it was time to turn their attention to more pressing matters.

"Any chance of getting a good cup of coffee around here?"

"We were waiting for you to arrive before heading to breakfast," Templeton answered. "Hungry?"

"Yes, ma'am," Richey replied. "Had a box lunch on the flight in—pretty bad stuff. I sure hope you Brits set a better table."

Neill nodded. "You won't be disappointed, Chief," he said, smiling at Templeton as he caught her eye. "I could get used to the hospitality around here myself."

THE LIEUTENANT LED THEM BACK THROUGH the passageway to a stateroom next door to the Marines' berth. Richey and Chau deposited their sea bags inside. With their gear secured, Templeton offered to join them for breakfast.

One of the many things that impressed Templeton about the Americans was their ability to consume food. The four of them wolfed down their breakfasts at a pace that truly amazed her. After the men had finished off several cups of coffee, the group exited the mess deck and headed aft, where she extended an invitation to tour the ship.

The carrier was a busy place, and seemed all the more so by the close quarters and narrow passageways. British seamen went about their duties, sometimes pausing to cast a curious glance at the American entourage being escorted by the pretty young officer.

The *Industrious* was the newest in the Royal Navy, and reflected the latest advances in hull design and ship-building. Most impressive was the hangar deck, where the group found a squadron of British Harriers and several helicopters. It was the same part of the ship that Neill, Crockett and Lieutenant Templeton had passed through on their way to the fantail earlier.

Maintenance crews busied themselves around the aircraft; several had their cowlings removed, enabling the sailors easy access to engines, hydraulics, avionics, and a host of other systems that Neill and his team were at a loss to identify. Some of the men were up to their elbows in grease, and the sound of tools clanging against metal filled the air.

Their tour eventually ended on the *Industrious'* well deck, a cavernous, warehouse-sized space at the rear of the ship and slightly below the waterline. The bulkhead at the very end of the ship served as the stern gate; the ship's crew could open the massive hatchway and partially submerge the compartment, allowing small boats and other craft to enter and exit by letting in a small portion of the sea. Neill identified a few small forklifts, cargo pallets, an overhead crane, and dominating most of the deck space, an air-cushioned landing vehicle, designed along the lines of the American Navy's hovercraft.

"Are we hitching a ride on that?" Richey asked, gesturing to the big watercraft.

Lieutenant Templeton shook her head. "Not quite, Senior Chief. Your vessel is on the other side."

She led them around the large vehicle where a group of sailors were preparing a Gemini inflatable boat, clearly intended for small team operations. The men were fitting a fifty-five horsepower outboard motor to the craft's transom.

"Shotgun," Crockett announced.

Amanda wasn't sure what that meant and didn't ask. "This will afford you a more stealthy approach to your destination. The motor is designed to be very quiet—on loan to us from your Department of Defense. We're also providing you with surveillance equipment—cameras, listening gear, night vision scope and the like. And you can hang on to that sat phone. It comes complete with next-gen OVERTURE encryption."

Simon's eyes lit up. OVERTURE was developed jointly by British and American intelligence agencies. The operating system was already in use by the cyber defenses office to reinforce their firewall. The software was so classified it was almost impossible to describe how it worked without disclosing state secrets.

Templeton turned to Neill and then reached into the cargo pocket on the leg of her uniform, producing a laminated map.

"As you requested, Leftenant. I'll leave you to coordinate your strategy. After you've finished, you can find me in Air Ops."

It was almost mid-morning now. Neill nodded his thanks as Amanda excused herself. As she turned and began exiting the compartment he watched her go with a slightly prolonged look before noticing the others were doing the same.

"All right, gentlemen," he said, unfolding the chart and spreading it out on a workbench for all to see. The four of them seemed to re-focus. "Let's get down to brass tacks.

"Operational planning begins now."

Chapter Nine ✷ Points on a Map

Chinese Naval Base
Hainan Province,
Southern China

THE CHINESE NAVAL OFFICER NORMALLY traveled with an aide—which meant a Lieutenant or an Ensign—but today he was alone. Ordinarily it proved helpful to have a subordinate along to take care of the little details that invariably cropped up. There was always some paperwork to sign, a bureaucrat to deal with or a line to wait in when it was impossible to circumvent the system. But that was for official visits, and trips like this one weren't exactly sanctioned by the admiralty.

There was still a certain degree of plausibility associated with this errand. It wasn't unusual for an officer to show up unexpectedly at a military installation. The possibility of a snap inspection kept the outlying posts on their toes, and if anyone questioned him about it—and he knew no one ever would—that would be all the justification he would need. Serving as he did in this role gave him the flexibility to bend the rules, and sometimes even the truth.

Being Admiral Lee's chief of staff kept Captain Zhu Ling very busy these days—and the variety of his responsibilities required every bit of his energy and intellect. He'd just returned from a meeting with ship-builders and industrialists in Russia when the Admiral ordered him on yet another assignment. Ling's trip north to the former Soviet nation was approved by the Chinese government; but what Lee had in mind for him now was a bit more unconventional.

The naval base at Hainan was near the city of Sanya. It was a common destination for members of the military. Ling had selected a commercial carrier—using military airlift might have attracted the Navy's attention—and booked the flight himself. He had flown in from Beijing the day before and wasted no time; there was a great deal to be done, and the window for accomplishing his task was a narrow one. The Captain was a man known for his careful planning and tried to minimize the effects of unforeseen problems; by their very nature they were difficult to predict. Building in extra time was one way to attenuate their impact. But that was an option Ling didn't have in this circumstance. If he intended to follow Admiral Lee's timetable, he would need to remain focused.

Arriving at the base, the Captain randomly selected an out of the way administrative office—there were many to choose from—and assumed a stereotype in character with his reputation. As an officer, Ling had learned early on that the absence of personality could work to his advantage. That was especially true when interacting with the enlisted ranks, which came to expect that from the brass. The Asian world had a long history when it came to castes and classes and the Chinese military perpetuated both.

Ling entered the small shop with little more than a *pro forma* introduction. He demanded to see the person in charge and insisted on receiving an overview of their workflow protocols. The supervisor was a senior enlisted man who was only too happy to cooperate, and Ling was surprised to find everything in order. Still, he nit-picked around the edges of their bookkeeping; this was merely subterfuge, to present himself as a staff officer looking for a means to justify his position. After an hour of examining their records, he encouraged the small staff of sailors to keep up the good work and then turned on his heel and left.

* * * *

LING MOVED ON TO HIS NEXT OBJECTIVE. HIS true mission required that he enlist the aid of a platoon of Marines. He smiled at the thought; his plan was more akin to pressing the troops into service rather than recruiting them, and he carried the authority to do just that. A barracks complex near the command post housed a dozen members of the PLAN-MC—the People's Liberation Army Navy-Marine Corps, an odd confluence of troops that would have maintained a distinctive separateness in the militaries of other nations.

Zhu Ling straightened his uniform and strode into the barracks with an emotionless expression on his face. The troops he found inside were part of the First Marine Brigade. A sharp group, they snapped to attention as soon as he entered the room. Ling's eyes narrowed as he searched for the non-commissioned officer in charge, and almost instantly a short, thick man named Wen stepped forward and identified himself as the platoon sergeant.

Ling surveyed the young non-com as if evaluating him on his fitness for leadership. Sergeant Wen's most distinguishing feature was an angry scar that ran from his temple down to his chin. Equally chilling was the snarl that seemed etched on his face. Once again, Ling adopted the tone of an imperious and aloof officer, this time displaying a slight disdain for the enlisted ranks. The persona had the intended effect. The Captain waved an official-looking document before the Sergeant and informed him that his Marines had been seconded to his command. After a few brusque directives to prepare his men for a four day assignment, Ling nodded curtly to the assembled platoon and headed back out the door.

* * * *

ALL OF THAT HAD TAKEN THE BETTER PART OF A day, and on the heels of his previous trip to Russia, Ling was tired. It was late in the evening before he finally had dinner and collapsed in his bed in officer country.

He woke early the next morning and got right back to work. There was one more detail that required his attention. Ling walked the docks and pier, surveying the available surface craft, and was drawn to one used by the Chinese Navy as a submarine chaser and patrol boat. Her master was a young and very nervous Ensign who complied with the Captain's every request. After a quick inspection, Ling used the authority granted to him by Admiral Lee to commandeer the vessel. He and his troops would use this craft to reach their destination.

With all the arrangements in order, Ling had made his way to the bridge for a look at the navigator's charts. A tall man, athletic and lean with jet black hair graying at his temples, Ling was no stranger to the sea. Using the basic tools of seamanship, he laid out the shortest course to their southern objective. The map he pored over was an older one, but the location he was looking for corresponded to the coordinates given to him by the Admiral. It was no coincidence that he was studying the same region as the Americans were doing at that very moment aboard the HMS *Industrious*.

* * * *

THE ENSIGN STOOD AT HIS SIDE, PEERING AT-tentively over Ling's shoulder.

"Here," the Captain announced. His index finger landed on a location in the center of the chart. "It should take no longer than six hours. Your boat is ready, Ensign?"

Ensign Tsao stiffened. "I will see to it myself, Captain. Whatever you require will be done." If he was alarmed by their intended destination he didn't let on; in fact, he seemed quite pleased with himself, being selected by such a high-ranking member of the naval staff.

Ling maintained a stony countenance, never taking his eyes from the map. "It is what Admiral Lee requires, Ensign," he said icily. "Don't forget that."

The young officer's confidence melted a little. There were rumors about the Admiral; stories whispered when no one else could hear. For the first time, he noticed that beads of sweat had formed on his nose and upper lip.

"I will remember, Captain Ling."

* * * *

FAR TO THE NORTH, AT A PIER LOCATED ON THE Chinese naval base in Qingdao, Senior Captain Wei Lao stood on the bridge of a Type 051C destroyer—designated as the *Luzhou* by NATO forces—and pored over a series of charts detailing sea lanes to the south and southeast. The ship was the command element of a task force with vessels that dated from the 1970s to the present. Embedded within the group was a squadron of minelayer/sweepers; eight Chinese T-43s for the most part, but many were of Soviet origin, or at least based on Russian naval design. Several had seen service in the Japanese Navy, and in years past—ironically—decommissioned warships bought from the U.S. had been used, but these were long since gone.

Lao's group of surface ships also included two frigates, four smaller gunboats, and an additional complement of destroyers in the same class as his vessel, all ready to sail for what had been described as an exercise; war games scheduled months in advance and not at all unusual for this time of year. Few suspected anything more, but the Captain knew that story to be a ruse. Lao stood erect and surveyed his fleet through the large, angled windscreen that enclosed the compartment. Two older 033 Type diesel submarines were moored nearby. These boats would travel with the task force to provide protection from below. Their presence reassured the Captain, but the subs would also serve another purpose. That thought brought a smile.

Like any other voyage, there were logistical preparations to be made before leaving port. Lao returned to his study of the map and the navigator's plotted course to the grid square the fleet would be operating in. Peering over his glasses, one location was of particular interest.

Lao heaved a sigh. A report just brought to his attention warned of an approaching series of storm fronts in the very patch of ocean where he planned to take his task force. That would not do. On the other hand, it might work to their advantage. He took in a deep breath and caught himself before sighing again. The weather might force a change in plans—but not in Admiral Lee's resolve.

The ship's Executive Officer came through the hatch and reported that all was ready. Lao considered the potential for squalls, but the decision had been made. He nodded silently and then gave the command to cast off lines. The order was relayed to the other vessels in the group, and one by one, beginning with Captain Lao's destroyer, the task force slipped away from the docks and quietly set sail for the Strait of Taiwan far to the south.

* * * *

"OUR MAIN OBJECTIVE IS THE HUO SHAN is-land chain," Neill said, marking their destination with a grease pencil. The small team had formed a circle around the map that Neill had unfolded. "There's a naval facility there that we've been asked to look into."

Senior Chief Richey leaned forward. "Doesn't that island belong to the Chinese?"

"It's disputed territory, Chief. And it gets a little more complicated than that." Neill spent the next few minutes bringing them up to speed, starting with the loss of the *Gansu Province*, the mysterious weapon that caused her destruction, and the discovery of the secret base they were charged with investigating.

"There's more," he added, and briefly touched on the submarine the HMS *Bradford* had tracked. He also told them what he knew about Admiral Lee—and his associations with the Russians. By the time he finished, more than a few eyebrows had been raised. Neill studied his audience for their reactions, but it was the look of concern on Lieutenant Chau's face that caught his eye.

"You're probably more familiar with this region than any of us, Lieutenant," Neill began. "Any insight you can offer would be helpful."

Being singled out for input only deepened Chau's expression. "I'm not sure how much I can add to your briefing," he said slowly. "But there is a bit of folklore associated with this area that we all might want to keep in mind."

Neill frowned. "Folklore?"

Chau looked almost embarrassed. "My grandfather sailed these waters many years ago; in the Navy, and then later on aboard merchant vessels. He used to tell me stories."

"What kind of stories?" Crockett asked.

"*Ghost* stories," Chau answered. "He said that these waters were haunted. And that Huo Shan was the home of demons."

"Demons?" Crockett repeated. "I had a drill instructor like that."

A grin spread across Senior Chief Richey's face. "I told you he was a historian," he chuckled.

"Go on, Lieutenant," Neill encouraged.

" ' *Demons* ' might not be the right word. '*Spirits*' is probably more accurate," Chau continued. "Grandfather said these waters were cursed—and that the spirits of sailors lost at sea could find no rest there."

"He might have a point, Mike," Crockett offered. "I mean, things didn't turn out so well for that Chinese sub."

Neill decided now wasn't the time to weigh in on the subject of ghosts. But he didn't want to offend Chau by discounting what he'd said, either.

"Anything else we should know?"

Chau looked thoughtful. "The islands were formed by molten lava thousands of years ago—*Huo Shan* is Mandarin for *volcano*. Fishermen in the region sometimes call it Fire Island. The Chinese Navy has always steered clear of them—sailors can be very superstitious about such things. It could be that someone took advantage of that fact when they chose the island."

"So you think the legends about this place would keep anyone from wanting to take a closer look?"

"Seems logical to me."

"What about the weapon that sank the sub?" Crockett asked no one in particular. "Any ideas about that?"

Richey had been mulling that over. He drew his hand across his chin, a habit he'd picked up from Captain Beacham back on the *Meyer*. "I think I might be able to shed some light there, Lieutenant. But I need to do a little research first."

Neill nodded. "Okay, Chief. But you might want to do it quick."

Another thought came to mind. "Oh, by the way, everybody remove the name and service tapes from your uniforms." Neill checked his watch. "We'll shove off just before sunset. That'll give us time to familiarize ourselves with the boat before it gets dark." He studied the faces of the two Navy men. While he and Crockett were well rested, Neill knew that Chau and Richey could probably use some rack time after their trip in from Pearl. "In the meantime, I want everybody to catch a few Zs and pack an extra MRE before we go," he said, referring to the pre-packaged Meals, Ready to Eat. "I'll coordinate with Lieutenant Templeton about getting the rest of our equipment."

Crockett's eyes lit up. "You might need a hand with that." He turned to Lieutenant Chau. "What do you say, Navy man? Care to help out a couple of jarheads?"

Chau nodded with a grin. "I'd be happy to," he replied. Crockett had an unpretentious and personable way about him. Chau was beginning to like this Marine.

Neill pocketed the grease pencil and folded the chart. They began moving as a group toward the bow and then up a few decks. Amidships the three younger men parted company with the Senior Chief as he headed in search of the *Industrious'* library.

Richey found what he was looking for in short order. The ship hosted a fairly extensive compartment dedicated to MWR, or morale, welfare and recreation. From the moment Neill described the weapon, the Senior Chief had his suspicions. In the next half hour he would confirm them.

Chapter Ten ✻ Karaoke and Barbecue

CAPTAIN LING APPEARED TO BE GROWING more impatient. This time it wasn't an act. The Ensign's patrol boat hadn't even cleared the dock before a mechanical problem with the engines halted their departure. For the next two hours, Tsao anxiously shuttled between the bridge—where he assured the Captain that his vessel would soon be ready—and the spaces below decks—where he cajoled, pleaded, and nearly cursed the chief engineer to hurry the pace of his repairs.

Ling walked the deck, arms folded across his chest, making his displeasure very clear to the Ensign. Inwardly, he found Tsao's efforts almost comical, but he couldn't let the young officer know that. Even the Captain had to admit that Tsao was doing his best, and that these circumstances were beyond his control. He decided it might be best if he removed himself from the boat, at least briefly, to give the crew time to deal with the problem without having a senior officer watching over their shoulders. Much to Tsao's relief, he turned and left the bridge, promising to return soon.

* * * *

THE MAIN GATE WASN'T FAR. LING'S LONG strides took him to a busy shopping district that butted up against the naval base's fence line. There he found a small restaurant serving meals native to the province he called home. He ordered a bowl of food, selected a table and read the local paper while he ate. After his light lunch, he decided he had time for one more stop before heading back to the boat.

Ling discounted any belief in coincidence. In his world-view, everything happened for a reason, and the delay in leaving port gave him the opportunity to take care of one last item. He stepped out of the restaurant and surveyed the other businesses shouldered together on the busy street. He was window shopping for one in particular.

His search took him two blocks further before he found just what he was looking for. The Captain adjusted his cap and uniform, cast a glance over his shoulder, and then disappeared into a small shop on the corner. Anyone paying attention might have seen him pull a small notebook from his jacket, but no one seemed to notice as he entered the building.

* * * *

"WHAT'S THIS?" CROCKETT STARED AT THE booklet Neill handed him. It was small with a dark green card stock cover.

"Terminology," Michael replied. Chau stood nearby. The three had reunited near their staterooms after gathering gear. "Phrasebook for the mission; code words for locations, time-lines and actions we might engage in," Neill explained. "Take some time to familiarize yourself with it. You too, Simon."

"Radio protocols. Gotcha." Crockett flipped through the pages. "Where'd you get it?"

"Lieutenant Templeton. Came from Willis Avery's office. Emailed as a pdf, then collated and bound by the ship's crypto-logic section."

Crockett nodded. "The Brits are very thorough. Anything in here about shooting people?"

"Page two," Michael said without missing a beat. "Rules

of engagement," he raised a finger for emphasis. "No shooting people. And forget about pouting." Equipment was stacked in a small pile near the hatch. A very large machete in a sheath rested on top. "Got everything?"

"How about extra MREs?" Nate answered.

Neill laughed. "I'll get a case of the British variety. They call them ration packs. Lieutenant Templeton can help with that."

"I'm sure she can," Crockett called after him with a grin. "And none of that vegetarian stuff, either," he instructed, his voice rising to be heard as Neill disappeared around a corner.

* * * *

"So what's your deal, Simon?" Crockett asked. They had collected their gear and were headed aft toward the well deck. "You a linguist for the Navy full-time?"

Chau shook his head. "No. Cyber Defenses office in San Diego. But the Navy had me at Pearl as part of the control element for the arsenal ship."

"Oh," Crockett grunted. "I've heard of that. So you're big into electronics and stuff, huh?"

"I dabble in it," Chau said modestly.

"High speed, low drag," Nate observed. The plan was to stage the equipment in their inflatable boat prior to departure. Each man carried an armload, and the further they went, the heavier it seemed to get. "Ever put to sea?"

"Not for long." Simon admitted. He recalled his first introduction to small watercraft—when his family escaped from the Chinese mainland. "Most of my career has been behind a desk."

Crockett picked up on the anxiety in his voice. "Nothing wrong with that. I've got a cousin who joined the Air Force— and he's afraid of heights. Besides, somebody's got to stay in the rear with the gear." He tried to put his new comrade at ease. "Going out in the field is pretty routine stuff. Just stick close. Me and Neill will take good care of you."

"Thanks," Chau said. He decided it was time to distance

himself from the uneasy memory. "I didn't know officers were allowed to be snipers."

"We're not," Crockett answered. "That was my primary MOS as an enlisted man. Once I became an officer they made me a platoon leader," Nate explained. "I'm still a pretty good shooter, or so the Corps tells me. They just don't let me out to play much. That's why I jumped on this assignment."

That wasn't entirely true. Crockett's shooting skills would have been handily employed for HEAVY ANVIL. He'd been looking forward to the mission in Somalia, but at the same time he wasn't entirely at ease letting Neill go off on his own.

Chau mulled over Crockett's words as they continued down the passageway. "Sounds like you've had an interesting career."

He shook his head. "I'm not very complicated," Nate deflected. "Just a simple jarhead. I've been known to enjoy karaoke and barbecue," he smiled. "But not at the same time."

Chapter Eleven ✴ The Tempest

"WHAT DID YOUR RESEARCH TURN up, Chief?"

An hour had passed since the team left the well deck. Neill and the others had re-assembled in the officer's wardroom. Light from the portholes on the starboard side shifted and dimmed as the big ship turned due north.

"Your description of the weapon used against that sub got me thinking," Richey replied. "So I did a little checking online. Reminded me of something I read about several years ago. At the time I thought it was all just science fiction, but now I'm not so sure."

Chau and Crockett's ears perked up.

"The speed this weapon was traveling . . . it could only be one thing, really. A super-cavitating torpedo."

Richey's audience just stared back at him.

"A what?" Nate finally asked.

"Easy on the big words, Senior Chief," Neill grinned. "Anything with more than two syllables confuses Crockett."

"That's real funny, Mike."

"It's not really a torpedo; more like an underwater rocket," Richey went on. "I'll try to break this down so even you Marines will catch on.

"It all started with the Russians. Several years ago there were rumors that they'd come up with a new weapon. They called it 'Tempest', or 'Squall'; something like that. I'd heard a few details, but then the stories just kind of died down and went away. Everybody seemed to forget about it after that. Which is probably what the Russians wanted."

Each man was listening intently now. Being a history buff, Chau seemed particularly interested.

"It has to do with Bernoulli's Law and the theory of cavitation, and a whole lot of science that I don't pretend to understand. But it basically works like this: when water moves across an object at high speed, the pressure gets reduced at the point of contact. If the pressure is *low* enough, and you can manage to introduce enough gas in the water, you can form a cavity around that object."

"And that's where the word 'cavitation' comes in?" Neill asked.

Richey nodded. "Exactly—well, not *exactly*. But close enough. Anyway, this cavity of gas is more or less just a bunch of bubbles, and if you can generate enough of them it forms an envelope around the object."

"The torpedo, in this case," Chau offered.

"Right. The more gas, the greater your chance of creating an envelope that expands around the length of the torpedo."

"But I thought cavitation was bad—especially for submarines, or anything below the surface," Crockett replied, scratching his head.

"Ordinarily that would be correct," Richey agreed. "Because cavitation creates noise. All those bubbles eventually collapse, which can be heard underwater. And if you're a submarine, that can give you away."

Neill looked thoughtful. "So the Russians figured that if they couldn't *eliminate* cavitation—they'd take advantage of it?"

"Right again," the Senior Chief replied. He grinned. "You've got to admire them. The Russians are pretty cagey. They came up with a torpedo that makes the most of cavitation; in fact, their goal was to *increase* it. And they went a step further." Richey was spun up. "They designed the torpedo's nose so that it would inject gases around the weapon, to reinforce the envelope."

"And that causes it to move faster through the water?" Neill asked.

"It helps. What really gets it moving is a liquid-fuel rocket mounted on the back end. Once the cavity is formed around it, the rocket kicks in, which gives it incredible speed."

Chau was thinking over the science of the weapon. "So the envelope surrounds it and reduces drag, creating the fastest torpedo the world has ever seen."

Richey nodded. "That's it in a nutshell. But apparently it's a very unforgiving weapon system—anybody remember the *Kursk*?"

"The Russian sub that sank back in . . . what was it?" Neill asked.

"2000. That's the one," Richey replied. "An Oscar II class boat. Anyway, some people think the *Kursk* was testing one of those torpedoes. According to the theory, the rocket motor ignited prematurely and destroyed the sub."

Nate shook his head. "Submarines are dangerous enough; Russian submarines even more so. On top of that they used one as a test bed for an unproven weapon?"

"How fast was the torpedo going that took out that Chinese submarine?" Simon asked.

"Over three hundred miles an hour," Neill replied. He had a very thoughtful look on his face. "So this weapon was developed by the Russians. And our intel suggests the sub was sunk by a rogue element of the Chinese Navy. If that's the case, then it's not hard to see where they got their hands on one." Neill recalled Willis Avery's words aboard the *Lexington*. "The survivors said their boat was destroyed in a 'tempest of fire.' "

"Appropriate." The Senior Chief slowly stroked his chin. He preferred the word 'tempest' to 'squall.' It was easier to pronounce, for one thing. "Sounds like Admiral Lee struck a deal with the devil. He got his country to buy ships from the Russians—and they must have thrown in a super torpedo to boot."

Michael was about to comment when Lieutenant Templeton stepped into the compartment. She greeted the group with a smile. "Commodore Wainwright would like to meet your team before you disembark."

Neill nodded in reply. *Better to get this over with now*, he thought. There were still plenty of details to go over, but they were aboard one of Her Majesty's ships—protocol and simple good manners couldn't be ignored.

The four men filed out of the compartment as Templeton led them forward. Final preparations would have to be postponed.

Chapter Twelve ✴ The Colonial Rifles

COMMODORE HARRY WAINWRIGHT'S STATE-
room aboard the *Industrious* was much larger than
Neill expected. Befitting his rank and station—in life
and in the British Royal Navy—Wainwright's accommodations were functional, but also plush and richly appointed.
A few modest-sized oil paintings adorned one bulkhead.
Embroidered curtains draped the portholes of the other.
Next to the hatch, a swallow-tailed flag with a St. George's
Cross hung in a simple wooden frame—the pennant used
aboard British naval vessels whose masters wore the rank of
Commodore. Ornately embellished furniture was arranged
in the middle of the room around a mahogany coffee table,
while an antique desk was positioned in one of the corners—
seemingly at odds with the very modern laptop that sat front
and center on its cluttered surface. Neill thought back to the
Lexington. An officer's berth on that ship would have seemed
austere by comparison.

Movement at the desk caught Neill's eye as Templeton led
the team into the compartment. Hearing the group enter, a single figure stood slowly and turned to face them. Neill didn't
recognize the rank on his shoulder boards, but he didn't have
to. Clearly this man was the *Industrious'* commanding officer.

"*Attention on deck*," Michael ordered. Everyone, including
Amanda, braced and became still, their eyes locked on the far

bulkhead.

Harry Wainwright was a tall, drawn man whose features had been weathered by more than twenty-five years at sea. As lean as any first-year seaman, the senior officer projected an athletic appearance and commanding presence that instantly but quietly demanded respect. He crossed the deck and surveyed the four men and one woman who had assembled before him, his face creased with a broad smile.

"You may stand at ease." His voice bid for their attention just as much as the rank on his shoulders, but also had a calming effect. "I trust Leftenant Templeton has made you feel welcome." He didn't wait for an answer, and as the team relaxed a bit Wainwright stuck out a hand toward Neill. "*Dobre ootra*, Leftenant." *Good morning.*

Michael was momentarily caught off guard, but responded in kind. "*Dobre ootra. Vy gavaritye pa-Rooskie*? You speak Russian, sir?"

"*Da.*" The Commodore nodded as he shook each hand and regarded the team warmly. "A consequence of being the Royal Navy's attaché to Moscow—some years ago." His smile widened. "And the efforts of my wife, I might add. She was my counterpart in the Soviet Navy during the Cold War."

Neill was impressed. "How did you know—"

"Your Mr. Avery and I are old friends." Wainwright explained. "But let's not totter over mutual acquaintances."

"Totter, sir?" Neill asked. He was fluent in three languages but had learned English primarily from only two people—his parents. Occasionally a word or phrase in his mother tongue could throw him.

"Yes, totter," the Commodore chuckled. "Moving unsteadily about, if you take my meaning." He saw the amused looks on everyone's faces, especially Amanda's. "But now that we've overcome the barrier of language, let's discuss your mission."

* * * *

"WE'LL BE IN POSITION SHORTLY BEFORE dusk," Wainwright said. He gestured to the chairs and waited until everyone had taken a seat, and then eyed the group as a whole. The Commodore studied the two American Navy personnel more intently. "I understand you chaps came aboard just this morning. Let's wrap this up so you can get some rest before departure." He faced Neill. "I have my own theories, but do you have any idea what you're up against, *Leftenant*?"

Neill repeated the briefing Senior Chief Richey had given earlier. Occasionally, Wainwright would nod his head during the presentation, but didn't seem the least bit surprised when Michael brought up the Tempest torpedo. The mention of the weapon only seemed to sharpen his interest.

There was a pause after the Marine finished. "An unexpected development, but not altogether surprising." Wainwright's words were carefully measured. "There were ripples about this back in the day. I thought they were just rumors, or disinformation. How much confidence do you place in this intelligence?"

It was Richey who spoke up. "There's not really anything else it could be, Commodore."

Again, a nod. "Understood," Wainwright said simply. "And I agree." He stood and moved toward a bulkhead where a chart was in place. "A look at the map, gentlemen?"

The team stood as a man and joined the Commodore as he illuminated the chart with an overhead lamp. He planted an index finger on a position in the South China Sea more than a hundred kilometers from the island of Hainan.

"Your destination. The islands of Huo Shan." His finger slid a few inches to the south. "Your team will disembark the *Industrious* here. Twelve hours later we'll take up a position fifteen kilometers due east of the largest island." He traced a path to a point on the map already designated with a red pin. "We'll be waiting for you there." He turned and looked at each man in turn. "Your boat's been fitted with an extra fuel bladder, so there's no worry about sufficient petrol to make the transit. Do you have everything you need?"

"Aye, sir," Neill replied. "Rations, equipment, and weaponry. We're good to go."

"Very well, then." Commodore Wainwright liked what he heard. One more thought tugged at him. "Have you christened your team, Mr. Neill?"

Michael didn't quite understand. "Sir?"

"A *name*, Leftenant." Wainwright's smile returned. "Some operational designation."

Neill considered the phrasebook he carried in his pocket. There was no mention of a code-word being assigned to the group; apparently Avery had left that to them.

"Anything but the Light Brigade," Richey said. "Or the *Old* Guard." He ran a hand through his slightly graying hair.

An awkward pause followed. The subject had caught them off guard. Nothing else was said, and then Amanda's voice was heard.

"The *Colonial Rifles*."

Everyone turned to give her a look. She smiled confidently.

Neill nodded in agreement. "Sounds good to me." He thought it over. "In fact, that sounds perfect. Any objections?"

No one challenged the name or had any other suggestions. Michael looked around the room and then back to the Commodore, who nodded his own approval.

"I'd suggest you get some sleep, then," Wainwright said at last. "If you have need of anything else, run it by Leftenant Templeton."

The Commodore had done his part; the team had received their official send-off and felt ready. Only one more thing needed to be said. The senior officer issued one final directive.

"Dismissed."

Chapter Thirteen ✷ Departures

McBride Defense Industries
Luzon, the Philippines

EMORY MCBRIDE HAD ALREADY DONE A walk-around of the sleek company helicopter and now entered the cockpit to start his pre-flight checks. His excursion this evening wouldn't really be questioned, which was one of the advantages of being the boss's son, as well as the head of the company's Far Eastern offices. Still, to cover himself, he'd casually mentioned to his secretary that he wanted to take the chopper out to test some new electronics gear that the technical department installed. That only raised her suspicions.

This bird had extra fuel capacity, which extended its range. McBride had chosen the aircraft for just that reason. He'd watched as the ground crew topped off the chopper before climbing aboard to go through the checklist. That process had taken a little time, but now, satisfied that all the systems were flight-worthy, he activated the GPS and input the coordinates for tonight's destination.

In the seat next to him was a canvas backpack embroidered with his name. He reached inside and pulled out a small, silver case, the contents of which would make him even wealthier than he already was.

It wasn't just greed that compelled McBride to do what he did; he certainly loved money, but that wasn't the sole reason for his actions. There was a part of him that liked playing with fire; he didn't want to get burned, he just wanted to see how close he could get to the flame. It seemed to almost defeat the boredom of his privileged life, and fill the void he felt deep inside.

McBride dropped the small case back into his pack. The sun's glare hurt his eyes. He put on his sunglasses and spun up the rotors. Within minutes he was ready to go.

* * * *

MCBRIDE'S SECRETARY TOOK IN THE VIEW from her office as the helicopter lifted off the pad. She was a perceptive woman, and couldn't recall any updated electronics being installed on the company's aircraft. Besides being observant, she was also very tech-savvy; and after McBride's departure, she dug into the company's files where she quickly found the chopper's maintenance records. According to those, nothing new had been fitted on the helicopter in over a year. From there she marched into McBride's office and checked all the recent activity on her boss's computer. Ordinarily, her access to this information would have been difficult to retrieve—McBride was a careful man, and always wiped the hard drive's memory. But in this case, the secretary had been supplied with recovery software—courtesy of the U.S. government—that made it easy to see what McBride had been up to. What she found alarmed her, so she hurried back to her desk and picked up the phone.

* * * *

"I WON'T BE GONE LONG," NEILL SAID INTO THE phone. "Just thought I'd give you a call before I left."

Halfway around the world, Daniel Neill looked at the

clock on his night stand. It was entirely too early—even for the retired Marine.

The elder Neill hid his grogginess. "Glad you did." He sat up, swinging his frame over the bed and planting a foot on the carpet. His prosthetic leg leaned against the nightstand. "I was just about to pour myself some coffee."

"At this hour?"

"I'll save you a cup." He ran a hand through his scalp. It was time for a haircut.

The two Marines spent a few minutes 'catching up'— it was more about their family bonds than anything else. Michael felt the need to stay connected. The younger Neill offered no details—operational security prevented that—but Daniel could always count on his nephew to contact him just before an operation.

After mutual assurances, the call ended. The Master Gunny replaced the phone in its stand and sat quietly in the darkened room. Alone with his thoughts, he whispered a prayer for Michael, lamenting the fact that the young man had so few family members left that he could rely on.

* * * *

THE TEAM MET AGAIN AT THE STERN IN WHAT Neill called the press box—a room filled with instrumentation located just above the well deck and dedicated to launching boats and other watercraft into the sea. From here, all operations below could be monitored and controlled. Each of the men had eaten another meal and grabbed a few more hours of sleep—with the mission planned as a night operation, none of them knew when they might get another chance for food or rest.

One by one, the technicians who worked in the control room began filing in. The process of opening the well deck to the sea was about to start. Neill and the others exited the compartment and made their way to the ladders that led below.

The team arrived on the well deck to find Lieutenant Templeton waiting for them. She wished the group fair winds and following seas and then fixed her eyes on Neill.

Crockett took the hint. "Come along, gentlemen. Let's make sure *Leftenant* Neill's kit is properly stowed."

* * * *

"IT'S NOT THAT OBVIOUS, IS IT?" AMANDA asked. The blush had returned to her cheeks.

Neill watched as the team headed for the boat before turning to face her. "Is *what* that obvious?" he answered, feigning ignorance—with a broad grin.

She downplayed the question. In the space of a heartbeat her demeanor went from playful to something more serious.

"You'll need to be careful out there; it's a big ocean and we don't have a lot of friends in this part of the world."

"We'll stay sharp," Neill promised. He decided to tease her a bit. "I'll bring you a souvenir. They might have t-shirts on the island."

She smiled at that. *Americans*.

"You know, when a lady gifts a gentleman, it's customary for him to return the favor," Amanda said softly. She had gone right back to being coy.

Neill had no clue what she was talking about, but he was intrigued.

"And what gift is that?" he played along.

She gave him her best alluring look. "Without my contribution, your team would be nameless."

"Ah—that," he said. He adopted a more official tone. "The *Colonial Rifles* extend their appreciation to the Leftenant for a truly inspired moniker." An exaggerated frown crossed his face. "I may be mistaken, but don't christenings usually involve champagne—or at least some sparkling grape juice?"

She smiled; the young Marine was catching on. "I think I can find some by the time you return."

"Outstanding. And I know a little restaurant on board. I believe it's called the Crown and Jockey."

Amanda laughed. "Such a refined sense of humor, Leftenant Neill—I had no idea. But I believe it's called the officer's wardroom."

"It's a date, then," Michael announced. "Just keep the bubbly on ice till we get back."

* * * *

THERE WAS A LOT OF ACTIVITY GOING ON around them now. The British deck hands wore hard hats as they readied the ship to take on several hundred metric tons of seawater. Amanda watched as they checked their packs and applied war paint to their faces. Each man wore their Gore-Tex, including the matching all-weather trousers, as well as tactical gloves. They had opted against Kevlar helmets for the mission, choosing instead to wear the classic eight point covers common to both the Navy and Marine Corps. Chau stowed his laptop and then he and Richey helped Neill and Crockett as they made sure the gear was positioned low in the boat. With everything in order, they all stood back to wait for the gate to open and begin the controlled flooding of the *Industrious'* stern.

The process didn't take long. As the massive hatch opened, seawater began to slowly fill the compartment. The sight was a bit alarming at first. Neill and the team stood on a platform just above the rising water, their boat tied securely to a series of bollards. As the sea swirled below, the small craft strained against its tether. In the control room, engineers monitored the flow as it came aboard and adjusted the ship's buoyancy to compensate for the added weight. The Americans peered aft through the opening for one last glimpse of the sun before it dipped below the horizon.

"You all prayed up, boss?" Nathan asked with a grin.

"Always."

Michael looked up at the technicians. The officer in charge checked his instruments, and then gave the Americans a thumbs-up. Neill nodded his acknowledgement and regarded the team.

"Things will start happening faster now. Keep in mind this is a simple mission—no John Wayne stuff. We'll make our way to the big island and land, if we can. Then we'll gather the intel we need, shove off again, and head for the *Industrious*. Watch your back, and watch your battle buddy's back. There are certainly risks to what we're about to do—keep your focus and stay safe. Any questions?"

No one said a word, and the excitement had built for each of them. With their adrenaline flowing, Neill motioned toward the boat and the four of them stepped aboard. A British seaman untied the mooring lines as Richey took up a position near the outboard motor. Once again, the Marines checked their canvas rifle bags between the inflatable's rigid gunwales. As Neill pulled the GPS locator from his pack, Crockett and Chau used oars to maneuver the craft toward the stern gate.

Richey looked over the side into the water beneath them. Satisfied with the depth, he adjusted the outboard until the propeller was fully submerged, and then started the engine. The group was surprised by how softly the motor hummed as the propeller's blades began to churn the water below the surface. Within minutes the small boat had cleared the gate and was heading out to sea.

Behind them, Amanda Templeton waved, and then threw them a casual but very British salute. Neill made sure to return the gesture. Templeton smiled. In the short time the Americans had been aboard, she'd grown accustomed to their presence. Her only regret now was that she wasn't going with them.

* * * *

"DID SHE JUST BLOW YOU A KISS?"
Chau and Richey grinned at Crockett's jibe but said nothing.
"Shut up, Nate." Neill consulted the hand-held GPS. The

Industrious still loomed very large, but slowly began to diminish in size as they continued their journey. Leaving the confined environment of the ship and emerging into the open sea was quite a contrast. "Our course will be north by northwest. Weather shouldn't be a factor on the way in, but there is a front moving down from the north. We'll reach our destination ahead of it. Transit time should be about an hour, maybe an hour and a half."

"I thought it was a three hour tour," Richey said with a smile. Neill gave him a blank look. The reference was lost on the younger men.

THE SEA HAD A LIGHT CHOP, WITH AN OCCAsional swell that the boat handled with ease. Senior Chief Richey manned the outboard, with Chau and Neill in the center. Lieutenant Crockett pushed the case of ration packs up front to the bow and used it as a seat. He looked ahead through the night vision scope the Brits had supplied to see what might be in their path. After getting in position he turned to see Neill grinning at him.

"What's so funny?"

"Glad to see you're protecting our most vital assets."

Nate patted his rump with a gloved hand. "Just keeping them close to my heart."

As the light faded, the men began to notice the glow of phosphorescent marine life as it was churned up in their wake. It had an eerie look to it as the twilight sky grew dimmer; and it brought to mind the stories of ghosts that Lieutenant Chau had told them about earlier.

The White House

"HE'S ON THE MOVE." RICHARD AULTMAN stepped into Willis Avery's office. He was a little out of breath.

"The CIA just got a call from his secretary."

Avery looked over his mug of coffee with a frown. It was barely seven in the morning. He found it odd to see Aultman in at this hour. In fact, he was surprised to be in himself, but he'd slept well the night before and decided to make an early go of things. "Who's on the move?"

"McBride," Aultman took a moment to compose himself. "He took a company helicopter and left more than an hour ago." McBride didn't know it but the breaches in security had left a trail that led back to him.

Avery looked clueless. He had been briefed on McBride's activities and received updates on a regular basis, but nothing new had come up in over two weeks. And there were always other concerns that cried out for his attention. Aultman could excuse him for not catching on right away.

"Where's he headed?"

"He didn't say—no flight plan," Aultman said, handing Avery a sheet of paper. "He also took this."

Avery scanned the page quickly. Recruiting the secretary to keep an eye on her boss had paid off. McBride's greed had made him a little sloppy, which, in turn, had made the CIA's job easier.

Avery cursed under his breath. "I thought we had people watching him."

"We do," Aultman answered. "But our satellite got fried by a solar flare. The NRO didn't get tipped off about it until after he'd left."

Avery paused long enough to absorb what he'd just read. "Looks like McBride's treason has jumped to the next level," Avery mumbled. "He's downloaded some very sensitive infor-mation." He swore again. "Is this everything?"

"No," Aultman said bluntly. "There's a level of encryption within the data. Langley hasn't cracked that yet."

"What are they looking at?"

"The secretary sent a zip file of everything McBride took."

"Good girl." Avery checked his watch. "You said an hour ago?"

Aultman nodded. "How bad is it?" He had read the report but hadn't fully understood its meaning.

Avery scanned the print-out again. "Depends. McBride Defense Industries has a lot of irons in the fire; securing our encryption codes, designing new weapons systems—their west coast branch built the arsenal ship." He shook his head. "They also work closely with other key defense contractors, so shared information is common. On top of that, they help maintain our comm network in the Pacific—and everything on this list can be used to compromise those systems." He wore a scowl on his face. "It's the encrypted material that really worries me. We'll need a closer look. Get that MDI representative on this—what's his name again? Farrell?"

"Farris," Aultman corrected.

Avery gulped from his mug. "I want an analysis of everything he took. Next we need to find out where he's headed," Avery declared. "Get on the horn to the base commander at Kadena—" he was referring to the U.S. air base on Okinawa—"Tell him to scramble whatever he's got to keep tabs on that chopper. Alert our assets in the region to be prepared to intercept Mr. McBride—wherever he might be going." His thoughts were racing now. He had a knack for thinking two moves ahead. But his next words came very slowly. "Before we do that, have the CIA forward the file to the Cyber Defense group in San Diego."

Aultman asked, "You want more eyes on it?"

"Many hands make light work." Grandpa Avery's words echoed in his memory. "Our Navy people have a lot of experience protecting against cyber-attacks," Avery explained. "Doing that requires creative thinking; maybe they can decipher it."

"I'm on it," Aultman said, heading back to his own office.

Avery continued to frown as he read over the page again. He considered the chronology of events, reminding himself that the Philippines were twelve hours ahead of the east coast. Laying the memo aside, he began thinking about his next course of action. At the moment there were too many unknowns. Once they knew where McBride was going it would be a lot easier to decide what the next step would be. The plan had always been to gather enough evidence against him for a quick and easy conviction. It occurred to Avery that they may have waited too long.

Chapter Fourteen ✶ Eyes in the Sky

EMORY McBRIDE WAS GETTING HUNGRY. He'd been airborne for nearly two hours, with at least another hour and a half before he reached Huo Shan. The coordinates given to him by his contact indicated he was headed for the big island. He checked the GPS display. The outline of his destination, represented by a luminescent, meandering green line, had just begun to form on the extreme edges of the screen.

Not long now, he smiled to himself.

Next he checked the weather. In addition to the GPS, the helicopter had a satellite Doppler feed, and McBride could access real-time weather maps for any part of the world. Before leaving Luzon, he'd pre-selected the region encompassing the target area to monitor the massive front moving south. He knew he could expect heavy cloud cover, but right now the radar displayed only moderate rainfall. McBride wasn't concerned about how that might affect his arrival. But it could impact his departure, depending on how long he stayed on the island.

* * * *

CAPTAIN HECTOR NOYES WAS LOITERING; NOT in the sense of hanging around and being an unwelcome pest, but more in the way the military defined it. At an altitude of seventeen thousand feet, and traveling at an air speed of over four hundred miles an hour, Noyes was flying his F-15 Eagle in a triangular pattern, maintaining a constant presence over the region. Noyes' wingman flew an identical aircraft a thousand feet from his right wing.

Like any good pilot, the Captain checked the data being fed to him by his instrumentation frequently. At the moment his eyes were following the progress of a contact on his radar scope. The small image on the screen was the sole reason for tonight's mission.

With a name like Noyes, it was inevitable that Hector got the nickname 'Maybe.' But for this mission, Flight Ops at Kadena—directed by Willis Avery's office—had assigned him a different call sign. Noyes took his eyes away from his heads-up display and looked down toward the sea.

"DENMOTHER, this is BIG LEAGUE," he called over the radio. "PIPEDREAM is continuing north by northwest at an altitude of four thousand feet—how copy?"

"Lima Charlie, BIG LEAGUE," came the reply. 'Lima Charlie' was military-speak for 'loud and clear.' "Has PIPEDREAM caught on to your presence?"

"Negative," Noyes answered. "His current course will take him directly over CATHEDRAL in five-five mikes." Again, radio terminology meaning fifty-five minutes.

CATHEDRAL was a reference to Huo Shan—a code-word substituted to confuse unwanted listeners. Checking his map—and noting the absence of any other land mass in the area—Noyes concluded that the island chain had to be PIPEDREAM's destination.

Hector pulled his night vision goggles on and his eyes swept the horizon. He was too far from his target to actually see him, but he thought maybe he'd catch a glimpse of his running lights. No luck there; the distance was just too great, so getting a visual was out of the question. But that really didn't affect Hector's tracking abilities. Noyes relied on radar, as well as the transponder signal beamed from PIPEDREAM, to get a constant fix on his location.

It was that transponder that identified Hector's target as an extended-range helicopter, owned by McBride Defense Industries. Hector considered the chopper's pilot to be something of an amateur—if he wanted to maintain a low profile, he should have deactivated the device. But Noyes was glad that he hadn't; it just made his job that much easier.

* * * *

"WE ARE SIX HOURS BEHIND SCHEDULE," Captain Ling declared. He didn't need to add that he was not pleased.

Tsao could feel the beads of sweat returning. "My apologies, Captain." He swallowed hard. "We are making the best possible speed. My chief engineer is doing everything possible to make up the time."

The Ensign was a little young to be a ship's master; even for a craft as small as this patrol boat. And he had risen in rank without political connections—a rare thing in China's Navy. He had done so through diligence and hard work, and while Ling would never admit it, he was impressed by the young man.

Ling looked out the window into the night, but there was not much to see. Hainan and the naval base had dropped from their view. Ahead, the sky was black, and it was difficult to pick out the horizon. He could just make out the lights of a ship sailing east—probably a cargo vessel bound for the Philippines. Behind the chaser, a front was pushing a line of thunderstorms to the south. *At least the wind is in our favor*, Ling thought.

To his right, outside the bridge cabin, a few of the Marines leaned against the rail, passing the time with stories and cigarettes. Ling noticed that Sergeant Wen was not among them. That didn't surprise him. The Captain had detected a rather nasty disposition in the swarthy NCO. None of the other troops seemed to spend much time in his company.

Ling didn't dwell on that thought. He turned back to the weather. He knew that as long as they stayed ahead of the front, they could expect clear skies. He checked his watch again—he had a deadline to meet on Huo Shan and didn't want to be late. Still, the delay was unavoidable; and whoever this American was, he would wait. With any luck, they might even make up some of the time they'd lost; *if* the boat's engineer could just nurse a little more speed from the engines below.

That thought had barely crossed Ling's mind when they all heard a muffled *whump* astern. The steady hum of the power plant went silent and their forward momentum slowed. Within seconds they were simply drifting, and standing at the wheel, the pilot was having a difficult time keeping the bow from moving to port or starboard.

The wheelhouse grew very quiet. Ling shot a look at Tsao, whose eyes were wide with fear.

"More problems, Ensign?"

The young officer ordered the pilot to hold his rudder amidships, and then darted from the bridge to see what he could do to avoid any more of Captain Ling's frustration.

The White House

At first glance Avery thought the font manager on his computer had suffered a system error. He checked the rest of the files on his desktop but discovered that nothing else was amiss. It was then that he realized what he was looking at.

"I can't read this," he muttered.

Richard Aultman stepped into the room. The boss was glaring at his monitor and clearly in a foul mood.

The ground level of the West Wing boasted a Navy mess and kitchen—the cafeteria that fed the White House staff. After getting word of McBride's departure from Luzon, both men had grabbed an early breakfast. The meal had been quite filling, and Richard Aultman regretted not pushing himself away from the table sooner. He knew that in time he'd be fighting the urge to nap. Now the two had returned and Avery found a message waiting in his inbox.

"Read what?" Aultman walked around Avery's desk.

"This email. It's in Russian."

"How do you know that?" Aultman regretted the question as soon as he asked it.

"I might not be able to read it, Richard, but I can certainly recognize the Cyrillic alphabet." Avery rubbed a hand across his face. The omelets served up by the Navy had alleviated his hunger but did little for his disposition. "Where's Neill when I need him?"

It was a rhetorical question, but Aultman couldn't resist having a little fun with it. "Right about now he's doing that other thing you asked him to do. I know he's a Marine and all that, but he can't be in two places at once."

"Get on the phone with State," Avery ordered. It annoyed him that someone could send him an email from the outside, in a foreign language no less. But he was intrigued. "No, hold on," he said, a curious look on his face. His expression changed to a smile as he sat down again. "Disregard that."

Aultman was puzzled by his boss's reversal. "Do we need a translator or not?"

"Yes, we do. And I know just who to call."

* * * *

"IT IS KIND OF SPOOKY," NATE CROCKETT declared as the boat moved through the water. Darkness covered everything; the *Industrious* had disappeared behind them, and the only source of illumination came from the scattered stars overhead. Using the night scope, Crockett could occasionally see the lights of a ship before it disappeared over the horizon.

From the rear of the boat, Richey chuckled. "*Lord, the sea is so big, and my boat is so small.* Is that what you're thinking, Lieutenant?"

"Roger that, Senior Chief," Nate replied, making his voice heard over the low hum of the outboard. "I'll bet you're used to this."

"I've been at sea most of the past eighteen years. But always aboard ships—not a little dinghy like this." *And not sailing into the dragon's mouth*, he didn't add.

Neill consulted the GPS. "Right on course. We should be able to see the island soon."

Crockett continued scanning. "There's something in front of us. Looks like a mountain. Covered in mist—or one of Chau's ghosts." He grinned. "Just kidding, Si."

Simon said nothing. Nate blinked and re-focused on what lay before them. "Belay that—cloud formation. Stretches across most of my line of sight." He handed the scope back to Neill. "Take a look."

Neill studied the skyline. "Got it. And there's our destination," he said, handing the scope to Chau. "Directly ahead, that small hump on the horizon."

"I see it," Chau answered. "What are the coordinates?"

Neill gave him the GPS. A key on the device featured a 'point of origin' option. Chau selected it and read the digits showing the position of the *Industrious*. The little hand-held mechanism was deceptively simple to operate. The Lieutenant tabbed to the next field on the display and checked his watch. He handed the device back to Neill, and estimated their speed at eight knots.

"What's our ETA?" Nate asked.

"Hang on, let me scroll back to preview mode." Neill once again referenced the GPS. "Probably—"

"Forty-three minutes," Chau finished for him.

No one could see Neill's frown in the dark. "How'd you know that?"

Chau ignored the question and just grinned. "Think we'll get there before that storm?"

"Might be dicey," Neill replied. He stared ahead at the approaching front. It was moving in faster than he'd expected.

"But we're all amphibious, right?"

The team was quiet for the next half hour. Crockett had acquired some protein bars from the *Industrious'* mess hall. He reached into his ruck and passed them around. The night air had awakened their hunger, and they would need the energy once they reached the island.

* * * *

THE MOONLESS NIGHT AFFORDED THE TEAM A great deal of stealth. But below the waves, the sound of their outboard provided a constant fix on their position.

A quarter of a mile astern, a mast housing a periscope/antenna array slowly and silently broke the surface. The optics were quickly focused on a point due north. After thirty seconds, the bulbous tip of the mast was lowered back into the sea, leaving only a foamless wake that was absorbed by the swells.

* * * *

EACH MAN TOOK A TURN AT THE OUTBOARD. Neill felt it was important for everyone to be familiar with its operation. Senior Chief Richey was a seasoned hand when it came to small watercraft, patiently instructing his teammates on handling and proper seamanship. After thirty minutes, Malcolm proclaimed them all to be experts.

Huo Shan soon began to take shape in front of the little boat. The largest island—Greater Huo Shan—featured a promontory on its eastern side. Nearly a mile and a half long, and the product of volcanic activity, the big island was crescent-shaped, its mass the remnant of a large crater jutting up from the ocean floor. More than half of that had collapsed ages before; but the high ground remained, rising nearly five hundred feet, a craggy finger of rock covered mostly by dense, tropical vegetation.

To the west were two smaller islands, Lesser Huo Shan

and Huo Shan Nua, which varied in shape and size according to the tides. Neither was very long or stood much higher than half a dozen feet above sea level. In truth, these smaller strips of land were merely part of the undersea ridge that formed the big island. They had borne the brunt of many storms and typhoons, and in time, both would probably succumb to erosion and disappear below the waves, becoming nothing more than a shallow breakwater.

Nearing the islands, a steady rain began to fall. Each man zipped his Gore-Tex jacket a little higher, and with the aid of the scope, Neill began to look for a spot to land the boat. He could make out a few man-made structures hugging the promontory and on the beach, but these only became visible as they drew closer. It appeared that the buildings further inland sat under large outcroppings of trees and other native vegetation—clearly an attempt to hide their presence from the casual observer. Neill could also see that a narrow dock had been built, running two hundred feet from the base of the crater wall out to sea. This was covered by a low, angled metal or aluminum roof that extended far over the water. It was covered on top by camouflage netting. Neill concluded that this must be the submarine pen Willis Avery had briefed him about. Even without the aid of the night scope, he could see that nothing was moored there at the moment.

Not a soul could be seen, and no lights were visible anywhere. This worried Neill; if the intel was true, and Admiral Lee had troops on the island, where were they? Had they detected their approach and now waited to spring a trap? And where was the submarine that British Intelligence had warned them about?

As the team leader, Neill was responsible for the lives of the men in the boat with him. While certain risks were acceptable, he decided that caution would rule their next steps.

"Let's take her completely around the island for a look-see, Senior Chief," Michael suggested. "I'd like an overview of the entire shoreline before we go in."

"Roger that, El-Tee," Richey agreed. As they edged closer, he could also see some of the features of the base. It looked deserted—for the moment—but the Senior Chief liked Neill's plan. "Low and slow, aye aye, sir."

"THERE'S SOMETHING MORE TO ALL this; but right now I just don't know what it is," Lloyd Farris admitted. Sitting in the office across from Willis Avery, the McBride Defense Industries representative was nothing if not honest.

"Your suspicions were correct; the bulk of the material deals with encryption codes and the like." He continued, reading from a memorandum he held in one hand. "There's even information on the metallurgy used to build the arsenal ship. The content is all classified material; no question there. But it's not the brass ring."

McBride's secretary had been very thorough. She'd received just enough training from her handlers to know how to retrieve everything her boss had downloaded. She bundled the material together and uploaded it to a server managed by the CIA, who kept a copy for analysis. On Avery's orders, it was immediately turned over to the MDI field bureau in D.C. From there, Lloyd Farris and his team went right to work. Now, barely three hours after the secretary had sent the data, Farris sat in Avery's office.

Avery listened intently. The National Security Advisor had been jotting down notes, but the concern in the MDI official's voice gave him pause.

Richard Aultman stepped into the room and pulled up a chair. He got his boss's attention with a glance—clearly he had news, but it would have to wait.

"Could you elaborate on that?" Avery asked.

Farris gave a nod. "It contains some good stuff. Mr. McBride made no attempt to hide the material—I found it in less than five minutes. And in the right hands it could prove very useful. But that's just window-dressing; embedded in the stream of data is an encrypted thread that I can't get into." His frustration was evident.

Avery decided to stop him there. "The CIA is having the same problem. What else can you tell us?"

"Not much beyond that. It's very easy to miss at first glance. I'd pat myself on the back for even finding it. But without knowing how to interpret the code—"

"—we're still no closer to knowing what it is," Avery barked. He softened his tone and asked, "Anyone on your staff have the necessary cryptologic skills?"

Another nod. "I have people on it as we speak," Farris answered. "Of course, you could always ask McBride. Does anyone know his whereabouts since he left Luzon?"

"We're working to ascertain his location," Avery said vaguely.

"Any clue as to what the encryption might be?" Aultman asked. He was ready to entertain wild speculation at this point.

Farris looked thoughtful. "McBride could have tasked a couple of teams to develop something new—our R and D department in the Philippines is pretty extensive. Compartmentalizing the project would have prevented anyone from getting the full picture."

"Clever," Avery observed. "So he is hiding something." An idea came to mind. "I'd like you to interview your staff in Luzon. See if you can piece together what McBride was up to."

"I'll see to it myself."

Lloyd Farris was only too happy to help. He looked a little frazzled. His normal routine had been interrupted, and the pace of today's events was catching up with him. He wouldn't get any rest soon. Considering all the contracts MDI held with the

Department of Defense, damage control was now his most pressing concern.

Avery got slowly to his feet and extended his hand. The meeting was over.

"You work fast, Lloyd. We appreciate you coming by. Give Mr. Aultman a call if you come up with anything else."

* * * *

"YOU'VE GOT THAT LOOK ON YOUR FACE," AVERY intoned as an aide escorted Farris out. "What's up?"

"Got a call from Langley," Aultman answered. "Justice signed off on monitoring McBride's financial activities—and one of his accounts just received a wire transfer worth a bundle."

"How much?"

"Five million."

"Probably just a down payment," Avery carped. "Where'd the transfer originate?"

"China. Beijing, to be specific." Aultman replied. "Admiral Lee?"

Avery smiled. "You cut right to the chase. But that's probably on the money—no pun intended. Anything else?"

"A Chinese task force set sail from the base in Qingdao twenty-four hours ago. A nearly identical group left Dalian about the same time."

"Destination?" As if he couldn't guess.

"The ships from Qingdao are headed south into the Strait of Taiwan. The other group is moving toward the northern side of the island." Aultman watched as Avery stood and retrieved his jacket from the coat rack in the corner.

"It is spring. All surface ships?"

Aultman nodded. "Sixteen in each. DoD can't confirm it, but they suspect both groups are traveling with submarine escorts."

"Most likely, if they're following standard naval doctrine," Avery surmised. He slipped on his jacket and had a thought, then stepped toward the door. "Did Defense give you a breakdown on the rest of the ships?"

"Destroyers, a couple of frigates—and minesweepers," Aultman answered, then asked, "You going someplace?"

"Pentagon. I'm briefing SECDEF. We need to tease this out. You line up our interpreter yet?"

"I got through to Gleeson over at CIA." Aultman checked his watch. "We're meeting in about an hour."

"All right, then." Avery chuckled at this news. "Tell Mr. Orlov I said hello."

Chapter Sixteen ✶ The Shores of Huo Shan

RICHEY STEERED THE BOAT TO PORT, AND they began circling the island from a distance of three hundred yards. The water was shallower here, and breakers began rolling under the inflatable, gently lifting them up and down as the waves moved inland. Reaching the western tip of Greater Huo Shan, Neill retrieved a small, hand-held device from his ruck. Like the GPS, it was sheathed in a protective rubber skin, and resembled a cell phone, but was about twice as long. Michael ran a finger across the handset's control pad and depressed the activation key.

The display began to glow as the device powered up. From the back of the boat, Richey recognized the small piece of hardware as a signals interceptor. Neill allowed the handset to become fully active and then began testing it, holding it above his head and pointing it from side to side.

"Anything?" Richey asked.

"Not a peep," Neill murmured evenly. "The display shows that it's interrogating the area, but nobody seems to be transmitting." He looked toward the front of the boat as they turned north and began rounding the end of the island. "Keep your eyes peeled, Nate," he called softly.

Crockett looked intently through the night vision scope, studying the shoreline. "I've got nothing," he answered. "It's like a ghost town." He took his eyes away from the beach and looked back toward Chau, a big grin on his face. "Sorry, Simon."

IN ANOTHER TEN MINUTES, THE BOAT BEGAN its turn south as they made for the eastern tip. There wasn't much to see, and they all noticed that the waves grew rougher here. Neill focused on the rocky wall of the crater, at the point where the cliff reared up into the night sky. Without the scope it was hard to tell, but it looked as if there might be a cave or grotto at the waterline.

Coming around on a westerly course, the naval facility abruptly came into view. Again, there was no sign of activity. The team got a closer look at the pier from this vantage point—mooring lines rolled up neatly on the deck, and a row of long buildings tucked away under more camouflage netting—but no boats or vessels of any kind. Chau retrieved one of the cameras the Brits had provided and began taking pictures as Richey continued to motor.

Neill looked back out to sea. This close to the island, they risked being spotted from someone on the beach, but other threats might be waiting offshore. He scanned the surrounding waters, then borrowed the scope from Nate and panned the horizon. There were no ships anywhere in sight.

Leaving the facility behind, they turned their attention back to the shore. Again, nothing out of the ordinary—just a line of uniformly similar palm trees, pushing out from the center of the island toward the sea.

* * * *

McBRIDE COULD NOW SEE THE ISLANDS. SHEETS of rain pelted the windscreen as the aircraft got closer. He brought the helicopter down to an altitude of one thousand feet and checked his fuel. Satisfied with what the gauges told him, he banked to the north and began his approach, using his own night vision goggles to search for the promised landing spot.

* * * *

FROM THE BOW, NATE TOOK HIS EYES OFF THE beach and looked back at Neill, a frown on his face. Something wasn't right.

"You hear that?"

Neill turned his head. For the moment, the only sounds were the hum of the motor and the occasional wave as it splashed against the side of the boat. Chau sat up, his ear to the east.

"I hear it," Simon announced. "Sounds like an engine—"

Nate fixed his gaze in the same direction. His senses were on full alert. Then his eyes locked on something in the sky.

"There—three o'clock." He kept his voice low, but very precise so each man could clearly hear him.

Neill looked but didn't see anything. Big raindrops began to thump down on the boat's gunwales and flooring. "What have you got, Crockett?"

Nate was pointing now. "Lights from an aircraft, about a thousand feet up."

Richey shut off the outboard and looked skyward as well. "Helicopter." He craned his neck and listened intently. Soon each man could hear the *thwump-thwump-thwump* of a rotary aircraft.

"Smaller than a Seahawk—" Richey continued. "—probably a commercial job. Or a Chinese bird." He hoped it wasn't the latter.

As the launch drifted in the rain, they watched as the aircraft's light moved north and passed behind the towering wall. When it appeared on the other side, they could make out the faint outline of a helicopter against the dark backdrop of the night sky.

"We've got company," Chau's voice was nearly a whisper. "But who?"

"No clue," Neill answered. He switched off the signal interceptor and stowed it back in his ruck. "If our people were sending back-up, they would've told us."

"Well, you'd think so," Richey answered. "It'd be a little rude if they changed the op and didn't tell us about it." There was more than a hint of sarcasm in his voice.

Neill shook his head. "That's not Avery's style. Besides, the mission is all about stealth. This is something else—has to be."

"What's the plan, Mike?"

"We'll sit tight for now; see where this goes," Neill answered. "Maybe it's a corporate aircraft. Might belong to some oil company, coming back from a rig and headed for the Chinese mainland."

"Sounds reasonable," Richey conceded from the back of the boat. "But I'm not so sure—"

Neill could see what the Chief meant. The chopper had slowed its speed, and descended further. Now it banked and began a leisurely turn high above the tall outcropping of volcanic rock.

"Looks like he's fixed on the big island," Chau said. "Could be looking for a place to land."

"I think you're right, Simon," Neill said, turning to Richey. "Let's make for shore, Senior Chief. Directly ahead looks good. We'll get in position on the beach and wait this out."

* * * *

MCBRIDE GRIPPED THE COLLECTIVE AND CY-clic and began his descent toward the island. Without any illumination below, he considered switching on the searchlight mounted between the landing skids. First, he pulled off the NVGs—besides being uncomfortable, he didn't want to be looking through those when he lit up the night.

His hand had barely touched the controls when he picked out a perfectly square clearing beneath the aircraft. There it was—although the pad was a bit close to the massive rock formation for his tastes. It annoyed him that he hadn't seen it sooner; his momentum prevented him from landing on this pass, so now he would have to go around. As he banked south again, he flipped the switch and night became day.

* * * *

"Big light," Nate warned.

"I see it," Neill answered.

Richey had just cut the motor and the boat rode the waves toward the beach. For an instant, the chopper's spotlight flashed in their direction and then pointed directly ahead of the aircraft.

"Looks like he's going to make another pass," Chau observed. "Getting lower, too."

Michael pulled one of the paddles up from the flooring. "Let's make landfall before he swings around."

* * * *

From ten thousand feet, Hector Noyes made note of PIPEDREAM's descent toward the island. He'd felt all along that the chopper was making for Huo Shan. Now he was sure of it. Noyes watched as the aircraft abandoned its northwesterly path and began circling the big island. He banked the fighter to the west and began a slow turn back toward Huo Shan so he could continue to monitor the helicopter's progress.

* * * *

"Wait—light just flashed—reflected off something."

The boat landed on the beach as the receding waves tried pulling it back out to sea. Crockett was the first to leap into the surf, but kept his eyes on the helicopter as it came back around. Chau splashed into the waves next, taking hold of the gunwale and steadying it as Neill did the same on the other side. In the rear of the boat, Senior Chief Richey tilted the outboard into the transom.

"Lieutenant Crockett, you have incomparable eyesight," Neill complimented his friend. "What did you see?"

Nate took hold of the bow line as Richey jumped out, and the four men began pulling the inflatable up on shore.

"Don't see it now. That searchlight caught something." Even as he spoke, the heavy rain had become a downpour.

* * * *

HALFWAY UP THE CLIFF, CLINGING TO THE SIDE of the rocky crater wall, a satellite dish sat perched on a ledge. The dish's receiver pointed toward the Chinese mainland. Anchored in place atop a thick concrete base, the device intercepted satellite and radio transmissions intended for the facility hidden below.

The dish could be adjusted for maximum reception, but at the moment it sat immobile, lashed by the wind and rain as its concave surface pointed north. A thick, metal framework had been erected nearby, jutting out and away from the outcropping. Power cables and fiber optic lines were strung from the control box at the base of the dish, and then draped over the top of the cage-like assembly. Standing even further out, a tower—shaped like a three-pronged trident—stood high above the dense vegetation that gripped the small mountain. Its purpose was to elevate the sensitive cables above any branches that might entangle them. Running from the frame, the cables were hung tautly over the tower and then down to a communication center tucked neatly away in the jungle below.

As the cables ran down the length of the rock wall, they easily cleared the tops of the trees by fifteen to twenty feet.

To further protect them, the cables were wrapped in a black, conductive casing. For increased visibility, these would have ordinarily been marked; but everything about the naval base had been designed to hide its presence. And now, with the rain coming down in sheets—

* * * *

IF ANYONE NEEDED TO SEE WHAT NATE Crockett had caught a glimpse of, it was Emory McBride. Coming around again, McBride swung the chopper west, and then pointed the nose down as he angled the aircraft toward the helipad he'd seen on his last pass. The rocky outcropping was just off to his left now, and although he couldn't see it yet, the satellite dish was less than a hundred feet below.

A sudden gust of wind caught him by surprise and forced the helicopter closer to the mass of rocks. McBride cursed under his breath; it was a rookie mistake. He should have expected something like that, especially near the tall, vertical cliff face, and in a growing storm like this one. He gripped the controls tighter and turned the chopper out into the open.

McBride dipped the nose again and descended further. Out of the corner of his eye he saw that the barren rock had given way to tropical plants as the jungle clawed its way up the crater's side. Ahead, the rain intensified and was making visibility difficult. McBride thought about switching off the spotlight and using the NVGs when the radio dish appeared below.

With the rain rolling down the windscreen, he couldn't tell what it was at first. Instead of banking away from the object— to get a better view of it from the side of the chopper—he pointed the nose toward it, thinking he could see it best from the front. He would have been better off not yielding to curiosity at all.

At that moment, another violent gust lifted the tail rotor and pitched the helicopter forward. Suddenly the promontory began to grow in McBride's field of vision and he realized that he was rushing toward it. He froze for the briefest of moments and then regained control and jerked to the right. The chopper's tail swung back in the direction of the dish; the aircraft powered forward and began moving down again. In order to intercept the helipad, McBride banked west, thinking he was well clear of the cliff's face. He was right on that count, but in the midst of the storm, he hadn't seen the cables directly in his path.

* * * *

"THERE IT IS AGAIN." CROCKETT WAS STANDING on the beach, peering through the night lens at the descending chopper. The rain coating the length of the cables now reflected in the spotlight's beam. From his position, Nate had a much better view of the events taking place nearly half a mile away. He watched as McBride fought the winds and struggled to regain control of the aircraft.

"*Shut the front door*—you might want to watch this," Nate advised the other three.

"That pilot's in serious trouble."

* * * *

MCBRIDE SAW IT TOO LATE. IN THE BLINK OF AN eye, the rotors whirling above his head clipped the cables running just below the tower, severing them at the point of contact. The aircraft lurched down and the tail rotor swung against the metal framework that supported the lines. Sparks flew in every direction as metal clashed with metal.

The impact of the rear section created a vibration that ran through the entire airframe. The blades on top continued to spin and kept the aircraft aloft, but then the rotors bucked violently. The propeller assembly, on top of the cockpit, was no longer stable, and the rotor mast shifted on its mountings and broke free. What happened next was nothing less than the complete disintegration of every major component of the helicopter's fuselage.

The cockpit remained intact, as it was designed to do, but only briefly. Two of the grips on the main rotor assembly came loose, and the blades were flung away from the aircraft. The other two came to an abrupt halt, torqueing the fragmented aircraft in a violent shudder. The tail section crumbled and broke away as the front half sheared off and began tumbling down the side of the rock wall. Tree branches slowed its descent at first; then the wreckage bounced away from the cliff and plunged two hundred feet to the jungle below. Cartwheeling as it went, the remaining fuel ignited, and the mass of twisted metal burst into flames.

* * * *

LIEUTENANT NOYES WATCHED FROM ABOVE AS the McBride Defense Industries helicopter spiraled around the tall cliff face and suddenly dropped off his radar screen. Now at eight thousand feet, he banked the jet and looked over his left shoulder.

Noyes had no problem finding what he was looking for. At the instant he began searching the darkness, he saw an erupting fireball that illuminated the cliff. His eyes followed it down as it came to rest near what looked like a landing pad.

Noyes leveled off and keyed his radio. He'd have to call this in.

"DENMOTHER, this is BIG LEAGUE. PIPEDREAM is down."

There was a long pause. "BIG LEAGUE, say again."

"PIPEDREAM is down," Noyes' voice seemed detached of emotion; but he did feel empathy for the chopper's pilot. "Hard impact on CATHEDRAL. I don't think he could have survived."

"Copy that, BIG LEAGUE."

Noyes continued to watch as the debris burned. He could see no other activity beneath his circling aircraft.

"What are your instructions, DENMOTHER?" Noyes asked. His body relaxed now as he sat in the cockpit—with the crash of PIPEDREAM, his job was done.

Another pause. "BIG LEAGUE, we consider this mission complete. RTB."

The Captain took one more look below. The driving rain had begun to extinguish the flames at the crash site, and the darkness began to reclaim the jungle. Noyes shook his head and wondered who the pilot had been, and what had brought him all the way from the Philippines to meet his fate on the islands of Huo Shan. Sending a flight of F-15s to follow the aircraft meant something was up, but Hector realized that he'd probably never know all the details behind this mission.

Noyes pointed the nose of the aircraft toward the northeast and began to climb. Adding thrust to the engine, he keyed the radio again.

"Copy that, DENMOTHER," he replied. "BIG LEAGUE is returning to base."

Chapter Seventeen ✭ Interpretations

The Pentagon

"**Y**OU'VE BEEN THINKING ABOUT THIS A lot, haven't you?"

SECDEF asked the question with a frown. Seated across from him, the man in the rumpled suit with the equally unruly head of hair watched as his host thumbed through a series of photographs. The question was somewhat rhetorical, but before Willis Avery could answer, the Secretary started in again.

"Not a week goes by that a picture of this gentleman doesn't cross my desk," he snorted. "I'm getting a little tired of seeing his face." SECDEF pushed the photos aside, then leaned back in his chair and looked over his bifocals at the National Security Advisor. "Does the intel support your assessment?"

Avery drew in a deep breath before stating his case. The four walls that surrounded the two men were decorated with framed pictures of various administration officials, but these were outnumbered by the more prominently placed photos of the SECDEF with members of the American military. In the Secretary's world—and Avery's, too, for that matter—they were the real rock stars.

"What we've gathered suggests a correlation," Avery ventured. He considered that in another time and place his friend's title would have been Secretary of *War*. He couldn't recall exactly when the change in designation had occurred. "And I certainly think we have to be prepared for such an outcome."

Allan Hayes wasn't the typical appointee to government office. Nor was he like other bureaucrats who saw their job as just another rung on the ladder to retirement—with a lucrative private sector position waiting in the wings. Hayes ignored expedient solutions and strived to do what was right. His worldview had caused him to butt heads with the rank and file of both political parties, and sometimes even the President himself. He would never be accused of being just another *yes man* in the administration.

"Agreed," SECDEF finally conceded. "But it is spring, Willis; you know as well as I do that the Chinese conduct their naval exercises at this time of year."

"I'm aware of that, Mr. Secretary," Avery answered softly. "And as a rule, those exercises have a tendency to play out in Taiwan's back yard, which is no accident." It was nice to have an intelligent discussion with someone about military affairs. Too many of the politicians in the Beltway these days had never worn the uniform. Hayes had been an Army tank commander back in the nineties, with a son now serving in the Air Force and a daughter in the Marines. He definitely had skin in the game, as the saying went.

Hayes continued. "All right, I'll play along." He glanced back at the photo on his desk. The soulless eyes in the image seemed to stare back. "It's not much of a stretch to see that your theory could be correct." He shook his head. "My opinion of Admiral Lee soured after he ordered the destruction of that submarine."

"*Allegedly* ordered, Mr. Secretary," Avery said with a thin smile. He almost imagined that he saw Hayes roll his eyes.

"Let's deal in 'what-ifs' for a moment. How does he plan on gaming this whole thing?"

"It's been generally assumed that China is willing to accept the status quo, so long as Taiwan doesn't do anything out of the ordinary." The words came easily. Avery had rehearsed this over and over in his mind.

"Of late, Admiral Lee hasn't been quite so accommodating," Hayes added.

Avery gave a nod. "Very true. Throw in a madman like Lee and all bets are off. Now he's decided to stir the pot. To understand his methodology, we have to flesh out his ultimate goal—which, in a word, is re-incorporation."

He had the SECDEF's full attention now. Beijing had made it quite clear that in their eyes, Taiwan was little more than a breakaway province that needed to be brought back in line. Tensions had grown lately. Most Asian nations with any appreciable coastline or navy had built up their submarine and surface fleets—as a hedge against an increasingly aggressive Chinese military. The U.S. had been inadvertently drawn into the dispute and was essentially in the midst of a brand new Cold War.

"Are you suggesting they'll take military action against the island?" Hayes asked. He already knew the answer to that, and while he wasn't baiting Avery with a trick question, he wanted to emphasize the hazards of such an approach.

"I'm suggesting something short of military action, Mr. Secretary. But equally effective," Avery replied. "The Chinese know they can't act with force of arms against Taiwan. Doing so wouldn't be in their best interests. For one thing, their goal is re-unification. Attacking Taiwan would just escalate things—giving us a reason to intervene. And they certainly don't want a shooting war with one of their biggest trading partners."

"Go on."

Avery leaned forward slightly. "Along the same lines, they just don't have the ability to land a large enough invasion force. Mounting an operation like that just isn't possible given their current capabilities. Besides, Taipei would see it coming. They'd be more than ready to apply stop-gap measures."

"So attacking and occupying the island is out."

"That's correct, Mr. Secretary," Avery said. "This leads me to believe they'll go at it in a different way, and initiate a two-pronged offensive."

"Starting with—?"

"Decidedly unconventional warfare," Avery went on. "The first stage will begin with an attack on their infrastructure. This provides them an advantage in two ways. For one, it gives them deniability. They're already quite adept at hacking into other countries communication networks—and masking their efforts." He recalled a story he'd seen on Fox News the night before. "Three days ago they breached domestic grids on the west coast; shut down basic services in Seattle and Oakland."

"Are we sure that was the Chinese?" SECDEF asked.

Avery's posture seemed to convey a shrug. "Well, it's not a slam-dunk—but our cyber office in San Diego is ready to hang it on them." Avery continued, "Taking that a step further, I suspect they'll try to breach Taiwan's telecomm, cellular, and internet grids. Bring those down and you can easily create chaos. If they're serious about it, that could happen within days." He paused to let that sink in. "Now, we can *assist* Taipei in countering those attacks, but if Beijing hits first—"

"We'll be playing catch-up," Hayes responded. He imagined the social unrest such an attack would bring. Not to mention the economic impact. "What's phase two?"

"After crippling their dependence on all things electronic, they enforce a blockade," Avery answered.

SECDEF looked incredulous. "Could they do that?"

"It's not an impossible proposition," Avery replied. He'd seen the estimates. "They have plenty of ships in their Navy. Stationing a heavy destroyer at the mouth of each major harbor would stop traffic going in or out. As you know, Taiwan is heavily dependent on imports. With the island cut off from shipments of food and energy resources, things would deteriorate very quickly."

Hayes shook his head. "You can't enforce a quarantine like that just by blocking their ports."

"No, but if you task another two dozen ships—with air assets—to patrol the coastline—" He didn't finish the sentence.

"And now, two fleet groups have set sail from Qingdao and Dalian—each with an inordinate number of minesweepers." Avery didn't have to bring up the submarine escort they were traveling with; those boats were equally capable of laying mines—and deterring the commercial trade Taiwan depended on. Most scenarios predicted their use in any confrontation between Beijing and Taipei.

SECDEF gave a nod. "Point taken. And by that time we'd be hard-pressed to affect any type of assistance—or counter China's hand."

"Countermeasures could be implemented after the fact," Avery reasoned. "So long as the ROC continues to build up its stores of resources—food, fuel and the like—they could fight back, in a manner of speaking." They'd discussed this strategy before. "Being able to hold out against a seige forces your attacker to prolong their campaign. That gets expensive for the bad guys after a while. And it also gives you the leverage to force your adversary to the negotiating table."

"There's a bit of a silver lining. But Taipei would also suffer politically."

Avery added, "They would look weak, unable to effectively guard their own recognized territory." He'd almost said *sovereign*, but that wasn't accurate.

"What happens next?"

"Well, their actions are pretty predictable at that point," Avery offered. "The Chinese would press their advantage and demand that Taipei accept their terms—re-incorporation with the mainland as an administrative province."

"You make it sound almost simple."

The National Security Advisor nearly smiled at that. "I didn't say it would be easy. And I'd wager the Chinese would dangle a carrot or two."

"How so?"

Avery shrugged a shoulder. "I'm just spit-balling, but it's all about saving face in the Asian world. China might make some bold promises, like offering Taiwan continued autonomy, or assurances that they could preserve their own internal security. Maybe they'd waive any type of structured taxation that would ordinarily be paid to the central government." There were other incentives that Avery could list, but he didn't want to get too far into the weeds. "I can imagine a couple of different ways that Beijing comes out on top. By re-acquiring the territory, they benefit economically. Then there's the strategic advantage."

"Probably their intention all along," SECDEF grunted. He knew what Avery was getting at.

"Yes, sir," Avery replied. "When it's all over, Beijing adds more territory—finally achieving their One China policy. And Taiwan experiences a fairly seamless transition. If Chengdu's smart, he won't rock the boat too much." There was one other payoff Avery had only slightly touched on. "Ultimately, the People's Republic would be free to forward position their ships all around the island, dealing them a much greater hand in the region."

"And diminishing ours," Hayes grunted. "Timeline?"

"The first task force is in the Strait now," Avery said. "The second is moving northeast. If I were them, I'd proceed with the exercise. Let Taipei see that it's just another routine military maneuver. After a few days they'll relax and things will calm down. That's when I'd make my move, pivoting to launch the blockade."

Hayes leaned forward and planted his elbows on the desk, a shrewd look in his eye. "But somewhere between those two events there has to be a trigger. A causal effect Beijing can use to justify their actions to the world." A pause. Avery had spoken Chengdu's name moments before. "And I don't see the Premier signing off on this. The analysts at Langley are singing the same tune about Chengdu; they think he's somewhat impartial on the subject of re-unification—at least for now."

"That part does have me stumped," Avery admitted. "Lee's got something up his sleeve. I just haven't figured out what it is yet. As far as Chengdu goes—maybe he's unaware of what Lee's up to."

SECDEF thought over that possibility. "A rogue in their admiralty?" Hayes shook his head. "That's a little hard to accept, Willis. Lee would need a lot of help. To pull that off he'd have to be willing to stage a coup."

"It just might come to that, Mr. Secretary," Avery allowed. Something else came to mind. "I understand you've ordered additional assets into the region?"

Hayes nodded. "Jim LaSalle's carrier battle group is just over the horizon. He's projecting a very obvious presence to our friends in Beijing. Hopefully that will persuade them of our interest. The *Victory* and the *Meyer* left Pearl four days ago; they should be on station within twenty-four hours."

"What about ground forces?" Avery asked.

"All of our posts in the Pacific Rim have been advised," Hayes announced. "Our air bases in Osan and Kadena are now on a heightened alert status as well."

Avery hoped that would be enough. China had an imposing arsenal at their disposal. Coupled with the political will to use it, things could change very quickly in that part of the world. The international community would condemn the action, but for the People's Republic that would be a small price to pay for regaining control over the island.

"Worst case scenario?" SECDEF asked.

Avery considered that for a moment. "The PRC's been stoking their military advantage for years," he returned. "State-of-the-art radar systems, satellites; and a boatload of surface-to-surface and anti-ship missiles. And that's just the stuff they'd use in a naval engagement. In a conventional war, we'd probably win, but not before they targeted our bases in Okinawa, South Korea—maybe even Guam and Japan."

"*Probably?*" Hayes glared. He didn't like the sound of that. "Those are not acceptable odds, Willis."

"No, Mr. Secretary. They are not," Avery sighed. "And if we step in and try to stop them from enforcing the blockade, things could get pretty ugly."

SECDEF said nothing, but began contemplating possible

options. Having the battle group in the area was a heartening thought. The USS *Bush* was a strong antidote to aggression. The presence of the *Victory* upped the ante.

There were still a few cards left to play.

Chapter Eighteen ✷ A New Ally

2nd Floor Conference Room,
CIA Headquarters,
Langley, Virginia

RICHARD AULTMAN SETTLED INTO HIS chair and remembered the last time he'd been in this room. It had been nearly a year since he, Willis Avery and Lieutenant Neill had met here, listening as Neill hatched a plan that few intelligence operatives would have dared dream of. But that had been the beauty of it. Many agents would have viewed the Marine's proposal as naïve, but in the past several months the strategy had paid off in ways no one could have imagined.

Maybe that was why Avery had chosen Neill for this assignment—the National Security Advisor had selected him personally to gather intelligence on Huo Shan. Aultman had to agree that there was no arguing with Neill's record so far; the young officer certainly got results.

Fresh coffee was brewing on a credenza in the corner. Richard got up and selected a mug from among many others and poured himself a cup. He was adding cream and sugar when the door opened and two familiar figures strode in.

Ike Gleeson was first; the CIA case officer crossed the floor and shook Aultman's hand. Behind him, Ivan Malyev smiled and greeted Aultman warmly. Richard was immediately struck by how different his mood seemed from their last meeting—oddly enough, right here in this room.

"Zdrahstvooytyeh," Malyev said. He employed the formal Russian greeting, and then switched quickly to English. "Mr. Aultman—how are you?"

"I'm good, Ivan—or should I say, Mr. Orlov?" He shook Ivan's hand as well. "And you?"

"Ochin kharasho," he replied. He chuckled at the mention of his *nom de guerre*. "Very well."

"How's Mrs. Lenkov these days?"

Ivan's expression turned. He seemed to shudder. "For a tyrant, she is well. It's as if the Tsars have returned." A smile now. "She lets me get away with nothing, and makes me study—" he seemed to struggle for the right words. "—*kazhday dyen*? Yes. Every day."

It was Richard's turn to smile. "Sounds like she's earning her pay. Coffee? Or maybe some tea?"

"No, thank you," Malyev replied. "Mr. Gleeson has told me that you need my help."

Aultman nodded. "That's right." He gestured toward a chair. "Shall we sit down?"

The three men took their seats around the table. Aultman sipped from his mug then continued. "You are adjusting to life here in America?"

Malyev seemed quite at ease, and smiled again. "I like your country very much," he replied. His English was much improved since their last meeting, although his accent was unmistakable. "And here I have honest work."

Honest, indeed. Aultman could almost see a light in the Russian's eyes. "Willis Avery sends his greetings. And his appreciation—your work here over the past few months has been very helpful."

That was something of an understatement. Ivan Malyev was the linchpin in Lieutenant Neill's plans. Plucked from

Ukraine—and a dismal future as a state-sponsored Russian terrorist—Malyev was now helping the West. The information he'd provided so far had been used to put pressure on President Arkadi Murovanka, frustrating his plans of re-unifying the Soviet Union. Under the direction of the CIA—and with Neill's friendship—Ivan had completely turned his life around.

"I understand you require the services of—" Malyev looked at the ceiling. "—a Russian translator, yes?"

"That's right, Ivan," Aultman said. "Ordinarily, we'd ask a State Department linguist. But in this case, we'd prefer someone who grew up speaking the language—it's possible your insight could provide us with some answers." He reached into his briefcase and produced a folder. Taking another sip of his coffee, he opened the folder and removed a single sheet of paper. It was a print-out of the email Willis Avery had received.

"Before we begin, I'd like to remind you that this is a matter of national security. Any information you provide today should be treated with great sensitivity." Aultman had repeated this speech many times during his career. "We've placed great trust in you, Ivan. Mr. Avery is once again acknowledging the confidence he has in your abilities—and your character. Do you understand?"

"Completely," Ivan replied. He reached into his jacket and pulled out a pair of reading glasses. "I will speak of this to no one."

"Good," Aultman said. With that out of the way, he slid the paper across the table.

Ivan looked over the words on the page. It was a short message; only one paragraph. The Russian held a pen in hand, and after reading through it once he began translating the words into English in the space below. Within five minutes the task was complete, and he slid the page back across the table to Aultman.

Richard scanned it quickly, and then re-read the message more slowly, digesting each word. Willis Avery needed to hear this as soon as possible. Aultman considered using his cell phone, then thought better of it. Slipping the paper back into the folder, he turned to the CIA case officer sitting next to him.

"Mr. Gleeson, I need to make a phone call. Can you get me access to a secure line?"

Gleeson smiled. "This *is* the CIA, Mr. Aultman. I think we can accommodate you."

Aultman got up out of his chair, leaving his coffee unfinished. He extended his hand to Malyev.

"*Spaseeba*, Ivan," he said. "Once again, we appreciate your help." He meant every word.

Ivan nodded. "It is my prayer that I can continue to be of service."

Prayer? Aultman was struck by the former terrorist's mention of the word. Clearly Neill's influence had made a difference in the man's life. But that was what faith was supposed to be all about, wasn't it? With the meeting at a conclusion, Aultman filed that thought away as Gleeson escorted them to the door.

Before they exited, Malyev paused and turned toward Aultman, a curious expression on his face.

"You said my insight might give you some answers."

"That's right," Aultman said.

"Then perhaps there is something else you should consider."

* * * *

"THERE ARE FOUR THINGS YOU NEED TO KNOW," Aultman said into the phone. "I can read this word for word or just summarize."

Ike Gleeson had found a smaller conference with a protected line, and while he arranged for a car to take Malyev home, Aultman placed a call to Avery's cell.

"Just hit the high points." Willis Avery had just concluded his meeting with SECDEF at the Pentagon. He leaned back in the car seat as his driver headed toward the White House. He held a pen in one hand and a small lined pad in his lap.

"First of all, McBride *is* selling classified information to

Admiral Lee," Aultman began. "We already suspected that, but the email confirms it. And there's more."

"I'm listening." Avery cradled the phone on his shoulder and began taking notes.

"Two—Lee is sending someone to meet McBride on Huo Shan—and he's bringing a dozen troops with him. They left Hainan aboard a patrol boat yesterday."

Avery thought that over. Their assessment of McBride's motives had been correct.

"What's number three?"

"The Admiral is planning something big—he intends to use whatever McBride's selling to expand China's military capability and threaten Taiwan."

"I figured as much," Avery grunted in reply. "The stuff he pulled off his computer would definitely help level the playing field. Then there's the encrypted data Farris can't get into." Avery paused. A soft tone buzzed in his ear. "Stay on the line. I've got another call coming in."

Aultman heard a click on the other end as Avery took the call. Staring at Malyev's translation, Richard considered the danger involved. If Admiral Lee made use of the classified information McBride had provided, peace in Asia could be jeopardized.

Richard had been fully briefed on Beijing's growing military. Over the past decade, China had been working to broaden their arsenal of weaponry in an effort to oppose the American Navy. Several U.S. ships had even been harassed by the Chinese as they sailed in international waters. And it was common knowledge that the People's Republic had developed a cruise missile capable of destroying any surface vessel it targeted.

Aultman shook his head. For more than thirty years, the presence of the U.S. Pacific fleet had calmed the fears of nervous governments in Japan, the Philippines—and especially Taiwan. But with the growing Chinese threat, more Asian nations began to wonder.

* * * *

"YOU STILL THERE?" AVERY'S VOICE BROUGHT Aultman back around.

"I'm here."

"You're not going to believe this," Avery grumbled. "That was the base commander at Kadena. The pilots they scrambled to follow McBride just reported in. Sounds like we caught a break; it's good news for us, but bad news for McBride. His helicopter just crashed on Huo Shan."

Aultman blinked. "How?"

"No details. Happened about half an hour ago. Probably weather-related; there's a storm front moving over the islands right now."

"How bad was the crash? Could he have survived?"

"Pilot doesn't think so. He reported seeing a fireball that fell into the jungle."

Aultman considered the sudden change in circumstances. This would certainly frustrate Admiral Lee's plans. Still, he knew Avery would want some boots on the ground, to make sure Lee never got his hands on the information McBride had been carrying.

"What about Neill and his team—have they reached the island yet?"

"I'm calling him next—the Brits gave them a satellite phone." Avery checked his watch and calculated what time it was in the South China Sea. "They should be there by now." He shifted gears. "What about number four?"

Aultman was caught off his game. "Number four?"

"You said you had four things I needed to know. What's number four?"

"Oh, yeah—the email's author claims to be White Dragon." Aultman said. "But here's—"

Avery cut him off. "Save it till you get back. We're coming

through the gate now."

Richard heard a click that signaled an end to the call. As he clipped the phone back on his belt, he wondered how White Dragon got Avery's email address; but the mysterious informant had proven himself to be very resourceful in the past.

Aultman stuck the message Ivan had translated back in the folder, then grabbed his briefcase and headed out of the building. *The threads are all coming together*, he thought to himself. *And they're converging on the islands of Huo Shan.*

Chapter Nineteen ✳ Reconnaissance

NATE CROCKETT RETRIEVED HIS M-4 FROM the shooter's bag in the bottom of the boat. Adjusting the rifle strap, he slipped the weapon over his shoulder and let it hang, muzzle down, across his back. Next he picked up his rucksack and turned to the rest of the team.

Chau, Richey and Neill stared in the direction of the crash site from the edge of the tree line. On Neill's orders, the group stayed put in case another aircraft was headed their way. None had appeared. Fifteen minutes had passed, and the falling rain and the waves breaking on the beach were the only sounds they heard.

In the distance, at the foot of the cliff, the wreckage of the helicopter burned, casting eerie shadows on the crater's rim as it rose above the jungle. That didn't last long; the downpour soon extinguished most of the blaze, and the remaining fuel seeped into the wet ground only forty feet away from the helipad.

"Snap out of it, people," Nate quietly said to his comrades. "Nothing to see here."

Neill looked at his friend; with their eyes glued to the cliff, none of them had even noticed as Nate slipped into scout sniper mode. Michael reached into the inflatable and pulled out his own weapon.

"Nate's right. I don't think anyone else saw the crash." He checked his rifle. "Let's get started."

The four men took hold of the boat and moved it deeper into the jungle. Waiting for their eyes to adjust to the dark canopy of palms, they found a good spot to hide it. Within twenty minutes, they'd covered it with fronds and other natural residue that littered the jungle floor.

Nate brushed the sand from his tactical gloves. "You think that pilot survived?"

Neill shook his head. "Not a chance." He looked back toward the beach, scanning the horizon beyond for any activity. Nothing moved.

"What's next?" Richey asked.

"Now we'll start the reconnaissance phase of the mission," Neill went on. "We'll hug the tree line and make our way east along the beach. I want a closer look at that crash site."

The men's voices were low. "Roger that," Nate said. "I'd like to find out where that pilot came from."

"And what he came here *for*," Lieutenant Chau added.

Michael nodded. "I'll take point. Nate, you bring up the rear. Go ahead and lock and load—but remember, we're here for intel."

Nate inserted a magazine into his weapon and pulled the charging handle to the rear. Re-seating the handle, he thumbed the catch, sending the bolt forward and chambering a round.

"Keep your weapons on safe—and practice good noise discipline. We'll make our way to the chopper first. After that, we check out the naval facility. Everybody got your gear?"

"I'm good to go," Senior Chief Richey replied. "The more we can get done while it's dark, the better."

"Agreed," Neill whispered. "Remember, slow is smooth—"

"—and smooth is fast." Crockett finished for him. He watched as Richey readied his M-4. Chau tried to imitate the movement but seemed to have a little trouble. Nate stepped in to assist.

Neill started to move toward the beach, and then Crockett

reached out and stopped him.

"Hold up—you hear that?" His voice was even lower now. The four men stopped in their tracks and became very still.

Chau was the first to move; he stepped past the Senior Chief and came up behind Neill. He reached into Michael's ruck and pulled out the satellite phone. The muffled sound they'd heard was the phone's electronic chirp. Chau looked at the digital display—this particular model even had caller ID. His eyes widened and he handed it to Neill.

"It's for you."

* * * *

"HAVE YOU REACHED CATHEDRAL YET?" WILLIS Avery's voice was crisp and clear. Michael turned down the volume on the device; the sound was too loud, especially on a deserted jungle beach.

"Copy that, sir," Neill answered. "We were about to begin our reconnaissance—but there's been a complication."

"There usually are," Avery grumbled. "That complication wouldn't happen to involve a helicopter, would it?"

Neill turned to his companions. The rain had begun to let up and the three men leaned in to hear the conversation. He held the phone slightly away from his ear so the team could listen.

"That's affirmative—but how did you know that?"

"We've had some eyes in the sky doing over watch. Were you there to see it crash?"

"Yes, sir. Not a pretty sight. Anything I should know about that bird?"

"Where do I begin?" Avery took a deep breath. "You've heard of Emory McBride III?"

"McBride Aerospace Industries?"

"Defense," Avery corrected. "That's the one. Apparently Mr. McBride got bored with his family's money and decided to spice up his life with a little treason."

Avery spent the next few minutes detailing McBride's recent

activities, and his connection to Admiral Lee. By the time he'd finished, Neill was shaking his head. "What type of intel was he going to turn over to the Chinese?" he asked.

"McBride Industries built the arsenal ship, for one thing. He downloaded details about her construction that might give an attacker the edge. The company is a big player in maintaining our communications net in the Pacific, too."

Senior Chief Richey whistled softly. "He was giving away the store."

"Selling it is more accurate," Avery quipped. "And McBride added a layer of encryption we can't break. We suspect he's embedded something of greater value within the intel."

"Moot point now, sir," Neill said. McBride's betrayal was regrettable, but he certainly posed no threat in his current condition. "If McBride was flying that helicopter, he's dead."

"Understood," Avery replied. "But there's more. You're going to have company."

Company? "Say again?"

"McBride was planning to meet someone on the island— Admiral Lee's personal representative, along with some troops."

Neill frowned. "So McBride was carrying the information with him on board that chopper?"

"His secretary has been keeping an eye on him for us," Avery confirmed. "According to her, McBride downloaded everything to a thumb drive. He and Admiral Lee must have chosen Huo Shan because it was a safe, out of the way place—a location under Lee's control."

"What's the Admiral's game?"

"We suspect he plans to blockade Taiwan."

It made sense. "Any idea when we can expect our guests?"

"We know their patrol boat left the naval base at Hainan yesterday, which isn't that far, so—"

"We don't have much time," Neill finished for him. *If they haven't arrived already*, he thought. "What's the force strength—and how did you find out?"

"As far as we know, it's the Admiral's proxy—and about a

dozen PRC Marines. We just received confirmation from an unexpected source—White Dragon," Avery answered.

That was a surprise; but before Neill could reply, Avery continued.

"Lee's men are going to be looking for McBride. They've been told that he's flying in. When he doesn't show, they'll search the island. And one way or another, they're going to find that helicopter."

"And the information McBride was carrying—unless we get there first." Neill realized their mission had suddenly changed.

Avery thought it over. "It might be too late. How long did you say you'd been on the island?"

Neill consulted his watch. "Going on an hour now."

"Any activity since your arrival?"

"Negative," Neill answered. "All quiet here. We circled before landing—there's not a soul in sight. No boats tied up at the dock, and none on the horizon."

Avery relaxed a little. Maybe they'd caught another break.

"Sounds like you've arrived ahead of Lee's men. That's good news for our side." The time for talking was done. "Get to that helicopter," Avery ordered. "Find the thumb drive—if it survived the crash. If it did, destroy it—we can't let that information fall into Lee's hands."

"Roger that," Neill replied. "We'll be in touch."

* * * *

NEILL ENDED THE CALL AND HANDED THE phone back to Chau. He looked through the opening in the tree line and out toward the black horizon. The Admiral's troops were out there somewhere. Knowing that added a new sense of urgency to their mission.

"All right," Neill began. He paused long enough to draw in a deep breath, letting it out slowly. "You heard the man. Our weekend in paradise just turned into real work." Even in the dark, he could make out smiles on each man's face. *Good,* he thought to himself. *Confidence is still high.* That could change in a heartbeat if things started going south.

"Just one question," Richey said. "Who's this White Dragon Avery's talking about?"

"An informant; probably Russian," the Marine answered. "I'll fill you in on the way."

"THE FIRST THING WE NEED TO DO IS GET TO the crash site." Neill began methodically laying out their course of action. "We need to retrieve that thumb drive—before Lee's troops get here."

"There's only one place that boat can make a landing," Richey said. "And that's the pier."

Chau now had a worried look on his face. "If they're coming from Hainan, they'll be approaching from the north."

"I see your point," Neill replied. "That's on the other side of the island. Unless we can get to high ground, we'll never see them coming."

"Then we need to get some elevation," the Senior Chief announced. "Anybody want to climb a tree?"

Neill grinned. "Good thought, Chief. But knowing where that boat is won't get us to the chopper any faster—and that's where we need to be." He squared his shoulders and adjusted his ruck, holding his rifle in front of him. "We'll reconnoiter from the cliff—after we've recovered that drive. Keep your eyes open—and remember, they could approach from either direction." Instinctively, they turned around to look west. "Crockett, this is your territory. Any instructions before we move out?"

Nate nodded. "The natural inclination will be to move in a crouch—but that's a mistake." He gestured to the tall palms around them, adopting an instructive tone. "The dominant vegetation is vertical, and spaced about eight or ten feet apart. We want to match our surroundings, in case someone's watching from the sea. Keep that same ten foot distance between you and the man in front. No sudden movements. Slow, fluid steps—nothing jerky."

Neill looked to each man; he could tell the team was ready to go. "Okay, the time on deck is—" He checked his watch again, "—twenty-two hundred. Let's get to the crash site and retrieve that drive before midnight."

The cloud cover hung in thin sheets over their heads. With the front passing to the south, the stars returned, but their pale light did nothing to illuminate the path. The rain slackened, and the four men moved away from the jungle and onto the beach with Neill leading the way.

Chapter Twenty ☆ Island Objectives

THE SEA HAD BEGUN TO ROLL. AS ONE FRONT pushed south, another followed. Between the two was a patch of relatively untroubled ocean, but the line of squalls bearing down from mainland China promised a rough voyage for any vessel in their path.

Ensign Tsao was doing his level best to avoid those storms. The young officer had gone below to the cramped engine room and rolled up his sleeves, working with the crew to get the power plant back on line. After an hour of drifting, Tsao's chief engineer had finally diagnosed their mechanical problems and had come up with a solution. Fortunately, everything they needed to effect repairs was on board. No permanent damage had been done to the engines, and with luck—something they seemed to have in short supply—they would soon be underway again.

Tsao used a rag to wipe the oil from his hands and face. His dress shirt was stained with grease, and drenched in sweat—even with the engines silent, this was still the hottest compartment on board. Tsao decided to head topside and change into a clean uniform. There was nothing more he could do here.

He was met at the top of the ladder by the expressionless Captain Ling. At least he had some good news to give to him now.

"Have you made any progress, Ensign?" Ling noted Tsao's

appearance and silently gave him points for his efforts.

"Yes, Captain. We should be able to re-start the engines soon and continue south."

"What was the problem?"

"The oil in the engines has begun oxidizing. It will require changing," the Ensign explained. "The ST-339 has sat idle for almost a year—this class of vessel was being transferred to the reserves. Newer ships were scheduled to replace her, but—"

"—they have been delayed." Ling finished for him. He had seen the reports. Poor weather and a shortage of materials had plagued China's shipyards of late—just one more reason for Admiral Lee to lobby for Russian-made vessels.

Tsao's answer made sense. Between the Chinese fleet and the naval reserve forces, no one had taken responsibility for the vessel. She had become an orphan. The delay of the replacement ships made it necessary to recall the old sub chaser to operational service, but by the time the Navy reclaimed her, she was no longer a well-oiled machine.

"The repairs can be made at sea?"

The young Ensign relaxed. Captain Ling seemed to regard his explanation as legitimate. An excuse, still, but—

"Yes, Captain. The level of corrosion is minimal, and we have sufficient oil on board for replacement. The crew should be finished within an hour or two."

Ling nodded. Tsao's answer seemed to satisfy him—to the Ensign's relief.

"Good work," Ling replied. "Now get yourself cleaned up."

As Tsao excused himself, Captain Ling returned to the wheelhouse. He checked the ship's onboard GPS and marked their position on the charts, and then did a little math in his head. If the Ensign was right, the patrol boat would be underway by midnight, and if they could avoid further complications, they would arrive at Huo Shan long before dawn.

* * * *

THE TEAM TRAVELED HALF A MILE, STAYING close to the copse of trees that defined the boundary between the jungle and the beach. Crockett was in his element, scanning ahead, out to sea, and then behind the group as they made their way silently toward the eastern tip of the island. There was nothing to be seen, and the only sounds to be heard were the waves lapping up on the shoreline and the wind gusting in the palm fronds above their heads.

Neill slowed his pace and crouched down. Using hand signals, he gestured to the squad to halt their movements. He looked over his shoulder to see Chau, Richey and Crockett all take a knee.

"We're close." His words were low, but not at the level of a whisper. He saw nods in acknowledgement. "The chopper should be directly to our left, about seventy-five yards on the other side of these trees."

The jungle looked pretty thick. "Machete?" Chau asked. He eyed the long knife Nate had strapped to his thigh.

Crockett grinned at his friend. "Trying to do things the hard way?" He knew that hacking through the undergrowth could take hours. "Let's move toward that rock formation. The vegetation should thin out as we get near the base."

Neill agreed with a nod. The four continued to stay close to the trees. They were moving toward the structures they'd seen crowding the foot of the crater wall. In the darkness, it was difficult to distinguish their shapes; the netting and natural camouflage of the thicket hid them from casual view.

Nate was right. As they neared the larger buildings, they came across a well-worn path that led away from the facility and into the tropical woodland. Michael peered ahead, but without illumination the trail revealed nothing.

"We'll have to be extra careful here," he advised. "There's no telling where this path leads—but it's clearly seen a lot of use. Everybody keep your head on a swivel."

Once again, Neill took point and started down the path. The clouds overhead were heavy with moisture, and they opened up just as the team left the beach and entered into the jungle.

Aboard the carrier USS George H.W. Bush,
75 miles southeast of Taiwan

DEEP IN THE SHIP, ADMIRAL LASALLE STUDIED the cartographic display in the Combat Information Center, or CIC. Captain Paul DeSouza stood at his elbow, his eyes fixed on the same screen.

"I count thirty-two."

The Captain nodded. "Thirty-two it is," he concurred.

"And we're getting all of this from the UCAV?" Jim LaSalle asked. He was referring to the Unmanned Combat Aerial Vehicle that was overflying the island of Taiwan and the East China Sea.

"Yes, sir; backed up by satellite," DeSouza replied. "Telemetry in real-time, too." He seemed very proud of that fact.

LaSalle grinned. "Well, at thirty thousand feet you'd expect some pretty good line-of-sight." He looked around the compartment, softly lit and bathed in the glow of instrumentation. Everyone looked very busy. The Admiral reminded himself that a flag officer on deck could have that effect on people. He regarded the display once more. "Still, thirty-two's a lot for an exercise."

"Sixteen in each task force." DeSouza used his index finger to gently tap the screen. "The first group continued south, thinning out and establishing overlapping areas of responsibility; the second is moving around the northern part of the island. And that's not all, sir. They've got three oilers and a supply vessel at anchorage in the Strait—closer to the mainland." He shook his head. "That's a lot of muscle."

"Almost as if they're in it for the long haul; what's Xinhua saying about all this?" LaSalle asked. Xinhua was the official news agency of the PRC.

The Captain sighed heavily. "Day two of a seven day drill—with a strictly peaceful purpose. Their Foreign Ministry spokesman is saying the same thing."

"Uh-huh," LaSalle muttered, a little sarcasm beginning to creep into his voice. "*Normal and defensive in nature; intended to ensure peace in the region*—we've heard that line before."

DeSouza lowered his voice and asked, "Do you think SECDEF's suspicions are correct?"

The Admiral drew himself up to his full height and stretched. "Mr. Hayes isn't completely sold on this theory; the suspicions belong to the National Security Advisor." LaSalle was a stickler when it came to details. He also liked giving credit where it was due—and more often than not, Willis Avery's hunches had panned out.

On the screen, the display remained fluid and changed slightly as the system updated the position of the Chinese naval armada. These vessels were depicted on the monitor as red squares. Out of the corner of his eye, LaSalle noted the presence of two newcomers, appearing on the edge of the screen in the western Pacific and digitally represented as yellow triangles. Their course followed that of the carrier group.

"That must be the *Victory* and her escort," LaSalle said.

"Captain Beacham?" DeSouza asked.

"That's right. You know Bob?"

"Only by reputation," the Captain replied. "A solid officer, from what I hear."

"You hear right," LaSalle agreed.

The Admiral stepped to the display and gently tapped one of the triangular icons. The Identification/Friend or Foe software, or IFF, was now active and relayed critical information between the American ships. With a simple touch of the screen, LaSalle pulled up a small dialog box that presented data about the approaching flotilla.

"Looks like Captain Beacham's in a hurry," the Admiral chuckled. The screen displayed some impressive figures for the *Victory* and the *Meyer*. "At this rate he'll be in position within ten or twelve hours. Maybe sooner if the weather holds.''

DeSouza silently did the math. Comparing their force strength with that of the groups fielded by the PRC, he hoped the two newcomers could help balance the odds. His thoughts were interrupted by the Admiral.

"I'm going to catch a few Zs. Wake me with anything out of the ordinary.''

DeSouza smiled. " 'Out of the ordinary's' a bit hard to define these days. Breakfast in the wardroom?''

LaSalle shook his head. "My stateroom. I'll be up early. We have a few tactical decisions to make.''

Aboard the USS Meyer

THERE WAS NO DENYING THE FACT THAT BOB Beacham had a passion for speed.

In his youth, Beacham's exuberance for anything capable of powered locomotion nearly crowded out his pursuit of a Navy commission. Conventional wisdom, common sense—and a few strong words from his mentors—got him back on track, and he managed to balance his priorities. Classmates at the Academy still teased that he was far better suited to be a fighter pilot than a ship's Captain.

His family lived an hour from Annapolis, and on weekends his younger brother would drive up the coast in an old Chevy the two enjoyed tinkering with. Unfortunately, Beacham's studies left little time to indulge his tendencies as a motorhead, so he took the long view and put those aside. After graduation, his interests resurfaced.

The years had passed, and when the *Meyer* wasn't at sea, Beacham could often be found straddling a Harley-Davidson touring bike. He enjoyed testing the limits of its rumbling twin-cam as he cruised the San Diego Freeway. The Navy—and his wife—gave him leave to relish time away from his ship, encouraging him to make the most of the freedom that only two wheels and a powerful, air-cooled engine could provide.

Sometimes, Angela Beacham rode with him, tandem-style, her arms wrapped around his waist as the sun-drenched landscape rushed by. Those were good times, but lately the impromptu trips up and down the coast had become rare. With his command responsibilities before him—and the current opstempo required—it was difficult for the Captain to break away for such diversions.

Those thoughts were on his mind now as the *Meyer* sailed westward. A cheap, plastic lei hung around Beacham's neck as he made his way aft. He was returning to his stateroom after just such a diversion; the MWR Chief had sponsored a Luau Night in the enlisted mess. It was a poor substitute for missed shore leave in Oahu—but an attempt to revive the crew's morale, nonetheless. The Captain had debated even putting in an appearance there—he wasn't sure how he'd be received—but in the end, he decided that avoiding the event just wasn't good public relations.

Someone rounded the corner ahead. "How was the party, Skipper?" The Petty Officer grinned as he came to attention in the passageway. "Looks like things got a little festive."

Beacham paused, a frown on his face. It was then that he realized the colorful decoration he sported.

"Just like being on Waikiki, son."

Chapter Twenty-One ✶ Scavenger Hunt

The White House

"SYNTAX," AVERY GRUNTED. HE STARED at Richard Aultman as they walked the portico by the Rose Garden. "His word or yours?"

"Mine," Aultman allowed. "Ivan was having a little trouble explaining himself. His English has improved, but not that much."

The National Security Advisor uttered something unintelligible, but to Aultman it sounded like agreement. Then Avery said, "That's what I thought. Somehow I just can't picture him using a word like that."

It was early afternoon and the two were headed to yet another meeting. "To be honest, I had to look it up to make sure I had the right definition," Richard admitted.

"Okay." Avery seemed detached. "So what does it mean? I gather it has something to do with how a phrase is worded."

"Bingo," Aultman said. "It deals with how words are strung together and ordered in a sentence, that kind of thing." The meaning had dulled somewhat in his mind since he'd consulted the dictionary. "Overall, Ivan had some concerns about the grammar. He said the message was written very formally. Textbook vocabulary; 'high Russian' was how he put it. The way it's taught at the university level."

"What's his conclusion?" Avery asked.

Aultman drew in a deep breath. He wanted to convey Ivan's words just as he'd heard them. "He believes that Russian isn't the author's native tongue. Should we turn the message over to another interpreter?"

Avery considered this new information carefully. Malyev had done more than just translate the missive White Dragon had sent; he'd provided an important clue that might help reveal the informant's identity.

"No need. I trust his judgment. But this does add a new fly to the ointment."

Even as he uttered the phrase, he wondered about its origin.

* * * *

THE CANOPY OF TREES OVERHEAD ENDED abruptly and the trail gave way to a wide, open space in the midst of the jungle. The rain was falling harder now and as the team stepped cautiously into the clearing, each man's eyes became riveted to the macabre display laid out before them.

On their right was the promontory. Close to the vegetation clumped near the rising rock wall was a helicopter landing pad, neatly imprinted with symbols that would have been easily discernible from the air. A large circle decorated the perimeter of the pad, and what looked like cross-hairs had been painted in the center. These had been placed as a guide. Oddly enough, the markings on the flat surface gave the impression of a large target—one that Emory McBride III had tragically missed.

It was the object in the middle of the clearing that attracted their attention. The pile of misshapen wreckage that had once been McBride's chopper sat in a heap not less than fifty feet from the pad. Only the main cabin retained some recognizable features; the rest of the aircraft was a jigsaw puzzle of twisted metal and composite materials, most of it concentrated in one spot, but with many smaller pieces lying haphazardly around the impact site.

The cables that had contributed to the crash lay in the grass and across the tropical growth near the crater wall. The thick bundled strands of wiring snaked away from the clearing and toward the base of the cliff. The smell of fuel was heavy in the night air but the fire had long since gone out. In places, oil puddled on the ground near the wreck. The deluge from the sky fell in sheets and created a metallic, rhythmic sound as it landed on the broken frame.

Nothing moved; there was an eerie finality to the whole scene. It was some time before any words were spoken, but eventually it was Crockett who broke the silence.

"Wow," he said simply. He raised his voice to be heard over the downpour. A steady stream of water ran off the muzzle of his weapon as he pointed it toward the ground. "I am not looking forward to this."

Neill unslung his own rifle. He glanced at Chau and Richey from beneath the hood of his Gore-Tex jacket. "We'll stack arms right here. Drop your rucks, too. Hey, squeamish one—" Michael grinned at Crockett. "Keep your eyes open in case our guests arrive." A quick glance showed him that each man still wore their tactical gloves. Those would come in handy as they searched for the drive among the debris.

"Do we know what we're looking for?" Richey asked. The Senior Chief took the rifles and arranged them into a tripod. For a Navy man, his efforts were spot on.

"We'll know it when we see it—I think." Neill answered. "Now let's start earning that overtime Uncle Sam's paying us."

Naval Fleet Command,
Tsoying District,
Republic of China—Taiwan

THE CHOICE BEFORE ADMIRAL LUNG SHIH evoked memories of better days. With those in mind, a subtle smile spread across the old man's face.

Shih's mentor, Captain Li Zhuh, had been a senior officer and member of the admiralty during the Cold War, and could also recall the unpleasantries exchanged between the two Koreas. When Shih had served him as a young Lieutenant, Zhuh had burned the central tenet of ROC doctrine into his brain; *protect the shores and sea lanes against an attack or blockade from the mainland.* That mission had been the foundation for every action taken by the Taiwanese Navy, and as long as tensions existed between the two governments, that strategy—more an article of faith—was not likely to change soon.

It was spring again, and the Navy of the PRC was once more conducting maneuvers around the island. Each Fleet Command on Taiwan was acutely aware of these exercises and monitored the ships of the much larger Chinese force—right down to their individual course changes—with keen interest. When possible, the ROC tracked the movement of the submarines that acted as escorts for the task forces operating near their coastline. Two variables had made that job easier than the tacticians had imagined. One was tied to the geography of the region. The East China Sea was relatively shallow, and its superficial depths made it easy to follow the undersea craft as they left port. Another factor was related to the acoustic signature of the boats—except for the newer Type 095 class, the Chinese submarines were incredibly noisy.

With the exercises now proceeding full on, Admiral Shih had considered his options and let the advice of his long-gone counselor determine his steps. Zhuh had many sayings, but one always stuck with Shih; "*A ship is hard to maneuver when it's moored to the pier.*" With those words echoing in his memory, Admiral Shih had ordered all the ships under his command to set sail.

Just as Li Zhuh had done for Shih, the Admiral now passed on his wisdom to a younger generation of Taiwanese naval officers. Shih's most trusted adjutant—Hao Hsu, newly promoted to Captain—now served as the commander of the fleet patrolling the coastline.

Some of the ships in the tiny group were newer vessels, bought from the United States, France, or the Netherlands; many were old, and a few had been constructed right on the island under the supervision of foreign contractors. The Admiral's group had recently been modernized with new combat systems to meet the threat of the People's Republic. It was a diverse fleet, specifically tailored for the strategic needs of a David facing a Goliath in a confrontation everyone hoped would never happen.

A blockade had always been the greatest threat, but there were other means available for deterring the Admiral's worst fears. The ROC had embraced a three-fold approach. First, they had been stockpiling critical supplies for years. Food was the greatest concern. Secondly, Taiwan had shored up their port defenses, hardening their facilities against military action. The third step was more offensive in nature; sending the destroyers and surface ships of their fledgling Navy on patrol to deny aggressors from the sea.

That prospect had always been the stuff of nightmares. If the Chinese Navy could get close enough, their vessels could enter Taiwan's harbors and begin mine-laying operations. The shallow-water explosives were a hazard that didn't differentiate between military combatants and cargo-laden transports. Hostilities would one day cease, but even if the ROC successfully repelled the Chinese Navy they would still have to contend with the presence of the ship-killing weapons. Mine-sweeping actions would probably be effective in removing the threat, but assurances from Taiwan's leaders might not be enough to persuade nervous commercial shippers. The Admiral reminded himself that even the *possibility* of one mine below the waves was enough to close a harbor.

Shih had ordered constant updates, and one of his junior officers now presented him with the latest report. The Admiral was pleased to see that nearly every vessel had cleared their home ports and hugged the shallows surrounding Taiwan. A back-channel message from the American ambassador in Taipei urged Shih to be especially vigilant. No other details were given, but the Admiral didn't need additional warnings. The PRC ships now surging around his homeland—in numbers unusual for a mere exercise—were enough of a reason to be wary.

Admittedly, the PLA-Navy was a formidable foe, but whatever their condition, the ships of the ROC were manned by crews devoted to their island nation. Admiral Shih took comfort in the fact that his fleet had sailed, and he was determined to put those ships to good use—to counter whatever plans the Chinese armada had for Taiwan and her people. What he hadn't prepared for were the vulnerabilities of his Navy's Achilles' heel.

Chapter Twenty-Two ✴ A Closer Look

THE UCAV HAD A MAXIMUM ALTITUDE OF WELL over thirty-five thousand feet. Looking like a miniature version of the Stealth bomber, the aircraft acted as the eyes—and ears—of Admiral LaSalle's carrier task force, and was now loitering in position high above Taiwan and the East China Sea.

Looking down, the UCAV—it was a Specter variant—used a combination of radar and IFF software that identified the American and Taiwanese ships far below. The friendlies transmitted a specific signal; anything that didn't was automatically classified as belonging to the other side. This information was sent downrange to the U.S. Navy ships, and the data transmitted gave the forward deployed commanders a moment by moment picture of their area of responsibility.

The Specter wasn't just focused on hardware. Delicate instrumentation packed in the nose of the aircraft had been finely tuned to monitor weather patterns as well. The UCAV noted the passing of several squall lines as they moved into the South China Sea from the northern Pacific basin. Another disturbance had long been forming near Shanghai, and was officially designated as Tropical Storm Ulysses. The violent front was a hundred miles northeast of the Strait between Taiwan and the mainland, swirling loosely at first and then gathering momentum and building in strength. It was still very early in the season for a major storm, but conditions were ripe—warm seas, a low pressure zone and the humid weather created by the showers moving ahead of it. As a result, the gale organized quickly. Within six hours, it would be classified as a typhoon.

* * * *

THE TEAM DID A WALK-AROUND OF THE CRASH site before focusing on the helicopter itself. Aside from finding more scattered remnants of the aircraft, the inspection turned up nothing related to the drive they were searching for.

Crockett followed a length of cable lying in a loose coil on the grass at his feet. He bent down and examined the frayed end with his tactical light. Strands of fiber optics were clearly visible in the center of the bundle.

"This is what caused the whole thing," he announced, holding it up for the rest to see. "The rotors must have made contact with these up near the top. Pilot lost control after that." Nate's eyes followed the wall of the crater towering over their heads. "Probably comm lines. It's hard to tell, but it looks like there's a dish up there."

Crockett dropped the cable and pushed through the undergrowth to the base of the cliff. Using the natural vegetation and handholds in the rocks, he scaled the wall to a point where he could see over the trees. If there were some way to gain a perspective on the northern side of the island, this would be it.

The group watched as Nate's form blended in to the wall. Using the night scope, he scanned the horizon just as he had done on their approach to Huo Shan. From his elevated vantage point he could see the circular shape of the fuel depot to the west. After several minutes he climbed back down to the jungle floor and returned to the team.

"Nothing on the water," he reported. He handed the scope back to Neill. "If there's a boat out there, it's running without lights."

"Anything else?"

"I saw where they keep their gas," Crockett grinned.

Neill nodded and turned to face the crash site. "Nice work, Nate." He stepped forward and began moving to the helo. "Let's get started."

Chau seemed reluctant to get any closer to the wrecked aircraft. Standing in the drenching rain, the young officer patted his pockets as if searching for something.

Neill noted his hesitation. "You okay, Si?"

"I don't have a flashlight."

"Hang on." Michael sloshed through the long grass to where he'd left his ruck. He pulled out two LED lights from one of the side compartments and then rejoined Chau and Richey at the front of the wreck. Crockett was now in a position near the northern edge of the clearing and began looking for an opening in the thick vegetation.

The two sailors weren't moving. The Senior Chief was illuminating the front of the crumpled cockpit with a beam of white light. Neill handed him one he'd retrieved from his gear.

"Use this, Chief," Neill offered. "Has a red filter on the end; if there's anybody nearby it'll attract less attention."

Richey switched off the beam. "Sorry," he said. His voice was emotionless. He wasn't thinking tactically and had been momentarily distracted by what he saw through the shattered windscreen. Neill had seen it too. It wasn't a pleasant sight. The laminated glass hung in sheets, punched out from the cabin frame; some of it lay on the ground, along with a grisly reminder that a human being had once piloted the craft.

"Let's move around to the passenger side," Chau suggested. He seemed to have found his voice again. "The cabin's not as badly damaged there."

That was an understatement. The cockpit had been severely crushed in the free-fall as it tumbled down the crater. The fire had done the rest. Beginning their search where the pilot sat just wasn't an option.

Richey led the way. Reaching the wreck, the Senior Chief stared first at the front of the chopper and then let his eyes roam to the ground a few feet away. "Closed casket funeral for this guy." Richey's dark humor broke the silence. Before them lay the tragic end to a privileged life. Something else occurred to him. "You don't think he was carrying the drive on him, do you?"

Neill hoped not. "We'll search the rest of the cabin first. If we don't find it in there—"

"Understood." The Senior Chief snapped on the flashlight and pointed it into the cabin. A mixture of oil, hydraulic fluid and blood decorated the helicopter's interior. Being bathed in the red glow of the flashlight only heightened the eeriness of the scene. It also made it hard to distinguish the difference between the fluids.

"Hold the beam there, Senior Chief," Neill instructed. He stepped across the debris, careful to avoid some of the more jagged pieces of metal that protruded from the fuselage. Chau joined him as Michael reached in through the passenger side and tugged on a big chunk of polyvinyl covering the buckled door. It came free easily. Neill took hold of the door frame and tested it for strength, then turned to Chau and said, "Give me a hand, Simon."

As Michael pulled himself up toward the opening, Chau reached out and supported the Marine from behind. The rain continued to fall heavily and ran down the metal surfaces, but Neill's gloves gave him the grip he needed. Balancing his weight on the frame, Neill slowly eased his legs through the narrow entryway and into the shattered cabin.

There was almost as much of a downpour inside the cockpit as there was outside. The interior was a jumbled mess. Michael avoided looking directly ahead, and using his own flashlight he focused his attention on what remained of the floorboards and the compartment behind the seats. Almost instantly his actions gave him pause. He shook his head and chided himself; to find what he was looking for it would be necessary to search every available inch of the confined space. He couldn't ignore the task simply because—

The sudden sound of crunching metal was unexpected. The ground where the smashed helicopter had come to rest was slightly uneven, and Neill's weight had unbalanced its remains. It shifted beneath him; not by much, but enough to send him awkwardly in just the direction he didn't want to go.

Neill instinctively tried to steady himself. The hand he put out landed on Emory McBride's corpse. In the split second it rested there, Michael thought that the soft tissue was still warm, but with the glove on it was impossible to tell. He chocked that up to an overactive imagination—the presence of the lifeless body was a powerful one.

"*Whoa*—easy there," Richey reacted. He pulled himself up to the opening and looked in, careful not to shift the fuselage further. His bulk acted as a counter-weight. Neill still held the light in one hand and the beam flashed near his feet as he re-gained his balance.

"What's that on the floor?" Simon asked.

A wrap-around windscreen near the nose and in the belly of the aircraft offered another view into the cockpit. Richey lowered himself down to the ground and knelt in the wet grass. He directed his light into the cabin from below, shivering as the hood of his jacket pulled away and a stream of rainwater ran down his neck.

North Island Naval Complex,
Office of Cyber Defenses
San Diego, California

KELSI PRESSMAN STARED AT HER SCREEN, THIS time in admiration. Emory McBride—or whoever had written this code—had done an excellent job of embedding something within the data crowding the file. She was equally impressed that anyone could look past the obvious to find the encryption in such a short space of time. From what Commander Fitzroy had told her, this piece of intel had come to light earlier that morning—in D.C., she reminded herself. California was hours behind the east coast, which meant—

"Got anything yet?"

Pressman's concentration was now broken. She gave Fitzroy an agitated look and then turned back to her monitor. The young sailor had already powered up a number of her favorite decryption programs and was preparing to put them through their paces.

"You do realize I haven't had my coffee yet, right, Commander?" Kelsi said. Fitzroy had noticed that at times like these, Pressman could be a bit testy.

"We could delegate some of the other stuff on your desk," Fitzroy offered. "That way you could focus—"

Pressman was way ahead of him. "I put Purcell and Ettinger to work on the remote app upgrades," she said. "What I really need is a decent breakfast."

The Commander checked his watch. The dining facility at Mercer Hall was closed. "How about I run down the street and get you a breakfast burrito?"

Kelsi scrunched up her face and said, "Too greasy. Cinnamon apple oatmeal, and it's on. Now *shoo*."

Fitzroy made a face of his own, but was on his way. Pressman returned to the task at hand—coming from the office of the National Security Advisor, there was an elevated priority associated with this request. Ordinarily Lieutenant Chau would have taken point, but he and the USS *Meyer* were now at Pearl—or so she thought. It had been several days since she'd heard from him. That puzzled her. Kelsi decided he was probably soaking up the sun on Waikiki or Bellows Beach, and just hadn't had the time to make a phone call or send an email. Wherever Chau was, she hoped he was enjoying his little island vacation—so long as there weren't too many *wahine* nearby.

Pressman let that go and got back to work. She began tinkering around the edges of the code that protected the encrypted data. In short order she located an obscure algorithm that was common to other programs engineered by McBride Industries.

The electronic signature was one she'd seen before, while vetting a software upgrade being prepared for commercial sale. Kelsi remembered it clearly now; before joining the cyber defenses group in San Diego, she had been brought in as part of a team to pass judgment on the product—and its potential risks to operational security. Simon Chau had been included as well; in fact, that was how he and Kelsi had met.

Contractors like MDI had many clients and didn't answer solely to the DoD. On occasion, customers wanted something they couldn't just buy off the shelf. Pressman had seen her share of military-grade applications tailored for use in the private sector—or the armed forces of a friendly ally. It was strictly routine, and at the time, her team had flagged the program for continued development and signed off on the system's integrity.

The young Ensign stared at the wall and her expression darkened. *McBride Defense Industries*. Pressman considered the data before her and reflected on the software she'd evaluated in the past. Kelsi let her mind wander and played devil's advocate. If there was a link, who could benefit from it?

A small, distant light started to glow in the furthest corners of her mind. Very slowly, she began to see a connection.

* * * *

"Looks like a backpack—and a pair of night vision goggles." Neill pocketed the NVGs and handed the pack to Simon through the space where the window had been. "Check inside."

Something caught Chau's eye as he examined the exterior. "It's personalized." He turned it around so Neill could take a look. The embroidered name of Emory McBride could clearly be seen.

Simon unzipped the top and looked in. After a moment's pause he reached into the pack and pulled out a silver attaché with a handle. He dropped the pack and went to work opening the small case.

Neill pulled himself back through the opening and re-joined the sailors in the rain. He caught a glimpse of Crockett as he skirted the perimeter of the clearing.

Simon paused. "You don't think it's booby-trapped, do you?"

Richey grinned at him. "Only one way to find out, El-Tee."

Chau decided to throw caution to the wind. The case was secured with two simple clasps that held the halves together. Simon flipped one and then the other and popped it open.

The results were a bit anti-climactic. The beam of Richey's flashlight revealed a simple USB flash drive in a black casing. Chau removed it from the attaché and turned it over in his hands.

"One hundred and twenty-eight gigabyte, high-capacity model," he remarked, reading the specs stamped on the side. "One of the more pricey types, but nothing out of the ordinary. I've got one just like it back at the boat."

Neill nodded. "I think we found what we came for, gentlemen." He held out his hand. "I'll smash it with the butt of my rifle."

Chau continued to examine the drive. "Avery said there was some encrypted data on this. Mind if I take a look at it first?"

Neill blinked, and then remembered that Simon had brought his laptop. He looked over at Richey.

"Why not?" the Senior Chief asked. He started to smile and said, "He didn't bring that computer all this way just to surf the internet."

"You can decipher it here?" Neill asked. "Don't you need special software for that?"

Simon grinned mischievously. "Trust me. I came here with more than just Solitaire."

"All right," Michael nodded. "It's worth a try." He got Crockett's attention with a wave.

Chau pocketed the drive and tossed the case onto the grass. "Now what?"

"Now we check out the facility around the corner," Neill said, cocking his head in the direction of the path beyond the clearing. He suspected the other end of the trail led to the buildings hidden at the base of the promontory. "I want to see what this so-called secret base is all about."

Crockett arrived and eyed the group expectantly. "Find it?"

"Roger that." Michael moved to the weapons and slung his rifle across his shoulder. He handed Chau and Richey their M-4s and then picked up his ruck. With their gear in hand, the team prepared to move out again.

It seemed darker now. Neill turned to face Nate, but could barely make out his camouflaged features under the bill of his cover. "You see anything through the trees?"

Crockett shook his head. "Too thick. And no trails that I could see leading to the fuel depot, or the beach on the north side. We're boxed in here, Mike."

Neill noted the concern in his friend's voice. "Understood."

The rain had let up. Once again, the team found themselves between downpours. Neill adjusted his headgear and tightened the straps on his pack. They had accomplished one mission for Willis Avery. It was time to attempt the other.

Chapter Twenty-Three ✷ Test of Leadership

The Strait of Taiwan

BINOCULARS IN HAND, CAPTAIN HAO HSU watched from the bridge of the *Kee Lung* as two Chinese frigates paralleled his course. At this late hour it was only possible to see their running lights. Hsu imagined the masters of those vessels were doing the same, monitoring his passage south through the Strait as the ROC flotilla sailed eight miles offshore. Riding low in the water, their bows rising and falling in the heavy seas, the PLA-Navy ships were fully fueled for what were described as routine exercises. Captain Hsu couldn't begrudge them their maneuvers, but he suspected there were other motives involved.

Since leaving port, Hsu's task force had sailed in a single file convoy. The individual ships protected a one mile stretch between them as they patrolled the western side of the island. Hsu's orders were explicit; the spaces between each vessel were to remain constant and inviolate. That was especially true for the smaller frigates and cruisers in Captain Hsu's group. A break in the chain could invite an attack on an isolated ship—should hostilities break out—or allow the Chinese Navy to simply push through and challenge the integrity of their shore defenses.

Two other squadrons of surface ships followed the same procedure on the eastern coast. Their goal was to deploy a maritime force capable of deterring any military action that might be contemplated by the Chinese. To that end, appearance and presence were everything, and the strategy worked both ways. For the ROC, showing their flag in the waters around Taiwan demonstrated their resolve to stand up to an aggressor. Putting to sea sent an unmistakable message—*we see you and are prepared to protect ourselves.*

China's Navy was free to navigate in the Strait so long as their ambitions didn't cross the line into belligerence. Their exercises each spring were a reminder of their interest in the region, and the obvious placement of weapons aboard their ships signaled an overwhelming capability. It was a game both sides played every year, but judging by the number of PLA-Navy vessels shadowing him, Captain Hsu feared the worst.

The weather had deteriorated, and the decks below the wheelhouse were awash with sea and foam. A blanket of clouds now stretched beyond the horizon and a steady rain had begun to fall. It was growing more difficult to stand without holding on to a rail or bracing against a bulkhead or control surface.

Warm air gusted into the compartment. Hsu turned as his Executive Officer, an affable young Lieutenant named Yang, entered the bridge just as the eight thousand ton destroyer plowed into a trough between swells. Hsu issued a one word directive; "Report."

Yang wore a weather-resistant smock over his uniform but peeled it off after closing the hatch. He stood at a respectable distance before shaking it free of water.

"The destroyer *Luzhou* has launched a Kamov helicopter from her stern." The insect-like Kamov was an anti-submarine warfare platform. "It is conducting low altitude drills, but nothing more provocative than that."

"What about navigation?"

It was the second time Hsu had posed that question since leaving port. Yang could understand his Captain's concern. Taiwan's self-reliant streak had grown, and the ROC had launched four satellites into medium earth orbit. The StarPoint

Series I vehicles were purposed to provide a global positioning system independent of the spacecraft put in place by the U.S. The ships in the fleet had recently undergone a few minor upgrades to their electronic architecture; this was necessary to link their navigational consoles to the satellites above.

"Operating as advertised, Captain." The younger officer had already checked. "I've just come from CIC. They report no problems."

Hsu appeared pleased but thoughtful. The new system had been in place long enough to clear out the bugs. And it had worked surprisingly well since its inception, requiring only minor adjustments.

Yang noted Hsu's concerned look. A smile spread across the Lieutenant's face. "The forecast calls for rain, Captain." He cast a glance in the direction of the frigates some miles away. "Do you think our brothers across the Strait will cancel their plans?"

Hsu expressed mild amusement. "I doubt we will be so lucky." He lifted the binoculars to his eyes. It was difficult to see the Chinese ships as the downpour increased. Then, with mock gravity, he said, "We have no need to worry, Lieutenant. These exercises are purely routine and will bring peace to the region."

Yang draped his wet jacket over one of the few high-backed chairs on the bridge. He knew when his Captain was being sarcastic.

"Of course, sir," Yang quipped. "And my grandmother is a fat Irish woman who smokes cigars."

Hsu chuckled. The humor of the moment helped to calm the Captain's apprehensions. He would revive them periodically; it was his job to worry. But for now there was no need. His fleet continued patrolling the shoreline, and the software that helped guide them was performing just as it had been designed.

Hsu hadn't concerned himself with the varied technical minutia of the system. There was just too much involved, and too many other details aboard that required his constant attention. But if he had taken the time to educate himself, he would have discovered that the application piloting each ship in the task force bore the imprint of McBride Defense Industries.

* * * *

FROM FIFTY MILES ASTERN, CAPTAIN LAO marked the progress of the opposing Navy's ships as they steamed south. There was little to see in the darkness. Like Admiral LaSalle, Lao had access to technology that tracked the vessels of his fleet and those fielded by the ROC. The plot board on the *Luzhou* wasn't as advanced as the American Navy's, but it was capable enough. Lao used it to locate the *Kee Lung* as it neared the port of Taichung. He was familiar with Taiwan's lead destroyer—and the man who stood on her bridge.

Lao decided it was time to test Captain Hsu's leadership, and the readiness of the ships under his command. He ordered the gunboats that paced his armada to begin a series of runs toward the smaller vessels in Hao Hsu's convoy. Doing so under the cover of night would sow confusion. The idea was to provoke some kind of isolated reaction; should the PLA-Navy achieve that and force their hand, Lao could gauge just how disciplined his adversary was.

For that reason, Captain Lao secretly hoped that his harassing strategy would fail. Hsu was a competent seaman and tactician, and Lao suspected that his counterpart would issue strict orders regarding the rules of engagement. If they were to cross swords, Lao wanted to go head to head against an opponent who could match his own mettle—anything less would be an insult to his skills as an officer, and the Navy of the People's Republic.

The Captain could bide his time. These exercises were only a few days old. By morning, Lao would order his ships to begin a lazy tack to the west. He would watch to see if Hsu's ships relaxed their posture in response. It might be possible to lull the ROC maritime force into complacency, but Lao had no real expectation of that.

He smiled. It made little difference. Once the Captain received word from Admiral Lee, everything would change, and

Hsu would be powerless to stop him.

* * * *

THE TEAM LEFT THE CRASH SITE AND FOLLOWED the path out of the clearing. Neill was anxious to leave the open spaces behind. The trail was the only way in or out, and with troops on the way, he didn't want to be caught there with one exit.

Hemmed in by the narrow passage through the trees wasn't much better, but at least they were moving. Neill pulled the NVGs from his cargo pocket and looked ahead. Fifty yards away he could dimly see the vegetation opening up and yielding to the beach.

"Everybody hydrate," Michael ordered softly over his shoulder. Each man's ruck contained a bladder filled with water connected to a tube. After a few long sips they reached the end of the trail and took a knee on the wet, gravelly sand.

"Same drill," Neill whispered, looking at each one in turn. "We'll check out the facility and gather whatever intel we can. But first we do a recon of the beach and the area around that pier. I'll take point."

He started to stand but Crockett stopped him. "Hold on there, pilgrim. I'll take point this time."

"Suit yourself," Michael agreed; adjusting roles and responsibilities was a function of leadership. He checked his watch; it was nearly midnight. "Just don't trip over those big feet."

Nate grinned. "Roger that."

Neill passed the scope to Crockett, who edged ahead, careful to avoid matter brought down from the trees by the heavy rain. Nate stopped once he had a clear view of the pier, and the buildings shouldered against the crater wall. He looked back at the team, pointed to his eyes and then ran a hand across his throat. The gesture was clear to everyone; *nothing to see.*

Crockett stepped off a little faster now. His movements were still cautious and followed the smooth and deliberate pace they'd established earlier. Within a few minutes the group left the cover of the tree line and arrived at the pilings supporting one end of the dock. It was even darker here and they instinctively took shelter under the boardwalk to conceal themselves.

The series of storms and tidal action had layered a variety of organic matter on the beach. This part of the shoreline was littered with palm fronds, leaves and vegetation blown out to sea and re-deposited on the sand by the waves. It might have been a nearly tropical setting in fair weather, but now had the smell of brine and decay.

Crockett trained the night scope along the length of the pier as it jutted out to sea. Neill's unaided eyes tracked along the same path. Neither Marine saw any activity, except for the breakers as they crested in the shallow waters and rolled ashore.

"No lights, no boat—and no submarine," Nate whispered, lowering the scope. "Didn't Avery say that McBride was meeting someone here?"

Michael nodded. "That's what I heard."

"Maybe they were delayed," Richey suggested. "Or maybe McBride got here early and just planned to wait. Either way, it's good news for us."

"It is a bit odd," Neill said. "A naval facility with no Navy."

"And no one in sight."

Neill didn't want to assume anything. "That remains to be seen, Si. Let's knock on a few doors and see if anybody's home." He saw a ladder on the opposite side of the pilings. "I say we go topside for a closer look."

Aboard the USS Meyer

A TROPICAL STORM WAS MOVING THROUGH THE Strait of Taiwan, but in this patch of the northern Pacific—the eastern boundaries of the Philippine Sea—the *Meyer* was enjoying fair winds, giving Captain Beacham ample opportunity to indulge his preference for swift acceleration. The *Victory* had long since passed through the chain of the Northern

Marianas Islands; the *Meyer* followed closely behind, mothering her charge ever westward. Both ships in the small convoy were traveling at nearly full speed.

It was peaceful now, but in another age the Philippine Sea had a storied history of war and conflict. The United States and Japan had fought a pitched naval battle here during World War II, the Great Marianas Turkey Shoot, and like the Battle of Midway, the outcome meant disaster for the Japanese Navy. These waters were also home to some of the deepest reaches of the world's oceans. The undersea canyons of the Marianas and Philippine Trenches lay miles below the surface. Each had been formed by a head-on collision with massive tectonic plates. Man seldom ventured there; few vessels were able to withstand the crushing pressure of those depths—not even the most advanced submarines in the American Navy could achieve that feat. As a rule, Davy Jones kept that part of the ocean floor all to himself.

As pertinent as those facts were to the region, neither was of concern to Beacham as his ships sailed to the rendezvous point. His focus now was to reach the western edges of the Philippine Sea where it met the Strait of Luzon. Standing on the bridge, Beacham could clearly see the lights of a Seahawk helicopter as it flew between the *Meyer* and the arsenal ship. Presently the aircraft banked north and accelerated.

The bridge crew performed their duties quietly, probably a concession to the late hour, Beacham decided. Subdued lighting allowed the sailors present in the wheelhouse to view the sea without distraction; those included the Officer of the Watch, an Ensign, and the pilot, a Petty Officer First Class. An Able Seaman stood as lookout.

The personnel on duty now were especially attentive. The Captain's presence helped, but each man was a dedicated professional. They reminded themselves that they had a job to do no matter who stood on the deck, and as a group, they willed themselves to relax—just as the *Meyer*'s Executive Officer entered the compartment.

Commander William Towle was tall and severely lean. A

marathoner and triathlete, Towle had faced challenges with his physical training aboard a sea-going vessel. The lack of open spaces on the *Meyer* forced him to confine his workouts to the treadmills and ellipticals down in the ship's weight room. He loved his career, but like the Captain, he reveled in his time ashore and the chance to break free and hit the open road—on foot, in his case.

"Evening, Bill," Beacham said in greeting. He'd just checked the time; almost eleven forty-five—2345 in military parlance. "What are they serving down in the galley?"

The ship's mess specialists served midnight rations—or mid-rats—starting at eleven-fifteen for all hands coming on or going off watch.

"Sliders and fries, Skipper." At times Bill Towle was a man of few words.

"Sounds like a winner," the Captain replied. "You have any dinner yet?"

He'd almost said breakfast; just coming on duty, that would have been true in Towle's case. It was easier to give the meals a name based on the beginning or ending of the watch.

Towle nodded. "Yes, sir." A grin crept across his face. "But I could go for a bowl of chili."

"Let's get to it, then." His voice carried enthusiasm, but Beacham was tired. "After that, we'll head down to Operations—I want a look at the video feeds from the *Victory*." Occasionally he felt the need to see things from the arsenal ship's perspective. "We can also check on the status of THRIFTY NICKEL."

Commander Towle continued to smile. He knew the Captain preferred another label for the prototype system aboard the *Victory*. THRIFTY NICKEL was the project title, but the nickname Beacham came up with seemed to have stuck.

"Aye, aye, Captain," the XO concurred. "First, some food. Then we'll give PEASHOOTER our undivided attention."

Chapter Twenty-Four ✲ Gathering Intel

Naval Facility,
Huo Shan

THE SEA HAD GROWN ROUGHER. GUSTING winds caught the waves and sent spray flying upward, showering the dock and the pilings below. The rain began to fall again—more heavily now—and as it struck the metal roof over their heads, it created a deafening clatter.

Every moment they were alone on the island increased their chances of success. But Neill also knew they were operating on borrowed time. Gathering the intel they came for required swiftness and sharp eyes.

Over watch was their primary concern. None of the team wanted to be surprised by the arrival of Admiral Lee's men. Crockett had taken up a position on the far end of the dock. From there he could see any boat approaching from the northeastern tip of the island. While that was the most likely ingress point, Nate continued to scan the western reaches of the shoreline as well.

Using the night vision scope his eyes swept the beach, but there was little movement to see aside from the tops of the trees swaying in the wind. To the north the storm endured, sending lightning across the sky and promising the torrent above would persist as the front thundered in their direction.

Neill, Chau and Richey eyed the series of buildings huddled low at the base of the crater wall. Before moving closer, the three wanted to determine if anyone might be stirring inside. None of the structures appeared occupied; as near as they could tell, the facility was empty.

With Neill in front, the team moved cautiously forward. The muzzles of their weapons were pointed down but at the ready. The dock itself was narrow, only about a dozen feet wide. The roof over their heads extended another forty feet over the water, the far side supported by beams planted deep in a man-made jetty running parallel to the pier. Fire bottles were attached to the dockside beams and heavy ropes were neatly coiled on the deck as they passed by.

"Just the kind of mooring lines you'd need to tie up a submarine," Malcolm noted. His voice was low, but he made himself heard over the din of the falling rain.

"Roger that, Senior Chief." Neill's eyes never left the structures before them.

Ahead, a separate building joined the others and sat off to the right side. This had the appearance of a mechanic's bay and stood twice as tall as the rest. Above, high up in the rafters, a bridge crane spanned the gap between two tracks running the length of the dock. A hoist swung lazily beneath an electric motor. All three of them saw it, but only Richey took the time to give it a second look.

"Probably what they use to load their weapons and equipment," he remarked.

By now the group reached a double-door entryway at the foot of the pier. Neill moved to the side and peered into one of the large windows framed in the center of each hatch. The interior was dark. He could make out the far wall, but the room itself was sparsely furnished. From behind, Richey attached the tactical light to a rail on the front of his rifle.

"We need to get in there," Neill said. He reached for his belt and retrieved a Gerber utility tool. The rain blew in under the roofing, and stood in puddles on the uneven surfaces around their feet. "I've got something here we can use to wedge—"

Chau stepped forward and took hold of the knob. With a turn of his wrist he pulled and the door swung open.

Neill looked at the smiling Navy men, and then broke out in a grin of his own.

"Well, if you want to do it the easy way—"

WITH A NOD FROM NEILL, SIMON PULLED OPEN the door. The Marine was wearing the goggles they'd found at the crash site. He slipped in quickly and turned left, weapon up. His eyes moved from one side of the room to the other.

The Senior Chief was right behind him, sweeping right, the red glow of his beam illuminating the darkness. There was nothing to see but office furniture, cabinets and charts decorating the walls. In one corner was another set of windowed double doors. These led into the large, two-story bay hugging the cliff. Neill announced *"Clear,"* and then turned to face Chau.

"Keep an eye on Crockett, Simon. He'll signal you if he sees anything. If he does, be sure to get our attention—we might need to bug out in a hurry."

Chau nodded as Neill and Richey headed off for the double doors. Michael hoped this entryway might be unlocked as well, but a tug on the handle proved disappointing.

"Maybe now's the time for that tool you're carrying," Malcolm suggested.

Neill pulled the Gerber from his belt and went to work. Richey trained the red glow of his flashlight on Michael's hands as he attempted to gain access. His movements were awkward, but he managed to find enough skill to disengage the bolt's simple locking mechanism—without breaking it. In short order both men were inside the large bay.

The two surveyed the room, leaving the doors open behind them. It was even darker here. Neill stowed the NVGs and pulled the tactical light from his pocket.

"No windows," he observed. "Let's risk a little light."

He switched on the beam and pointed it low and toward the center of the room. There was no need to look elsewhere.

Neither man spoke for several seconds, using the time to take in the view. Resting on twin racks were two bullet-shaped cylinders facing a large roll-up door. Each was narrow and very streamlined. Neither displayed any noticeable surface features, but the one closest to them appeared to be disassembled on one end.

Neill swung the light around the rest of the bay. Workbenches equipped with lathes and milling tools lined the walls. Open carts were positioned near the cylinders, and over their heads was a bridge crane identical to the one mounted in the rafters above the pier. Everything seemed organized around the missile-like objects dominating most of the floor space.

Richey kept his eyes forward as Neill lowered his pack to the floor. He unzipped his ruck and began searching inside till he found what he was looking for.

They were going to need a camera for this.

* * * *

"JUST LIKE THE DIAGRAM I SAW ONLINE," RICHEY observed. "Longer than I expected, though—but I guess you'd need the extra length to carry the rocket fuel."

Neill found a tape measure on one of the benches. Richey held one end as Michael walked to the nose of the first weapon.

"Nearly twenty-seven feet," Neill commented softly. "How long are the tubes on an Oscar class?"

Malcolm shook his head. "No clue," he answered. "My research didn't get that far. My guess is that these weapons would have to be similar in size to Russian conventional torpedoes—otherwise they'd have to modify their launchers."

Neill pointed his light at the torpedo's nose. "What are these?"

The Senior Chief walked to Michael's side. "Gas ejector ducts." He removed his glove and ran a hand along the smooth surface of the outer casing. "This is how they form the bubble cavity."

The bay was warm and the air humid. Neill powered up the camera and made sure the flash was on. He moved down the length of the torpedo and stopped near the middle.

"There are two seams here," he noted. "A couple of inches apart. Running lengthwise, about two feet long." He snapped a photo.

Richey nodded. "Control skids. These spring out during transit and act as stabilizers."

Neill continued taking pictures as they made their way to the rear of the undersea missile. This part of the weapon ended abruptly and had been opened up; a cowling of sorts had been removed, exposing intricate gadgetry within. Four narrow fins branched out at perpendicular angles.

"More stabilizers?"

"Probably," Malcolm guessed. "Some kind of device on the ends, though. Must have an additional purpose—steering, maybe?" He pointed his light downward. "This is the rocket nozzle; these smaller jets are the igniters. Once those are lit, this thing's off and running." He moved back to the center of the casing and rested a hand on the weapon. "Rocket fuel's probably stored here, along with the tanks for the gas used to create the envelope. The warhead should be between this point and the nose."

Charts were spread out on a cart between the two missiles. Neill picked one up for a closer look. "Schematics," he announced. "These are in Chinese." He handed them over to Malcolm and picked up another set. "Here's more; in Russian."

"Should we get Lieutenant Chau to translate?"

Michael shook his head. "No need; we'll photograph them and let the CIA's brain trust make an analysis."

Aboard the USS George H.W. Bush

ADMIRAL LASALLE HAD LEFT THE CIC FOR SOME much-needed rest. Captain DeSouza was about to do the same.

Before heading off to his cabin he wanted a firm sit-rep on the status of the Chinese task force and the ROC Navy ships plying the seas surrounding Taiwan.

"What have you got for me, XO?"

DeSouza could have gotten the information he wanted by studying the plot board; having the Executive Officer brief him assured the Captain that his relief was up to speed. Given the tensions that now existed between the two—actually, *three*—navies, now was not the time for anyone to drop their guard. Vigilance had to be the order of the day.

Lieutenant Commander Casper "Ghost" Lipford had expected this. Before relinquishing the conn, DeSouza always seemed to ramp things up; checking on navigation, speed or the disposition of the ship's tactical systems, and sometimes more. Lipford had noticed the tell-tale signs half an hour earlier when the Captain downed his third cup of coffee.

"Haze gray and underway, Skipper." His assessment summarized the condition of the carrier battle group. He was prepared to offer a more detailed appraisal of the respective Asian fleets.

"The PLA-Navy has two groups operating in Taiwanese waters; both have expanded their reach, deploying their shipboard platforms and splaying them out across the Strait of Taiwan—to the northwest—and on the eastern coastline of the island in the Pacific."

Lipford kept his eyes on DeSouza. The Skipper followed his narration by consulting the digital images on the big screen. "Any provocative actions on their part?"

The XO snorted. A crooked smile spread across his face. "They've sent a few gunboats out to challenge the ROC ships; racing in—broadsides—trying to goad them into a fight." He shook his head. "Taiwan's not buying it. They turned on their radars and painted the targets, but nothing more."

"A disciplined response," DeSouza noted. He'd read the bio of the officer in command of the Taiwanese fleet. "This isn't Captain Hsu's first rodeo."

The Skipper mangled the name badly. *Must be tired*, Lipford decided with a grin. He wondered how the Captain planned to sleep with all that caffeine coursing through his veins.

"What about the *Meyer*?"

For the first time the XO checked the cartographic display. "Moving up nicely; she's not experiencing the weather we've encountered—yet." As if on cue, the watchstanders in the CIC felt the deck rolling slightly beneath their feet.

"Very well, Mr. Lipford. You have the conn."

"*Aye*, sir," the XO announced in a loud voice. "I have the conn."

An entry was made in the log. The time on deck was 0015. Commander Lipford now had control of the ship, and a series of *ayes* rippled through the compartment as the officers and enlisted men acknowledged the shift in command.

Chapter Twenty-Five ✭ Back to the Beach

The White House

THE TECHNICIAN FROM THE SIGNALS OFFICE had just finished when Avery returned.

"Let me guess," the National Security Advisor began. "No luck, right?"

The tech shook his head. "These days there's not much point in trying to track down an IP address," he responded, putting a few devices back into a case. One looked like a small external hard drive. "There's a lot of masking software available. And whoever sent that email utilized some high-test stuff."

"Can you narrow it down to any specific region?"

The man offered a shrug in reply. "Somewhere between Eastern Europe and the Philippines." He saw the look of surprise on Avery's face. "But I'm not even sure about that. It appears the message was sent from someplace with a run-of-the-mill firewall. It got washed through a dozen servers before it reached you."

"Well, it was worth a try."

"Yes, sir," the tech replied. "I just hate not knowing."

Avery nodded. "I know how you feel, son."

Huo Shan

THE ROYAL NAVY HAD SUPPLIED TWO DIGITAL cameras. Over the course of an hour Neill photographed every feature of the Tempest torpedoes. First came wide shots capturing the full length of the weapons. Richey stood next to them for perspective. Michael then snapped away at the nose ejector ducts, the stabilizer fins and the rocket motor at the rear of each missile. He spent a great deal of time on the open cowling and the exposed wiring of the first device.

Senior Chief Richey used the second camera to document the interior of the bay, as well as the schematics they'd found. After a hundred photos, Malcolm stopped and glared.

"What's wrong?" Neill asked.

"Battery's starting to go."

Michael nodded. "Mine too. Indicator's been blinking for a while now." He turned it off and dropped it into his pack. "No matter; I'm pretty much finished. You?"

"Yeah," Richey growled. "You ready to get out of here?"

Another nod. "Let's switch places with Chau and Crockett. I want them to be a witness to this."

* * * *

"YOU LOOK COLD." NEILL RAISED HIS VOICE SO he could be heard above the rain falling on the roof overhead. "Should have relieved you earlier—sorry."

Crockett was nonplussed. He continued to stare out to sea. "No worries. Just wet." He shivered just a bit and then gave Michael a look. "What did you find in there?"

"Just what we came for," Neill answered. "The Senior Chief's giving Simon a tour now. I want you to see it too—but don't take too long."

"Roger that. I'll signal you when we're done."

After an hour of staring into the storm, Crockett was glad

to be relieved. He hadn't been bored. The storm's ebb and flow kept things interesting. The salt spray stung his eyes as the wind whipped up; and the threat of a patrol boat rounding the remnants of the crater wall kept him on his toes. Taken together, it was not unlike many other days he'd spent in the field—with long stretches of inactivity. In this case he was grateful for that.

Nate moved off toward the weapons bay leaving Neill alone with his thoughts. All the evidence they'd found pointed to the facility being used as a submarine base. The presence of the two weapons inside confirmed it. But the sub itself was nowhere to be seen.

Neill shrugged it off. They'd been there for less than five hours; the boat was probably out on patrol—and thankfully so. The team had accomplished two major objectives, neither of which could have been achieved if the sub—or its crew—had been on the island.

The lightning that snaked across the sky moved south. Even in the darkness Neill could tell more storms were headed their way. The wind and rain had slackened for the moment, but under the Gore-Tex his uniform was wet from the humidity. Neill felt a chill and rocked slightly on his heels, water shifting inside his boots.

Michael pulled out the NVGs and scanned east and west. There was still no sign of an approaching patrol boat. He expanded his search area and looked seaward. To the extreme south a light was moving, crossing the horizon and dipping below his line of sight. The *Industrious*, maybe? That wasn't likely, Neill decided; Commodore Wainwright would have moved his ship closer to the pick-up point by now. What he saw was probably a merchant vessel.

There was nothing to see above except a thick canopy of clouds. As he looked out over the ocean, two red flashes reflected off the support beams and caught his eye; the rest of the team had finished, and Nate was signaling him. Neill surveyed the water approaches before heading down the dock to re-join them.

"NO BOAT, HUH?" CROCKETT ASKED.

Neill shook his head. "Nothing. What'd you think of those torpedoes?"

"Bigger than a fifty cal," Nate grinned, referring to the ammunition of choice for a Marine sniper. "Anybody hungry?"

Simon perked up. "That would be me; Senior Chief?"

Malcolm gave a nod. "Never had British ration packs before."

"Sounds like a plan," Neill agreed. He checked his watch. "Zero one-thirty. We retrieved the thumb drive and got some outstanding intel—I think we've earned some breakfast." He gave Richey a look. "Did you leave everything the way we found it?"

"Roger that, El-Tee. Locked the doors to the bay, too. They'll never know we were there."

"I'm not so sure," Nate breathed. He kept both eyes trained on the waves breaking against the base of the crater wall. "Lee's men will go after that chopper once they get here. And if they don't find the drive in the wreckage—"

Neill was way ahead of him. "I've been thinking about that." He stole a glance in the direction of the eastern tip of the island, sharing Crockett's watchful attitude. "We'll replace it with one Simon brought."

"What if the drive doesn't match?" Richey asked.

"Doesn't have to." Neill replied. "My guess is they'll be satisfied just to find one. I doubt they know what it looks like."

"Very clever." Nate was smiling broadly now. "You're a sneaky preacher man!"

Neill patted his stomach. "And hungry, too." Once again he adjusted his ruck and cradled his weapon. "Let's get back to the boat."

* * * *

THE TEAM RE-TRACED THEIR STEPS, TAKING the ladder down to the beach and under the dock. The rain stopped completely as Neill took point and Crockett brought up the rear. Eddies of water rolled in and swirled at their feet, then receded, borne inland by the storm's tidal action.

"Hold up."

Senior Chief Richey had spied something in the dim light. Planted at the foot of the pilings was a small pumping station, nearly obscured by the jungle foliage. A series of pipes ran horizontally from the base of the mechanism and up to the dock. At the top was an open fitting with a flow control valve.

"Must be how they fuel the sub," Malcolm decided. "But how do they get it to this point? I don't see any supply lines leading from the depot."

"That's a good question—but why would they need to? Oscar class submarines run on nuclear power." Neill was unaware that the Brit's intel pegged the boat as a diesel. "In any case, we'll have a look at that storage tank on the way back."

They continued to move slowly and cautiously, but each man was buoyed by their success so far. As they followed the tree line Nate lifted a displaced palm frond from the sand and began brushing over their footprints.

"Yo, Simon," he called softly over his shoulder. "I've got a question for you."

Chau followed behind Richey and took a sip from his water supply. "What's on your mind?"

"I was just thinking," Crockett continued. "What would your grandfather say about this place—I mean, what we've seen so far?"

Simon's thoughts went back to the crash of the helicopter. "He would say that this place is bad luck." He chose his words carefully. The young officer didn't want to dishonor his grandfather's memory. At the same time, he wanted to distance himself from superstition. "He would probably feel that McBride's greed brought on his death—and his punishment would be an eternity here on the island."

"So it's like karma."

"I suppose," Chau said evenly. "There are those who believe that if you wrong someone, they can summon an evil spirit to come against you."

"A curse, right?"

"Yes."

Richey was listening intently to the conversation. The subject disturbed him, but he remained silent.

"A curse," Crockett repeated. He dropped the palm frond. The four were now navigating the detritus of the jungle's edge and were no longer treading the damp, hard-packed sand. Small crabs skittered across the beach, their white carapaces seeming to glow in the dark. "I wonder what our intrepid Lieutenant Neill would have to say about that."

Neill smiled but kept his eyes ahead. "Are you asking my opinion, or just thinking out loud?"

Nate continued to scan the shoreline and the eastward approach to the island. "I guess I'm just in the mood for a theological discussion," he answered.

Neill thought it over. "What I think doesn't count," he began. "In spiritual matters you need a reliable source; I'd recommend the Bible."

"I had a feeling you'd say that," Crockett quipped.

"The New Testament says that sin entered the world through one man," Neill went on. "But it also says that God's grace can be received through Christ—and He gave some pretty specific instructions about curses."

Neill hadn't expected to hold a Bible study but now everyone was listening.

"Jesus said to bless those who curse you. He didn't give us any fancy spiritual formulas; we're just told to do good to them by our actions." He shrugged. "Reach them by taking the high road—with an attitude of compassion."

"That's it?" Nate asked.

"Pretty much. And I don't believe God's people can be hurt by curses. The Bible teaches that Christ has rescued those who put their faith in Him. If you're living under His grace, but still vulnerable to curses, what's the point?"

"Somehow that's . . . very comforting." Senior Chief

Richey was surprised to hear the words coming from his own mouth; for the first time in the conversation he felt a measure of peace. He wore a serious look and was puzzled, but at the same time he sensed the truth in the Marine's words.

Nate turned to make sure he'd heard right. The big Navy man seemed to be the gruff, hard-edged sort, and not given to comments of a particularly sensitive nature.

"Sounds reasonable," Nate said simply. He was eager to put the discussion on a less serious footing. "Does the Bible talk about how to get along with women?"

"It does indeed," Neill grinned.

Malcolm became his taciturn old self again. "I should have read those chapters years ago," he grumped.

* * * *

LIEUTENANT COMMANDER LIPFORD KEPT A weather eye on the cartographic display before him. In the dark, early morning and in rolling seas, Ghost and the other watchstanders made use of every advantage afforded by the technology at hand. Posting lookouts was just a matter of procedure; human eyes were of little value in picking out hazards under these conditions.

Fortunately, Lipford had a host of other resources at his fingertips to monitor vessel traffic. Orbiting satellites were tied in to the ship's GPS navigational suite, and highly classified sensors—rarely even hinted at—were online to track the positions of the battle groups in the region. Radar became the electronic eyes of the carrier and was the most reliable source of information. The UCAV currently aloft over the Taiwan Strait was another link in the chain. And then there was AIS.

The primary function of the Maritime Automatic Identification System—usually referred to simply as AIS—was to assist in avoiding collisions at sea. Signals were transmitted to ships, AIS base stations and a network of satellites, enabling the complex system to track a vessel's course, speed and position; and by exchanging data between watercraft, the chances of two or more meeting in a catastrophic event were greatly lessened.

Over the years the AIS receivers and transponders had been upgraded and installed on thousands of ocean-going vessels. Yet it was still just a supplemental aid. As effective as it had proven to be, the system played a close second to marine radar—and showed no signs of replacing it.

Lipford moved to a control pad centered in front of the electronic plot. Using a mouse, he drew a marquee around selected points on the map and then tapped a few keys. This allowed him to enlarge a specific area of interest and gain more detailed information. Similar to mapping software found online—but much more sophisticated—the view could be toggled between simple graphic representations and actual, real-time satellite imagery. He chose the latter of the two and watched as the screen jumped and then resolved into a high resolution display.

The area of operation Lipford was most interested in were the sea lanes surrounding Taiwan. Arranged in neat groups, spaced at tightly controlled increments, the XO watched as the ships of the Republic of China patrolled their national shorelines. These vessels formed an inner ring. Positioned in a broader perimeter was the armada that had sailed from the mainland. The two distinct groups moved in a counter-clockwise direction in the waters of the Strait of Taiwan and the western Pacific.

"*Two worlds collide,*" Ghost mused quietly.

A young Ensign looked up from his monitor. The officer was charged with monitoring the ship's navigation. "What was that, Commander?"

Lipford shook his head. "Nothing. Just some lyrics to a song on my playlist." He binked at random on a few of the red squares present on the monitor. Dialog boxes popped up, giving Lipford information on those particular ships' speeds and the types of vessels they were. In some cases, the intelligence was good enough to provide class names.

"Looks like everybody's playing nice," the Ensign remarked.

"For now," the XO agreed.

So far, all their scrutiny had been directed at the PLA-Navy ships participating in the 'exercise.' China had massed a large fleet for the spring maneuvers, but Lipford knew they had plenty more where those came from. It occurred to him that they might miss the forest for the trees. By deploying their naval forces in such a concentrated way, it would be easy to miss what the People's Republic might be doing elsewhere.

Lipford used the mouse to reduce the scope of the view on the monitor. His focus went from a magnified image of Taiwan to a larger, overall picture of the entire region. Seeing nothing awry there, he next panned far to the southwest and the area of the South China Sea. The screen was momentarily empty, but then the pixelated image once again coalesced and a solitary red square appeared in the center of the display.

"Hello," Lipford said as he stepped forward. "And what are you doing there all by yourself?"

Normally, the XO preferred using the mouse to control the monitor's functions. Now, with his curiosity piqued, he used his fingertips and touched the screen to call up data on the vessel moving due south.

There wasn't much to tell. Lipford knew the object intriguing him belonged to the Chinese Navy. The software also gave him the ship's course and speed, in addition to the gross tonnage.

"Navigation."

"Aye, sir?" The Ensign looked up again.

"What do we have on this vessel?"

The Navigation Officer eyed the screen and noted the ship's size. "Her displacement suggests a patrol boat or submarine chaser." He turned back to his monitor and tabbed through a few fields. "We have information on that area going back four hours; I can pull up her course during that time."

The Ensign went to work. Momentarily, a solid red and slightly crooked line appeared on the screen, emanating from the square and running north. Where it ended marked the limits of the available data.

"She's headed south," the XO remarked. "Can you extrapolate on her port of departure?"

Navigation selected a program running in the background. This application factored in what they knew and used other variables to predict the ship's point of origin.

Once again the screen jumped, and a yellow line joined the red one. This projected route hinted at the nearest land mass—and the suspected area of embarkation.

"Hainan." This came from the Ensign, but he didn't need to say it. Lipford was very familiar with the naval bases used by the Chinese Navy.

"Where's she headed?"

Nav worked his magic once more. Another line appeared—this one green—and snaked ahead of the vessel. The software was designed to locate ports of anchorage, or harbors within a given region. The Ensign used the mouse at his station and selected the terminus chosen by the computer.

"*Huo Shan*. Did I say that right?"

Lipford shrugged. "My Chinese is a little rusty. Tell me about this place—I've never heard of it."

The Ensign consulted his monitor again. "Small chain; looks like two or three islands. Not very big."

"The Chinese don't have a base there," the XO said. "At least not one I know about. What's she up to?"

It was a rhetorical question, one that the Ensign didn't have an answer for. Navigation figured that the actions of this particular vessel probably weren't significant—especially with the current naval activity around Taiwan—but he knew the XO would want to keep an eye on her.

The Ensign didn't wait for further instructions. He pulled up the electronic SOE—the sequence of events database—and entered the contact in the ship's log.

Chapter Twenty-Six ✳ The Fuel Depot

ZHU LING HADN'T INTENDED TO SLEEP, BUT as the night wore on he found himself nodding off. The air was warm aboard the patrol boat, and the motion of the deck below his feet had a calming effect on the Captain.

Ensign Tsao was courteous enough to offer Ling the use of his stateroom. The stoic Captain accepted—without any outward signs of gratitude. He ordered the Ensign to fetch him at the first sign of land.

Ling changed out of his dress uniform and into a set of utilities. He settled into a chair and put his feet up on a desk in the corner. The Captain drifted off immediately, his head bowed and his chin in his chest.

THE ENGINEERING CREW OF THE ST-339 MADE swift work of their repairs; the small vessel had been chugging through the rolling seas for more than three hours. The weather they encountered was part of the growing storm system to the northeast. Bands of wind and rain from the developing typhoon reached far to the south, offering only brief respites between gales. For a time the squall line produced a predictable pattern of swells, but as the boat sailed on the waves became more violent.

Zhu Ling slumbered lightly, rousing himself at the first knock on the door. His unfamiliar surroundings gave him a momentary pause before drowsiness left him. He became fully aware when he heard Tsao's voice calling his name from the passageway. Ling steadied himself as the boat began a slow roll to starboard, getting to his feet and easing open the narrow hatch.

"Have we arrived?" the Captain asked curtly.

Ensign Tsao appeared pleased to offer Ling some good news. "Within the hour, Captain." He turned on his heel and ascended the stairwell to the pilothouse.

Ling considered his next steps; the series of mechanical problems had put the mission far behind schedule. McBride would have reached the island by now, unless the storm—or some other circumstance—had delayed him. But that wasn't likely.

Ling straightened his uniform and exited the compartment, closing the door behind him and heading away from the stern. His contingent of Marines was bunking toward the bow. He wanted to give them one final briefing before arriving on Huo Shan. As he moved forward, Ling's hand went unconsciously to the sidearm he wore on his belt.

* * * *

NEILL STOPPED IN HIS TRACKS. "I DIDN'T SEE this before."

Crockett stepped forward from the rear of the group. "No, me either." Overhead, the wind was picking up, bending the trees in an eastward direction as more rain began to fall. "Probably because we were focused on the dock."

The team had passed the trail that led back to the helipad. Organic debris had littered their path between the tree line and the beach, but the stretch of sand before them now was mostly free of clutter. On closer inspection the scene had an artificial appearance to it.

"Slightly different here," Neill observed. He advanced and extended a hand toward a vertical expanse of vegetation. Vines and other plant life intertwined and masked a rough, horizontal framework that spanned a twelve-foot distance. It was patchy and inconsistent, with gaps spaced unevenly. Each end of the obviously man-made structure was supported by posts set into the ground. Both stood at chest-level.

"It's a gate," Richey announced. Rope around one of the posts secured it. "Camouflaged to hide something."

All four men peered over the screening. The trees were higher here, intentionally cut back for greater clearance. They could see an opening on the other side.

"Looks like a road," Chau said. "I'll bet it leads back to the fuel depot."

"Simon's right," Nate agreed. "I could see it from the cliff. A path here would take you directly to it."

A sudden gust swept in from seaward and howled in their ears. Neill faced the beach and scanned the horizon with McBride's NVGs, pausing to focus on the pier. Breakers were edging closer to shore, and whitecaps were stirring further out. The storm seemed to be gaining strength. Michael lowered the goggles and gripped the gate to steady himself; the force of the wind threatened to unbalance him.

"Let's get a quick look at what's back there," Neill ordered. "And then we'll replace the drive. After that—weather permitting—we'll shove off for our rendezvous with the Brits."

"We still have a good six hours before they'll be in position," Malcolm pointed out. "If I might make a suggestion—"

"Be my guest, Senior Chief." Neill navigated around the nearest gatepost with the others in tow. They were now following the path deeper into the jungle toward the heart of the island.

"Timing will be important. In fair seas, reaching the pick-up point wouldn't be an issue." Richey cast a glance left and right, eyeing the jungle on both sides. The downpour wasn't quite as bad here. "But the weather being what it is right now, things could get a little sketchy."

"He's right, Mike," Nate chimed in. "It would probably be a good idea to minimize our time in open water."

Neill's head bobbed under the bill of his cover and hood. He turned to Richey. "No argument there. Your sea legs are better than mine—we'll gauge our departure with respect to conditions later on."

The trail widened. The palms and tree branches overhead offered a shifting ceiling, allowing sheets of rain to land around them as the winds blew steadily over the island. The team soon reached a clearing. Neill paused to survey the opening; as if on cue, the gusts billowed, drawing back some of the foliage like a curtain.

"There's the depot," Neill said.

Nate stepped up, a grin spreading across his camouflaged features. "Okay, I get it—that's how they transport the diesel."

An antiquated fuel truck was parked next to the towering storage tank, and a small, windowed shed butted up against the rounded steel of the reservoir. Located a few feet away was a pumping station, not unlike the one they'd seen back at the dock. Hoses looped in coils were stacked nearby.

"Hence the need for a road," Richey opined. "The fuel is kept here, away from prying eyes. When the sub comes in, they truck it out to the dock."

"You people stay here; I want a closer peek." Crockett moved out into the clearing.

Simon was right on his heels. "I'll tag along."

* * * *

IN THE WHEELHOUSE, CAPTAIN LING TRAINED A telescopic lens on the sea directly ahead. The optical device was calibrated to adjust instantly to changes in available light. It was a feature designed to protect the user's vision and make the scope more adaptable during storms. To the south, sporadic lightning split the sky and silhouetted the chain that sat on the edge of the horizon, prompting the instrument to toggle between modes.

Ling became aware of a presence at his side. "The currents will be treacherous near the eastern tip of the island." Tsao's voice was low as both officers observed their destination. "I've instructed the pilot to steer south by southeast to avoid the shallows."

"Very well." Ling was impressed. Consulting the charts, he had noted the presence of an undersea ridge, the invisible backbone of Huo Shan that lay just below the surface of the roiling waters. The Ensign had seen it too, and had exercised common sense along with a sailor's instincts—the basic requirements for practical seamanship.

The Captain continued his observations to the south. The menacing clouds marching across the sky erupted with more electrical discharges, and thunder echoed around them, seemingly muffled by the sheets of rain. Rising like a spire, the crater wall on Greater Huo Shan soon came into view.

* * * *

"Not a fan of storms, I take it," Nate said, grinning. He'd seen Chau flinch as the lightning arced above them, immediately followed by a loud clap of thunder.

Simon recalled his childhood experiences at sea. "You could say that," he said in reply. But Crockett's devil-may-care attitude inspired him to adopt a little more bravado, and Nate could see him smiling back.

Crockett was the first to reach the shed. He shined the beam of his tactical light through the window.

"Not much inside," he said. "Some jerry cans and rags. That's about it."

"Jerry cans?"

"Yeah. Gas jugs," Nate explained. "You know, containers for *petrol*, as our British cousins might say."

Crockett knelt at the base of the pumping station. The

mechanism had few moving parts and appeared simple to operate. The Marine gripped a control valve and twisted it in both directions. The low moaning of air escaping the pipe could be heard, followed by a louder gulping sound. Nate could feel a slight vibration as a small amount of diesel fuel spilled out at their feet.

"There's a lot of play in this—hasn't seized up, so they must use it frequently." He closed the valve. "I've seen enough. You still hungry?"

"I'm still hungry," Simon said with a nod. He marveled at Nate's ability to switch gears.

Neill had taken a few photos by the time Simon and Nate returned. Getting intel on the depot wasn't as crucial, but the team's extra efforts might be appreciated by whichever agency ended up analyzing the data.

The weather had not improved. Dropping the camera in his ruck, Neill led the group as they re-traced their steps on the road back to the beach. He had a nagging feeling that bordered on claustrophobic. Being bottled up on the path explained part of it. The imminent arrival of Lee's troops and the mystery of the sub's whereabouts just added to his anxiety.

It was the unfinished business that kept tugging at him. Replacing the thumb drive wasn't critical, but doing so might buy some time. For whom, Michael wasn't sure, but if it helped the team—or frustrated Beijing's aspirations—that was a good thing.

None of that mattered if the Admiral's men reached the island before they had a chance to make the switch. Neill gave that some thought, and by the time the four had reached the gate he had come to a decision.

"When we get back, you three grab some food and get the boat ready." He had to raise his voice to the level of a shout just to be heard. "I'll take Simon's flash drive back to the crash site and replace the one we took."

"I'll go with," Richey said.

Michael shook his head. "I can handle it," he said. "Besides, I need you to assess the weather—and our chances of getting off the island."

Malcolm insisted. He had taken a liking to field work. "You don't need me for that. Besides, don't they preach the 'battle buddy' concept in the Corps?"

Richey was right. "Okay, Senior Chief," Neill grinned. He was silently thankful for the support.

"You're on."

Chapter Twenty-Seven ☆ Dangerous Currents

THE PILOT HAD TROUBLE KEEPING HIS RUD-
der steady. Surging below the waterline was a swirling mass of violent energy, pushed first in one direction and then the other. Waves lashed the hull, alternately
lifting the forward and aft sections clear of the sea—and then
sending the patrol boat crashing down again into the next
swell.

Through it all Ensign Tsao displayed a remarkable calm.
Bracing before the windscreen that wrapped around the bridge,
the young officer watched and waited for the next upheaval.
Steadying himself behind Tsao, Captain Ling smiled evenly;
the Ensign's confidence had grown as the voyage progressed.

"The currents here fight us, Captain," Tsao informed him.
"The sea divides as it flows around the island. But we'll pass
through it shortly." He smiled. "We will fight back—and meet
the swells head on."

The wheel shuddered in the pilot's hands as he wrestled for
control.

"You seem to have found your stride, Ensign," Ling observed. Not since hours before—when Tsao explained their
mechanical problems—had the Captain offered his praise. This
was a rare event.

"*Xie xie*," Tsao replied. *Thank you*. They lurched forward and down again, and as the bow plunged below the waves the twin screws astern spun wildly in mid-air. "Of course, if you prefer another approach—"

Ling shook his head, gripping a railing tightly as he fought for balance. "Indulge your instincts, Ensign. I defer to your judgment."

PLA-Naval Division headquarters,
Beijing

THE LOW-LEVEL BUREAUCRAT HELD THE PHONE nervously. He was barely an Ensign, fresh out of one of the Navy's technical schools and ill-suited for working behind a desk.

His shift was normally uneventful, but tonight he had received several messages. Each had something to do with the exercises being conducted in the waters surrounding Taiwan; progress reports mostly, detailing the status of various ships in the fleet and intended to bring the Admiral's staff up to speed.

The man he spoke with now was a Senior Captain, the commander of the battle group encompassing the island, no less. This flustered the Ensign. The officer's rank gave him a start, and with his nerves shaken, he misunderstood the reason for the Captain's call. In the absence of clarity, the Ensign fell back on his training.

"Should I have someone wake the Admiral, sir?"

The satellite feed relayed his question almost instantly to the operations center of the PLA-Navy destroyer *Luzhou*. Pacing the deck, the phone pressed against his ear, Captain Wei Lao frowned and then reminded himself of the time. A digital clock on the bulkhead told him it was well past two in the morning. Lao was expecting too much; the personnel in the admiralty at this hour wouldn't include the best staffing available.

Lao kept that in mind as he moderated the impatience he felt.

"No, Ensign," he answered slowly. "There is no need to wake the Admiral." Such an action might prove disastrous for everyone involved. Lee might be sound asleep—or worse yet, entertaining one of several women with whom he maintained liaisons. "Our operations proceed without impediment. Simply relay that message—along with my concerns for the weather. The Admiral and I can discuss both topics tomorrow."

That had been the real reason for his call. Reporting to the admiralty was a task ordinarily delegated to a more junior officer. But coming from a Senior Captain, apprehension over the typhoon brewing to the north could not be ignored. Lao wanted to give Admiral Lee every opportunity to reconsider his plan.

The Captain didn't wait for a reply. He had a fleet to command. There were operational details to work out, complicated by the threat of the storm. To the Ensign's relief, Lao ended the call and replaced the phone in its cradle.

* * * *

NEILL DROPPED HIS RUCK AT THE BOAT'S SIDE. Richey, Chau and Crockett did likewise. Simon retrieved his laptop and searched the case for a suitable memory stick. He finally settled on a substitute that resembled the one they had pulled from the wreckage of McBride's helicopter.

Crockett pointed the night scope toward the sea. The place where they'd stowed the boat was a deep hollow, offering natural cover and concealment. At the same time, the foliage restricted Nate's field of vision.

"What's the forecast, El-Tee?" Richey asked.

"Choppy whitecaps close in, with big swells further out." He lowered the scope.

"Maybe things will settle down by the time we get back," Neill suggested.

"I'd make this a quick trip if I were you," Crockett advised. He reached down into his ruck and produced the last of the protein bars, which were hungrily accepted by each man. "How long do you plan on being gone?"

"Only as long as I have to." Neill tore open the wrapper

and bit off one end. Then he turned to Simon, who handed him the drive. "It's not quite a mile there. We'll make this fast," he said, laying out his plan. "The Senior Chief and I will work our way to the crash site and plant this in McBride's pack. Then we'll high-tail it back here."

Chau asked, "What do you want us to do?"

"Get the boat ready," Neill instructed. "But one of you will have to take up an over watch position where you can see the dock. Keep your eyes open in case that patrol boat gets here. If Lee's men arrive while we're back in the jungle, you'll have to figure out some way to warn us."

Crockett frowned. "How do we do that?"

"You'll come up with something," Neill grinned.

"I dunno, Mike," Nate continued. "I'd prefer to tag along and cover your six."

"If I had my druthers, we'd keep the team intact. But if we have to split up, it's best if each pair has someone with recent marksmanship training." Neill eyed the two sailors. "No offense, gentlemen."

Richey grinned between bites. "None taken," he said. "You want trigger-pullers with experience; a tactically sound decision, if you ask me."

Michael turned to Simon. "Don't let Nate eat all the ration packs." He held up the drive. "What's on this, anyway?"

"Old prototype software," Chau answered. The downpour seemed to have found them; the canopy over their heads provided little protection from the driving rain. "It's not even properly formatted, just a lot of random code." Simon began to smile. "It should confuse them for a while until they figure out it's useless."

Neill liked the sound of that. "You ready, Senior Chief?"

Malcolm nodded. "Let's move out."

Crockett was more concerned than he let on. "Just don't screw this up," he warned.

* * * *

THE PATROL BOAT HEAVED FROM PORT TO STAR-board as it sailed past the eastern tip of the island. Under orders from Ensign Tsao, the pilot steered a course south against the currents sweeping around Greater Huo Shan. As they made their approach, the skies seemed to open up and a deluge poured down from above.

Tsao was concerned about two hazards to navigation. The first was the unpredictable tidal action, amplified by the surging storm and displaced waters of the powerful sea. He answered that threat by giving the island a wide berth. His next worry was the depth below the keel. The ST-339 was a shallow draft vessel, but the undersea ridges here rose abruptly from the depths.

The Ensign scrutinized the charts. They were older than he would have preferred, yet still accurate. Using those, and a small sonar scope, Tsao navigated away from the island; getting too close, they would risk running aground. At its closest point the vessel passed within three quarters of a mile from shore.

The PRC Marines were on deck now, along the railing port and starboard. Captain Ling watched as Ensign Tsao skillfully navigated a course that would take the patrol boat through the swift-moving currents and the furrow of volcanic rock below the waves. The bow crashed through a series of swells, and the troops outside the wheelhouse held their weapons with one hand, while steadying themselves by gripping the rails with the other.

Through the rain, Ling could sometimes make out the black, foreboding silhouette of Huo Shan as it was framed by lightning in the sky. He lifted the night scope to his eye and scanned the long dock as it came into view. The Captain half expected to see the rounded hull of a submarine moored there, but the enclosed basin appeared to be empty. That was good, he thought.

And according to plan.

* * * *

SIMON BEGAN REMOVING THE PALM FRONDS and other foliage concealing the boat. The squall lines that pummeled the area had deposited additional clutter, and rain had collected in the bottom, rising nearly an inch high. With the added weight, he knew the craft would be harder to man-handle out to the beach.

He staged their small cache of supplies next to the inflatable and began looking for a drain plug. He found one at the base of the transom. Simon popped it open and lifted the bow a foot or two above the wet, sandy floor. Water sloshed in the stern, and then started to spill out the hole.

Nate crouched at the mouth of the jungle hideaway and watched Neill and Richey all but disappear as they moved down the beach. Sheets of rain came and went, obscuring his view. After a few minutes, he was able to catch a glimpse of their progress using the night optics.

Crockett frowned again; the worsening weather complicated things. Over watch was only effective during times of good visibility. And as the tropical storm pushed south, that became less and less of an option.

Back at the boat, Simon seemed to read his mind. "See anything?"

"Too much rain," Nate called over his shoulder, loud enough to be heard. He kept his eye trained eastward. Occasionally the downpour relented, allowing him to see two figures edging along the trees near the promontory; both were moving more quickly than they had on their first trip to the crash site.

* * * *

AS THEY CLEARED THE BOUNDARY OF THE CURrent flowing on the southern side of the island, Tsao ordered the pilot to come about and steer a course due north. The Ensign matched the data from the GPS system and radar display and lined up the bow for a slow, parallel approach to the dock. Under normal conditions it would have been no problem, but the swells worried him.

"The seas are rough, Captain. We should make anchorage here." Tsao had no intention of tying up his ship to the dock—only to have her continually dashed against it by the waves.

Ling looked ahead. "There's a breakwater on the opposite side of the pier; the basin itself is much calmer."

He offered him the lens. The Captain was right; the man-made jetty that stretched the length of the pier protected the inlet from the weather lashing the island.

"Very well," Tsao announced. Ling could hear the authority in his voice. "We'll moor the boat to the dock. But if the weather deteriorates further—"

The navigational lights were dim. These were of no use in showing the way. Tsao subdued the bridge illumination for better visibility as he and the pilot nudged the patrol boat forward. Nearing the pier, the Ensign reached overhead to the handle of a small spotlight affixed to the roof. He flipped a switch on the grip and a bright white beam pierced the night.

* * * *

OUT IN THE OPEN, THE WIND WAS MUCH STRONGER. Chau knelt in the sand next to Crockett, but with his unaided eye, he could see nothing. He stared ahead for a moment and then felt his body tremble.

Nate caught the movement out of the corner of his eye. "Got the chills?"

Simon shook it off. "Felt like the hair on the back of my neck just stood up." He wasn't ready to vocalize an opinion, but the gusts had a ghostly howl.

"Probably all this moisture," Crockett offered. "Humidity and sweat combined with the rain. My uniform's pretty damp under this jacket." He maintained his concentration on the shoreline ahead and then thought of something else. "I hope you didn't forget to close that drain plug," he grinned. "Leaving it open would be like having a screen door on—"

Crockett stopped in mid-sentence. Something on the water got his attention.

"Hold the phone," he announced. Nate scrutinized the horizon. The torrential rain abated just long enough to give him a better view.

"*That's a light.*" Chau could see it now too, even without a scope. They'd been expecting this since they spoke with Avery. Simon started to get to his feet.

"Easy there, big guy." Nate reached out to stop him. He remained calm but focused, training the scope on the source of the light. Through the lens he saw the shape of a small watercraft—not as big as a corvette, and much smaller than a frigate. It had the characteristics of a vessel designed for coastal defense.

"Definitely our patrol boat," Crockett told Chau. "Looks like the Admiral's men have finally decided to show up. They're almost to the pier."

He looked below the spotlight and picked out the bridge. Nate began applying his skills as a scout, trying to identify anything that might prove useful. Three or four sailors were now on deck. From the port side a navigational light shone dimly. A bundle of short antennae sat atop the wheelhouse, and a small Chinese flag snapped in the fierce breeze.

Painted in white on the bow were numbers; to Crockett's eyes, these appeared to read *three three nine*. The rest of the boat was a typical battleship gray. Beyond those details, the vessel was unremarkable.

"Any sign of our people?" Simon asked hopefully.

Nate had lost the two just before they reached the trail. He looked away from the patrol boat and focused on the jungle; the tree line was the most obvious place to search. His trained eye scanned the vegetation, but he detected nothing unusual.

The beach was next, yet Crockett didn't expect to see his

friends there. Tidal action had brought seaweed and palm branches ashore; but the long, dark clumps offered nothing in the way of concealment.

Nate grumbled under his breath. The narrow strip of sand was empty. His efforts were in vain.

Neill and Richey were nowhere in sight.

Chapter Twenty-Eight ✶ The Arrival

Aboard the USS George H.W. Bush

THE NAVIGATION OFFICER WATCHED AS THE contact proceeded south and then swung around. He'd been bird-dogging its progress since Commander Lipford expressed an interest in her.

"Change in course?" Ghost was already aware of the vessel's actions.

"Roger that, XO," Navigation replied. "She's come about, heading due north now."

Lipford nodded. "Making for those islands," he observed. "Very odd."

He looked to the flight status board next to the cartographic display. It might be prudent to sortie some Hornets to get a bird's-eye view of things, but the XO checked that impulse. He'd wait till they had daylight before suggesting something along those lines.

* * * *

THE TRAIL FELT LIKE A WIND TUNNEL. NEILL and Richey pushed on, but they were fighting against the gale. The two trudged forward single file to avoid the lashing foliage as it was whipped by the gusts. Below their feet the ground was a mixture of grass and sand; the soil and their boots were saturated with rainwater.

Each had left their rucks back at the boat, which gave them a little less weight to carry. They still held their weapons; neither man felt comfortable leaving those behind. With Neill leading the way once again, the clearing soon opened up before them.

The weather seemed to improve immediately. The wind and rain ebbed to a fraction of their former strength. It was tempting to think that the storm might be weakening, but that was a false hope. Both men knew the feeder bands came and went, and the slackening between gusts was just temporary.

* * * *

"WHAT NOW?"

Crockett continued to observe the events unfolding before them. "We sit tight—and wait to see what happens next."

Chau was growing more anxious by the moment. "Do you think they saw the boat?"

"That's a very good question, Si," Nate answered. "Let's think about that for a minute." He lowered the scope and assumed a prone position. Simon did the same. "If they did see the boat, they've ducked into the tree line for cover. And that's a good thing."

Simon followed Nate's line of reasoning. "Or they've reached the trail and are on the path back to the crash site."

"Which is not a good thing—if that's the case, then they don't know we've got company." The Marine raised the scope back up to his eye. "The boat's reached the dock—looks like the crew is ready to tie her up."

In spite of this news, Simon seemed to relax. Thinking it through helped to steady his nerves. "Neill said we should warn him. How can we do that?"

"I'm working on it," Nate assured him. This wasn't the

time for rash action. It occurred to him that Neill and Richey could be between them and the trail, hiding in the trees and waiting for a chance to make their way back to the boat; that was a more encouraging prospect. Until they knew more, creating a diversion might only invite disaster. Crockett had done the math—if Avery was right about their force strength, a dozen Chinese troops carried much more firepower than the four Americans could ever muster.

That reality sparked a thought. A slow smile spread across Nathan Crockett's face.

The beginnings of an idea had taken root.

* * * *

Two of Ensign Tsao's sailors made the leap from the ST-339 to the narrow dock. Two others stood by fore and aft with coiled mooring lines in hand. Once in position, the deck crew tossed the ropes across and secured the looped ends to the pier. The seamen made quick work of it. Within minutes the patrol boat was hugging the dock, gently rising and falling with the swells that filled the inlet.

Taking direction from the boatswain, Sergeant Wen and his troops swung into action and positioned a gangplank across the gap. This was attached loosely, to give with the boat's movement on the water. With the bridge in place, the boatswain looked up at the wheelhouse and gave a nod.

The pilot returned the gesture and reduced power to the engines, taking them down from an idle to all-stop. He cast a glance between the island and Tsao, getting the Ensign's attention. The young officer repaid the look with a curious expression; neither man knew that there was a naval facility on these forbidden islands.

Standing next to Tsao, Zhu Ling watched the PRC Marines from the port side of the bridge. Sergeant Wen formed his men up in two ranks on the narrow deck and brought them to attention. Ling recognized this as his cue.

The Captain expected to find McBride waiting for them in the clearing. He was aware of what the American had been paid to do; he just had no idea how long it would take. Admiral Lee's instructions made it sound simple enough, but Ling was out of his element when it came to technology.

"We may be gone for several hours," the Captain told Tsao. "If the weather worsens, cast off and make anchorage in the shallows. Should that happen, I'll signal you from the dock when our mission here is complete."

Zhu Ling turned, adjusting his cap and drawing in a deep breath before pulling open the hatch and stepping out into the rain. Closing the door behind him, he descended the ladder well to the deck below—leaving Ensign Tsao and the pilot to wonder just what that mission might be.

* * * *

THERE WAS AN ODD TRANQUILITY IN THE OPEN spaces of the clearing—despite the carnage of the smashed chopper near the helipad. Gale force winds were now replaced by warm, light breezes, and the rain had become little more than a light drizzle.

Neill wasted no time taking in the scene. He marched purposefully toward the helicopter's remains, his eyes sweeping the ground. The persistent drafts of air swept softly through the grasses like waves on the sea.

Richey fanned out to Michael's right side. "Do you see it?" he called out.

Neill shook his head. The case that held the drive was nowhere to be seen. "I remember Simon tossing it aside; I just don't recall where."

"Well, it didn't just sprout legs and walk off," Malcolm grumbled. "Has to be closer to the chopper."

Neill silently agreed and narrowed his search. He moved toward the helicopter's cabin, edging around small pieces of the aircraft as he went. Nearing the passenger side, a slight movement on the ground caught his eye. He crouched down and pulled back a palm frond blown in during the storm. Underneath was the inverted case, lying open and resting in the grass.

"Got it," Neill announced. He stood to his feet and turned it over in his hands. The dark foam interior had absorbed a lot of rainwater.

"Pretty wet," the Senior Chief observed. "You still want to plant it in the case?"

A frown. "It would look a little suspicious if we do that—and then close it up and put it back in McBride's ruck," Neill said. He finally decided on a solution. "Let's not get too creative with this scenario. I say we just leave it open on the ground—with the drive inside—below the busted windscreen."

Malcolm nodded in agreement. "Make it look like the whole thing spilled out during the crash. Logical enough."

* * * *

"THEY AREN'T WASTING ANY TIME," CROCKETT told Chau. The break in the storm gave him a fairly clear view of the dock. "I count thirteen . . . no, make that fourteen troops. Disembarking the boat now."

He watched as one of the men moved away from the rest. Taller than the others, Nate guessed this was their leader—probably an officer, given his swagger. This figure stopped at one of the beams supporting the roof. There was a fuse box attached to the pole at chest level. Crockett had noted its presence while the team collected intel inside the weapons bay, and he knew what was coming next.

"Time to change modes," he said, lowering the optics.

Before Simon could ask why, the length of the dock was suddenly bathed in bright light. He took in the view as Nate tabbed the selector switch on the device. With the night vision function disabled, he brought the scope back up to his eye.

"Got any ideas?" Chau asked.

Crockett paused before answering. The officer barked an order—at least that's what it looked like—and then spun on his heel, his troops following at a brisk pace.

"Patience, Simon," Nate replied slowly. "We can't warn them now—it's too late for that. But there's still something we can do."

* * * *

"That should work," Neill said. "How does it look?"

"Does it matter?" Malcolm asked with a grin.

"Guess not," Michael replied. He stepped away from where he'd positioned the case on the grass. It was lying open and upside down—he didn't want to make it look too obvious. "We're done here."

"Roger that, El-Tee." Richey slung his weapon back over his shoulder. "Let's go home."

* * * *

"They're on the beach."

Nate handed Simon the telescopic lens. He'd just followed the movement of the Chinese troops as they scaled the ladder that led down to the sand. "I was hoping they would stay on the dock a little longer. Maybe go inside for some tea or something."

It was hard for Simon to tell when the Marine was being sarcastic. "No such luck," he told his friend. "I'm no scout sniper, but it looks to me like they're headed right where we *don't* want them to go."

They watched as the troops trudged by twos through the sand. Marching away from the well-lit dock area, the new arrivals followed the tree line west. After a moment, Nate could only pick out jumbled motion and bobbing heads as they advanced on the path that led to the crash site.

* * * *

THEIR MAIN CONCERN NOW WAS GETTING OFF
the trail and back to the beach. Neill would have preferred
another way out, but an alternate exit didn't appear to exist.
Nate had been right; they were bottled up here. From a tactical
standpoint, it was not a position that afforded them much of
an advantage. And using the same route over and over grated
against Neill's training and instincts.

The wind had increased as they marched south. Once again
the two forged ahead single file. Neither man looked back.
Michael considered how fortunate they'd been in achieving
both of their mission objectives, and whispered a silent prayer
of gratitude. He prayed that the grace and mercy they'd been
given would hold out just a little longer.

Neill kept his eyes open—and his rifle at the ready—re-
calling the last time he'd fired a weapon in close quarters.
That had been a warning shot in the Ukrainian port city of
Odessa—against an adversary he now called his friend.

The path began to widen, intersecting with the beach and
giving Neill a clear view of the sea beyond. But something
was different now. The breakers rolling in didn't look right;
the white-caps further out seemed brighter, almost glowing
as they swelled close to the shoreline. As if they were reflecting—

Light.

* * * *

"I SEE THEM." SIMON DIDN'T SOUND PLEASED.
He handed Nate the scope and dropped his head.

Crockett pointed the lens toward the path. He understood
Chau's reaction as his own worst fears were confirmed. What
had been a lonely stretch of beach during most of their time on
the island was now very crowded.

Staring ahead, Nate watched as Neill and Richey came face to face with an entire platoon of PLA-Navy troops.

Chapter Twenty-Nine ✶ Playing Nice

Aboard the HMS Bradford
One mile south of Greater Huo Shan

IT HAPPENED EVERY FOUR TO SIX HOURS, THE activity infrequent enough as to be unpredictable. Working with the seaman controlling the planes, the Diving Officer moved to his station and ordered the boat to periscope depth. The Chief of the Watch repeated the command and activated two valves at the ballast control panel. Compressed air entered the trim tanks, forcing seawater out of the submarine and creating more buoyancy. Simple physics took over at that point as the *Bradford* began her ascent.

Rising slowly toward the surface, the hull began to creak as the sea around the boat relaxed its grip. At about sixty feet below the waves, the ship leveled off, giving the Executive Officer—sometimes called a First Lieutenant aboard Royal Navy submersibles—the chance to raise the retractable mast and take a peek in every direction.

"*Up periscope.*"

At Lieutenant Christopher Adley's command, the optical array nudged its way up through the fairwater. The swells in this part of the South China Sea made visibility a little more difficult, and even at her current depth, the *Bradford* experienced an occasional roll from side to side. It took an extra minute before Adley was satisfied that no surface vessels were nearby; the safety of the ship rested in his hands, and it simply wouldn't do to be run over by some container ship or fishing boat plying these waters.

A low, commanding voice at his side alerted Adley that the Skipper now shared space in the compartment.

"I'll take the conn, Number One."

"Aye, sir. Captain has the conn and the deck—I stand relieved." Adley stepped back from the eyepiece.

Commander Miles Wickett—'Sticky' as his crew affectionately called him—strode into Control and regarded the other watchstanders with a nod. The crewmen already on their feet braced, and those sitting at consoles came to attention. Wickett gave them all an 'as you were' as he scanned the display boards clustered along the bulkheads. Wearing a navy blue woolen pullover—or 'wooly pully'—the Skipper hovered briefly at each station, getting a read on the ship's status. Normally he would be asleep at this hour, leaving Adley or some other junior officer in command, but the tropical storm rolling down from the north had changed all that.

Wickett checked their plot as the communications officer appeared from the comm shack. Leaning into the compartment, he caught the Commander's eye and handed him a printed message.

"VLF traffic, Skipper."

Very low frequency transmissions were intermittently beamed to submarines operating below periscope depth. Boats like the *Bradford* trailed a signals antenna from her sail that listened for those messages. The VLF bursts prompted the sub to raise her communications masts in order to receive orders and instructions from orbiting satellites.

Wickett grunted in reply and read the communique. "Most likely another weather report." He was expecting that.

"Raise the mast?" Number One asked.

The Skipper shook his head. "Not here." He didn't want

to go topside just yet. They were vulnerable near the surface, and their mission in these waters required an extra measure of stealth. The submarine they'd been tracking had been curiously absent of late. Besides that, this was the mystery boat's backyard; if she made an appearance while they were this close to the island—

"Make your course due east," Sticky ordered. "We'll raise the satcomm mast two kilometers from here." He moved to the periscope and draped his arms over the handles. Looking through the viewfinder, he rotated the shaft in a full circle as he studied the horizon. With Huo Shan in his sights he stopped; what he saw surprised him.

To the northwest, light reflected off the swells as they rose and fell in a direct line to the island. Wickett could clearly see the source of the illumination. A series of floodlamps in the ceiling enclosure lit the pier. He narrowed his eye—using the periscope required only one—and gazed on a corvette or frigate as it bobbed snugly against its berth. The boat's navigational lights were on, and a searchlight atop the bridge cast a beam ashore.

"Belay my last order, Mr. Adley." The Skipper collapsed the handles on the 'scope. Receiving instructions from the satellite would have to wait.

"Secure the mast and prepare to come about."

* * * *

NEILL STOOD ROOTED TO THE GROUND. RICHEY did likewise, and both men kept their weapons pointed down.

In his haste to leave the trail behind, Neill assumed that the beach ahead would be empty. Stepping abruptly into the open, he still had his guard up; but he wasn't expecting to see a dozen armed Chinese troops advancing on the path. It was like rounding a corner and realizing that the blind spot on the other side was a collision just waiting to happen. And that was a perfect description of their current circumstances.

The wind suddenly rose at their backs, ushering in a fresh wave of showers. Even in the dark, the first thing the two Americans noticed was the look of shock on the faces of the men before them. An uncertain moment passed as the two opposing forces adjusted to each other's sudden presence. Michael realized that the reactions of both groups during the next few seconds would determine how it all played out.

Captain Ling collected his wits and was the first to act. The stillness was broken as he stepped forward and unsnapped the holster on his belt. He pulled an automatic pistol and pointed it in Neill's direction. Michael's eyes met the Chinese officer's, with Ling offering only a frown and the muzzle of the sidearm in return.

It was clear that the Captain intended to remain in charge of the situation. He barked a command, and one of the shorter troops—a man with a long scar on his face—raised his weapon and aimed it ahead. Richey decided he was probably the platoon leader; an NCO, most likely. On his orders, the rest of the troops began pointing their rifles as well.

Ling stepped forward and continued to regard Neill exclusively. The Marine found the scrutiny a little odd, but at the same time he felt perfectly at ease. Michael issued a silent prayer, but remained still. At his side, Senior Chief Richey followed his lead.

SHEETS OF RAIN WERE FALLING AGAIN. THE downpour had become annoying. For the first time, Simon heard Nate swear under his breath. The night scope remained fixed to his cheek as he watched the drama unfolding nearly a mile away.

Chau strained to see; details were hard to make out, but he could distinguish the group halted at the opening to the trail. From the patrol boat, the spotlight swung around to illuminate the unintended rendezvous.

"This is a big surprise for Lee's men, I'm sure." Nate tried to anticipate their next move. "We know they're here to meet

McBride. My guess is they'll continue toward the helipad—that's priority one."

"Do you think they know about the crash?"

Crockett shrugged. "How could they? And even if they do, they're not going to scrub the mission just for that. These guys will try to find what they came for."

"Can you see what they're doing now?"

Nate pointed the optics ahead. "Everybody's playing it real cool—for now, at least."

* * * *

SERGEANT WEN DIRECTED TWO OF HIS MARINES to relieve the Americans of their weapons. Neill decided it was best not to resist; the Chinese hadn't shot anybody yet. Acting aggressively now wouldn't help their situation.

"If this were a movie, we'd be giving them our name, rank and serial number right about now," Richey muttered under his breath.

Neill managed a grin. "Let's hope the credits don't start sliding up anytime soon, Chief."

Richey was about to reply, but Captain Ling wasn't in the mood for conversation. He spoke almost no English, but was able to come up with an appropriate word for the occasion.

"*Up*—up!" he barked.

Both men raised their arms high. Sergeant Wen roughly patted down Neill while another PRC Marine searched Richey. The NCO then grabbed the collar of Neill's jacket and gave it a tug. There was a pause, and then he issued another directive and did the same to Malcom.

"I think they want us to remove our rain gear," Neill decided.

"What's the magic word?" Richey's growl matched the icy glare he gave Wen.

Michael slowly began to unzip his top layer. "Let's cooperate for now, Senior Chief," he advised. "I'd hate to go home with holes in my uniform. It would come out of my pay."

Neill's eyes swept the troops, taking in details about each one. None of them looked particularly fearsome; in fact, some appeared just a little nervous. He hoped that wouldn't impact their actions. He also noted a few fingers on triggers; a practice frowned upon among American Marines. That was a bit worrisome. The last thing they needed now was some jumpy kid squeezing off a round in their direction.

In less than a minute their jackets were off and being searched by Ling's men. Finding nothing more than a half-eaten protein bar in Richey's pocket, they turned to the Americans.

"I'm gonna need that back," the Senior Chief brazenly quipped. His comment was ignored.

Neill's thoughts went briefly to the code book Avery's office had provided, but then he relaxed. He'd left that in his ruck. Michael was also thankful not to have the original flash drive, and in a stroke of providence, they'd also left the cameras back at the boat. All told, there was nothing in their possession that could seriously jeopardize the mission's success so far.

Another pat-down ensued, but the Chinese Marines collected only a pen, a flashlight, and an empty notepad for their efforts. At a word from Sergeant Wen, one of the troops came forward and produced two sets of plastic ties. He said something to Neill in Mandarin, and then held his balled fists together. Michael understood and mimicked his actions. The enlisted man secured Neill's hands in front of him and then did the same for the Senior Chief.

"Handcuffs," Nate observed. "Those plastic kind, I'll bet." He kept watching. "Now they'll do one of two things."

Simon had already considered that. "Take them to the boat; or herd them back to the clearing."

"Give that man a cee-gar. I'm betting on the clearing, now that they've finished searching them."

"Searching—but not finding." Simon was catching on.

"Roger that," Crockett replied. "Next they'll look for the

chopper—and McBride. The only other place the drive could be."

Chau thought about what they'd found at the helipad and projected ahead. "They're in for a rude awakening," he said.

Chapter Thirty ✷ Flash Point

"SORRY I GOT YOU INTO THIS, SENIOR Chief."

Richey shook his head. "No apologies necessary, Lieutenant. If you go to Vegas, you might as well gamble."

The search had been very thorough. Sergeant Wen examined what his men took from the Americans. Each item was just what it appeared to be. Whatever it was the Captain had hoped to find was still missing.

Ling kept his eyes—and his pistol—trained on Neill. The rain was falling harder now, and without their weather gear the sailor and the Marine were soon drenched. The drive was nowhere to be found—at least not on these two. It suddenly occurred to the Captain that there might be more U.S. troops on the island.

"Sergeant Wen."

"*Sir!*" The NCO stepped up.

"Take four men with you and clear this path. You'll find an opening at the other end. Secure it and wait for me there."

Wen nodded and picked three of his Marines to accompany him. He regarded Richey coolly before setting off down the trail. Neill watched them go and then heard the sound of Ling's voice once more. His tone suggested that the Captain was speaking to him. Neill turned to see him gesture to the trail behind them.

"You speak any Chinese?" Richey asked.

"No. But by the way he's waving that pistol around, I'd say he wants us to follow his men to the clearing."

* * * *

CROCKETT HANDED CHAU THE SCOPE. WITHOUT a word, he backtracked toward the hollow where the inflatable was hidden. His movements were somewhere between a low-crawl and a crouch.

The first thing he did when he got there was to pop open the drain plug at the boat's stern. With the rain falling again—and their departure delayed—he didn't want water up to the gunwales when the time came to leave.

His next action was to open the box of rations. He pulled out one of the packaged meals and tore it open. A sealed bag of condiments had just the item he was looking for. He stuffed it in his cargo pocket and dashed back to Chau.

"What's up?" he quizzed Simon.

"They've just left the beach. The tall one has a pistol on them."

"Headed down the trail?"

Chau nodded. "And completely out of sight."

That news seemed to lift Nate's spirits. "Awesome. You ready to go?"

"Go where?"

"Just follow me. And stay close, Si. It's time for a little harassment and interdiction." What he had in mind carried some risks, but Neill and Richey depended on them.

They had to do something.

* * * *

FOUR OF LING'S MEN LED THE WAY. THE CAPTAIN and the rest brought up the rear, with the two Americans trundled up and marching in-between.

Neill's first thoughts turned to his friends back at the inflatable. So long as the PRC troops were headed toward the helipad, Crockett and Chau were relatively safe. The Marine considered ways that he and Richey could keep their captors occupied and together as a group. Few options came to mind. Ultimately—unless some opening presented itself—Neill realized that variable was beyond their control.

Richey grated out a question, his voice subdued. "You think our friends with the boat saw all this?"

The corner of Neill's mouth crinkled into a half-smile. He replied in a whisper, "No doubt about it."

Michael suddenly pitched forward. A rifle butt was rudely thrust between his shoulder blades. He caught himself and turned to glare at the Chinese Marine behind him, but thought better of challenging the man.

* * * *

NATE LED THE WAY, FOLLOWING THE TREE LINE at a steady pace. The Marine stopped twice to survey the beach ahead and the patrol boat moored to the dock. Crouching behind thick vegetation, he used the scope to study the newcomers.

The metal roof high over their heads offered little protection against the rain as the winds blew. Crockett could make out a handful of sailors on the boat's deck. These few soon took shelter inside the wheelhouse.

"Can they see us?" Simon was breathless as he took a knee next to Crockett.

Nate shook his head. "No way—their night vision's compromised by all that light coming from the pier." He shoved the optics into his pocket. "Let's go."

Crockett got to his feet and dashed off. Within a minute, the two had reached the camouflaged entry point that led back to the fuel depot. Nate shot one more look to the east and then squeezed around one of the support posts. Simon did the same and followed closely behind. The path was wider here to accommodate the passage of the fuel truck, and like their comrades on the trail to the helipad, Crockett and Chau could feel the winds buffeting them as they moved deeper into the jungle.

* * * *

Sergeant Wen's Marines stood facing the helicopter. As the rest of the group entered the clearing, the dusky NCO trudged to Captain Ling and made his report. Without hesitation, Ling replied with a string of dialogue that neither American could fathom. When he finished, Wen nodded with a curt bow and began issuing orders to his troops.

"Not much has changed since we were here last," Richey grunted. Lightning flashed overhead, illuminating the scene and casting stark shadows. The PRC Marine carrying their weapons dropped them near the trail, along with their rain gear. As before, the gale bent the tree tops and swept through the long grasses covering the ground.

Neill didn't reply, watching the Chinese troops as they fanned out around the chopper instead. He took in the view with a casual eye, and noted that the case with the drive still lay where they'd left it. With his men forming a tight circle around the crash site, the tall Chinese officer stepped forward and began inspecting the aircraft's remains.

Ling paused long enough to view the more grisly aspects of the setting. He produced a flashlight and pointed its beam into what remained of the cockpit, stepping gingerly around the wreckage that littered the clearing. For the moment he ignored the bits and pieces of the shattered aircraft; it was more reasonable to assume that Admiral Lee's prize could be found somewhere in the cabin.

The Captain barked an order to the troops, keeping his eyes locked on the interior of the forward section of the helo. Sergeant Wen repeated the command and two of the troops positioned themselves on the passenger side of the fuselage.

Gripping the bent frame where the windscreen had been, one of the men pulled himself up and carefully squeezed into the very opening Neill had used earlier.

* * * *

CROCKETT WAS RUNNING AT A GOOD CLIP AS HE made for the fuel depot. Chau expected to see him slow his pace, but the Marine barreled ahead. Reaching the small tool shed in front of the reservoir, he raised his boot and planted it squarely in the center of the door.

The window splintered in its frame, fracturing and crashing to the floor as the narrow door violently swung open. Nate took hold of the jerry cans stowed in the corner, shifting them to test their weight. Both containers were full. He removed the lids and inspected their contents—gasoline.

So far, so good, he thought. With the broken glass crunching underfoot, he turned and stepped out of the shed and back into the rain.

"Simon, take one of these and park it next to the truck. Put the other one by the pumping station."

Chau nodded. Gripping the handles, he double-timed over to the vehicle and then to the piping that sprung from the steel-ribbed storage tank. He deposited the second fuel can in front of the valve assembly and ran back to the shed. His adrenaline was pumping now.

By the time he returned, Crockett had found a wooden broomstick inside the tiny shack. It was old and dry, and Nate had no trouble snapping it in half across his knee. He took a couple of the grease-stained rags he'd seen earlier from the corner, and wrapped them tightly around one end.

"Head back to the truck and unscrew the fuel cap," Nate instructed.

Simon had a pretty good idea of what the Marine planned to do. He raced back to the truck and did as he was told. Crockett followed, crouching as he ran and protecting the dry rags from the falling rain as best he could. He jammed the end of the make-shift torch into the neck of the vehicle's fuel tank and lifted the jerry can at his feet.

Nate dumped the fuel on the rags and down the side of the wheeled tanker. He emptied half the container just below, allowing a generous amount to collect in a puddle. He poured the rest of it on the ground between the pumping station and the truck, and then tossed the empty can aside.

"One down—"

"—one to go," Simon called out with a grin.

* * * *

THE PRC MARINE SEARCHED AS MUCH OF THE cockpit as he could. It didn't take long to locate McBride's backpack. The young troop displayed it triumphantly and then handed it to his comrade standing in the rain.

Sergeant Wen took the ruck and unzipped the main compartment. He dumped its contents onto the ground, tossing aside a sandwich and some personal items the American had brought along for the trip. The NCO checked the other pouches, but found nothing else.

Looking up at Captain Ling, the Sergeant shook his head.

* * * *

THE RAGS WERE SOAKED WITH FUEL. THE ground beneath the truck was also saturated, as was the short trail that led to the pipes. Nate used half of what remained in the second can to drench the wet, sandy soil around the pumping station. The rest he kept in reserve.

Bending down, the Marine opened the flow control valve on the assembly. The pipe gulped and sputtered, and then a heavy volume of thick diesel began spilling out. Nate stepped back and watched as the two fuels mixed.

"We'll use the gasoline as an accelerant," he explained. "It's got—"

"—a much lower flash point; I know. But if it's a diversion you're after, wouldn't it be easier to just fire a round into the air?" Simon asked.

"*Easier*, yes." Nate patted his weapon affectionately, and then fished around in his cargo pocket and pulled out the condiments bag. Avoiding the gushing diesel, he stepped over to the truck. "But the sound of gunfire would just put the bad guys on a war footing. We don't want a bunch of trigger-happy troops in the neighborhood."

Nate broke open the bag. Just like American MREs, the ration pack included a box of matches. He crouched again, protecting one of the sticks as he struck the side of the box. Flame jumped at the tip, but the downpour snuffed it out. For his second attempt, Crockett used two matches. Cupping his hand around them, he managed to bring the fire close enough to the fuel-soaked rags to ignite them.

The sensation of heat was instantaneous. The torch blazed to life with a low *WHUMMPF*, illuminating the setting as Nate stepped back. He tossed the still-burning matches to the ground; the fuel there flamed up as well. The process had been set in motion, and the growing fire traveled to the pumping station.

The air grew warmer as the flames spread and the diesel began to ignite. An orange light bathed the scene, and Chau could see a broad grin on Crockett's face.

"Combine the right amount of fuel, heat and oxygen and you can get anything to burn—even in a rainstorm," Nate said. He grabbed Simon's arm and then headed off for the trail.

"Time to ride the bullet train to Splitsville."

* * * *

ONE OF THE MORE OBSERVANT MEMBERS OF Wen's platoon thought he heard something. A low, deep rumble—like the thunder, but muffled and localized several hundred meters distant. A flash of light followed. At first, the young Corporal assumed it was just the storm. Glancing westward, he could make out a dull red glow defining the shifting clouds above.

* * * *

THEY WERE HALFWAY DOWN THE ROAD BEFORE Nate took one last look over his shoulder. Two separate fires now burned. The torch was fully involved, with pieces of singed rag falling to the ground.

Aided by the gasoline, the diesel fuel at the pumping station reached its flash point and erupted; not even the rain could stop it now. Crockett and Chau watched as the valve assembly was engulfed.

The truck went next. Fumes rising from the fuel tank met the torch as the flames consumed it. The petrol seemed to resist at first, but then combusted into a fireball. As the tank of flammable liquid ripped in half, supply lines and hoses connected to the vehicle's main reservoir ruptured. A heavy amount of fuel gushed out and fed the blaze. Burning hotter now, the conflagration expanded; hot yellow tendrils began to lick the open wounds of the tanker, and the entire back end of the truck was instantly enveloped in flame.

The two Americans were moving again, but each could feel the air pressure change as the old vehicle exploded with the force of several small munitions. The sound was deafening. Light and heat radiated from the blast as it rocked the clearing. When the intensity of the moment had passed, a billowing shroud of black smoke curled up and met the storm clouds above.

* * * *

THE TROOPS UNDER CAPTAIN LING'S COMMAND flinched and then spun around to face the source of the sudden din. Through the drenching rain, the Corporal was sure of what he saw now. Barely half a kilometer away, a fire was burning in the jungle as a dark mushroom cloud rolled upward and smudged the sky.

For the Chinese troops, this was the morning's second unexpected turn of events. Sergeant Wen's first thought was to set off in the direction of the bonfire. Seeing the smoke and flames, he looked to the Captain.

Ling's raking gaze went to the two bound Americans. Their faces were expressionless, reflecting only traces of the firelight that glowed from the windswept tree tops. He kept his pistol pointed at them and then returned Wen's questioning stare.

"Take your men—you'll find a fuel depot in the next clearing."

"Or what's left of it," the NCO snorted.

The Captain had considered that. He could see the pulsing aura in the distance. As the ferocity of the eruption diminished, one thing was clear to him. Ling had visited the island once before, and was well aware of the depot's storage capacity. Looking back at Wen, he shook his head.

"I doubt that. See to it, Sergeant—the diesel stored there is vital to naval operations on this island."

Wen regarded the two prisoners. "I'll leave men here to—"

"*Take all of them.*" Ling's voice carried a commanding tone. "I can manage these two. That fire didn't start by itself. There are probably more Americans on this island."

Wen was hesitant, but then nodded and growled an order to his men. As the rain continued to fall, he set off for the trail with the PRC troops following him.

* * * *

CROCKETT PULLED THE MACHETE FROM ITS sheath and hefted the blade in a downward arc. The coil of rope that held the gate broke free. Gripping it with his gloved hands, he swung it open. Chau edged out onto the beach and looked eastward.

"Do you think we got their attention?"

Nate smiled at the question. "They'll come runnin'." He

started off again, heading for the boat.

"And you *want* them to see the open gate."

"We missed it the first time—I don't want them to," Crockett called over his shoulder.

* * * *

THEY WERE COMPLETELY ALONE NOW. WITH Sergeant Wen and his troops dispatched to the fire, only Neill, Richey and the Captain stood in the clearing.

Ling's eyes went to the ground. The case with the flash drive lay at his feet, and he seemed to notice it for the first time. He stooped and turned it over, probing the wet foamed interior with his fingertips. When he stood again, he held the small storage device in his hand.

The tall officer relaxed his grip on the pistol. He paused briefly, and then appeared to be overcome with urgency. Facing the two men, he holstered the weapon, snapping it in place at his side. Neill watched, disbelieving, but what the Captain did next shocked the Marine even more.

"You look surprised, Lieutenant Neill," Ling said simply. Something like a smile appeared on his face. "Do my actions puzzle you?"

Richey was listening intently. He noted the distinct change in language; the foreigner's words still weren't clear to him, but Neill seemed to catch on right away.

And with good reason. Captain Ling's Russian was nearly flawless.

Chapter Thirty-One ⭐ White Dragon

FLOATING SERENELY ABOVE AN UNDERWATER ravine, the *Bradford* was lined up on a direct path to the dock. Commander Wickett draped his arms around the periscope mast and gazed through the viewfinder. The man seemed to have a talent for picking just the right moment to survey the surrounding seas.

"Wicked good fireworks. Looks like they're throwing a party." An understated British wit was evident in his voice. He watched the fireball roll skyward. "Sonar, conn."

"Conn, sonar, aye sir." The Leading Seaman's eyes never left his console.

"Any side-scan contacts?"

"Conn, sonar; no contacts at this time."

He needn't have asked. If the sonar man's equipment had detected anything, the young sailor would have let the Commander know immediately.

Wickett viewed the scene for several more minutes. Some kind of fire now lit the skies in the center of the island. He stepped back from the pedestal to give Lieutenant Adley a look. His Number One rotated the 'scope as the boat swung to the east.

Adley acknowledged the spectacle with a grunt and moved away, allowing Wickett to study the horizon for a moment more. At length the Commander snapped the handles against the mast and began issuing orders.

"Down 'scope."

The hydraulics hissed quietly as the optics were retracted. Wickett turned to navigation. "Helm, make your course due east—and trim her up quietly. Speed five knots. Maintain current depth."

The Navigation Officer nodded and checked his display. "Aye, sir; my rudder is due east, course zero nine zero, speed is five knots. Maintaining current depth."

* * * *

ENSIGN TSAO'S VIEW OF THE ERUPTION WAS hindered by the glare coming from the pier. He wouldn't have seen it at all if he hadn't been facing west. Only the initial burst was visible as it rose above the jungle.

He considered sending a few of his sailors ashore to offer assistance. That idea was immediately scrapped; Tsao had his orders, and Ling had a dozen Marines at his disposal. Counting the Captain—and that squat, severe-looking Sergeant—the PRC troops outnumbered the Ensign's crew by three men.

* * * *

CROCKETT AND CHAU SPRINTED THE LAST HUN-dred feet. Nate reached the boat first, dropping to the hard-packed sand in a prone position. Simon arrived seconds later, and the two turned to face the chaos.

The Marine retrieved the night scope from his jacket and pointed it toward the open gateway. Training the lens further east, he saw the bulk of the Chinese troops spill out onto the beach and begin a dash in their direction.

"We got back just in time," Nate breathed.

Simon followed their movement with his unaided eye. "Let's just hope they're more interested in the fire—and not us. I guess we'll know in a minute or two if your diversion worked."

Crockett gave his friend a smile. "Our diversion, Si. And trust me, it will." He lowered his head a little and spied forward. "The whole idea is to divide their forces—give Neill and the Chief some wiggle room." His grin widened. "Hey, I didn't know you squids could run like that."

Chau smiled but otherwise ignored the comment. "What's next?"

"We wait till they disappear down that road," Nate answered. "And then we take the boat out for a little spin."

* * * *

Neill instinctively checked his blouse. Their ID tapes had been removed before leaving the *Industrious*.

"He knows you," Malcolm blurted. He couldn't understand anything else being said, but he was fairly sure that *Neill* sounded the same in any language.

"Yeah, I caught that." Neill stared at their captor from beneath his visored cover, rain dripping from the bill. The Chinese officer had initiated the conversation; Michael waited to see if there was more to come.

"*Gospoda.*" *Gentlemen*, he continued. "Captain Zhu Ling, People's Republic of China. No heroics, Lieutenant Neill. You and I must come to an understanding."

"*Vy gavaritye pah-Rooski.*" *You speak Russian.*

"*Da,*" Ling answered.

"And how do you know my name?"

"We don't have time for that." Ling's accent suggested northern Russia, probably Moscow. "There's a great deal I must tell you first."

"You're both speaking Russian?" Richey asked nervously. "Is there something here I should know?"

Michael nodded, but skirted Malcolm's second question.

"I'm listening, Captain."

* * * *

CROCKETT LOWERED THE SCOPE AND GOT TO HIS feet. The PRC troops had found the gate and were following the road toward the depot.

Without a word, the Marine ran back to the boat and waited for Simon to take his position on the other side. Nate gave him a nod, and the two men took hold of the gunwales and began carrying the launch toward the water.

"As long as we're moving, there's a chance we can help," Crockett explained.

"What if Neill and the Chief manage to get free—won't they try to get back to the boat?"

"That's what I'd do. But we'll signal them long before they get that far."

THE INFLATABLE FOUGHT TO MAKE HEADWAY AS the two pushed it forward. Once they were knee-deep in the surf, they hopped over the gunwales and into the boat. Chau lowered the outboard and started the engine. The props churned below the surface as they motored through the breakers to the open sea.

Richey had taught them to take swells head-on and the rigid little vessel soon cleared the most treacherous waves. Nate patted a pocket and was reassured by the presence of his tactical light. One more thing occurred to him, and he turned to face Simon.

"Check that screen door, willya?"

Chau didn't have to. He'd reset the drain plug before they dragged the boat out onto the beach.

* * * *

LING PALMED THE DRIVE AND HELD IT UP FOR Neill to see.

"You came for this—am I correct?" He smiled and shook

his head. "But when we met, you were leaving—empty-handed. Did Willis Avery send you all this way for nothing?"

The Captain was full of surprises. Neill kept a poker face and didn't say a word.

"Suppose I tell you what it is you're after. Will you trust me then?"

The Marine considered his options. Ling had shown a measure of good faith when he put away his weapon. Even with their hands bound, the two Americans could have easily overpowered him. Neill decided to step out and reciprocate the foreign officer's trust.

Suddenly the truth dawned on him. Only a handful of individuals would have guessed at their mission on Huo Shan; even fewer could link them to Willis Avery. Ling had done both.

"You sent that letter to our ambassador—as well as the message to Willis Avery."

The Captain nodded. He'd contacted Avery before leaving Hainan from a small internet café.

"You're White Dragon." Neill was going out on a limb, but his statement fit the facts. He stared at Ling intently.

The Captain didn't react. "The information on this drive— or at least a drive somewhere on the island—" Ling eyed the device suspiciously—"contains critical navigational software. Have you ever heard of the Squall torpedo, Lieutenant Neill?"

"We call it the '*Tempest*'." Michael allowed himself to relax. "It's easier to say—and way cooler. We couldn't help but notice that you've got a few of them stashed around the corner."

Ling's eyes widened. "Then you have been busy. Do you know anything about the weapon?"

Neill gave a nod. "It's very fast—and very deadly. As I understand it, one of your country's submarines was destroyed by just such a weapon." He saw the pained look on Captain Ling's face and decided to press the subject. "We also know that Admiral Lee had something to do with it."

Ling dodged the issue. "Your assessment of the device is correct; it can travel at tremendous velocity. But it suffers from two design flaws. The first is created by the mechanism that makes those speeds possible."

"The rocket motor?"

The Captain shook his head. "You're getting ahead of me—the booster is the second problem; the first lies in the torpedo's nose."

"The ejector ducts." Neill focused on Ling's words; he wasn't about to miss an opportunity to replace conjecture with fact. "What about them?"

"The ducts are the conduit for the gas that envelops the casing." The Captain slowed the pace of his words, taking on an instructional tone. "But during operation, they produce a great deal of interference—effectively neutralizing any possibility of guidance."

Senior Chief Richey stood by patiently, watching the faces of both men as they spoke. Things seemed to be going well between them. But he couldn't ignore the plastic ties around his wrists, digging into his skin.

"Hey, El-Tee," he broke in. "Maybe this fella could get us out of these now, huh?"

Neill wasn't thinking about the handcuffs. His mind began filling in the blanks. "Without guidance, the missile would have a very limited effective range."

Ling was impressed. "Essentially rendering the rocket—what would you call it?—a 'fire and forget' weapon. If the target changes course *after* the torpedo leaves the tube—"

"—then it's a miss," Neill finished for him. "And McBride found a way around that?"

A nod. "His software is designed to do two things; the first interfaces with guidance pods built into the stabilizer fins. An additional algorithm stabilizes the weapon for shallow water use."

Michael eyed the Captain shrewdly. "Shallow water—as in the coastline of Taiwan?"

A slight cringe. The expression was answer enough.

Neill thought back to the exposed tail section of the torpedo in the bay. Richey had been half right; the devices on the stabilizers were tied to steering. Taking it all together, another question came to mind.

"What was McBride's plan in coming here—aside from delivering the drive?"

"The Admiral paid him to install the software and test its function. A very simple process, really. Once complete, all of us would leave the island."

Neill frowned. "And what about the weapons?"

Ling lowered his eyes and spoke slowly.

"Somewhere out there is a submarine, Lieutenant Neill. An Oscar class boat waiting until we leave. And once we do—"

* * * *

THE TRUCK AND THE PUMPING STATION WERE in flames. The Sergeant and his Marines got as close as they could, but the fire was just too hot. Wen saw a possible angle of approach at the rear of the valve assembly. If he could get in from behind and shut off the flow of diesel, there might be a chance to stop the fuel that fed the blaze.

The depot itself was still intact. Wen knew that wouldn't last long. If it got too hot, the steel reservoir would rupture, and the containment would fail. The resulting blast would dwarf what had come before.

The NCO gathered his courage and circled the fire. Ducking behind the small shed, he was protected from the heat. If he could edge along the wall of the giant fuel tank, he might be able to keep some distance between himself and the scorching air.

* * * *

"TELL ME ABOUT THE SUB."

"It was purchased years ago—off the books. She has a crew of nearly two dozen, led by a man named Zhen and hand-picked by the Admiral. The boat is called *The Talon of the Seas*."

"Sounds like a pirate ship," Neill said. There was a measure of disgust in his voice.

The Captain shrugged. "A rogue vessel crewed by brigands—guilty of crimes against their own countrymen. Your appraisal is a fair one, Lieutenant."

Neill sensed more than just agreement in Ling's tone. He seemed to genuinely disapprove of the boat's mission.

"You said the rocket booster was a problem."

Ling turned to face the path. Sergeant Wen and his Marines were still tending to affairs at the fuel site. "On occasion, the motor ignites prematurely. The Russians believe it has something to do with the liquid fuel mixture."

Neill recalled the Chief's research. "Is that what happened to the *Kursk*?"

The Captain gave a humorless smile. "Let's just say we were warned."

A rushing sound of more wind and rain came from the west. Another round of showers swept across the island, the downpour increasing as the storm grew in strength. The three men braced themselves against the powerful gusts.

Richey couldn't make heads or tails of what was transpiring before him. He felt at ease because of Neill's rapport with the Chinese officer. Malcolm trusted the Marine's judgment, but he couldn't ignore the gnawing sense that staying here put them in danger.

Michael raised his voice and asked, "What's Zhen's mission?"

Ling cleared his throat. "After we leave, he'll slip into port and retrieve the torpedoes. Then he sails for Taiwan—where he will sink one of our own ships."

Had he heard right? Neill mulled that over and realized just how diabolical the Admiral really was.

"Let me guess—Zhen sinks a Chinese naval vessel, but keeps the *Talon* out of sight. Giving the PLA-Navy—"

"—an excuse to blame Taiwan and strengthen the blockade." The Captain cast another nervous glance at the trail; there wasn't much time left. He pulled a long knife from a sheath on his belt and stepped forward.

* * * *

THE SWELLS WERE MUCH HIGHER THAN BEFORE. In the back of the boat, Simon cringed each time the inflatable smacked against one. Nate instinctively burrowed into the bow, adding ballast and lowering the tiny vessel's center of gravity. At times, both men feared they might capsize.

* * * *

SERGEANT WEN FLATTENED HIS BACK AGAINST the curved surface of the massive storage tank. He could still feel the intense heat of the flames as he inched toward the pumping station. His uniform was drenched, and the rain jacket he wore was fire-resistant. The NCO hoped that combination would protect him long enough to reach the valve assembly.

At that moment, the torrent of rain increased, tamping out some of the blaze and giving him just the opening he needed.

* * * *

"STEER LEFT!" NATE CALLED. THE BOAT WAS taking a pounding as the waves rolled toward shore.

Simon angled the tiller to starboard, causing the launch to move in the opposite direction.

"You mean *'port'!"* the sailor called back.

Crockett tumbled backward as the vessel changed course. *Port, starboard; left, right.* He knew the difference—he was a Marine, after all.

"Whatever—just navigate this thing between swells." Taking them head-on wasn't working anymore.

* * * *

LING SLIPPED THE BLADE OF THE KNIFE BE-
tween Neill's forearms and cut through the plastic. Stepping
before the Senior Chief, he did the same. Now free, the two
men began rubbing their wrists, feeling the pain fade as their
blood started to flow freely again.

"You should leave, Lieutenant. I assume you have a way
off this island."

Neill had a few more questions. "Why are you doing this?"

Ling said nothing, but gave the Marine a knowing look.
He stooped down and knelt on the wet soil, producing his
flashlight from a pocket. He flipped it on, pointing the beam
downward. Using the tip of the blade, he traced a simple arc
in the sand.

"Do you understand now, Lieutenant?"

Michael knelt at Ling's side and took the knife. He du-
plicated the arc, inverting his so the two curved lines now
intersected on one side. On the other, the lines joined together,
forming a point. With the drawing of the *ichthus* complete,
Neill handed the long blade back to the Captain.

"We both know what the Admiral plans to do," Neill began. "You could stop him."

Ling stared at the ground. "That would require great sacrifice."

"True," Michael allowed. "In this case, I'm guessing that
only you can do the right thing; it's not always easy. But for
those who have responsibility thrust upon them, it's the only
correct path."

The Captain's eyes were still cast downward. Neill waited
for him to respond as the clouds opened up, obliterating the
drawing at their feet.

* * * *

THE RAIN HAD DONE ITS JOB. THE FIRE HAD
been beaten back by the downpour, and Sergeant Wen was

able to reach the pumping station unscathed. Shielding himself with one upraised arm, he was able to grip the control valve and shut off the flow with his gloved hand.

The PRC Marines recognized their own need for self-preservation, but that meant taking some risks. One of the men jumped into the cab of the truck and released the brake. The rest took up positions on either side—as far from the burning rear section as they could—and began the laborious task of pushing the vehicle away from the base of the reservoir.

A brief cheer went up as they managed to get what was left of the tanker out of the fire zone. Sergeant Wen ran back to the protection of the shed. He checked his limbs and was surprised to find that he was uninjured. The NCO then slogged back to his troops.

Wen surveyed the scene. The truck was now clear of the depot—the cab was intact, but the big fuel tank on the back had collapsed in the blast. The residual flames were all but gone. The fire at the pumping station shifted, dampened as the rain fell and chased it to points where only small pockets of diesel remained.

The Sergeant had succeeded. The blaze had been reduced, and the depot itself was out of danger. There was nothing left for the Marines to do now but report back to Captain Ling.

* * * *

RICHEY DECIDED HE COULD BE MORE USEFUL gathering their gear. He went over to where the Chinese Marine had dropped it and put on his Gore-Tex. Slinging his rifle over his shoulder, the Senior Chief picked up Neill's raincoat and weapon.

Ling sheathed the knife and looked toward the path as Malcolm returned. Neill decided to try again.

"You'll need incontrovertible evidence if you want to stop the Admiral."

The Captain smiled but offered a non-committal answer.

"The proverbial 'smoking gun?' "

"Something like that. Do you have one?"

"You should go," Ling repeated.

Richey handed Neill his jacket. The Marine slipped it on and took his rifle.

"What about you?"

A smile. "The two of you overpowered me. I was unable to stop you. During your escape, I was injured by a blow to the head."

Neill gave him a sideways look. "Think you can convince your men of that?"

Ling nodded. "If I apply enough blood." He studied the interior of the smashed chopper. "And I think I can find plenty of that."

Michael watched as the Captain fingered the small storage device. "Just one question, Lieutenant—is this the drive that McBride brought with him to the island?"

Even if it was, the point was moot. Neill grinned. "I think you know the answer to that."

Ling thought it over. "I suppose so," he agreed.

The current circumstances offered Ling a wide range of options; he could always claim that the device was never found, or that it was destroyed when the helicopter crashed. In any case, he had no intention of turning it over to Admiral Lee.

"Do the right thing, Captain," Neill urged.

Through the rain he saw the Chinese officer nod. Neill returned the gesture, and a moment later, he and Malcolm were racing down the path.

As he watched them go, Ling made his choice. He knew now that the device he held couldn't be the one he'd come for. No matter how much they might trust him, the two Americans would never leave the island with the real drive in Chinese hands.

Ling placed the small object on a chunk of volcanic rock. Raising his boot, he crushed it under his heel. The Captain gathered the fragments in his hand and then tossed them into the shattered cockpit.

Chapter Thirty-Two ✶ Cracking the Code

San Diego

FITZROY EYED THE CLOCK ON THE WALL. TIME passed, yet Ensign Pressman still toiled at her computer. It was clear that she was on to something, but the Commander had no intention of pressing her for details. At least not yet.

Earlier he'd toyed with the notion of scooting out early; that was before the tasking from the office of the National Security Advisor. Now the priority had been set. Fitzroy sighed. Quitting time might come and go, but without measurable progress—or even with it—no one would be headed home any time soon.

The Commander had resigned himself to his fate when he saw a flurry of activity from Pressman's cubicle. The young Ensign gathered up a stack of notes and got to her feet. She paused long enough to collect her thoughts before crossing the floor to Fitzroy's office. Her stride suggested purpose, and she stopped in front of Fitzroy's desk.

"You cracked McBride's encryption?" The Commander gestured to a chair.

The young woman took a seat. "The code was complicated—layered with no apparent rhyme or reason."

"You chased a few rabbits."

"A whole brace of 'em." *Or was it a covey?* She shook her head. It didn't matter now. "Anyway, here's what I've got."

"Just give me the Reader's Digest version," Fitzroy cautioned.

Kelsi found her starting point. She shuffled her notes and squared her shoulders. "Tangents are fundamental to differential geometry. McBride's math takes into account anomalies that exist under only a few conditions; number one, extremely high speeds, and two, an underwater environment."

Fitzroy leaned back in his chair, a somewhat puzzled look on his face.

Kelsi smiled. "It's all about navigation and steering. Flow dynamics, hydrologic variables; how they relate to the passage of sound waves within thermocline layers." The Ensign glanced across the desk. "There's even some Euclidean spatial equations thrown in, and an algorithm intended to interface with some kind of guidance protocol."

"To what end?" Fitzroy grabbed a notepad.

She drew in a deep breath. The answer to that question required a little speculation.

"Paired with the right hardware, this operating system would be ideal for a high-velocity weapon—like a torpedo."

The Commander's brows were knit together. He was taking a few notes of his own now. "Effective enough to be a game-changer?"

She gave a shrug. "As long as it works—and there's no reason to believe it wouldn't. The science behind it looks pretty sound."

"Okay." Fitzroy considered his next move. "I'll contact Mr. Avery's office."

"Hang on," Pressman said. "That's just the first part."

"I'm listening."

"I've seen this line of code before," she continued. "It's got McBride's fingerprints all over it—and I've come up with a scenario that fits in with current events. I just need you to authorize something."

Huo Shan

"I TAKE IT THAT WAS WHITE DRAGON."

"You'd be right," Neill called out as they ran.

"You want to explain what just happened back there?"

Neill and Richey reached the point where the trail opened up on the beach. Light from the pier still reflected on the choppy seas—but this time there was no reception committee to surprise them.

"We'll have time for that later."

Michael wanted a few answers himself. The question of how White Dragon knew his name was first on the list.

NEILL'S EYES SWEPT THE SHORELINE TO THE west. There was no activity to be seen. He switched on his tactical light and signaled in the same direction: one long, two short.

Neill expected a reply in kind, but his sign went unanswered and the beach remained dark. He flashed again. Still nothing.

"*There!*" Richey pointed. Out of the corner of his eye he saw a red beacon, flashing one short and two long. The source came from a point several hundred yards out to sea.

"That's Crockett's counter-sign—they're in the boat," Neill announced. He sounded relieved.

As he watched, the red beam came on again—steady this time—and pointed toward the dock. The message was obvious.

"He wants us to head for the pier." Neill turned to face Richey. "You ready to get wet?"

Malcolm smiled. "You mean more than we are right now? I don't think that's possible."

Neill was about to reply when his eyes returned to the tree line.

"Uh-oh."

Richey saw it too. A quarter of a mile away, Sergeant Wen and his Marines had exited the road and were moving back toward the trail.

* * * *

DRAPED ACROSS THE BOW OF THE BOAT, NATE pocketed the flashlight. He turned to Simon as he guided the inflatable between swells.

"*They saw us*—make for the end of the pier."

With the spray in his face, Chau nodded and nursed a little more speed out of the engine.

* * * *

SERGEANT WEN STOPPED IN HIS TRACKS AND turned his head to one side. He blinked as he looked ahead. There on the trail—moving toward the beach and away from them—were two figures. The NCO recognized the Americans, but Captain Ling was nowhere in sight.

Wen growled an order to his men and took off in pursuit.

* * * *

RICHEY ASKED, "ARE YOU SURE THIS IS A GOOD idea?"

Their boots kicked up sand as they got closer to the dock. "Would you rather go the other way?"

The Senior Chief followed the Marine as he ducked under the pier. A quick glance over his shoulder helped him decide.

"I think I see your point."

NEILL SCALED THE LADDER AND FOUND HIM-self topside. The bow of the patrol boat heaved in the swells just a few dozen feet away. Rain was blowing in at an angle. Pointing his weapon ahead, the Marine could see no one.

Malcolm joined him seconds later. The glare of the overhead lights was more intense than either man had expected; the last time they'd been here, the entire facility had been dark.

Neill's eyes tracked west again, but it was impossible to see the approaching launch. He focused next on the patrol boat's wheelhouse. A soft glow lit the interior. Two figures could be seen through the glass; one stood closer to the windscreen, peering through the beads of water that dappled its surface. Michael watched as a hand wiped away condensation that had built up on the inside. Now both watchstanders on the bridge had seen them.

Neill didn't wait for them to react. He slung his weapon across his back. Malcolm followed suit.

"Time to go."

Tugging on Richey's arm, the Marine took off at a trot. With the Senior Chief at his side, both men sprinted toward the end of the dock.

* * * *

WEN'S EYES FOLLOWED THE AMERICANS AS they made their way to the top of the boardwalk. Their intentions weren't clear; *did they plan to seize control of the cutter?*

He halted his troops as the two began moving toward the gangplank. Once they began their dash to the sea, the NCO dropped to one knee and shouldered his rifle. He was acting on instinct now.

He led them with the front sight of his weapon, keeping the muzzle just ahead of their advance. Neither man was a specific target; at this distance—and given their movements—the two seemed to blend together. Their rate of speed was consistent, and Wen had plenty of time to get an accurate sight picture.

It was almost too easy.

* * * *

ENSIGN TSAO OPENED THE HATCH. OVER THE sound of the wind and rain, he could also hear the clattering of the strangers' boots as they ran the length of the dock. He called out to them, but they ignored his challenge, racing past the gangway on a path that would end very quickly.

NEILL AND RICHEY LOOKED AHEAD. AT THE END of the pier lay a deep, black abyss. As ominous as it appeared, that was their only hope of escape.

From somewhere on the beach, the two heard what sounded like the crack of a rifle. The report came just as they took their leap from the edge.

For a brief moment, Neill felt weightless as he sailed in an arc over the dark waters. That sensation was replaced by a sharp pain in his back—the round from Sergeant Wen's weapon had struck a glancing blow to his shoulder.

The force of the bullet's impact spun him around. As he twisted in mid-air, his eyes turned upward. Lightning flashed overhead, and the rain stung his face.

His descent felt like an eternity. Neill entered the cold water with a splash, his body plunging below the surface as the waves closed over him. The Senior Chief landed a split second later.

* * * *

CROCKETT HEARD THE GUNFIRE AND SAW THE muzzle flash. His eyes had gone immediately to the end of the dock, and he'd seen Neill's body twisting in the air. There was no doubt that his friend had taken a bullet.

In the space of just seconds, the scout sniper sank the butt of his M-4 into his shoulder. He thumbed the selector switch and readied the weapon for fire. The rear post was just inches away from his eye. Simon continued to guide the boat and watched as Nate lined up for the shot.

"I'll try to keep her steady for you."

"Good luck with that," Crockett called out.

Strangely enough, Chau was able to do just as he promised. Nate's eyes adjusted to the light and he picked out his target on the beach. He was almost ready when small chunks of ice began peppering the rigid gunwales of the boat.

Great, he thought silently. *Hail.*

As the inflatable rounded the base of an eight foot swell, Crockett exhaled and squeezed the trigger.

* * * *

SERGEANT WEN SAW THE SPLASH AS THE TWO Americans hit the water. He felt exhilaration in knowing that he hadn't missed.

Movement directly ahead caught his eye. He squinted into the darkness. The presence of whitecaps was consistent, giving uniformity to the seascape. But plowing through the pitching waves, a small shape pushed eastward, leaving a telltale wake behind.

The NCO got to his feet; the action saved his life. As he rose, a single rifle shot rang out. Wen's senses told him where it had come from, and he could almost feel the approaching danger.

At that instant, he reacted sharply to contact with a 5.56 millimeter NATO round. The projectile struck the rifle's wooden stock, shattering the weapon and breaking Wen's hand. He was knocked to the ground, landing flat on his back as the PRC Marines looked on in surprise.

* * * *

THE BOAT WAS ONLY FIFTY FEET FROM WHERE Neill and Richey had met the waves. Drawing closer, Chau unzipped his jacket and removed his cover. With one hand holding the tiller, he grabbed Crockett by the shoulder and pulled him forcibly back to the stern.

"Take over!" Simon called.

Surprised by the sailor's actions, Nate did as he was told. He settled in next to the outboard as Chau stripped off his blouse. A few dozen feet to port, Senior Chief Richey's head broke the surface. There was no sign of Neill.

Chau considered removing his boots, but there just wasn't time. He crouched near the bow. With Crockett watching in amazement, the young Lieutenant launched himself into the air and dove into the next swell.

Chapter Thirty-Three ✶ Up from the Depths

THE HARD IMPACT HAD DRIVEN MOST OF THE air from Neill's lungs. The weightlessness he'd experienced before was now replaced by a cold, smothering pressure. Aside from those sensations, the Marine felt nothing—not even the pain in his back.

Michael tried to open his eyes; they remained closed. He knew it was important to move, to use his arms and legs to climb upward, but his sense of direction failed him. That didn't matter; his limbs seemed to belong to someone else, and refused to obey his commands.

At the same time, he was keenly aware of the surrounding environment. There was a rushing sound in this dark, new place. It came from everywhere. The din rose and fell in his ears. He could tell that his body was rising and falling with it.

Suddenly the coursing flow of sound dropped away, and he was bitterly cold. His faculties seemed to fade. Neill's perception of this black domain went to a different level, with words and voices intruding on the edge of his drifting consciousness. Unintelligible at first, they grew louder until becoming crystal clear in his mind.

" 'The LORD on high is mightier than the noise of many waters, yea, than the mighty waves of the sea.' "

Michael looked up from his hand-held game. "What makes

you say that?"

His father stared out of the window as the Ukrainian countryside rushed by, a serene look on his face. "Just the motion of the train. Sometimes it feels like riding a boat down the river."

The young teen took notice of the scenery. Lush forests filled his view. It was spring, and the train was headed north to Moscow.

"Do you remember learning that verse?"

Michael nodded. It was one of a few he'd memorized in English, Russian and Ukrainian. He almost grinned, recognizing his dad's penchant for waxing nostalgic—while including a reference to Scripture.

He went back to his game, noticing the rocking motion of the passenger car as it rolled down the tracks. A small table by the window separated the bunks on either side. Michael reached for the bottle of soda he'd left there—it was a Russian brand, and not too bad as long as it was cold.

He took a sip, but the beverage had the distinct taste of seawater. Michael wanted to spit it out, but then noticed that his father no longer sat on the seat across from him; in fact, he wasn't even in the compartment.

That was odd; Michael hadn't heard him leave. The sliding entryway was open, but there was no one within sight.

"Don't you think you've had enough to drink, son?"

Michael put the bottle back on the table. He could feel his throat closing.

"You can't stay here forever, Mike."

The voice had come from the passageway just outside the door. Michael got up and peered down the corridor.

The scene had shifted. It was dark now, the lights from an approaching station casting poorly-defined and phantom-like shadows in the narrow thru-way. But it was empty. Michael found that strange as well; moving from one car to the next, passengers routinely filled the small space.

Suddenly, he felt very cold.

"Where's your jacket, Mike?"

Michael turned, hoping to see his father. He noticed that his arms were bare. He was getting much colder.

"Don't forget about your friends, son. They're waiting for you." His father's voice was strong. The sound of it filled his ears, crowding out everything else.

"Dad?" Michael began to panic. The voice came from nowhere, but everywhere at the same time.

He called out for his father, more loudly this time. There was no answer.

"Dad?—Dad!"

He called again.

The voice seemed to have left him.

* * * *

"DAD!"

Neill bolted upright, his unexpected movements toppling Malcolm Richey. The Senior Chief landed in an awkward heap near the stern of the boat. Collecting himself, he regarded the soggy Marine with a broad grin.

Crocket found humor—and relief—in his friend's return to consciousness.

"From now on, your nickname's *Pappy*," he told Malcolm.

Neill coughed up a mixture of bile and seawater. His heart was racing. Leaning back, he rested against the gunwale. The pain in his shoulder had been replaced with a dull ache.

They were surrounded by rolling swells. The launch pitched up and down as Simon guided them with his hand on the tiller. Nate knelt at Michael's side and held a Marine Corps blouse and a Gore-Tex jacket.

Neill still felt cold—shivering—and realized that the uniform items were his. He was still gathering his wits when Crockett poked his finger through a hole in the rain gear.

"You're one lucky preacher man, Mike," he grinned.

"I thought you said I was sneaky." Neill's voice was hoarse.

"That too," Nate agreed. "You've just survived being shot

and nearly drowned."

The boat hit a rough patch and the four were doused with spray. Malcolm was concerned about the Chinese troops they'd left behind; he faced west, but there was no one in pursuit. To the east, the faintest trace of light began to glow on the horizon.

"What happened?"

Crockett gestured toward the stern. "After you hit the water, Simon jumped in and fished you out—took forever for the Chief to get you to empty your lungs."

Neill hadn't noticed, but save for Nate, each man's uniform was drenched with seawater. From the back of the boat, Chau threw him a casual salute.

Michael coughed again. "I thought you were afraid of water, Si."

"I am," Chau admitted. "But I couldn't let my teammate drown." No one could see his white-knuckled grip on the tiller. Simon had faced his fears, and managed to overcome them.

Nate was shaking his head. "I still don't know how he did it. The Chief dove twice and couldn't find you."

Richey thought back to Chau's parlor trick on the *Meyer*. "I think I've got a pretty good idea," he drawled. "I'm more curious about how you survived getting shot."

Nate fingered a small rip in the soaked blouse. He pulled out a small, rectangular wafer from the tear.

"Tevlite," he explained to the sailors. "Thin layers of composite material. Helps make combat troops a little more bullet-resistant." He slapped his friend on the leg. "Mike made sure we were both wearing it before we left the *Industrious*."

Neill reached over his shoulder. There wasn't a hole in his t-shirt; the bullet had been deflected by the tevlite, and hadn't even broken his skin. He would sport a dark bruise for a week or so, but he was alive.

Richey leaned in with a flashlight and checked Neill's shoulder. "Now count backwards from ten—in Russian."

Michael did as he was told. Richey smiled.

"Okay, I'll take your word for it. You don't seem any worse for wear."

Nate was quick to dismiss his friend's discomfort. "No doubt about it—that's gonna hurt a while. Eight hundred milligrams of ibuprofen. You'll be fine."

Neill's eyes tracked west as he squinted into the darkness. Two miles distant, the lights on the patrol boat glowed brightly.

Malcolm used the scope and focused on the island. "That chaser's bringing in her lines." Once they cast off, the Senior Chief had no doubt what course they would set.

"We can pat ourselves on the back later," Neill said. That brought a groan as he slowly rotated his arm. Fatigue and exposure were gnawing at all of them.

"We're not out of the woods yet."

The Bradford

"Do you hear it, sir?"

Commander Wickett pressed the headphone against one ear. He listened silently for a moment and then handed the device back to the sonar man.

"Low-thrust gearbox?"

Sonar smiled. "Aye, sir." The lad had a grating Cockney accent. "Slight Doppler shift. It's an outboard—same one we caught last night, by the sound of it."

And it's headed due east, Sticky thought.

Someone was leaving the island.

Aboard the Talon of the Seas,
Periscope depth,
Two kilometers southwest of Huo Shan

The massive submarine moved at less than five knots—forward momentum was barely enough to keep her from falling to the bottom. Her twin screws turned at a rate slow enough to ensure that she would not be heard, and the Diving Officer kept a close watch on his gauges; keeping the double hulled leviathan trimmed out was a challenge as the storms stirred the water under her keel.

The Russians had never commissioned her—that honor was reserved for the boats they could afford. She did receive a number designation, but that wasn't enough. For many sailors, a ship without a name was bad luck. The steel workers and craftsmen who built her cared little for superstition, yet they weren't entirely without sympathy. For that reason, some in the shipyard had been creative in supplying a few crude labels. *Whale* was one; *Vladimir's Folly* was another. Most of the monikers were conceived after the truth became obvious; this sub would never sail flying the red, white and blue pennant of the Russian Republic.

A part of the Oscar class—a Project 949A Antey series— she was one of the largest submarines ever built. Her keel had been laid down in 1997; but service in the Russian Navy was not to be. Nuclear boats were a drain on the Republic's coffers; the heavy expenditures surrounding construction far exceeded the sub's operating budget.

NATO's victory was complete. The West hadn't outfought the Soviets; they had simply outspent them. Fiscal constraints plagued every aspect of Russian life, and the military was not immune. And so the designers in Severodvinsk chose a radical and decidedly unconventional solution.

Instead of installing an atomic power plant, the naval architects went old-school. The shipwrights removed half of the reactor compartment, and a massive row of batteries were incorporated into the expanded engineering spaces—if *Vladimir's Folly* ever sailed, she would do so as a diesel submarine.

It was a bold move, but ultimately futile. With more than a dozen Oscars under construction or already in service, putting this last boat to sea could never be justified after the Soviet empire's demise.

Complete but unused, the boat languished at her graving yard for ten years. The stirring economies and militant aspirations of some third world countries offered her new life; Iran took an interest in building up their Navy and looked to their Russian neighbors for help. The ship was fitted out and sold for kopecks on the ruble.

Finding crews for the boat proved to be a problem. As the Iranians focused on land-based systems—long-range missiles and other weapons—the submarine sat idle at her pier on the Gulf of Oman. It became little more than a curious landmark, a navigational aid for ships entering the Persian Gulf. The giant spent very little time at sea.

In the new millennia, brazen ambition caused ownership of the boat to pass discreetly into the hands of Admiral Lee. His own nationalistic agenda was privately shared by many in the Chinese high command, but no other senior officer was willing to risk so much to advance the cause. Xian Lee quietly stepped forward—in silent opposition to Beijing's stated policies—in the hope of using his power and influence to one simple end; to bring Taiwan back under Chinese control.

To make that happen took years of planning. Sprinkled among the admiralty were men of like mind. Lee recruited enough officers to crew his boat; so many, in fact, that he rotated the ship's complement frequently to keep their skills from dulling after months at sea. These were men with complicated allegiances. Lee's plan required the absolute loyalty of patriots; but at the same time, it needed individuals who could ignore the core values that enabled them to serve their country.

At its heart, Lee's strategy depended on mercenaries.

CAPTAIN ZHEN WAS THAT KIND OF A MAN. Standing immobile at the *Talon's* periscope, the rogue officer stared through the viewfinder to a point onshore. Two concerns occupied his mind as he looked ahead. The first was the fire he'd seen raging at the center of the island. The blaze seemed to have diminished, but there was no denying its source. Something—or someone—had compromised the depot, the source of life and energy for the secret base on Greater Huo Shan.

The Captain was sweating now. The world of Zhen and his crew revolved around those stores of fuel. The diesel in that reservoir was their existence. It powered the tiny naval facility that hugged the island's crater, from the lights and generators to the electronics equipment, filtering down to the simplest of mechanisms necessary for operations.

And without diesel, the sub roamed on a very short leash.

Zhen stepped away from the pedestal as the intercom came to life. "Captain—Sonar room. New contact bearing zero six five."

"Can you identify?" Zhen's tone suggested irritation.

"It's very low." The sonar man strained at his headphones. "Something small; sounds like an outboard motor."

Zhen frowned. It might have been the cutter. "Has the patrol boat started her engines?"

"Negative, Captain. Single screw . . . very little cavitation, with correspondingly low revolutions." Sonar closed his eyes, trying to divine further details from what he heard. "It's a launch."

A launch? "What about the British vessel?" While the fire ashore preoccupied him, Zhen was not about to forget the *Bradford*—his second source of concern.

"Steady at five knots, eight thousand meters off our port beam; bearing is zero six two."

"Bring us closer." Zhen turned to his second in command. "What is our fuel status?"

The Executive Officer studied a display next to the navigation console. "Stores are at twenty-five percent."

Zhen bit his lip. *Not good news*, he thought.

"Continue to run on battery power."

Chapter Thirty-Four ✷ Surface Contacts

The Bradford

T HE LEADING SEAMAN SUDDENLY SAT UP IN his chair. "Commander—contact moored at the dock has started engines. He's churning up the water pretty good."

Wickett embraced the periscope pedestal and stared through the viewfinder.

"She's backing out of the garage now. Do you have a bearing on that outboard?"

A pause. "Affirmative, Commander. Signal fading, but still operating on the surface." *That patrol boat just stole the megaphone*, he didn't add. "Bearing is zero six five."

"Helm, course and sounding?"

Adley checked a display. "Course is zero six two, depth below the keel one hundred sixty-eight meters."

Wickett was still watching through the periscope. "Helm, come right three degrees, match course with that Gemini and make your speed ten knots. I want to ID the crew."

"Aye, sir—coming right three degrees, matching course, turn count on the screw is ten knots."

* * * *

ZHU LING STUDIED THE HORIZON. DIRECTLY ahead—the bow was now pointed east—the sky grew just a bit brighter. The Captain picked out the small launch as it fought its way through the swells, but at this distance he could make out few details.

The Chinese Marines reported that Sergeant Wen had shot one of the Americans. That disturbed the Captain. If Lieutenant Neill had been hit—or worse, killed—the Admiral's plan could still go forward. Ling strained to see further. He thought he saw four figures aboard, but until they got closer it would be impossible to do a proper head count.

Ensign Tsao stood next to the pilot at the wheel. The American inflatable was fast, yet it was hampered by rough seas. The patrol boat was less susceptible to the waves, and in time she could match the speed of the launch and possibly even overtake her.

Ling frowned and rubbed his eyes. His hair was matted with blood, and he made a show of touching his scalp from time to time. Tsao wondered if the Captain might have suffered a concussion. The Ensign silently cursed the foreigners, unaware that Ling's injury was all an act.

"Captain, you should go below and have that cut bandaged."

Ling nobly rejected the offer. "I'll be fine, Ensign. Do you have anyone aboard with medical training?"

"My boatswain," Tsao replied.

"Have him tend to Sergeant Wen's fractured wrist—his condition is much more serious."

* * * *

IT WAS THE STRANGEST CONVOY IN THE SOUTH China Sea.

Leading the pack was the launch crewed by the Americans.

The inflatable outpaced the patrol boat that pursued it, but that wouldn't last long. The ST-339 was building speed and began to close the distance.

Below the waves, the HMS *Bradford* trailed both vessels as they sailed east. Commander Wickett's course brought the sub within half a kilometer of the Chinese boat. Still close to the surface, he ordered the periscope mast raised and trained the optics ahead. Sticky was afraid of that—he could see the sub chaser but not the smaller vessel. The bigger boat was blocking his view.

"Helm, Conn—come right three degrees."

Adley responded, "Aye, Conn; helm is answering. Coming right three degrees."

"There you are," Wickett breathed. *It* looks *like a Gemini*, he thought—and it was clear the chaser was living up to its name.

The senior officer magnified the image in the viewfinder. Next he toggled from low-light to normal—although the sky was covered by clouds, the advancing dawn forced him to change modes.

The view improved immediately. Silhouetted against the beginnings of daybreak, Wickett could see the Gemini as it motored through the whitecaps. He increased the magnification again and waited for the ship's eyes to focus. As the image resolved, Wickett found himself looking at the four men who crowded the boat's interior. Three were wearing hats— the distinctive eight-point covers worn by U.S. Marines and sailors.

"*Americans*," the Commander announced. He snapped the handles against the pedestal and ordered the mast lowered. "Helm, increase speed to forty knots and maintain current course." He issued one more order. "And make your depth one hundred meters."

Wickett intended to position the *Bradford* between the patrol boat and the Americans. Taking the sub deeper was only prudent; he didn't want to collide with the Chinese vessel on the way there.

Once more, Adley repeated the order. "Conn, aye; increasing speed to forty knots, staying true on current course. Making my depth one hundred meters."

The Talon

"CAPTAIN, SONAR ROOM—SHE'S INCREASED TO flank!"

The Americans, Chinese and British weren't the only boats in the water. Seven thousand meters astern of the *Bradford*, the *Talon* followed the convoy at a snail's pace. In the submarine world, they were very close.

Captain Zhen was glued to the viewfinder, with perspiration and oil dotting his skin. The air was warm and reeked of fuel—a consequence of life aboard a non-nuclear submarine. Only the forward spaces provided some relief from the smell.

Zhen was sweating for another reason. The pressure was on now. Earlier, he'd witnessed their diesel supply go up in flames—or so he thought. He had been ordered to stay away from the island until Ling and McBride had done their work. But no one expected foreign visitors, and now that decision had cost them precious fuel.

His mind raced ahead as he considered possible options. Without the depot, the *Talon* would have to find alternatives to replenishing her stores. None were particularly appealing.

Using a PLA-Navy vessel was out of the question. The most obvious choice was to contact the Admiral. Arrangements would have to be made for a Russian oiler to resupply them. That would require some finesse and a lot of *quid pro quo* negotiating. Lee would grease a few palms to keep the operation under wraps, but it could be done.

The Captain put those distractions aside. Presently it appeared that the Chinese sub chaser was in pursuit of the much smaller boat. Zhen surmised that the crew in the launch had something to do with sabotaging their fuel stores. And now the British submarine was making revolutions to catch up.

Someone was going to pay for this.

"Continue to follow," he snapped at his Navigation Officer. "Fire Control, load two weapons and standby."

There was a pause, and then Zhen heard a voice on the intercom.

"Conn, Fire Control." The man sounded nervous. "Please specify *type* of warshot."

Zhen cursed aloud. "Fire Control, this is the Captain. *Load two Squall torpedoes.*"

More hesitation. "Aye, Captain. Loading two Squall torpedoes. Standing by."

* * * *

IT WAS TO BE A SUNLESS DAWN. THE INFLATABLE bounced from wave to wave. Neill pulled on his blouse and jacket in an attempt to warm himself, the ache in his shoulder forcing him to move gingerly.

He thought back to Captain Ling's words on the island. In hindsight, the man had to be White Dragon. Everything pointed to that conclusion. He'd given them details that only their informant could have been aware of—and he'd cut their bonds and let them go.

Neill tried to convince himself that Ling's intel wasn't just an attempt at disinformation. He smiled. Two facts argued against that idea. For one thing, the Captain knew his name— and Avery's. How he was aware of Neill's identity was still a mystery, and Ling chose to let it remain that way.

The second factor was the image they'd drawn in the sand. The simple graphic of the ichthus—a symbol of the Christian faith— was all the proof Michael needed.

In his heart of hearts, he knew that Ling was telling the truth.

The Marine looked west over Chau's shoulder. Half a mile

away, the lights of the patrol boat lifted and then dipped on the waves. The seas around them had grown rougher, fueled by the storm surge and the squalls being pushed south. The Chinese vessel was closing—but Neill was convinced that the pursuit was just for show.

Michael's concentration was broken by movement to his left. The whitecaps had a certain consistency to them, yet now something was different. Fifty meters to starboard, the sea rose up, and for an instant the swells were displaced by an elongated mound of water.

A rounded, man-made shape—completely black—broke through the surface, trailing a frothy wake that washed astern. The four men recognized the behemoth as a submarine, but its nationality was in doubt.

Straddling the center of the sub was the bridge fin, a smooth and nearly featureless tower that enclosed various masts. At the bow, twin diving planes cut through the waves and then disappeared as the hull leveled out.

The sail of the submarine was symmetrically rectangular, and the Americans could see seams in the deck plating. In the muted light of the new dawn, Neill spied a small Union Jack painted on its side.

FOUR MEMBERS OF THE BRADFORD'S CREW— including the coxswain—spilled out of a hatch at the base of the bridge. Each sailor wore reflective life vests.

One of the men raised a pair of light wands and got Chau's attention. He began marshaling the little boat closer, and then gestured to a point on the deck where it joined the sail. Simon nodded his understanding and gunned the engine.

With the submarine's decks awash, the launch rode the waves up the side. Chau killed the engine and lifted the blades clear of the sub's hull. Tethered by safety lines, the British sailors grabbed the gunwales as the inflatable came to a halt.

With the deck crew holding the boat steady, Neill and the others disembarked with their gear and weapons. They were surprised to find that the surface beneath their boots wasn't nearly as slick as they might have imagined.

Crockett was careful to retrieve the case of ration packs.

* * * *

CAPTAIN LING CAUGHT HIS BREATH AS THE *Bradford* broached the surface. Tsao saw it too and immediately eased back on the throttle. Both watched as the launch jetted to a sudden stop on the submarine's deck aft of the sail.

"Captain?"

Ling ignored the Ensign and studied the scene. He counted four men leaving the inflatable—each one moving under their own power.

But that meant nothing. He had no idea how many were in Neill's team; the Marine might have been the fifth—

Suddenly the Captain experienced a wave of relief. Standing on the sub's deck, one of the men turned and faced west. He snapped a picture-perfect salute and paused long enough for Ling to recognize him.

* * * *

"CAN YOU BRING THE BOAT ON BOARD?" RICHEY held the British sailor's tether and shouted above the howling wind. On the other side of the sail a massive wave slapped against the hull. Seawater swirled at their ankles.

The coxswain shook his head. "No, sir—not in seas like this. You'll have to leave her."

"That's a shame," Crockett called out. He pulled the machete from its sheath and stabbed each gunwale, running the blade down the length of each. Air in the rigid walls escaped and the little boat collapsed. The *Bradford's* crew were surprised by Nate's actions, but then shoved the ruined inflatable over the side. The twisted remains of the boat lingered briefly on the surface and were then pulled below by the weight of the outboard.

"So long, *Minnow*." Richey seemed upset. He'd grown fond of her since they'd left the *Industrious*.

Nate clapped him on the shoulder. "Women come and go, Senior Chief." He gave the man a grin. "You'll get over her."

* * * *

"CAPTAIN, SONAR—THE BRITISH SUBMARINE has surfaced!"

Zhen swiveled the mast. The Royal Navy vessel was riding the swells directly ahead.

"Fire Control, Captain—range to target."

"Conn, Fire Control, five thousand meters." The Talon had edged closer. "Speed has slowed to five knots."

"Weapons Officer, compute solution; we'll fire one Squall when he dives."

The Weapons Officer looked up from his display, an alarmed expression on his face. "Captain, the missiles need time to warm up—the rocket fuel has been sitting idle for weeks."

"The weapons are turned in their racks daily," Zhen barked. Still, the man was right. Zhen knew he was rushing the process. He keyed the intercom. "Fire Control; expedite pre-load. Send a current to the propellant tanks."

The Fire Control team in the bow repeated the order. Zhen returned to the periscope to mark the sub's progress. The game of cat and mouse had gone on for weeks, but now the British had gone too far—destroying their fuel stores meant the *Talon* was crippled.

Zhen smiled through his sweat. A vengeful man by nature, he had the means to inflict pain in return. Before the morning had fully dawned, he would show his enemy just how dangerous a wounded animal could be.

Chapter Thirty-Five ✯ Sting of the Tempest

Admiral LaSalle's stateroom,
Aboard the carrier USS George H.W. Bush,
75 miles southeast of Taiwan

"I T'S JUST SITTING THERE."

Jim LaSalle held a stack of reports and a weather map. In his other hand was a mug—this one bearing three gold stars. The coffee was hot, just the way the Admiral liked it.

In the center of the compartment, a mess specialist busied himself removing tray covers from a serving cart. Steam rose from a selection of breakfast foods. A decanter of orange juice sat nearby, and the steward placed silverware, glasses and napkins on the small conference table.

Captain DeSouza stirred milk into his cup and took a sip. He leaned back in the plush sofa and took in the surroundings. Except for the sound of jet aircraft overhead—and the low ceiling—they might have been seated in a finely-appointed hotel suite. The room was warmly lit, and through the portholes the sky took on a shade of mottled gray at the first hint of dawn.

LaSalle amended his statement. "Well, almost sitting." He began reading aloud. "Sustained winds of seventy-eight miles an hour. But barely moving. Ulysses is now a full-fledged typhoon, creeping southwest at two knots." He got up from his chair, the report still in his hand. "You hungry?"

The Captain grinned. It was well known that the Admiral rose early—and with an appetite. The aroma of eggs and bacon filled the room and stirred DeSouza's cravings. He stood to his feet and joined LaSalle at the buffet cart.

"I stopped by the CIC," DeSouza said. He piled hash on his plate. "Captain Beacham has reached the rendezvous point. He's sending the *Victory* north by northwest and is awaiting further orders."

"He's a few hours early." The Admiral grunted his approval and gave the steward a smile. "That'll be all for now, Eddie." The messman voiced an "Aye, sir," and started to go before LaSalle stopped him. Still grinning, he hefted the coffee carafe and said, "Make sure we don't reach the bottom of this."

With a smile and a nod, Eddie exited the compartment, closing the hatch behind him.

The two officers took their seats and dug in to their food. Several minutes passed before either spoke. Despite the early hour, both men were well-rested, and the Navy chow would bolster their stamina for the coming day. Glancing at the reports before him, the Admiral had a feeling they'd need it.

"This comes directly from SECDEF," LaSalle intoned. "The President has been briefed on the status of China's surface fleet, as well as their possible intentions. He's quietly—and I stress *quietly*—informed CINCPAC to provide 'all necessary resources' to assist Taiwan's government, should the situation deteriorate."

DeSouza took another sip of his coffee. "That sounds a bit vague. Any other details?"

The Admiral snorted. "The President's not too big on specifics. He wants his commanders in the field to handle things delicately; which means with an eye toward the politics of the region—and back home." His grin returned. "Welcome to my world, Paul."

DeSouza didn't envy the Admiral's responsibilities. Juggling political as well as military considerations went with the territory. He decided to take the discussion in a slightly different direction.

"What's our game plan?"

LaSalle leaned forward and poured more coffee into each mug. "For now we simply monitor the situation to the north-west. Our presence alone should dissuade Beijing from being too aggressive." He thought that answer over, and decided something a little more proactive was in order.

"We may have acted too late, Paul. Their military has grown, and precious little has been done to stop China from manipulating their currency." The Admiral's voice was low. "This administration has lost its way on the field of free trade—and now the enemy owns far too much of our debt. We can't afford to equivocate on the field of battle." *If it comes to that,* he thought.

The Captain was just a little surprised. LaSalle was seldom so blunt when it came to his political opinions. But now that he had shared this one, his intentions seemed clear.

The Admiral sat back in his chair. "Advise the fleet to maintain a heightened sense of vigilance. We need to keep an eye on our friends in the PLA-Navy. I want to anticipate their every move." He consulted the weather map and traced a finger north. "Order Captain Beacham to send the *Victory* into the Strait. Right up the middle, Paul. Have the *Meyer* follow at a practical distance—and by that I mean close enough to affect change at a moment's notice."

"Do you think one ship can make a difference?" DeSouza asked.

"I think the *Victory* can tip the scales in Taiwan's favor—should the Chinese overstep their boundaries."

The Captain nodded his acknowledgement. LaSalle's orders would send the *Victory* into the belly of the beast—two, quite possibly. He wondered which threat would present the most difficulty; typhoon Ulysses, or crossing paths with the PLA-Navy fleet.

Either way, the arsenal ship was about to make history.

The Bradford

LIEUTENANT ADLEY WAS WAITING IN THE cramped spaces of the sail's interior. One at a time, the sub's crew filed into the tiny compartment. The American servicemen entered next. The coxswain brought up the rear, dogging the hatch behind him before turning to give the First Officer a nod.

"Welcome aboard the *Bradford*." Adley wore a wide grin. "Going our way?"

"Hope so—otherwise, just let us off at the corner," Richey said, returning the expression. Then, almost as an afterthought, he said, "Permission to come aboard, sir." He would have given a proper salute, but the mixture of American and British personnel were standing shoulder to shoulder.

"Permission granted." Adley keyed an intercom on the bulkhead. "Crew is aboard; make revolutions for ten knots."

Almost immediately, the deck below their feet stabilized as the submarine surged forward. Gaining speed, the *Bradford* began to negate the effects of the storm-tossed waves on the surface.

"Oh, and this one here—" Richey gripped Michael's shoulder lightly, "—he suffered a bit of trauma as we were leaving the island. He should probably see a doc."

Adley nodded as Neill tried to protest. The XO regarded the newcomers. Water dripped from their uniforms, forming small puddles around their boots. They'd need something drier—the cool air aboard the submarine was enough to create shivers.

"You may have noticed that the bridge makes a poor conference room," Adley continued. "Let's go below and see to your needs."

* * * *

DESCENDING THE SAIL, THE DECK CREW TOOK charge of the Americans' gear and headed aft. Crockett was reluctant to part with his rifle—Neill as well—but Adley assured the Marines that their weapons were in good hands. Crewmen appeared with blankets. Neill and the team gratefully draped them around their shoulders.

With the Executive Officer as their escort, they found themselves in the midst of the submarine's control center. Banks of displays and monitors crowded the compartment. Subdued lighting filled the space, designed to make the instrumentation easier to see.

In the center of the room Commander Wickett stood at the periscope pedestal. He rotated the mast and scrutinized the horizon astern. He seemed amused by what he saw, and then stepped away from the viewfinder.

"Your pursuers are a little befuddled at the moment. They're still following us—but at a greatly reduced speed." His rich British accent put the men at ease. "Miles Wickett, Commander; Her Majesty's Royal Navy—at your service, gentlemen."

The group shook hands and proper introductions were made. Watchstanders on duty regarded their American passengers with curiosity, but only briefly. Wickett offered a jovial comment (or two) about fishing for Yanks, and then went back to tending his ship.

"Number One, is the deck crew aboard and accounted for?"

"Aye, sir."

"Is the ship secure in all respects and ready to dive?"

The Exec checked a row of green lights that glowed from an overhead console. The Officer of the Watch nodded from the navigation board. "The ship is ready in all respects, sir."

Sticky looked pleased and asked, "Sounding?"

"Two hundred and five meters below the keel, Commander," Nav called out.

"Very well. Submerge the boat."

"Aye, sir; Diving Officer, submerge the boat."

The Americans looked on as the British submariners ticked through their diving procedures. Neill made no effort to conceal a grin.

"You okay, El-Tee?" Richey asked.

The Marine nodded. "It's just nice to let someone else drive the bus for a while."

The Talon

SONAR HAD BEEN LISTENING INTENTLY. HIS ATtention was soon rewarded.

"Mechanical sounds emanating from directly ahead, Captain—target is flooding his ballast tanks."

Zhen noted the shift in terminology. That was good. His crew no longer regarded the British sub as merely a contact—it was now a target. He stepped to the sonar station and picked up a headset. Listening to the sounds relayed by the hydrophone, he could hear compressed air being forced from the vessel now in their sights. This was followed by creaking as the pressure of the sea began to close in around the hull.

The Captain dropped the headphones and stepped to the intercom. *"Fire Control*—weapons status."

In the bow, the technician checked his monitor. He'd sent an electrical current to the rocket's propellant tank to warm it up. Temperatures in the fuel cell were high—the Captain had ordered the process expedited, after all—but the readings were still within acceptable parameters.

"Torpedoes are in the tubes—breech is sealed and weapon one is ready."

Zhen looked through his viewfinder once more. His quarry had disappeared from the surface and was now descending. He issued a command to the Weapons Officer.

"Open the outer doors and flood the tube. Standby to launch the weapon."

* * * *

COMMANDER WICKETT SNAPPED THE HANDLES against the mast and ordered the periscope retracted. As

Lieutenant Adley repeated his orders to the crew, the senior officer turned to face the Americans. Neill started to speak, but Wickett seemed to anticipate his request.

"We've just gotten word from the *Industrious*. Our rendezvous is in two hours—enough time to get you fed and dried."

"That would be greatly appreciated, Commander." Neill shivered in the new environment. "Commodore Wainwright supplied us with ration packs, but we've been too busy to eat." He gestured toward Nate. "Lieutenant Crockett's a little disappointed about that."

Sticky regarded the group with a smile. "We witnessed a fire on the island. Perhaps you could brief me on a few operational details. I'd like to hear what you chaps have been up to."

The Leading Seaman on sonar held his headset a little closer. His trained ears heard something.

"Conn, Sonar—towed array has a contact directly astern."

Wickett's head snapped around. "Can you identify?"

The response was instant. "Aye, sir—it's our lost Oscar." He closed his eyes, interpreting the incoming data. After a pause, he looked up, surprise on his face.

"He's opened a cap to the sea and is flooding a launch tube."

The Talon

ZHEN KNEW THEY COULDN'T WAIT ANY LONGER if they wanted to strike effectively.

"Weapons Officer—match bearings and fire the weapon."

There was no pause this time. With the press of a button, Weapons actuated the firing sequence. Highly compressed air was forced through a shaft, pushing water into the rear of the launcher. These actions produced a ram-jet behind the weapon. With no place to go but out, the Tempest exited the ship under tremendous pressure.

Everyone on board felt the boat shudder. The *Talon* rocked

back as the weapon cleared the tube. The streamlined torpedo slid into the sea with almost no resistance. True and level, the Tempest moved forward, designed to travel far ahead of the sub before the starter motors ignited the main engine.

Yet that didn't happen.

Barely five meters from the bow, the electrical charge warming the weapon spiked. Arcing through the propellant tank, the unstable fuel mixture reached its flash point prematurely, and the booster flamed to life.

Stabilizers embedded in the slender chassis sprung out. The fins did their job, keeping the Tempest on a pre-programmed course and adjusting the track as the rocket began to burn. The ejector ducts at the nose released their seals, allowing bottled gas stored within to flow forward. Everything was operating as planned—but the detonation that launched the missile had a catastrophic effect on the *Talon*.

Subjected to the underwater blast, the sub's outer hull cracked like an egg. At the bow, the concussive effects snapped the joints connecting the *Talon's* layers of skin. The inner hull protecting the torpedo bay went next. Titanium framing failed at its weakest points. Under high pressure, water jetted into the torpedo room. Terrified, the Fire Control team had just enough time to escape the compartment—and seal the hatch—before the bulkhead collapsed completely and the sea rushed in.

IN CONTROL, CAPTAIN ZHEN PANICKED AS HE realized something had gone terribly wrong. An ear-splitting din radiated from the forward section; it sounded like metal being ripped in half. The boat lurched forward and down. The extra weight in the bow altered the ship's equilibrium. Vented to the surrounding ocean, the *Talon* took on a sickening angle as she began to slide into the depths.

With his world collapsing around him, Zhen began issuing commands. The Diving Officer reacted instinctively, opening air valves and forcing seawater out of the *Talon*—even voiding the ballast in the trim tanks.

Reluctantly at first, the submarine began to slowly rise to the surface.

* * * *

NEILL AND THE OTHERS WATCHED AS THE Leading Seaman ripped the headset from his ears. The scene playing out before them now had become quite surreal.

Sonar fought to keep his emotions in check. "Commander, the Oscar has launched a weapon—bearing is two four five, west-southwest!"

Wickett reacted. "All ahead flank. Sound the alarm for collision," He needed more clarification. "Sonar, what's his distance?"

"Incoming is four thousand meters. Speed is—*good God!*"

Sticky had never seen the operator react so violently to a submerged contact—clearly, something wasn't right.

"Can you identify the weapon?"

The sound coming from the phones could be heard by nearly everyone in the compartment. Sonar adjusted the gain and slid the headset back on.

"Conn, weapon is *not* a torpedo." The sailor gave Wickett an imploring look. "Unless it has a Saturn V rocket strapped to its tail."

It might have been a cruise missile. But that type of weapon against another submarine—and at such a short distance—didn't make sense. *Why hadn't the towed array detected her?* Wickett already sensed the answer.

The Chinese sub must have been drifting—staying behind the *Bradford*—keeping her plant noise to a whisper. The boat rose and fell like an elevator, only going to periscope depth when she had to. The Oscar had simply gotten lucky; there was no other way for the giant to defeat the advanced systems aboard the British vessel.

"Time to impact?"

The Leading Seaman's math was a little shaky. "Conn, Sonar, forty-five seconds. Velocity is off the chart."

"Saturn V?" Neill shot a glance at Richey. "Did I hear right?"

The Senior Chief nodded. He turned to Wickett. "Skipper, if it helps—that Oscar's just launched a Tempest torpedo."

"A what?"

Richey licked his lips. He'd have to choose his words wisely.

"A *Squall*, sir—rocket torpedo built by the Russians. Ever heard of it?"

Wickett nodded. "Impossible to out-run."

He wore a tense look on his face. Wickett's instincts and training told him to get his boat far away—to go deep, where the sea floor would confuse his adversary's targeting system. But doing so against this weapon might prove fatal. By turning, he'd give the torpedo a broader cross-section to aim for. Wickett was also laboring under the assumption that the Tempest could track his vessel. In the space of seconds, he made his decision.

"Helm—standby with countermeasures; maintain current course, give me maximum speed."

Neill recalled Captain Ling's words. His mind cleared, allowing him an inspired thought.

"Commander, the Tempest's guidance system doesn't work—to propel it at high speeds, the missile uses ejector ducts in the nose cone. I have it on good authority that it's blind once it leaves the tube."

Richey jumped in. "He's right, sir. The weapon's not designed to house a functioning navigational suite." That thought hadn't occurred to Malcolm, and he wondered how Neill knew about it. *"Did White Dragon tell you that?"*

Wickett was unsure what the Chief meant and didn't wait for an answer. "How does it find its target?"

"It doesn't," the Marine replied. "It's a point and shoot weapon; aim, fire—and hope for the best." He looked at his watch. Time was running out. "Your best course of action is to simply get out of the way."

"Time to impact?"

Sonar gauged the distance. Increasing their speed had bought them a little time—but not much.

"Conn, Sonar—thirty seconds."

"Is it using active sonar to locate us?"

"Negative, Commander." Sonar considered Neill's words. "The weapon's engine noise will keep the Oscar from tracking us." A hard turn in either direction—and the sound generated by the Squall—would prevent the Chinese boat from locating the *Bradford*. Forcing the weapon to bank to port or starboard might snap its guide wire—if it had one.

Wickett was faced with a hard choice. Against a weapon that his ship couldn't out-run, conventional wisdom told him to make his attacker work for a kill. His knowledge of the Squall was limited, but Sticky was aware of its basic operating principles. He even had some recollection of the way it formed an envelope to reduce drag.

It was hard to imagine a weapon system like the Squall without a guidance system, but if the young Marine standing before him was right—

"*Helm*—left ten degrees rudder, make your course zero five five, continue all ahead flank. Take her deep and launch countermeasures."

Wickett turned to Neill. "Lieutenant, for all our sakes—I hope you're right."

Chapter Thirty-Six ✫ Taking on Water

I T WAS DOME-SHAPED, A CANOPY OF GREENISH-
white light erupting below the surface of the water.
Through the rain, Zhu Ling caught a glimpse of the flash
on the starboard side. Like the lightning above, it lingered
for a few seconds and then diminished. Before it disappeared
altogether the Captain got the impression that it was moving
east.

The morning dawned slowly, and Ling no longer needed the
scope. Ensign Tsao had brought them within a mile of where
the British submarine dove below the waves. The blades on the
windscreen operated at full speed, giving the men a clear view
of the pitching seas before them.

Without a word, Tsao nudged the patrol boat forward. Some
of the PRC Marines were braving the inclement weather and
lined the bow railing. A few looked back at the wheelhouse once
the *Bradford* submerged, wondering what the Captain would do
next.

The HMS Bradford

THERE WAS NO SENSE OF FORWARD MOTION,
but the boat was banking to port at nearly twenty-five degrees. Everyone standing in Control braced themselves as the
bow of the submarine angled toward the bottom. Commander

Wickett's eyes swept a multitude of gauges and then settled on the sonar suite. The creaking of the hull increased as the sub dove.

Wickett tabbed the ship's intercom. "*Fire Control*—load two fish. Weapons Officer, compute a solution on the Oscar's last bearing. Firing point procedures and standby."

Weapons had already done his job. He gave the Commander a thumb's up.

Sonar was in a world of his own. He was frozen at his station, listening to the approaching missile and checking his board. The watchstanders in Control were too busy driving the boat; few paid him much attention, but the four Americans regarded the British sailor with increasing interest.

The sound grew in his ears, reached a high pitch—and then began to fade. The Leading Seaman's head came up. Neill was prepared for the worst until he saw a broad grin on the man's face.

"*Conn, Sonar*—weapon is passing aft, three hundred meters, starboard quarter. Intersecting our last plot . . . and continuing east by northeast." Beads of sweat dotted his forehead. He gave Neill an approving look. "Someone pat that Yank on the back!"

Wickett looked relieved, but pressed for more. "Let me know if it doubles back." He was about to cycle through a few more directives when Sonar raised his hand.

"*Conn*—sound cluttering up the surface." He frowned.

Sticky shared his expression. "He's prepared another weapon. *Fire Control*—"

"Negative, sir. Hull's making a racket; sounds like he's *hit* something." He paused, and then continued. "*The Oscar is taking on water*." Now a smile.

"He's emptied his tanks and driving to the surface—and he doesn't care who knows it. Screws are spinning like windmills."

Commander Wickett wasn't about to be baited into a trap. "Diving Officer, angle planes ten degree up; take us to periscope depth. Helm—make your speed ten knots."

The watchstanders repeated his orders, but Sonar wasn't finished. Once again he called out, *"Conn, Sonar*; engine cut-off on weapon—*and loss of contact!"*

That sounded like good news. "Where'd it go?" Crockett asked.

"Best guess?" Sonar checked his display. "Two kilometers due east—and falling into a deepwater basin."

The White House

FITZROY'S CALL WAS FORWARDED DIRECTLY TO Richard Aultman. The conversation was brief. The assistant to the National Security Advisor took down a few notes and then hung up.

He checked the time. Night was beginning to fall. Richard pulled out Lloyd Farris' business card and found the number for his cell. He stared at the MDI logo on the card's corner and shook his head; McBride's treason would put a whole new face on the contractor's work. He wondered if the company would survive.

Aultman punched in the number.

"I need two things, Lloyd." He wasn't surprised to find the MDI official still on the job—the man was doing yeoman's work, trying to salvage his company's reputation with Defense.

"Just name it." Farris sounded tired.

Aultman studied his notes. "Our cyber office on the west coast has made a request. They'd like all your files on the StarPoint Series I satellites—specifically the operating system and encryption architecture. Can you get your hands on that?"

Farris was working on a monitor as they spoke. "I can make that available—but StarPoint isn't a U.S. initiative. What's it got to do with McBride?"

Richard winced. Any other time he might have answered that question, but McBride's actions had altered a trusted relationship.

"Sorry, Lloyd. I'm going to have to cite the old 'need to know' clause."

There was an awkward pause, and Aultman could almost

hear a heavy sigh through the phone.

"Understood." Farris' voice was flat. *And so it begins.*

He pulled up a few files from a separate drive. "The data's firewalled, but I can disable that. Where do you want it?"

"Does MDI have an FTP site?"

"Yes." *Who didn't?* Farris kept the question to himself.

"Go ahead and upload it there."

Farris clicked a few icons and launched the server. "You'll need a user name and password—I'll forward those separately. Anything else?"

"That should do it," Aultman replied. A question nagged at him. "Just out of curiosity—could McBride have *electronically* sent material to foreign agents?"

"Sure—but not using our FTP site," Farris answered firmly. "We share administrative rights with the DoD. Essentially, it's the intellectual property of the company, but we've relinquished control to the government. The site is monitored 24/7, and every file transferred flags at least two separate watchdog agencies—one being the CIA."

That was reassuring. And it partially explained why McBride had flown all the way to Huo Shan.

"Thanks, Lloyd. Be sure to send me those passwords." He wanted to add something else before ending the call. "I'll be sure to let Mr. Avery know what a help you've been."

He'd said it as a professional courtesy—Aultman owed the man that much.

* * * *

THE TALON LIMPED HALTINGLY TO THE SUR-face, her massive hull down slightly at the bow. Only the submarine's bridge and stern fin stood above the waves. The decks fore and aft were awash as the leviathan rolled in the whitecaps.

The Chinese Marines had seen her first, broaching to the south and astern of the ST-339. Zhu Ling watched as the

Talon's crew escaped from the sail, and rafts were deployed from storage points in the bridge. Ling raised the telescopic lens and counted two dozen sailors—including Captain Zhen.

He trained the optics on the submarine's forward section. Between swells he could see buckling in the hull. Seams in the bow's plating were split wide open, and the sea flowed easily through the gaps. As the *Talon's* crew took to the rafts, the sub began listing to port. Ling could see less of the ship's damaged nose, and the white waters that swirled over her no longer stirred.

The *Talon of the Seas* was sinking.

From a mile away, another surprise awaited. A thin wake creased the sea, led by several black, narrow masts. The submarine that had collected the Americans was breaking the surface. The ship sailed north by northwest, and the men in the patrol boat could see figures emerge atop the towering sail.

Tsao started to speak, but the words caught in his throat.

"I see her, Ensign," Ling said. "Forget the British vessel for the moment—we have other business to attend to."

Tsao turned and regarded the crippled Oscar as she fought to stay above the waves. The submarine was heeling over hard, and the men who had escaped her corpse were now at the mercy of the pitching sea.

"Bring us about." A smile crossed Zhu Ling's face.

The junior officer nodded to the pilot. Tsao suspected he knew what the Captain had in mind. He was wrong.

"Go below and prepare the crew," Tsao ordered. "We'll render aid to the sailors of that submarine."

"Not aid, Ensign," Ling corrected. An unexpected option had just presented itself—one that would allow the Captain to honor Neill's request. "We will place those men under arrest."

Tsao was dumbfounded. "On what charges?"

"Piracy; treason—and murder. I will explain everything on our return trip." Ling turned to the pilot. "I want every available man on deck. And the Marines—with their weapons and sidearms."

* * * *

FROM THE TOP OF THE BRADFORD'S SAIL, Commander Wickett and a select few witnessed the death throes of a giant. Geysers shot into the sky as pockets of trapped air escaped the *Talon's* hull, and as she began to slide below the surface, the sub did a slow pirouette.

A full third of her stern was now visible, her screws and diving planes immobile. Below the waterline, the boat was painted a dull red that had tarnished over the years. She displayed no other color, and no flag, number or insignia marked her skin.

As the sea claimed her, the *Talon* descended more rapidly. With the rain falling heavily from above, the waters below pulled her down for the last time.

"There she goes." Neill rested his arms on the bridge coaming. Chau, Richey and Crockett stood at his side. The four Americans had been invited to the bridge by Wickett; a rare privilege, but fitting under the circumstances. At their backs, an array of masts towered over them. A digital camera in the periscope recorded the Oscar's demise.

"What killed her?" Nate asked. The *Bradford* had surfaced too late for the group to see the Oscar's damaged bow.

"Probably the sting of the Squall," Sticky suggested. "Or the *Tempest*, as you chaps have taken to calling it. The submarine's tube might have failed during launch, allowing a breach of her watertight compartments; or possibly the rocket ignited too close to the hull."

"Without even the sun to bid her goodbye," Richey said, sadly but with eloquence. Despite the fact that the warship had attacked them, the sailor in him mourned her loss.

Commander Wickett grunted and studied the scene through a pair of field glasses. The Chinese patrol boat had moved in to pick up the survivors.

Nate spoke up. "That's going to be one crowded ship."

The gusting wind sent spray over the sub. "It doesn't appear that her master is too concerned with guest comfort," Sticky commented. He handed the binoculars to the Senior Chief.

Richey lifted them to his eye. "Those troops are showing them the business ends of their weapons," he laughed. The memory of the PRC Marines on the island tempered his mood. "Better them than us, right El-Tee?"

Neill nodded soberly. He wondered if Admiral Lee's lust for power had just cost more lives.

The *Bradford* surged forward. One by one, the men descended the narrow passageway through the sail. Commander Wickett was the last one down. Within minutes the sub turned east and dove below the surface. Her pace would be unhurried now. The rendezvous with the *Industrious* was hours away, and there was no need to rush.

* * * *

TO THE STERN, THE ST-339 TURNED NORTH. THE promontory on Huo Shan stood as a mute sentinel, its peak hidden under dark, scudding skies. In every direction, the sea was empty, save for the swells stirred up by the storm.

From the bridge, Captain Ling watched as the PRC Marines handcuffed their prisoners—linked arm in arm—and forced them to sit on the rain-swept deck. He was surprised to see Sergeant Wen taking charge. His wrist was bandaged, and his arm was held in a sling, but Ling was pleased that the truculent NCO wasn't seriously injured.

The patrol boat knifed through the waves. Unlike the British vessel, she steamed at full speed. Her course would bring her home to Hainan. She would arrive in less than six hours, bearing a cargo Admiral Lee could not possibly anticipate.

Chapter Thirty-Seven ✷ The Black Ditch

The Industrious
15 Kilometers East of Huo Shan

THE SEAS WERE TOO ROUGH FOR THE ACCOM-modation ladder—the portable stairwell on the side of the ship. Instead, a dual outboard launch was dispatched from the well deck. The vessel edged away from the carrier and motored alongside the *Bradford*, matching the submarine's speed.

Moving personnel from one boat to another was a delicate operation. The storm didn't help. Both vessels maintained just enough speed for steerage, and in short order, the sure-footed Americans had traded decks. With the transfer complete, the *Bradford's* hatch was sealed and the launch turned again for the larger ship.

The sturdy boat plowed through the swells and approached the yawning stern. From a kilometer away, the *Bradford* signaled her departure. Neill and company followed her sleek lines as she disappeared beneath the waves. Their time aboard had been brief—but unquestionably memorable.

The *Industrious* turned her bow into the wind for the recovery effort. The coxswain maneuvered deftly, timing his approach with an eye toward the shifting seas. With the ship looming above them, he gunned the engines and entered the well deck. It was much easier guiding the boat in the ship's interior. The seaman idled the engines as a mooring party tied up the launch. Templeton was there to greet them.

She welcomed them back aboard and then lowered her voice. "It's a little early for champagne."

Neill gave her a smile as they disembarked. Shouldering his rucksack and weapon, it seemed to Amanda that he favored his left side.

"Right now I'd settle for a hot shower and some dry clothes."

Crockett nodded agreement. The group as a whole looked exhausted.

Templeton was her cheerful self. "A full-on English breakfast would stand you all in good stead."

"They fed us aboard the sub, *Leftenant*." Richey was glad to be back. "But I'd be grateful for some coffee."

"What happened to your Gemini?"

Neill knew that would come up. "Long story. You four go ahead." He unzipped his ruck and pulled out the sat phone. "I've got a call to make."

People's Liberation Army-Naval
Division headquarters,
Beijing, China

LIKE THE OTHER SENIOR OFFICERS BILLETED there, the Admiral's suite on the ground floor overlooked a landscaped courtyard. The complex was situated in the center of the military district, a massive bureaucratic edifice that dominated two city blocks. The separate wings of the building were connected by sidewalks, a configuration that loosely resembled the Pentagon in the United States. At the center of the quadrangle, the Chinese standard hung atop a flagpole, blowing listlessly in the breeze.

The mild spring day was in sharp contrast to the weather

felt in the Strait of Taiwan. Admiral Lee sat at his desk, poring over a stack of communications. They had flooded Lee's basket all day. Sent by the squadrons now beleaguering the island, most dealt with the storm; typhoon Ulysses was playing havoc with shipboard operations, but it was nothing the fleet couldn't handle.

Other messages focused on the status of the vessels in the task force plying the broad channel. With mild disinterest, Lee noted that one frigate was having trouble with her water purification system. In the Pacific, a cruiser reported two minor injuries when careless seamen got between pallets of supplies. But few of the dispatches bore details of real consequence, and the Admiral gave his Captains at sea the autonomy required to deal with those that did.

Lee grumbled. The most recent communique came from Captain Wei Lao. Once more, the master of the *Luzhou* brought up his concerns for the storm. The two had already discussed that topic, and Lee was beginning to doubt the man's resolve. That worried him. The Admiral's plans hinged on the efforts of three men under his command. Lao was generous with his reports, but bulletins from the other two were conspicuously absent.

Lee had arrived at his office early. The morning passed quickly enough, filled with the details and decisions required for a full-scale naval operation. A subordinate served breakfast and Lee spent much of the day sipping tea. He skipped lunch, his afternoon schedule a blur of more items needing his attention.

By late in the day, the Admiral had grown very concerned. He fully expected to hear from Captain Ling; his mission to Huo Shan should have been accomplished by now. Lee had even entertained the notion that McBride might try to contact him. But there had been no word.

Conversely, with Ling's task complete, the *Talon* should have signaled *her* status—yet no communications had been received from the submarine. Taken together, the silence from his subordinates in the South China Sea fueled his anxiety.

Lee picked up the phone. The Strait of Taiwan was full of his ships, and the Admiral needed assurances.

Aboard the Luzhou

IN THE OPERATIONS CENTER, SENIOR CAPTAIN Lao heard the chirp from the encrypted line. The display ID'd the caller, and he picked up the handset.

Lao apprised the Admiral of the battle group's status, again relaying his concerns for the storm barreling through the Strait. At this, Lee made no effort to mask his agitation.

To Lee, the typhoon offered an unexpected opportunity. Darkness and inclement weather could be their allies. What he needed from the Captain was an honest appraisal—would Ulysses impede operations or enhance them?

Lao's answer was contingent on two factors. The first concerned their ability to bend the curve in their favor.

"It's essential that we rely on the electronic measures at our disposal." Lao wasn't backing down. "Can those be guaranteed?"

He waited for an outburst, but Lee kept his composure.

Lao pressed him on another front. "And what of your contact at sea—have you heard from him?"

There was a pause before the Admiral answered. "We can proceed without him. His services are inconsequential."

The Captain dared to challenge that assumption. "That's not how it has been described to us in the past, Admiral."

Lee continued to maintain a cool-headed evenness. "This enterprise has been in the planning stages for quite some time. Its impetus will carry us forward to success—without additional naval intervention. The time to strike is now. Position your principals in their assigned locations. Are my orders clear?"

Lao consulted the plot board. Things were moving a little faster than expected. He'd have to shuffle a few key players, but beyond that—

"Crystal clear, Admiral. The preparations will be made."

* * * *

ORBITING HIGH ABOVE ASIA, TANGENT/CASCADE-6 had recovered from her previous difficulties. Fully active again, the satellite was back in business. Its electronic brain—actually, *brains* was more accurate, as the spacecraft housed several CPUs—swept aside the pesky encryptions intended to protect Admiral Lee's calls.

Along with brains, the satellite had big ears. Those were employed to listen in whenever specific communications networks were used. The conversation between Beijing and the *Luzhou* was dutifully recorded—and instantly passed along to several locations; the Office of Cyber Defenses in San Diego, the White House Communications Agency, the CIA—and the newly-created COMMAND/TACTICAL hub deep in the Pentagon.

Washington, D.C.
The White House

THE DATA FROM TANGENT/CASCADE-6 WAS FLAGGED PRIORITY ONE. In Chantilly, the NRO case officer saw the message and immediately called the White House. A signals operator there was already on it. His next call went to Richard Aultman, and forty-five minutes later, the lights went on in the office of the National Security Advisor.

* * * *

"GLAD YOU COULD MAKE IT." RICHARD AULTMAN stirred sugar into his second cup of coffee. He gestured to a mug as Willis Avery stumbled into the room. "Can I pour you some?"

"Just give me the whole pot." The boss looked more disheveled than usual—a consequence of arriving at four a.m., fully twelve hours behind Beijing. Unlike the past few nights, Avery had enjoyed precious little sleep before rising.

Aultman was oddly rested, to the point of annoyance. "You think it's bad here?" he chuckled. "San Diego's four hours behind us."

"Wrong, sunshine." Avery didn't even consult his watch. He unbuttoned his collar. It was much too early to be wearing a tie. "West coast is three hours different—it's one a.m. there. Did you call Commander Fitzroy?"

Richard nodded. "He's headed in now—along with his key people."

"What's the signals office saying?" Despite his fatigue, Avery was spooled up and ready for a full briefing. Aultman had told him about the intercepted call on the drive in—what Avery wanted now was an update on events taking place at sea.

"Increased chatter between Beijing and the fleet surrounding Taiwan," Aultman answered. "Routine stuff mostly; they're worried about the typhoon. You'd expect that. But they're also focused on the status of the ROC Navy—distances to shore, as well as their responses to PRC probing actions." He took a sip from his mug. "Overall, there's an uptick in traffic by thirty-eight percent over yesterday. That's to be expected, too."

"Granted. Same as last year. They're just repeating the pattern," Avery grunted in reply. "Then there's that cryptic message between Lee and the *Luzhou*. It appears Lieutenant Pressley is on to something."

Aultman grinned. "That's *Pressman*—Ensign, U.S. Navy. She's convinced China's exercises last spring were a dress rehearsal for something bigger."

"According to Neill, she's right—but their exercises every year are a dress rehearsal."

"So what's next?" Richard took a seat on the sofa across from Avery's desk. A glance at the wall clock told him the Navy mess wouldn't be open for another hour. That didn't matter much; he'd need more coffee before the thought of food would hold much appeal.

"I'll contact CINCPAC; have him inform LaSalle about Lee's call. After that, we continue to monitor radio traffic. Evaluate their chatter. Keep an eye on the respective navies of both sides." Avery hung up his jacket and found his way to the coffee. He looked pleased. Aultman had retrieved an ample supply of caramel creamer from the micro-fridge. "Any more word from Neill?"

"Nothing yet," Richard replied. "He's probably still sleeping off his island excursion." He shook his head. "The man certainly earns his pay. How do you think he gets so lucky?"

The National Security Advisor thought that over. Neill's call weighed heavy on his mind. The tale he'd spun about McBride's intentions—relayed by White Dragon himself, no less—and the intel regarding the Chinese Oscar were impressive. MI:6 had played an altruistic hand, forwarding images of the sinking sub to the American intelligence community. *Quid pro quo*—they'd insisted—for the Yanks' help in preventing a catastrophic end to the HMS *Bradford*.

What struck Avery the most was the confirmation of Lee's plans. White Dragon had been very specific. The Tempest/Squall torpedo had weaknesses that could be exploited, should they ever encounter it again; and now that the Admiral's strategy had been revealed—

"I don't think luck has anything to do with it," Avery said at last. The words *grace*—and mercy—crossed his mind, but he kept that thought to himself. He took a few gulps from his mug as a new idea stirred in his brain.

"Drink your coffee. At five we'll head to the cafeteria for breakfast. After that, let's take a little drive over to the Pentagon—SECDEF should be in his office by seven."

"You could invite him here," Aultman suggested. "We can monitor the play-by-play in the Situation Room."

"True," Avery allowed. "But they've just opened up their brand new COM/TAC suite. I'd like to see its capabilities first-hand—in a real-world scenario. And if things start breaking bad, I'd prefer to be someplace where we can exercise more strategic options."

Aboard the USS Meyer

THE FURTHER NORTH SHE SAILED, THE MORE Captain Beacham looked through the eyes of the *Victory*. Distances between the two ships had grown steadily over the past several hours. The arsenal ship was now in the heart of the vast channel, and Beacham deemed it time to begin turning the vessel to the east.

Formerly called the Formosa Strait, it was clear to see why the body of water had gone by another name; the *Black Ditch*. Beacham attributed that to the current weather conditions. Two of the four monitors tied to the ship's optical array displayed images in black and white. These formed a very somber view of the sea lanes. The color screens didn't improve much on the overall picture. Thick rainclouds blocked out the afternoon sun, and dusk came early as the *Victory* plowed through fifteen foot seas toward the typhoon lashing the region.

A host of other seamen and techs shared Captain Beacham's focus. Lieutenant Sanchez was seated at the main console and drove the *Victory*. Commander Towle stood nearby, his eyes glued to the cartographic screen. The monitor depicted the positions of the PLA-Navy ships participating in the exercise. It also displayed the locations of the ROC vessels patrolling Taiwan.

"Mr. Sanchez, any surface contacts within sight of the *Victory*?"

The Lieutenant had maintained good situational awareness of the waters surrounding his charge. "No contacts at this time, Captain."

"Any chance these seas will abate as she nears the eye?"

"That's affirmative, sir." This came from Towle. "Weather says things should calm down in the next hour. The typhoon has picked up a little speed, tracking south-southwesterly again."

The Skipper drew a hand across his chin. "Very well. Let's reduce her radar cross-section before we make the turn. Lieutenant Sanchez, flood her tanks fore and aft, starboard and port. Trim her out evenly and come to new course zero nine five.

Make your speed eight knots."

Sanchez repeated the Captain's orders. His hands moved across the keyboard, and then he adjusted the track-ball on the mouse at his fingertips.

Ninety miles to the north, the *Victory's* waterline shifted. Taking on ballast, the ship began to disappear into the sea. Her decks were nearly awash now, and only the rounded superstructure could be seen above the waves.

Captain Beacham smiled at the thought. Like a warship of old, and riding low in the water, the arsenal ship now resembled a Civil War ironclad.

The Industrious
Officer's Guest Quarters

NEILL STIRRED FROM SLEEP, OPENING HIS EYES in the darkened stateroom. He yawned and stretched, then swung his legs over the bunk and planted his stocking feet on the deck. Completely rested, the Marine had slept soundly for more than five hours.

Sitting on the edge of the rack, he was reminded of the dull ache in his shoulder. It had been more than half a day since he'd been shot, and the pain had greatly lessened. He stood and extended his arms over his head. His limbs felt fine. Squatting next, Neill listened to see if any other part of his body might complain. Everything was in working order; the months of physical conditioning aboard the *Lexington* had paid off.

Neill thought back to the brief time spent aboard the submarine. The doc on the *Bradford* had examined his wound—*bruise* was more accurate—and given him a clean bill of health. He prescribed nothing more than ibuprofen, which elicited an *I told you so* from Crockett.

Considering all they'd been through over the past twenty-four hours, Neill was thankful to be alive. With that thought in mind, he pulled a small New Testament from his ruck; there hadn't been time for devotions since they'd started the mission. He flipped on a light at the head of the bunk and spent the next few minutes reading Paul's words in II Corinthians; oddly enough, the apostle's account of his physical trials—including a night and day spent on the open sea.

Neill finished in prayer. He put away his Bible just as Nate eased open the hatch, holding two arms full of uniforms. A pair of black boots hung by their laces around his neck.

"Good. You're awake," Crockett announced. He moved to his bunk and dropped the bundle, then checked the corner—assuring himself that his rifle was where he'd left it. "Uniforms are done—but our boots are still drying."

"You washed our boots?" Neill was shocked. "I thought you said clean boots were the sign of an office pogue."

"I didn't *wash* them—just rinsed out the seawater," Nate grinned. "Don't worry. I left the dirt on."

Michael yawned again. "Where is everybody?"

"Senior Chief's next door. He and I have been doing laundry."

"What about Simon?"

Nate shrugged. "He found a quiet place to work. Took his laptop and McBride's memory stick with him. I think he's down in the ship's library."

Neill's eyes widened. "He's trying to decrypt the code. I forgot all about that." He was wide awake now. "Have you slept?"

Crockett nodded. "I crashed right after breakfast. Been up for two hours." He removed the boots from around his neck and tossed them to his friend. "Here—I got your size. *Leftenant* Templeton found these in ship's stores."

Neill looked at Crockett's feet. He was wearing an identical pair.

"Those aren't regulation."

Nate shrugged. "I won't tell Headquarters Marine Corps if you won't. Wear 'em or not. But you're gonna look awful funny running around the ship in your shower shoes."

Aboard the USS George H.W. Bush,
65 miles southeast of Taiwan

GHOST LIPFORD HAD THE MIDNIGHT TO NOON watch, but showed up in the CIC early. The compartment was somewhat crowded—and brimming with the 'shiny stuff,' the enlisted men's term for high-ranking officers.

"What'd I miss, Skipper?"

Captain DeSouza turned away from the plot board. "The Chinese Navy is still circling the island. No changes in their course over the past eight hours." He looked worried. "Maybe it's just me, but this is beginning to look less and less like an exercise."

Off to one side, Admiral LaSalle hovered over the navigation board. He gave Lipford a passing nod, a phone pressed against his ear.

Ghost focused on the display. "Copy that, Cap'n." The ever-present red squares—the PLA-Navy ships—still ringed Taiwan. Green ovals, the vessels of the ROC, formed a perimeter closer in. "Consistent formation—paralleling Taiwan's ships." Ghost stepped forward and traced a finger along the path of the Chinese task force. "Reminds me of a noose."

"And getting tighter," DeSouza grunted.

Admiral LaSalle replaced the phone and moved to Captain DeSouza's side. "That was CINCPAC. The NRO bagged a call between the mainland and their lead ship. Transcript to follow, but the upshot is that Lee has authorized movement among the Chinese 'principals'. We've been advised to watch for 'new activity.'"

Ghost's attention was once again drawn to the screen. Something had changed.

"You mean like that, sir?"

All three officers were now watching the display. The circular motion of the outer ring continued as before. But at equidistant points all around the island, six of the red squares broke formation. Their progress was slow at first. On the western coastline of Taiwan, the Chinese ships turned to starboard and then came about. Along the eastern shores, those vessels also reversed their course. They were now headed due south.

DeSouza stood at the control monitor. He moved the mouse from one ship to another, holding down the COMMAND key and clicking on separate icons in turn. Data callouts appeared next to the graphics.

"Two destroyers—*Luang* class, the *Shenzhen* and the *Taizhou*," the Captain intoned. "The *Luzhou*—that's the command ship. One from the *Luhai* class, and another from the *Sovremenny* series; Russian built."

"Bring up all of Taiwan's major harbors," the Admiral ordered.

DeSouza tapped a few keys. Six new icons appeared—white diamonds, sitting at points spread around the island.

LaSalle approached the big screen and gently touched them all. "The Port of Taipei; the Port of Kaohslung; Mailiao Harbor." He stepped to his right. "The Port of Huallen on the eastern side." The Admiral faced his officers. "I'll wager those ships will take up positions within sight of each one."

There was one other image the Admiral hadn't mentioned. In the center of the Strait, a yellow triangle—representing the *Victory*—had turned east. She was making for the Port of Taichung.

Chapter Thirty-Eight ✳ Pivot Point

San Diego

I T WAS TWO A.M., PACIFIC DAYLIGHT TIME, when Pressman arrived at the base. Traffic was light, and the drive from her apartment in Chula Vista was short. She showed her ID at the gate, and then navigated the narrow, well-lit roads to the shop, a typically non-descript facility facing the sea on Bisner Street.

Fitzroy had preceded her by twenty minutes. He would have gotten there sooner, but had stopped on the way in to pick up breakfast for his team. It was the least he could do, and the gesture might even blunt the shock of being there so early.

With a box of coffee and sacks of food clutched in one arm, he entered the building. Fitzroy dropped his load at the nearest desk—Lieutenant Chau's, as it turned out—and then switched on a few lamps. He moved to his own office and powered up the computer. Checking his email was the first order of business. The encrypted message from the NRO was in his in-box. He read it twice and printed it. It was something of an eye-opener, and explained the call from Richard Aultman. Fitzroy stepped away from his desk and surveyed the working spaces on the main floor. Choosing a suitable location for the buffet would come next.

The break room was down the hall, but the conference table

in the auditorium was much closer. The Commander gathered up the assorted meals and spread out the selection there. He had just retrieved mugs from the common area when Ensign Pressman walked through the door.

Kelsi greeted her boss with a sleepy grin. She wore her working uniform, blue and gray patterned utilities, and carried a matching backpack. Her short-cropped hair was still damp at the ends. She dropped the ruck at her desk and made for the food.

"Get any rest?" Fitzroy sipped from his mug.

She managed a few words in reply. "About four hours. I was here till seven working on a few things." Kelsi was slowly stirring to life. She poured some creamer. A shower had helped, but coffee was what she really needed. "D.C. called?"

Fitzroy handed her the printed message. She scanned it quickly; it was short read.

"Wow." She voiced the word with little enthusiasm. "Sounds like they might try it this time."

"Washington thinks so. And CINCPAC concurs." He offered her a smile. "Might be a busy day."

"Did you call Garcia?"

"He's on his way. Ettinger too. Purcell's a new dad—we'll let him sleep. I think the four of us can handle things."

"No doubt," Kelsi replied. "I'll access the schematics on StarPoint and prep the other software. We could use real-time interfacing with the battle group."

"And the Pentagon," Fitzroy agreed. "I'll coordinate with both. Pull up video conferencing on your machine. You can run it in the background, but if things get hot we'll need to be able to talk to our assets at sea."

* * * *

LaSalle studied the transcript once more. He didn't want to miss anything, and by now he'd memorized its key points.

"Looks like your bet's paying off, Admiral," DeSouza noted. "The big guns in Lee's fleet are moving into position—right at the limits of territorial waters." He considered the Chinese officer's next move. "If I were him, I'd do the same thing; wait till dark—and then pivot."

Ghost Lipford noted the time. "That won't be long."

On the screen, the six images were nearly in place as the others continued their counter-clockwise movement around Taiwan. The icon depicting the *Victory* continued a slow track to the east, with the *Meyer* was just north of the carrier task force.

"Relay the word to the rest of the group," LaSalle ordered. "—and activate PARTY LINE; I want Taiwan to know we're monitoring this."

U.S. Navy ships maintained an open channel with the ROC. PARTY LINE was an encrypted link to their grid. It always seemed to become more active during China's spring exercises.

At the southernmost reaches of the display sat a single yellow triangle. "Be sure to contact the *Industrious*; the Royal Navy's a long way from home, and I don't want to exclude an ally, especially when they've been so accommodating."

The Pentagon

ALLAN HAYES WASN'T IN HIS OFFICE WHEN THE pair from the White House arrived. His assistant was expecting the two, and directed them to an elevator at the end of the hall. Avery and Aultman traveled one floor down and had to pass through an additional checkpoint before gaining access to COMMAND/TACTICAL.

Even within the Pentagon's walls, few had the credentials or clearances necessary to enter COM/TAC. The suite was a high-tech extension of several other points in the building. Housed in a sprawling auditorium, the network of computer stations linked to outside sources and was the focal point for intelligence-gathering and reports from the field.

SECDEF saw the National Security Advisor as he was cleared

to enter the room. "First time here, Willis?"

Avery regarded the suite with a mixture of awe and appreciation. Technicians and operators manned the consoles, most wearing military uniforms of some stripe or another. A few personnel were coalition members from friendly nations. "Very impressive, Mr. Secretary. Can you get cable?"

"When necessary," Hayes chuckled. "Most of our programming is dish-fed." He greeted Aultman with a handshake. "I imagine you're here to bring me up to speed on a few things."

Avery nodded. *The man doesn't beat around the bush,* he thought silently.

"WE DISCUSSED ADMIRAL LEE'S STRATEGY DURing my last visit," Avery began. "At the time, I was a little fuzzy on details."

"What's changed since then?" SECDEF gestured to a conference room. The three entered and took their seats around a long table.

"One of our men in the field has gained some valuable intel," Avery continued, adjusting his frame in the chair. "As a result, we've determined the causal effect Lee had in mind to kick off his scheme—at least one of them."

He expected Hayes to press for details. White Dragon's identity would become an issue sooner or later. For the moment, Avery preferred to keep a lid on their source. But the Secretary seemed unconcerned about that.

"The trigger." Hayes' mind went back to their conversation the day before. "What's his plan?"

Avery drew in some air. "Originally, he intended to torpedo one of his own ships. Make it look like Taiwan struck first. That would give China an excuse to extend the blockade and seize the island. But that particular option is now off the table."

SECDEF mulled over that thought. "We've confirmed the sinking of that Oscar?"

Another nod. "The Brits have, Mr. Secretary. HMS *Bradford* tracked the hulk all the way to the bottom."

"Which puzzles me, Willis. I've read the intercept between Lee and Captain Lao. He mentions something about 'electronic measures.' " Hayes leaned forward. "What's he referring to? Can he really hope to succeed without naval interdiction—in the form of a rogue submarine?" SECDEF had his doubts, but the recorded conversation made it clear that Lee's resolve was unfazed.

Avery pursed his lips. It might be time for a little salesmanship; SECDEF wasn't entirely convinced, but he was edging closer.

"This whole thing has been in the works for a while, Mr. Secretary. China's military is bent on using force to re-acquire their wayward province. Her political leadership has been swayed in the same direction, even though the Premier has looked the other way. We don't know precisely what those *'electronic measures'* are at this point; but I'm guessing they're on a level that will effectively neutralize the opposition—and deal the Chinese Navy a winning hand. My advice? We stop them." He paused, allowing his words to sink in.

Hayes sighed deeply. The National Security Advisor had done his job. SECDEF would have liked to think otherwise, but there was no denying what Admiral Lee had in mind.

"He said it himself, didn't he? Something about their 'impetus' carrying them forward?"

"Yes, sir, he did," Avery acknowledged. "At some point, it's all about momentum."

SECDEF paused before continuing.

"And your man in the field—that wouldn't be the Marine connected to the Ukrainian incident—the missionaries' son?"

Avery found that question to be a little odd.

"One and the same, Mr. Secretary. He's very good on his feet."

Hayes chuckled. "A family trait, apparently—I've read their file."

Avery blinked. "I wasn't aware they had one. Anything I should know?" He and Aultman traded curious glances.

"When this is all over, Willis, you and I should have a conversation."

"What about?" Avery was caught off guard.

Hayes had a faraway look in his eye.

"The end of the Cold War—and something called IRON HARVEST."

The Industrious

THE KNOCK ON THE STATEROOM DOOR WAS INsistent. Crockett opened the hatch to find Malcolm Richey standing in the passageway on the other side.

"What's up, Pappy?"

Richey wore a concerned look, but his expression lightened when he saw Crockett. "Neill awake?"

"Yeah; Sleepy's been stirring for about an hour now." Nate stuck his head out, looking left and right. "Where's Si?"

"Radio room. On the command deck, in the CIC. He wants us all up there." Malcolm's eyes went to the deck. "Nice boots," he grinned.

* * * *

THEY ASSEMBLED AT THE FAR END OF THE COMM shack. Simon was seated next to one of several technicians. Banks of controls lined the bulkhead. It was much like the interior of the *Bradford*, only brighter and more spacious.

Chau was all smiles. Neill regarded the sailor with a knowing look. "You cracked McBride's code, didn't you?"

"It's what I do," Simon replied with a nod. Some of Crockett's swagger had rubbed off.

A second group entered before he could go further. Commodore Wainwright was followed by Lieutenant Templeton and the ship's XO. The room came to attention, and then the senior British officer yielded the floor to Chau.

"Go on, Leftenant—you were saying?"

Simon took a breath and started his presentation. "A while back, I was in a group that evaluated the guidance software for the StarPoint satellites—you've heard of them?"

"Launched for Taiwan's military," Wainwright reflected.

"Yes, sir," Simon nodded. "We vetted it thoroughly—or so we thought. There were some random lines of code, but nothing that raised any flags. We subjected those to a cursory analysis." He shrugged. "Our filters didn't catch anything."

"Who created the software?" Neill asked.

"McBride Defense Industries."

"And the encryption on the flash drive?" Michael pressed.

"The data on the memory stick was protected by the same line of code. That made me suspicious—so I dissected it."

A thin smile creased Wainwright's face. "And what did your autopsy reveal?"

"That the code from the StarPoint software had another application—something we missed on our first go-around."

Nate spoke up. "This is a little over my head."

"I think I get it," Neill said. "McBride added a back door; a code that would allow him—or someone else—access to the satellites. Is that it?"

Chau nodded approvingly. "That's close enough."

Wainwright looked concerned now. "What bearing could this have on China's exercises?"

"I'd like to speak with a colleague of mine in San Diego," Simon replied. "Maybe she can answer that."

"Feel free to do so, Leftenant." Wainwright traded looks with the XO. "Ring up the American battle group. We can't keep this to ourselves."

Naval Forces Garrison Academy,
Beijing, China

THE CALL CAME AT EIGHT P.M.—CHINESE Standard Time. The voice on the other end uttered a simple, coded phrase. Lin Yuan understood its meaning immediately and went right to work.

It was getting late, and the cubicles around him were occupied sparingly. Few could have guessed at Yuan's intentions.
He was discreet, but hardly secretive about his actions—for the
operators on this floor, there was little need to justify the proj-
ects they were involved with.

Yuan used a simple laptop. This was linked to a server that
relayed commands to several orbiting spacecraft. It also had the
capability to interface with Taiwan's sea-going network.

The Prober pulled up an app that pin-pointed the location of
the StarPoint Series I satellites. It didn't matter which vehicle
he selected; there were four in total, and Yuan only needed one.
Each carried powerful gear that could beam transmissions anywhere in Asia—on land or at sea.

He clicked randomly on one of the satellites. A drop-down
menu appeared, displaying a control panel. Yuan typed in an
alpha-numeric code from memory. The dialog box blinked, instructing him to repeat the string of data in the next field. He
followed the prompt and then hit the submit button.

For the Prober, this was the culmination of months of prepa-
ration. Admiral Lee's plan had been set in motion—all with the
click of a mouse.

Aboard the ROC Destroyer Kee Lung

CAPTAIN HAO HSU'S EYES SWEPT THE DARK-
ness. He could see the running lights of the *Luzhou*, three
miles from the *Kee Lung's* starboard bow. The Chinese vessel
was now sailing in a clockwise pattern—while the rest of the
fleet continued south.

Hsu knew that something was afoot. The destroyers of the
PLA-Navy had been playing a game. They would steam on a
parallel course and suddenly turn into the path of the closest
ROC vessel. When collision seemed imminent, they would turn
again and head back out to sea.

It was much too provocative for Hsu's tastes.

Lieutenant Yang was also on the bridge. He moved from one station to another, intent on checking the position of the surface fleet surrounding them.

"Recommend we slow our speed, Captain. The *Luzhou* has changed course for a reason."

Taichung was just off their port quarter. Yang studied a screen as the destroyer made her approach. A smaller, unidentified vessel seemed to follow the *Luzhou*. The swells further out made it hard to get a clear radar return. Probably one of their gunboats, Yang decided. "Captain Lao intends to goad us into a fight."

That threat had existed for decades. At the heart of it was the contentious issue of the island's status as a nation. Somewhere between *illegitimacy*—China's view—and *sovereignty*, the preferred opinion of Taiwan—the potential for armed conflict depended on who had power. For the moment, Premier and Party Secretary Tao Chengdu held the reins in Beijing. His perspective counted for much, but Chengdu seemed ambivalent about the island's political posturing. Like most of Taiwan's population, and his own countrymen, the Premier seemed to prefer the status quo. This was a position that guaranteed a measure of calm, both internationally and among China's teeming inhabitants.

But there was another group. A smaller percentage cried out for reunification—and their voices grew louder. They were the old guard, a generation of military men with the power and the will to see it done. The Republic of China could not ignore their growing ambition.

Although much smaller than the combined ships of the Chinese fleet, the Navy of the ROC enjoyed certain advantages. Friendship with the United States and the free world was one. The relative safety of the Black Ditch was another. Each acted as a buffer against hostilities, but in recent years, political developments and advancing technology seemed to have narrowed both.

Hsu was prepared to calm Yang's concern when something unexpected happened. The diffused light on the bridge winked out. The monitors were the next to go; numerical displays announcing the ship's speed and position went blank. Overhead, the ductwork feeding cool air into the compartment dropped to a whisper and became silent.

Yang and Hsu traded alarmed looks. Below their feet, the steady *thrum* of the ship's power plant faded—as nearly every vital system aboard ground to a halt.

San Diego

ENSIGN PRESSMAN STUDIED THE SECURE FEED from the *Bush*. A monitor in her cubicle was hooked to USPACFLT, the hub for command and control in the Pacific. The split-screen display featured an overhead satellite view, with links to other cameras in-theater. Most of the data streamed from the UCAV, and was beamed from an orbiting satellite directly to her station.

Kelsi jumped as her cell phone lit up. She certainly wasn't expecting a call at this hour. The number didn't look familiar. She decided to answer—and was shocked by the sound of a familiar voice.

"Okay. So where are you?"

From halfway around the world, Simon Chau paused before answering. "I'm not sure I can tell you that. Think Pearl—but further west. And I didn't mean to wake you."

A soft laugh; the kind that reminded Simon of how much he missed her. "No worries there, sailor. I've been up since one a.m.—I'm at the shop as we speak."

Chau blinked. *Had he miscalculated the time on the west coast?*

Pressman didn't wait for a response. "Things are a little busy here right now. Did you call for a reason?"

"Yeah." Simon looked around him. Some of the watchstanders in the CIC seemed a little more focused. "You remember that software we evaluated, two summers ago?"

That was an odd coincidence. "I'm looking at it," she replied.

Her concentration was suddenly broken. Radio chatter crackled from twin speakers on her desk. There was an urgency to the traffic that she couldn't ignore. Kelsi focused again on the split-screen view being broadcast from sea.

"Hang on a sec. There's something happening."

"Yeah. I know what you mean," Simon answered. He sounded detached.

There was movement in Control. Commodore Wainwright and the XO left the shack, with Amanda in tow.

Chau looked to Neill. The Marine had also noted the activity. He stepped off in Templeton's direction.

Aboard the USS Bush

THE XO ABOARD INDUSTRIOUS ASKED FOR THE Admiral. Commander Lipford handed off the phone to LaSalle and turned to face the cartographic display. Something on the screen just didn't look right.

"You see this, Skipper?"

Captain DeSouza nodded. A Petty Officer manned the station at his side. "Notch up the volume, Comm."

The seaman adjusted a dial. Excited voices filled their ears—in a language none of the crew recognized.

"Where's that coming from?"

"Traffic between the ROC ships, Captain. The broadcast we're listening to is from the *Kee Lung*."

"Hao Hsu's command," DeSouza said. His eyes locked on the plot screen. The red squares on the monitor continued to move as before—in fact, some of those were increasing speed. But the images representing Taiwan's Navy seemed frozen. The men watched for two full minutes as the board changed.

"They've stopped," Lipford announced. "What the Sam Hill are they up to?"

LaSalle replaced the handset. He shook his head, recalling CINCPAC's warning—and the intel he'd just received from Wainwright.

"Trust me, Commander. This isn't Hsu's doing." The Admiral faced Comm. "Raise Captain Beacham aboard the *Meyer*—and do it now, son."

Chapter Thirty-Nine ✶ General Quarters

Aboard the Luzhou

S ENIOR CAPTAIN LAO WATCHED AS ADMIRAL Lee's plan began to unfold. The *Kee Lung* had been surging ahead. Now her speed had greatly diminished, and the destroyer moved sluggishly.

Lao waited and checked his radar. Taiwanese ships up and down the coastline were also incapacitated. Lao's commanders in the fleet began transmitting coded messages. They reported the same results; all around the island, the ROC Navy was now dead in the water.

The Industrious

"YOU'RE FOLLOWING THIS?" PRESSMAN WAS A little surprised.

"I am now."

Simon's attention was divided. At the other end of Control, the *Industrious'* crew scrutinized a screen on the bulkhead. The display featured a satellite view of Taiwan—courtesy of Admiral LaSalle, and the telemetry provided by the UCAV. Chau listened as radio transmissions were piped in through speakers on either side of the monitor.

"Can you turn that up?"

Neill looked in his direction. "Is that Mandarin, Si?"

Chau nodded. He strained to pick out details of the conversation. "Taiwan's ships are reporting a loss of power."

"Which ones?" Wainwright asked.

"All of them."

The Meyer

CAPTAIN BEACHAM REPLACED THE PHONE AND studied the plot board. The ocean far to the north was laid out before him—a combination of the data sent from the UCAV and the *Victory*.

The Admiral's words were still ringing in his ears. *All actions authorized, subject to the Captain's discretion.* Beacham drew a hand across his chin and smiled.

LaSalle's orders had been specific—but vague at the same time. He had one outcome in mind, but resisted the urge to micro-manage one of his most capable officers. The Skipper surveyed the two-dimensional chess game playing out on the monitor. The *Kee Lung* still had forward momentum, but the inertia provided by the ship's bulk wouldn't last long. Two and a half miles to the south, the *Luzhou* doubled her speed and changed direction. The new course pointed her toward the port of Taichung.

Beacham did a little math in his head and turned to face Commander Towle.

"XO, set a new course for the *Victory*. Come right five degrees to zero nine zero and increase to flank. I want her to intercept that Chinese destroyer before it can enter the harbor."

Towle eyed the monitor. "Aye, Skipper." He turned to Lieutenant Sanchez. "Helm—new course, zero nine zero. Blow tanks fore and aft and increase to flank."

Sanchez repeated the order.

To increase speed, the arsenal ship would need to lose a little weight. The ballast she carried had reduced her radar cross-section, but the time for stealth was over. It was the Captain's plan to advertise the *Victory's* position—and send a clear message to the command element of the PLA-Navy.

Almost as an afterthought, Beacham said, "Spool up THRIFTY NICKEL while you're at it. We might need to get a little feisty."

Towle grinned. "Mr. Sanchez—coordinate with weapons and bring the PEASHOOTER online."

"Aye, sir." It was the Lieutenant who smiled now. He nodded to the Weapons Officer. "Bringing the PEASHOOTER online."

The Industrious

CHAU'S MIND RACED. IT WAS THE COMPUTER *uplink; it had to be,* he decided. He pressed the phone closer.

"Are you still there?"

"I'm here," Pressman answered.

"And you've got StarPoint on your screen?" Simon was at something of a disadvantage. Without access to the application, he was blind. But that didn't mean he was powerless—as long as he could rely on Kelsi.

"What do you want to know?"

"Check compatibility—could the software interact with a ship's communications?"

"Hang on."

She scrolled through paragraphs of code until she found what she was looking for. "Negative—that architecture is separate." With the truth staring back at her from the screen, Kelsi had found illumination. *"Which is why you can still hear them."*

Simon nodded excitedly. He turned in his chair and got Neill's attention.

"The StarPoint satellites are being spoofed."

Neill raised an eyebrow. "Excuse me?"

Wainwright followed Neill as he took a few steps in Chau's direction. Simon was glad for that; he didn't want to have to run through his explanation twice. There wasn't time.

"Spoofed—hacked into," Chau began. "Think of it like this. Four satellites; they provide Taiwan with an alternative to our

GPS system. Nationalistic pride meets low-budget software, I guess you could say."

The Commodore looked alarmed. "Hacked by whom?"

"China," Neill answered. "Did they use a virus?"

Chau shook his head. "They didn't have to—McBride's company sold them an app that wasn't totally secure. It's like you said earlier; a *back door* that gives them access privileges."

Templeton moved closer. "How does it work?" On the phone, Kelsi Pressman followed the discussion as Simon continued.

"Our GPS is protected against hacking. We use encrypted firewalls. It takes special technology to receive and process the signals. Taiwan's situation is a little different. Their Navy relies on StarPoint for navigation. The data is beamed directly to each ship from space."

"Is this where those random lines of code come in?" Wainwright asked.

"Yes, sir. They're like a Trojan horse, allowing a hacker to send coded commands—which apparently they did."

"Good Lord." A groan from the Commodore. "Tell me that it isn't really that easy. Is that why the ROC ships have stopped moving?"

"That's my guess, sir. An order's been relayed to Taiwan's Navy to shut down their power plants."

"What about the rest of their hardware?" Templeton asked.

"Comm and a few other systems are the only things not controlled by their onboard computers."

"Are there any effective countermeasures?" Wainwright pressed.

Chau looked thoughtful. He paused before answering, and then said, "Maybe—but we'll need to communicate directly with their ships."

"That can be arranged." Wainwright eyed the communications officer next to Simon. "But we'll need to be quick about it."

The Luzhou

THE VICTORY LEFT NO WAKE. IT WOULD HAVE been impossible to find one in the storm-tossed seas. Her displacement had changed as the hull rose from the waves and the ship turned to starboard. This new course would take her directly to the mouth of Taichung's harbor.

The lookout posted on the *Luzhou's* bridge saw her first. A brief flash of lightning revealed her presence. Another bolt arced across the sky before the sailor announced what he'd seen.

"Ship astern!" His voice was uneven. This was unexpected, and the young seaman hoped he hadn't just alerted the entire bridge crew to one of their own. "Half a kilometer—overtaking us on our starboard quarter."

Captain Lao now stood at the lookout's side. He trained a pair of binoculars aft. More lightning, and he could see her now that the ship moved up.

"American."

The sleek lines of the warship were too advanced to be anything else. Lao had heard rumors of a new high-tech weapon being built by the United States. He shot a look at Navigation.

"Do you have it on radar?"

The Navigation Officer studied his screen. "I have her now—but she has only just appeared."

Lao nodded. "A hybrid. Part submersible, part destroyer." Briefings identified the ship as fast and very nimble, with an unmatched sonar suite and electric drive propulsion. Most systems were said to be fully automated.

"She intends to reach Taichung before us. Increase speed." The American ship had begun to outpace them. Lao couldn't let that happen. He turned to his Executive Officer. "Bring up our gunboats. Have them send a few rounds across her bow."

The XO raised an eyebrow. Two riverine-type craft had accelerated past the *Kee Lung* and were approaching the *Luzhou* from the north, bouncing from one swell to the next. Individually, each boat wasn't much bigger than a good-sized launch. Lao's second in command relayed the order and the Senior Captain watched as they turned east.

The USS Bush

"ONE OF OUR LINGUISTS?"

LaSalle pressed the phone to his ear. He wore a surprised look. DeSouza and Lipford took their eyes from the plot board as the Admiral listened for a moment longer.

LaSalle covered the mouthpiece. "The *Industrious*," he explained. "Wainwright says they might have a solution." He turned to the officer manning communications. "Patch this call through the network. Captain Hsu needs to hear it." Once more the Admiral spoke into the handset.

"Standby, Harry."

The Kee Lung

LIEUTENANT YANG WAS FRANTICALLY RUNNING diagnostics when the call came through. He hesitated to answer; the ship was drifting, and his first priority was to restore power and steerage. If the Chinese destroyer ahead continued on her present course—

Captain Hsu stepped to the radio, allowing Yang to proceed. A glance at the board reassured him. The incoming transmission rode the frequency used by the U.S. battle group to the south. He picked up the handset and expected to hear English, yet the voice that addressed him spoke perfect Mandarin.

Simon Chau talked fast. First came a few brief introductions. There wasn't time to explain an ex-Chinese national's presence aboard a British warship—Hao Hsu took it on faith that the caller had Taiwan's best interests at heart. The Captain almost smiled. If this was some kind of trick, hearing the man out wouldn't make any difference. The *Kee Lung* was powerless in the middle of a typhoon; the damage had already been done. Hsu put the call on speaker and cradled the phone.

The Industrious

"YOUR NETWORK'S BEEN COMPROMISED," Simon began. He forced himself to proceed methodically, taking a deep breath and pacing his words. "The Chinese military has gained access to StarPoint—they're using it to relay commands across your grid."

Yang tried to restart the ship's central processing unit. The attempt had failed. "All of our major systems are interconnected. The interface runs deep—is there some way to bypass it and bring the ship's functions back online?"

Simon didn't have the StarPoint software in front of him. He translated the question for Kelsi's ears.

Pressman sifted through lines of code. She was familiar with McBride's odd formatting protocols, but her search took time. A full minute passed and she still hadn't found what she was looking for.

Back up, Kelsi, she told herself. *Take the long view—stop focusing on the details.*

By now, Fitzroy and Garcia were hovering behind her chair. She scanned her screen again, broadening the scope of her search. Suddenly, it all became clear. An algorithm embedded in the stream acted as a bloodhound, first sniffing out and then seizing command functions.

"Got it," she breathed. "Simon, it's a fool's errand—but very clever. McBride's code brackets specific control hierarchies and shuts them down. As long as StarPoint maintains a connection, the command will continue to cycle through. Taiwan's Navy has to break the link."

"They've already re-booted the system once. Power's still out." Simon was beginning to feel just a little helpless.

"Okay—hang on."

Kelsi was momentarily distracted. Intercepts from Taiwan were reporting attacks against servers across the island. They were widespread, but less than effective. Pressman smiled.

The Chinese had bitten off more than they could chew.

She switched to an app running in the background—the navigational software used aboard the ROC ships. The change in perspective helped immensely. She sat up in her chair and quickly read through the string of data. What she saw was unexpected, but Pressman could appreciate its elegant simplicity.

"Simon, you're going to like this. At start-up, the nav program links directly to the satellite—which is the problem."

"That much we know." Chau eyed the plot board along with everyone else in the CIC. The Chinese Navy was getting uncomfortably close to the island's harbors.

"McBride overlooked something," Kelsi pressed on. "The system allows for three hard re-starts—after that, it assumes a major problem—and breaks the connection."

* * * *

THE NAVAL INFANTRYMAN ON THE LEAD GUN-boat primed his weapon. The older style 12.7 millimeter machine gun was mounted squarely on the foredeck. Another sailor was standing by to assist with ordnance. The two steadied themselves as the small craft was tossed on the waves.

Directly ahead, and half a kilometer away, the sleek American warship knifed evenly through the swells. She pulled abreast of the *Luzhou* and continued eastward. The lights of the harbor were hidden in the distance by sheets of rain.

They were well within range. The gunner turned to face the small wheelhouse. At a nod from the pilot, the sailor swung the barrel slightly to port and fired a burst of three rounds. None of these were tracers, and it was impossible to accurately gauge their trajectory in the dark. The gunner had aimed far ahead of the advancing destroyer's bow, but the vessel showed no signs of changing her course or slowing down.

He shifted position; this time he pointed the muzzle closer to the target. He loosed three more rounds, but a trough between swells spoiled his aim. One of the shells passed overhead—but the last two found the ship's superstructure and ricocheted harmlessly into the sea.

The USS Meyer

Lieutenant Sanchez watched the video feed from the *Victory*. Color images dominated the split-screen view, with separate optics in the arsenal ship's bridge providing an infrared perspective.

Rain pelted the *Victory's* sensitive lenses, at times obscuring the ship's field of vision. The thermal shots gave an uncluttered look at the seascape. Sanchez and the other watchstanders in Control relied on both.

Movement to the north caught the Lieutenant's attention. "Skipper—small boats closing." He used the mouse at his fingertips and adjusted the cameras' track. "Two craft, half a mile out, broad on the port bow."

Captain Beacham squinted at the screen. "Was that a muzzle flash?"

Sanchez saw it too. It was especially pronounced in the IR range. "Aye, sir. Deck sensors indicate multiple contacts with the skin—but no breaks in structural integrity."

With all the armor enclosing her hull, small arms had little effect on the *Victory*. The Captain raised an eyebrow and smiled. "Probably just scratched the paint. A little provocative, wouldn't you say, Commander Towle?"

The XO nodded. "I concur, Captain. And they're approaching at high speed."

Beacham's mind went elsewhere. "Fishing boats."

"Skipper?"

"Can't remember who said it—but the Chinese Admiralty doesn't consider ships like the *Victory* to be a threat. One of their senior officers has said that a few fishing boats with explosives could defeat a high-tech warship."

"Like the attack on the *Cole*?" Sanchez asked.

Beacham's eyes were glued to the display. "That statement's on the record. And in this storm—under the cover of darkness—those two craft look an awful lot like fishing boats, don't they?"

Towle grinned. "Might be prudent to assume a more protective posture—given the nature of the Admiralty's comments."

"Agreed," Beacham snapped. "Mr. Sanchez, what's the status of THRIFTY NICKEL?"

"Warmed up and ready to roll, Skipper. Intermediate stores are fully charged." On screen, the watercraft had slowed their pace. It was clear they were focused on the *Victory*. Their intentions were a little murkier.

"Very well. Continue on present course. Bring the *Victory* to general quarters and deploy the rail gun."

"Aye, sir." Sanchez felt a surge of adrenaline. He tapped a few keys, initiating a sequence he'd only used during simulations. "Signaling general quarters to the *Victory* and deploying the rail gun."

* * * *

THERE WAS NO MISTAKING THE SOUND OF THE shells striking the hull. The gunner cringed. He'd never fired on a foreign vessel before—much less an American Navy warship—and now his carelessness had caused him to hit one.

The stealthy destroyer continued as before, seemingly unfazed by the attack. Forward of the command superstructure, panels fifteen meters long separated and revealed a rectangular compartment. In the space below was the shipboard cannon code-named THRIFTY NICKEL.

As the bay doors receded, hydraulics propelled the weapons array upward to the foredeck. Earlier versions of the PEASHOOTER were bulky affairs, and could be mistaken for shipping containers wired to elaborate generator assemblies. The rail gun on the *Victory* had few of those features, and with a ten meter barrel it could be easily distinguished as a massive weapon.

* * * *

LIEUTENANT SANCHEZ HELD A JOYSTICK. Toggling controls on the device, he activated servomotors in the gun mount and swung the PEASHOOTER'S muzzle to port. Optics on the big screen clicked into place and zeroed the weapon's sights on the lead boat. A soft tone followed; the sound from the speakers informed everyone in the CIC that the rail gun was locked on target.

"Lower your aim, Lieutenant," Beacham ordered. "There won't be anything left if you hit them there. Point the barrel about twenty meters in front of their bow."

Sanchez did as instructed, adjusting his sight picture.

"He's getting close, Skipper."

"He is indeed, Mr. Sanchez. Now let's see if a hypersonic bullet can deter his intentions.

"*Weapons free*—fire the first salvo."

* * * *

SANCHEZ WAS RIGHT.

For a weapon capable of sending rounds one hundred miles downrange, the small gunboat was very close. A strong message needed to be sent, and Captain Beacham knew that THRIFTY NICKEL could deliver it.

Far over the horizon, the Lieutenant depressed the firing switch. Propelled by a thirty mega-joule charge—the rail gun was powered by an electromagnet—a three and a half kilogram shell was launched from the barrel. The initial blast briefly turned night into day. An inferno of fire engulfed the end of the muzzle as more than a million amps arced through the system. The round left the weapon traveling at more than two kilometers per second, shedding its outer casing as it went.

Aboard the gunboat, there wasn't time to react. The shell's

impact vaporized a zone of water several feet deep, cratering the sea directly in front of the hapless craft. Her bow dove into the trough and then heeled over on her starboard side. The deck crew was thrown clear; the gunner suffered two broken arms as he gripped his weapon.

On the *Meyer*, no one was surprised when the second boat veered away.

* * * *

"SPLASH ONE," BEACHAM ANNOUNCED. "Weapons status?"

Sanchez had already checked his board. "Batteries at forty-eight percent. Re-charging."

Beacham looked pleased. "Nice shooting, Mr. Sanchez. I think they got the message. Now let's see if they understand something a little more diplomatic." Beacham turned to address the Petty Officer at his side. "Ready for some dictation, Comm?"

"Aye, sir."

"Tap the Chinese frequency. We'll be transmitting to the *Luzhou*." Beacham eyed Commander Towle. "You think anybody on their bridge speaks English?"

"That's a possibility, Skipper."

"We'll take that chance. Send them this—"

Aboard the Luzhou

THE EXECUTIVE OFFICER STANDING AT CAPTAIN Lao's side was educated at Cambridge and did speak English. He translated the message as it came up on the screen.

220016MAR14
RESTRICTED ACCESS/RECIPIENT ONLY

FROM: USS *MEYER*
TO: PLA-NAVY VESSEL *LUZHOU*

MESSAGE FOLLOWS

YOUR SITUATION IN DOUBT XX URGE YOU RE-EVALUATE
INTENTIONS XX RECOMMEND ALL PARTIES STAND DOWN
TO MITIGATE AGAINST FURTHER LOSS XX ESCALATION OF
FORCES NOT IN YOUR BEST INTERESTS XX STANDING BY FOR
CONCURRENCE XX VERY INTERESTED IN YOUR RADAR MAST
SHOULD YOU DISAGREE XX ALL OF OUR SHIPS – REPEAT –
ALL OF OUR SHIPS AWAIT YOUR RESPONSE

MESSAGE ENDS
CAPTAIN BEACHAM SENDING

The officer finished speaking just as an alarm chimed in
their ears. A glance at the ship's threat board told Lao all that he
needed to know; the American destroyer had her sights on the
Luzhou's antenna array two stories above the bridge.

The Kee Lung

LIEUTENANT YANG HELD HIS BREATH. HE HAD
re-booted the command processor three times—while keeping a wary eye on the *Luzhou's* progress. Something had happened on the other side of the destroyer. He couldn't tell what
it was, but a flash of light moments earlier had come from the
sea.

The instructions from the *Industrious* seemed simple enough.
Yang could only wait now. Before him the monitors tied to the
computer started to hum; one by one they flickered to life. The
past three attempts had all ended the same way; the screens
glowed briefly and then went dark again.

This time it was different. The American on the British vessel—*Chau, did he say his name was?*—had been right. Lights
began flickering on the bridge. The flow of air in the ducts above
was next as other systems began to come online.

The final evidence of restored power was the most gratifying. Beneath their feet, in the bowels of the ship, the *Kee Lung's* power plant came alive again.

Captain Hsu wasted no time relaying commands now that he had his ship back. He keyed the intercom and spoke directly to Engineering.

"This is the Captain. All ahead full." A nod to the pilot. "Helm, come to new course zero nine zero—put our bow ahead of the *Luzhou*."

The seaman at the wheel was only happy to oblige. As the *Kee Lung* built speed, steerage was instantly responsive.

"Helm is answering, Captain. Our course is now zero nine zero."

The Luzhou

"HE'S BLUFFING."

The Executive Officer watched the arsenal ship on the starboard beam. There would be no catching her now. The American was just too fast.

Captain Lao trained his binoculars ahead. Through the rain he could make out the weapon that had disabled his gunboat. The second craft was already rescuing survivors from the capsized vessel.

"No, Lieutenant," Lao breathed. "I don't think that he is."

Lao looked to his left. The lights aboard the *Kee Lung* had returned, and the ROC vessel was underway. She was increasing speed and moving to intercept the *Luzhou*. Between Captain Hsu's command and the *Victory*, there was little chance Lao could best either ship.

He studied the newcomer once more. Even at this distance it was obvious that his ship was in the crosshairs. With one shot, this new destroyer had melted Lao's resolve.

"Slow to one third and contact the fleet." The Captain's voice was steady. "Order each of them to expand their area of operations—*away* from the island. All principals close to shore are to disengage." He lowered his field glasses and sighed.

Perhaps next year—

Lao knew that wouldn't happen. Taiwan would be more pre-pared in the following spring. The Americans especially so. He could foresee the U.S. Navy's pivot to Pacific waters accelerat-ing after this incident.

The Captain stepped to the communications board and picked up a handset, resigned to the situation. Someone would need to inform the Admiral. That duty fell to Lao.

It was a task he would have preferred to ignore.

Chapter Forty ✵ Resolution

Beijing

Xian Lee sat in the anteroom of the Premier's office. He was understandably tense.

Twenty-four hours had passed since his plans had unraveled. A full accounting would now have to be made. The Premier would expect a comprehensive review; and as a former officer in the PLA-Army himself, nothing less than an analytical evaluation would do.

Lee forced himself to relax. He was a seasoned hand at after action reports. At the conclusion of each spring's exercises, he had laid out point-by-point summaries of naval operations in the Strait. Today his briefing would be a little different, although some operational details had been tweaked—or scrubbed altogether.

Lee had managed to disguise a few aspects of the Navy's maneuvers. A creative misrepresentation of the facts had helped. But there were specifics related to the exercises that not even the Admiral could keep secret. The Chinese armada had overstepped its boundaries. That was undeniable, and Lee had no intention of skirting the issue. To excuse his actions, he would appeal to a sense of nationalistic fervor—and the misplaced exuberance of his commanders at sea.

The Premier was well aware of Lee's political views. In the

past, Chengdu had been persuaded to rein in the Admiral. What had happened a day before—in confused circumstances, and at the height of a raging typhoon—was just one more example of Lee's patriotic enthusiasm.

The Admiral was ushered into the Premier's office promptly at nine a.m. A few things caught his attention. Standing on either side of the door as he entered were members of the Secretary's protectorate. These two men normally wore dark suits, but today they were clad in military uniforms. Neither acknowledged his presence, nor stood at attention as Lee came into the room. This provoked him to anger; their actions were odd and extremely disrespectful to the stars he wore on his collar.

He let that pass when he saw who sat across from Chengdu's desk. Captain Zhu Ling turned in his chair and stared at the Admiral. Seated next to him was an Ensign; his face was unfamiliar. The younger officer braced, and almost got to his feet—until Ling's hand restrained him.

"Thank you for coming, Lee."

The Premier's voice was devoid of emotion. He studied what appeared to be notes on his desk, never looking up. By contrast, Zhu Ling's gaze seemed to bore through the Admiral.

A slight bow. "I serve at your pleasure, Mr. Secretary."

The Premier grunted. "Perhaps at your own. But certainly not at mine." He looked up for the first time. "You are surprised to see Captain Ling here?"

Lee said nothing. He had a very bad feeling about what might follow.

"The Captain arrived yesterday. He spun a wild tale; submarines, torpedoes—" he paused for effect. "—and a covert scheme by the Admiralty to seize Taiwan. His testimony names you as a key player in this unauthorized plan."

Lee could feel sweat on his forehead. "A lie, Mr. Secretary."

The Premier stood slowly and walked around his desk. Out of respect, Ling and the young Ensign rose from their chairs.

"I considered it to be a fiction as well—until the Captain

produced evidence. Twenty four sailors. The crew of a Russian submarine, an Oscar class boat, yes, Captain? And each has signed affidavits corroborating his story."

"And you believe this, Mr. Secretary?" Lee protested, but felt a sickening in the pit of his stomach.

"I must confess, I had my doubts. But then the Captain did something quite unusual. Can you guess what that might be?"

Lee shook his head. His eye twitched, and his heart raced.

"No, Mr. Secretary."

The Premier nodded. "Captain Ling took his share of the responsibility. And he offered to place himself under arrest. Such a noble gesture is not to be ignored. In fact, considering the circumstances, I feel it should be rewarded. Wouldn't you agree—*Admiral?*"

Chengdu bit off that word with unmasked disgust. He stepped forward and came face to face with Lee. The two stared at each other, Lee's eyes on the Premier. He was a proud man—even in defeat.

A simple gesture brought the security detail to the Admiral's side. The two men were burly by Chinese standards. They quietly took charge of Lee and escorted him back out through the doors he had entered moments before.

* * * *

EAST OF BEIJING, IN THE CHANGPING DISTRICT, Qincheng Prison buttressed the Yanshan Mountains on the North China Plain. A maximum security facility, Qincheng had been passed from one state agency to another, but was now under the control of the military.

The number of residents there had recently grown. Twenty-four new detainees were flown in from Hainan during the previous night. For such a large influx, the provost marshal had arrived to oversee their processing. Oddly enough, each man had ties to the Navy.

Twelve hours later, the facility received another guest.

The provost recognized him immediately. This internee wore a military uniform, but had been stripped of his rank. The charges leveled against him were capital crimes—and the arrest warrant had been signed by the Premier himself.

For Xian Lee, the formalities of a trial would be expedited. A guilty verdict was a foregone conclusion. His sentence was automatic.

The death penalty was alive and well in China. Lee could not evade justice this time. His stay at Qincheng would be short.

Aboard the USS Bush,
The Luzon Strait

ADMIRAL LASALLE STOOD ON THE BRIDGE, staring out to sea. It was much quieter now—a few dark clouds lingered on the horizon, but typhoon Ulysses had moved far to the south.

From a naval standpoint, operations to the north had also settled down. China's fleet had suspended their aggressive maneuvers and now gave Taiwan a wide berth. The ships of the ROC kept a watchful eye. It would be some days before they relaxed their posture.

Captain DeSouza cleared his throat at the Admiral's side. "I take it Mr. Avery is pleased," he offered.

LaSalle nodded. "He is indeed. Things turned out well." His simple assessment gave rise to another thought. "This whole thing reminds me of Mr. Madison's war."

The Captain smiled. LaSalle often launched into soliloquies when summarizing operations. He was a student of history—especially where the fledgling U.S. Navy was involved.

"American vessels gained the upper hand in more than a few fights during the War of 1812," he pressed on. "Granted, they were single-ship engagements. The Royal Navy complained, naturally. They said the battles were unfair, and that they had been beaten by *'a few fir-built frigates, manned by a handful of bastards and outlaws.'* The English language was a curious mix of candor and elegance back then."

DeSouza silently agreed, and also noted the change in weather. He did a quick head count of the vessels under the Admiral's command. On either side of the *Bush* were the rest of the ships in the battle group.

Out of sight, far over the horizon, the *Meyer* cruised the waters of the Strait of Taiwan. The *Victory* sailed ahead, and had already rounded the northern tip of the island on an easterly course. In one more day, the small flotilla would be in a position to retrieve Chau and Richey, liberating them from their English hosts—and bringing an end to the association of the Colonial Rifles.

Aboard the HMS Industrious,
100 Kilometers west of Luzon,
The Philippines

"What's left?" Crockett asked.

Neill grinned. "Just the paperwork," he answered. The two Marines stood at the fantail, mesmerized by the ship's wake. The afternoon sun tinted the sea with shades of orange and gold.

"USPACFLT's arranged for a helo to pick us up tomorrow. One more night as guests of the Royal Navy—then back to the *Lexington*."

"And two days of box nasties," Nate grimaced. "Or is it three?" His sour expression turned to a smile. "I know your plan. You're hoping for more champagne with that bonnie English lass."

Neill heaved a sigh. "That wasn't champagne," he corrected.

Amanda Templeton had hoped for some quiet time alone with Michael, but the four Americans—along with the Commodore and Executive Officer—had toasted their way through the evening with sparkling grape juice. The team would be going their separate ways soon, and it just seemed appropriate to celebrate together.

A moment passed as Neill reflected on the young woman. He was flattered by her attention. She was both beautiful and engaging, with a coy personality that contrasted with his own. Her professional demeanor was the one characteristic that matched the two. Michael was drawn to Amanda, but the face of another woman came to mind.

The past few days had been a whirlwind. Thoughts of Huo Shan kept pushing to the surface, along with Simon Chau's words about curses. Neill considered that in a spiritual frame of reference. The four of them had enjoyed a certain level of protection while on the island. Neill attributed that to God's grace. It wasn't until their feet left Huo Shan—or more specifically, the pier—that the Chinese troops managed to direct violence their way. But those acts hadn't prospered against them.

Something else nagged at him. White Dragon had recognized him, and spoken his name without any real way of knowing who he was. There hadn't been time to get answers on the island. And now it was a mystery that would have to keep.

The surreal experience of hearing his father's voice was also heavy on Neill's heart. It flooded him with memories of his mom and dad—and the love they shared together.

Those feelings left him wanting.

Neill fished his cell phone out of his breast pocket. He wanted nothing more than to reach out to an old friend. He activated the device and scrolled through the directory until he found Christina Arren's number. It would have been nice to hear her voice, but the Marine doubted he could get a signal in the midst of the South China Sea.

"I'm gonna grab a shower," Crocket announced. "Si wants to meet us for dinner, so don't be late."

Neill chuckled softly as Nate wagged his finger. From behind, the hatch opened and Senior Chief Richey stepped out onto the deck. Crockett gave him a nod in passing, and then disappeared into the ship.

"Ready to go home, El-Tee?" Malcolm rested his forearms on the railing and drew in the sea air. Neill pocketed his phone and stared aft.

"Home is where you make it, Chief." At the moment, Arlington, Virginia was looking pretty good.

"Yeah," Richey drawled. "I guess you've got a point. Lately I've had a little trouble figuring out where that might be. At least in my case." He paused, and then turned to face the younger man. His words were awkward.

"You said a few things back on the island. About God rescuing people. That stuff about faith. Is all that real? I mean, does He still do that?"

"God keeps all of His promises; that's one thing you can be sure of in this world." Neill allowed himself a grin. "You remind me of another searching soul. A man named Jonah."

He couldn't recall the entire passage, but a few verses were familiar enough.

'In my distress I called to the Lord,
And He answered me.
From the depths of the grave I called for help,
And You listened to my cry.
You hurled me into the deep,
Into the very heart of the seas,
And the currents swirled about me;

. . . When my life was ebbing away,
I remembered you, Lord,
And my prayer rose to you,
To your holy temple.

. . . But I, with a song of thanksgiving,
Will sacrifice to you.
What I have vowed I will make good.
Salvation comes from the Lord.'

Epilogue ✶ Redemption

WU CHANG CHECKED HIS WATCH— again—as the car navigated the narrow streets of Beijing. He winced as he realized this would probably be regarded as impatience by his driver. Chang suppressed the thought and stared ahead. It seemed like every government official with a car was jockeying for position in the morning traffic.

That was to be expected. Chang recalled his own service here, many years before, when he served on the staff of the Chinese admiralty. As a young Lieutenant, he himself had driven many officers and bureaucrats, and experienced the hustle and bustle of making sure his superiors arrived for their appointments on time.

What he saw outside the windows of the government sedan seemed no different from those faraway days. He remembered the past with fondness, but the car's next turn brought his mind forward; in the distance, Chang could see the outline of the multi-storied office building that was to be his next destination.

The People's Liberation Army-Naval Division headquarters was a short drive from the hotel Chang had stayed in the night before. He'd arrived the previous day on a flight from his home in the Jiansu province, but the purpose of this invited visit was a mystery to him. Days before, a courier had delivered an official letter—with a cryptic request. Several high-ranking naval officers asked to meet with him. Beyond that, there was nothing to indicate the reason for their summons. He was understandably curious and concerned. It had been more than six months since Admiral Lee had terminated his career in the Navy and sent the former Captain home in disgrace. Was that what this was all about? Did Lee intend to inflict further punishment?

Chang put that thought aside as the car slowed and parked in front of the division headquarters. He reached for the door handle, but the driver gently laid a hand on his arm. Chang watched as the younger man jumped from the car and moved around to his side of the vehicle, coming to attention as he opened the door.

Surely he has no idea who I am; Chang thought to himself; *if he did, he certainly wouldn't be so quick to extend such courtesy.*

The driver waited dutifully with the car, and Chang made his way up the steps and into the entryway of the building. The exterior looked just like any other bureaucratic office complex, but once inside, Chang marveled at the mix of functionality and ancient Chinese décor. This building had been recently built, and was very different from the headquarters Chang knew. The lobby was a spacious area with a four story atrium. It was clear that someone with great respect for the country's culture and art had been given a free hand to decorate it.

As Chang gazed at his surroundings, a petite young Asian woman approached him and offered him a seat near a set of double doors. These undoubtedly led deeper into the facility. She returned to a desk not far away, picked up a phone, and after a short pause, whispered something Chang couldn't hear. He could only guess that she'd informed someone of his arrival, and he wondered how long they would make him wait.

"WU CHANG?"

The voice from behind startled him; turning in his seat, he saw two uniformed naval officers—one a Captain, who looked vaguely familiar; the other an Ensign, and each wearing their dress uniforms. Noting their appearance, he wondered if there might be some special event taking place.

"So good of you to come; may I offer you some tea?" The Captain smiled warmly as he shook Chang's hand, bowing slightly. "Forgive me; we met many years ago—you have probably forgotten. My name is Zhu Ling; this is Ensign Tsao."

Chang nodded. *Of course*; he now recalled Ling from his dealings with Admiral Lee. "I remember, Captain. It is good to see you again." *Or was it?* Chang was now concerned that his worst fears were coming to pass; the presence of one of the Admiral's underlings couldn't be a good thing.

The young woman from the desk had suddenly appeared with a tray and a full tea service. It would have been rude to decline, so Chang took a cup as she poured. Captain Ling thanked her as the three men took their seats on the sofa and chairs in the center of the room. "Have you had breakfast?"

"Yes, at my hotel, just an hour ago."

"And your accommodations were satisfactory?"

Chang nodded. "Very much so." *What was all this?*

Ling was a perceptive man. "Please be at ease, Captain Chang. All of this will be explained shortly." He turned to the younger officer. "Ensign, would you see if our hosts are ready?"

Tsao smiled and nodded curtly, then sprang up and disappeared behind the double doors.

Chang sipped his tea and made himself relax. He tried not to speculate as to whom their 'hosts' might be, but the image of Admiral Lee flashed through his mind.

"Ling, you need not refer to me by my former rank. I am no longer a Captain in the Navy."

Ling leaned back in the sofa, a mixed expression of surprise and pleasure spreading across his face. "You're quite correct," he said. "Again, I must ask your forgiveness."

Ensign Tsao reappeared before Ling could continue. He nodded and then stood attentively at the door.

"Shall we?"

Chang put his cup of tea down on the table and got to his feet. With Ling leading the way, they crossed the marbled floor and passed through the entryway.

IT WAS RARE TO SEE SO MANY HIGH-RANKING naval officers gathered in one place. Chang recognized several Captains, Senior Captains—and a smattering of Admirals; but one was peculiarly absent—Xian Lee was nowhere to be seen. Chang was silently thankful for that. But the truly remarkable thing was the presence of the man at the center of the room.

Premier and Party Secretary Tao Chengdu held a teacup and looked up as Chang crossed the threshold. He handed the beverage to an aide and strode over to take Chang's hand.

"Welcome to Beijing, Wu," the Premier said simply. "Thank you for coming."

For his part, Chang could only return the handshake and bow deeply. He spoke the only words that came to mind. "I serve at your pleasure, Mr. Secretary."

"So I have heard," Chengdu smiled. "And you have done so quite well, I am told." At this, the Premier turned and nodded to Captain Ling. "We have much to talk about, Wu. Walk with me."

It was a large room, and the Premier guided Chang toward a series of expansive windows overlooking an elaborate courtyard garden. As the two men moved forward, the multitude of officers parted before them.

"First, let me thank you on behalf of the officers and men you saved when your ship was attacked." He shook his head and a look of deep concern colored his face. "Truly remarkable that only four members of your crew were lost; I commend you."

Chang blinked. Considering his treatment by Admiral Lee, he now felt like he had stepped into an alternate reality.

"I'm curious," Chengdu went on. "The escape pod aboard the sub—you designed it?"

"Yes, Mr. Secretary," Chang replied. "I wanted to give the crew every chance to survive, in the event of an emergency."

"You value life," the Premier observed. Even Chengdu had to admit that such a characteristic was unique among his officer corps.

"I have only just recently read the full report of the board's findings. It would appear that some details were withheld from me. I must take the blame for some of that." The Premier looked remorseful. "I placed great trust in Admiral Lee. Delegating power is a necessary evil that comes with great responsibility, I'm afraid. Lee betrayed that trust." Now a smile. "Even I can be painfully naïve at times. But I have corrected that mistake. Admiral Lee is now paying the price for his treason, along with those who conspired with him." He looked Chang in the eye. "Of course, his departure has created an opening on my staff. Captain Ling?"

Ling moved to the Premier's side.

"*Attention to orders.*"

At the Captain's command the assembled group of officers stood ramrod straight. Ling produced a small case and handed it to the Premier.

"You have suffered a grave disservice at our hands, Wu," Chengdu said. "I would like to correct *that* mistake as well." He opened the case, and Chang saw Admiral's stars resting inside. "You would honor me by accepting these. I have ordered your record expunged; in place of Admiral Lee's reprimand, a letter of commendation has been placed in your file.

"Many years ago, I was in the military too," the Premier's voice was low. "The Army. I know what it is to aspire to honor, Chang—you have honored your crew, and the memory of those who were lost."

Chang trembled slightly as Chengdu placed the rank insignia in his hands. He could find no words to express his gratitude, bowing instead. As he rose, the men around him expressed their own approval and broke into enthusiastic applause as Chang fought to control his emotions.

Even the Premier was smiling now. "We will meet this week to discuss improved safety measures aboard our naval vessels—particularly submarines. I want to hear your thoughts on this."

Chang nodded. *So*, he thought to himself, *redemption* does *have a place in this world . . .*

* * * *

"YOU HAD SOMETHING TO DO WITH THIS, Captain?"

The two men were now walking the halls of the headquarters building. Ling was taking Chang to his new office.

"I can't take full credit—*Admiral*," Ling replied. "You might be surprised to learn that the Americans and British also played a part."

Nothing surprised Chang anymore. "I'm sure it will make an interesting story, Zhu," he said as they moved down the corridor. He paused when they came to a large office, the door standing wide open. Looking inside, Chang saw the overhead lights on, but the room was empty.

"Mine?" he assumed.

Ling shook his head. "No, Admiral. This office was formerly occupied by Xian Lee." Chang noted that the Captain did not refer to Lee by rank. "While it might be poetically appropriate for you to take this place, we would not be so cruel as to remind you of the indignities you suffered at his hand. Your office is down the hall."

Chang surveyed the room. Except for a desk and a few bookshelves, it had a hollow look.

"Why, Ling?"

Zhu Ling frowned. "Why?"

Chang nodded. "Yes. Why did it enter your mind to help me—to see justice done on Lee for my sake?"

Ling considered his words carefully. "We must always choose to do the right thing," he answered, stepping into the room. "Sometimes that is hard. *'But for those who have responsibility thrust upon them, it is the only correct path'.* An American told me that just recently." He moved casually toward the desk. "Do you see the layer of dust that has built up here?"

Chang thought that to be an odd observation. Lee's personal effects, as well as his files and computer, had been removed. No trace of his presence remained. And while the desk had been cleared, it had not been thoroughly cleaned. He watched as Ling leaned forward. With his index finger, he traced an arc along the top of the desk. The Admiral blinked and then recognized the significance of what Ling had just done.

Chang stepped forward, and with his finger he drew another arc, inverted from the one drawn by Captain Ling. Taken together, the simple graphic formed the shape of the ichthus.

Good, Ling thought. *You understand.*

"We live in a dangerous world, Admiral. Recent events have threatened the peace of many nations." With the palm of his hand he wiped away the image they'd made. "But there are many like us, serving around the world—wearing different uniforms.

"The time may come when we must all stand together."

Look for

the next book in

the Michael Neill adventure series.

Coming Soon!

Made in the USA
Charleston, SC
15 April 2014

His code-name is 'White Dragon'. His motives—unclear.

Somalia has split in two, with armed insurgents threatening American lives. China has emerged as a leading arms exporter, supplying weapons to Third World nations. But before National Security Advisor Willis Avery can deal with either danger, he faces a new challenge.

On her maiden voyage, Beijing's newest and most advanced nuclear submarine is destroyed by a weapon of unimaginable power. While the loss of the sub is kept secret, America and her allies want to know what happened. Avery believes a renegade faction of China's Navy is behind the attack, striking from a secret naval facility in the South China Sea, and assembles a group to investigate.

Leading the mission is Marine Corps Lieutenant Michael Neill. Fresh from his assignment in Ukraine, Neill and his team—with a little help from British Intelligence and the Royal Navy—must find a way to locate the weapon before it is deployed again. Along the way, they must stop a Chinese Admiral who plans on seizing control of an independent Taiwan. Neill's squad is aided by a mysterious informant—but is he baiting them into a trap?

Tempest of Fire

ABOUT THE AUTHOR

Steve Wilson is a multimedia designer and has worked in advertising for over 25 years. A prior service Marine, his military ties have taken him to Kuwait, Iraq, Afghanistan, and the former Soviet Union. He lives in Florida with his wife, and is also the author of *Red Sky at Morning*.

Fiction, War and Military

$15.95

ISBN 978-1-61808-071-

51595

9 781618 080714

White Feather Press